"NO ONE WOULD EVER HAVE TO KNOW YOU WERE A CAPTIVE."

At Hunter's words, Sarah felt as if a giant fist were squeezing air from her lungs. *Nobody would ever have to know she'd been a captive of the Comanche.* No shame to bear and none to pass along to an innocent child. She'd be married to a half-breed, but this man was nothing like the savages who had captured her.

"You'll want time to think it over," he said, rising.

Sarah stopped him with a cry. "No! I mean, don't go. I . . . I don't need to think. I just need . . ." She covered her burning cheeks with her hands and fought an absurd desire to weep. "You'd raise my baby as your own child?"

"A baby is easy to love, Sarah. Who could resist that chubby little sweetheart?"

Lots of people, thought Sarah. "Do you swear it?"

He smiled. "If it makes you happy, then yes, I swear it."

Sarah's mind was too full of questions to choose which were the most important. "I don't love you," she said instead.

"I don't love you, either," he said, "but I like and respect you. Love has grown in far rockier soil than that."

She considered the beauty of his words, and that more than anything won her. Then she remembered how he'd protected her the other night and thought about how it would feel not to be afraid anymore.

Quaking inwardly at the enormity of her decision, she managed a tremulous smile. "All right, Sergeant Tate. I'll marry you."

VICTORIA THOMPSON

WINDS OF PROMISE

ZEBRA BOOKS
KENSINGTON PUBLISHING CORP.

ZEBRA BOOKS are published by

Kensington Publishing Corp.
475 Park Avenue South
New York, NY 10016

First Printing: June, 1993
Printed in the United States of America

To my cousin,
Charles-Charlie-Chuck-Sonny-Brother,
and his new bride, Eileen. L'Chaim!

Prologue

Hunter smiled when he caught sight of the rider coming toward him. As usual, Eva was late, but Hunter didn't mind. He liked being alone here by the river in the relative seclusion of the willow trees. With the United States slowly crumbling, as one state after another seceded from the Union, and Americans killing each other at Fort Sumter, anyplace away from the constant talk of war was a refuge.

Here under the willows no one spoke of states' rights or secession. All Hunter could hear was the quiet rippling of the water, the lazy Texas wind rustling the trailing branches, and the sound of his horse cropping the crisp, green grass nearby. The war was very far away, and a beautiful woman was riding up to meet him.

He could see her now, her long blond hair whipping in the wind, her luscious lips smiling. Rising, he went to meet her, eager for her touch and the taste of her kiss. He caught her horse's bridle, and she slid from the saddle right into his arms. Her lips were warm and as hungry as his, her body pliant and yielding.

Without a word, he lifted her into his arms and carried her to the blanket he had spread beneath the trees. Their kisses grew feverish, their hands desperate as they tore at each other's clothes to reach the heated flesh beneath. Hunter caressed the softness of her breast, and for an instant he marveled at the contrast between her milky white flesh and his own coppery hand, made even darker by the sun.

Then her delicate white fingers closed around his manhood, and his other thoughts scattered, leaving only one driving need. Delving under her skirt, he found her warm, moist center and began to stroke the tender lips with the same urgency she was using on him. While their hands groped, their mouths clung, tongues tangling in an imitation of the ultimate union they were saving for their wedding night.

But they denied themselves nothing else of their passion, and within moments they were both gasping as desire peaked into ecstasy. When it was over, Hunter collapsed back onto the blanket, fighting the delicious lethargy that beckoned him to sleep. He reached for Eva, but she was busy with her clothes, covering herself again.

He thought of protesting her eagerness to end their lovemaking so quickly, of pulling her back into his arms and burying his face in the sweet pillow of her naked breasts, but he'd tried that before. She would only push him away, scolding, "What if somebody comes along?"

Which was ridiculous. Nobody would come along. That was why they'd picked this spot in the first place. But there was no arguing with her, as he'd learned. He told himself he should be glad he'd gotten a woman who was modest.

He opened his eyes to find her just finishing buttoning her bodice. Her skirt was already properly down around her ankles again.

"Hmmm, that was nice," he said.

She smiled at him, showing her small, even teeth. Her blue eyes shone with the aftermath of passion. "Yes, it was," she agreed. "There's nobody like you, Hunter."

He put his hands behind his head and smiled back at her. "You sound like you've been trying to find out," he teased.

As he'd expected, she blushed, the color turning her cheeks to roses. "Hunter, how you talk," she said, nervously smoothing her skirt and brushing imaginary lint from the faded calico.

"You can't blame me for feeling a little worried," he said with mock gravity. "After all, the prettiest girl in the county is bound to attract a lot of attention from other men. Why, if I remember correctly, I had to fight my way through a real crowd the first time I ever went to call on you."

"Oh, those *boys*," she said, dismissing them all with a wave of her hand. But Hunter could see she was still embarrassed. She wouldn't quite meet his eye.

Or maybe that was because he hadn't covered his own nakedness yet. He didn't intend to, either, not until he was sure Eva couldn't be coaxed into a repeat performance.

"Still, I'll feel a lot better when we're safely married and I *know* no other men'll be trying to steal you away," he said. "What do you say we set the date right now?" He reached for her hand, but she drew away.

"I don't know why you're in such an all-fired hurry," she said with a laugh that sounded forced.

"You don't want to be an old maid, do you?" he asked, still teasing but puzzled by her reluctance. She'd always been happy to talk about their marriage before.

"I won't be an old maid," she said stiffly. "I'm only seventeen. And you . . . don't you want to go back and finish college?"

Hunter had just completed his third year at the College of William and Mary in far-off Virginia, but the coming war promised to put an end to his studies for a while. And if he was called up for the Army to fight for the newly formed Confederacy . . . "I don't know what's going to happen, and neither do you, Eva," he told her solemnly. "I want us to be married so that if I have to leave . . . well, at least we'll have been together."

He reached for her again, and this time she scooted out of his range.

"Hunter, there's something I've got to tell you," she said, biting her lip and still not quite meeting his eye. She came up on her knees and looked at him so earnestly, he had to smile.

"So tell me," he invited, crossing his hands behind his head again.

"I . . . I *am* going to get married," she said, her hands twisting together apprehensively.

"I'm awfully glad to hear it, Eva," he said, feigning sternness. "You've kept me waiting a long time."

"I'm going to marry Owen Young!" she blurted, lurching to her feet.

"What?" Hunter demanded incredulously, pushing himself up to a sitting position.

Eva was already backing away. "I going to marry

Owen Young!" she repeated desperately. "Next month, the fifteenth!"

Hunter scrambled up, then realized his state of undress. Frantically, he started stuffing in his shirttail and trying to button his pants. "Then what in the hell are you doing here with me?" he demanded. "What was all this about?" He gestured toward the blanket on which they had just given each other so much pleasure.

"I told you," she whined, still backing away. "There's nobody like you, Hunter. I . . . I just couldn't help myself."

"Then why're you marrying somebody else?" he shouted.

Her blue eyes glowed with terror, but before he could even wonder why she should be afraid, she said, "Because he's *white,* Hunter."

The words hit him like a physical blow, and he just stood there, stunned by the pain, while she turned and ran and jumped on her horse and rode away.

He's white. The words echoed down the dark corridors of his mind, the black places he'd thought were sealed off forever. *He's white, and you're a half-breed Indian bastard.* That was what she hadn't said, hadn't needed to say, because they both knew it. Everyone in Texas knew it. Hunter Tate was the spawn of a white female captive and some filthy savage, and no decent white woman would ever have him as her husband.

He should have known. He should have suspected something was wrong when Eva had insisted on meeting him secretly. She'd said she wanted to be alone with him and that they'd never be alone at her parents' house. Indeed, whenever he'd tried to call on her there, he'd found the same crowd of young men that he'd encountered on his very first visit after returning home from school.

But now Hunter knew the real reason she'd wanted to sneak away to meet him. She didn't want anyone to know she was seeing a *breed,* not her parents or her friends and especially not any truly eligible young men who might also want to marry her.

And he also knew the other reason she wanted to meet him secretly. It was the same reason those Virginia girls had found him so attractive when he'd been at college: for some reason they just couldn't resist the idea of being with an Indian. They'd wanted the thrill of being at the mercy of a savage, but without the danger.

Hunter had never quite understood it, but he'd gladly fulfilled their fantasies. He'd just never expected a Texas girl to feel that way, not a girl who'd lived her whole life under the constant threat of Indian attack.

Eva Wilkes might really have been kidnapped by the Comanches, just as Hunter's mother had been, a prospect certain to make every woman in Texas shudder in horror. Eva might have been forced to endure captivity and the lusts of the fiendish Comanche braves. Instead she'd lain with Hunter Tate, a *safe* savage. She couldn't help herself, she'd said. Desire and curiosity and whatever other emotions drive young women had compelled her.

Now, curiosity satisfied, she'd marry another man. Another man would taste her kisses and touch her secret places and sate himself on her luscious body. A white man.

Hunter felt the rage rising in him, the fury and frustration he hadn't known in years, not since he'd learned to ignore the barbs thrown by the more ignorant members of his mother's race. He'd thought himself immune to them now, but he'd been wrong, so very wrong. The pain burned his soul like a brand.

Part of him wanted to ride after her, to drag her off her horse and take by force what he'd been too gentlemanly to demand before. Give her a taste of what a real Indian could be like. Another part of him shuddered at the thought of touching her. No, let her marry Owen Young, that bloodless whelp. She'd find her marriage bed cold indeed. Knowing what she was missing would be her everlasting torment.

But Hunter wouldn't be around to see it. He wouldn't stay to watch her marry another man, not when there was a war to be fought. They were saying the fighting would be over by Christmas, just a few months away. By the time he got back, she'd understand what she'd given up. Then Hunter would have the last laugh.

Chapter One

Bluff Creek, Kansas, 1865

Something important was going to happen. Sarah could sense it. In the months since she'd been captured by the Comanches, she'd had to learn to sense things because she still couldn't understand much of their language. Gibberish was what it sounded like to her, so much turkey gobble. She'd only learned enough of it to comprehend the commands they gave her so she could avoid a beating for not responding quickly enough to her master or his wife.

The rest she'd just learned to sense by watching their expressions and trying to guess what was going on, and lately a lot had been going on. First they'd moved camp.

Not that moving camp was so unusual. The Indians only stayed in one spot until the game was played out and the firewood used up, then they'd move on. In the thirteen months she'd spent as a Comanche slave, Sarah had moved five times.

But this move was different. They'd moved a lot farther than ever before, traveling as if they'd had a specific destination in mind and passing several likely campsites along the way. The place they'd chosen was apparently near several other Indian camps as well, since she'd seen a lot of strangers visiting the village and the men had been gone much of the time, probably visiting the other villages. Her questions about it had been ignored or answered in phrases she didn't understand. Still, she'd known this wasn't just an ordinary resettlement.

Something was going to happen. If Sarah had still been able to hope, she might have hoped it would be something good for her. She knew white captives were treated differently now than they had been in the old days. Oh, they were still tortured and abused and even killed if necessary, but no longer were they taken for the purpose of making them additions to the tribe. While some of the white children were occasionally adopted by Comanche parents whose own children had died, most of the captives were considered merely valuable trade goods to be kept only until they could be sold back to the whites.

As she walked slowly along the creek bank near the new camp, looking for deadfalls she could gather for firewood, Sarah considered the possibility that she might someday soon be ransomed back to her own people. The prospect both thrilled and terrified her. Certainly, she wanted to be rescued. The life of a Comanche slave was far worse than even the grinding poverty she and her husband had sought to escape by immigrating to Texas; far worse, in fact, than anything she had ever imagined.

So being rescued *from* the Comanche was her dream, but what would she be rescued *to?* Everything she'd had

16

was gone, destroyed by the damned Comanches. Not that they called themselves "Comanches," though. They called themselves "The People," or something very close to that, as near as Sarah could translate it. But they weren't people. They were animals, dirty, stinking animals who had killed her husband and her baby. And they'd killed her, too, or at least all the parts of her that mattered, like her heart and her soul.

Now she was as dead inside as her husband and her son, and she'd be dead outside, too, if it wasn't for . . .

Automatically, Sarah shifted the cradle board on her back and listened for any sound of discomfort from the little one nestled snugly in the mossy bed. She heard only contented cooing from the one her master had named Ebihuutsuuʔ, Bluebird, because her eyes had been so blue when she'd been born, as blue as her mother's. They were darkening now, as Sarah had feared they would. With her raven hair and coppery skin, each day her daughter looked more and more like an Indian.

But she'd never be an Indian, not really, because she was Sarah's child, and somehow, someday, Sarah would get her away from them. Somehow. Someday.

Frowning over her somber thoughts, Sarah made her way back to the camp, her arms full of firewood, the cradle board bumping insistently against her back. She was almost there when she noticed that the something she'd been expecting had suddenly happened. The camp was a flurry of activity with women and children darting everywhere and dogs barking furiously.

Heart pounding from a combination of hope and dread, Sarah hurried toward the lodge she shared with her master's wife, but she soon realized the flow of traffic was heading in the opposite direction, toward the

17

Civil Chief's lodge, and she allowed herself to be swept up in it.

Somewhere along the way, she'd dropped the wood, but that no longer mattered. Nothing mattered now except finding out what was wrong. All around her, the women and the children were chattering like magpies, but she couldn't understand their words, especially the one phrase they kept repeating, *taibo ekusahpana?*.

Then she saw them, the white men in the blue uniforms. Soldiers. *Union* soldiers, but what did that matter now? Dear God, had they come for her at last? Or did they even know she was here? They had to see her, they *had* to!

Pushing, jostling, she fought her way frantically through the excited crowd, ignoring the exclamations of outrage and the rude shoves she received. She had to get to the soldiers!

Closer now, just a few more feet to the edge of the crowd where she could call out and be sure they'd see her, when someone grabbed her arm and screeched a protest. Sarah turned, ready to swat off whoever was holding her, and saw the furious face of her mistress, Numu ruibetsu, She Invites Her Relatives. The woman was pulling Sarah away with both hands, dragging her back toward their lodge where the soldiers wouldn't be able to see her, so they wouldn't know she was there and they wouldn't be able to get her away.

Desperate, Sarah clawed at She Invites's clutching hands, fighting for her freedom, for her very life and for the life of her child, but She Invites wouldn't let go, and Sarah saw her master, Witawoo?ooki, heading toward them, ready to assist his wife.

Sarah turned back to the soldiers, a cry of despair on her lips. *See me!* she wanted to shriek, but the words

18

died in her throat when she saw the tall, dark soldier looking at her. He *did* see her, and he knew she was a white woman in spite of her Indian dress and the way they'd smeared her yellow hair with bear grease. He nodded once, very deliberately, and she knew he had come for her.

Her terror died, and an overwhelming sense of peace flooded her. It was over. It was almost over. She no longer even cared that She Invites was dragging her away. The soldier would find her. He would find her no matter where they tried to hide her.

She went along meekly, and allowed She Invites to thrust her into the buffalo-skin lodge and close the flap behind her. It didn't matter. Nothing mattered. Sarah sat down on her pallet of buffalo robes and slid the cradle board from her back. In a few seconds, she had freed her daughter from her mossy haven. The child shrieked happily and nuzzled the front of Sarah's doeskin dress.

Sarah lifted the edge of her top and offered the hungry child her breast, smiling at the baby's greediness. "We're going home, little one," she murmured, and once more her joy gave way to despair. Where was home now that the Indians had burned the dugout in which she'd lived and destroyed everything she'd owned? Where was home now that Pete and little P.J. were dead?

Everyone was gone now, her parents, her brothers and sisters, Pete and P.J. Every last person that Sarah had ever loved was dead except for this Little One in her arms. Memories of her losses brought tears to her eyes, and she let them fall as her precious baby suckled, crying out her grief for the past and her fears for the future.

19

Sarah didn't know how long she'd been in the lodge, waiting, when they finally came for her. Her tears had dried, and the baby had long since finished nursing and fallen asleep, but Sarah continued to cradle her in her arms, almost afraid to let her go and desperately needing the small comfort of the baby's tiny body against her own.

She heard their footsteps first, the unfamiliar sound of boots against the packed earth, in a place where everyone went about in moccasins. Her heart began to pound again, and her breath quickened as the footsteps came closer and closer and closer still.

"They're coming, little one," she whispered into the stillness of the tent. Then she heard She Invites jabbering in outrage, but a word from an unfamiliar voice silenced her instantly.

Sarah's breath stopped when the tent flap lifted and a man in a blue uniform ducked into the lodge. He straightened and looked around, blinking in the sudden dimness, and Sarah fought a wave of disappointment to see it wasn't the dark soldier she'd been expecting.

But her disappointment was short-lived. Immediately, another solder ducked through the opening, and when he looked up, she once again caught his eye, the silvery eyes that had found her in the crowd outside. He'd come for her, as she'd known he would.

"Mrs. Peters?" the first soldier asked. His voice was strained, as if he were very nervous. He'd pulled off his hat to reveal ash brown hair with a tendency to curl, and now Sarah could see his fair skin was pink with sunburn. A newcomer to the West, no doubt. "Mrs. Sarah Peters?" he asked again when she did not reply, less certain this time.

20

Sarah had thought she might never be called by her right name again, and for a long moment, she could only gape up at him, drinking in the wonder of it.

Her hesitation seemed to unnerve the blond soldier. He turned to his companion. "Do you think she's lost her wits?" he asked uneasily.

The dark soldier frowned at the blond soldier and turned his silvery gaze to Sarah. "You *are* Mrs. Sarah Peters, aren't you?" he asked in a deep voice, so full of confidence that Sarah would probably have admitted to being Sarah Peters even if she hadn't been.

"Yes," she said, her own voice soft in the stillness of the tent. "Yes," she repeated more firmly. "I'm Sarah Peters. It's just . . . it's been so long since I heard English, I almost forgot how to speak it."

The dark soldier smiled, showing straight white teeth that contrasted sharply with his deeply tanned face. "I'm Hunter Tate," he said. "Sergeant Tate," he amended, "And this is Lieutenant Irwin. We're with the United States Army. We've come to take you home."

Sarah felt the sting of tears again and had to cover her mouth to hold back a cry of joy. Or was it a cry of anguish? *Home.* Where would she go now?

Away from here, she told herself sternly, blinking away the tears. Anyplace else but here. That was all that mattered. She and her child would be free once more.

"Can I go with you right now?" she asked, thinking of She Invites waiting outside the tent. Never again would she have to fear a kick or a slap or a jab with a burning stick from out of nowhere. Never again would she walk in fear of assault by anyone she encountered. She was free!

But the blond soldier was still frowning. He cleared

his throat. "We just have to settle one thing, Mrs. Peters," Lieutenant Irwin said. His voice cracked, and Sarah wondered why he was so nervous. Perhaps being in a Comanche camp disturbed him. Perhaps he didn't know the Indians wouldn't attack someone who was a guest in their camp.

"What?" she asked, wondering if she should be worried or if she should start gathering her meager possessions.

"It's . . . it's about your . . . your baby," he stammered. The light was bad, but Sarah thought he was flushing.

Instinctively, she held her little daughter closer to her bosom. "What about my baby?" she asked, frightened anew. Would the Army refuse to ransom a child born in captivity? A child that was half Indian?

"We need to know . . ." The lieutenant glanced at Sergeant Tate, who stood impassively, offering no help. The lieutenant cleared his throat. "We need to know . . . do you want to take it with you?"

It? What did he mean, *it? "My baby?"* she cried in outrage, crushing the child to her breast until she whimpered in her sleep. "Of course I want to take her with me!"

Sergeant Tate scowled at the lieutenant, then took a step forward and hunkered down until he was on her eye level. "Mrs. Peters," he said, his deep voice gentle now, as if he were afraid of startling her, "think about this very carefully. Think about what you'll face when you leave here and go back to your home. Think about what people will say when they see you have a half-breed child."

Sarah stared at him, mesmerized by his kindness, something she hadn't experienced in so many months,

22

yet terrified by his words. She wanted to jump up and run away to someplace where she could hide her baby from the lieutenant's disapproving glare. Instead, she sat stone still and listened while Sergeant Tate continued with his argument.

"Your little . . ." He glanced down at the naked child. "Your little girl would be well taken care of if you leave her here. The People love children, as you probably already know. Someone would adopt her, and she'd grow up perfectly happy, never knowing any other kind of life."

The People. He'd called them "The People." She studied his face, the high cheekbones, the deeply tanned skin, the raven hair that hung straight and thick across his forehead. Then she knew. In spite of his blue uniform and silver eyes, he was one of *them*.

But he hadn't been raised an Indian, of that she was certain, not with his perfect English and his polished manner. Oh, no, he'd been raised a white man, and here he was telling her to leave her baby behind in this filthy, stinking place with these filthy, stinking savages!

Suddenly furious, Sarah thrust her face towards his. "And what about you, Sergeant? Your mother didn't leave you with the Indians, did she? Or your father, whichever of your parents was white."

"My mother," he said, calmly. "She was a captive, too."

Sarah's heart contracted with the pain she heard in his voice, but she couldn't let herself be distracted. "And she took you with her, back to her people, didn't she?"

He nodded, his expression inscrutable.

"And I'm taking my baby with me, too!" she cried, the tears blurring her vision. "They killed my husband

and butchered him like a pig, and they took my son by the heels and smashed his head against a tree, and they . . . they did things to me that . . ." Things that she couldn't speak of, not now and not ever, ever again. "But they're not taking this baby! They took everything else, and she's all I've got left. I won't leave her here! I won't!"

She braced herself, ready for whatever argument he might throw at her, ready to throw it right back in his face, but instead he smiled again.

Sarah blinked in surprise, but before she could figure it out, Lieutenant Irwin said, "Be very sure, Mrs. Peters. Without the child, you could start over. No one would ever have to know you were a captive—"

"*I'd* know!" she cried, furious. "And I'd know I had a child out there somewhere, being raised as a squaw! How could I live with that? Tell me, Lieutenant!"

"I . . ." he tried, but words failed him.

"Won't the army ransom her?" she demanded of Sergeant Tate.

"Yes, they will. In fact, they already have. We just signed a treaty with several Indian tribes at a place not too far from here. This group of Comanches was among them, and one of the provisions of the treaty was the return of all captives. You're free, and so is your daughter. You can come with us right now."

Sarah thought her heart might burst. "Right now?" she echoed incredulously.

Sergeant Tate nodded. "Just get your things together, anything you want to take with you, and we'll go right back to our main camp tonight."

Sarah thought she might weep again, but she fought the tears, biting her lip and lifting her chin in defiance. "There's nothing here I want to take but my daughter."

24

Sergeant Tate smiled again. "Then put her in her cradle board, and let's get out of here."

A few short minutes later, Sarah was ready. There was an awkward moment when both men stood back to allow her to go out ahead of them, a courtesy she hadn't known in so long that at first she couldn't figure out what they were doing. Then she ducked out into the sunlight, her daughter's bed in her arms, a free woman for the first time in over a year.

From the corner of her eye, she saw She Invites Her Relatives squatting in the dust beside the smoldering remains of their fire, the same fire for which Sarah had been gathering wood not too very long ago. Never again would she have to serve this woman, or fear her wrath, or endure any of the other myriad tortures the Comanche could inflict.

Sarah turned and caught She Invites's dark gaze. The older woman glared at her, eyes full of all the hatred and contempt Sarah returned in full measure. She Invites spat in the fire and muttered an imprecation Sarah didn't try to understand.

"You won't get my baby," Sarah told her in her halting Comanche, knowing this was the one legacy she could leave which would extract a small measure of revenge for the agonies she had suffered here.

She Invites spat again, and Sergeant Tate took Sarah's arm.

"Let's go, Mrs. Peters," he said, a warning in his voice. No use causing trouble now, it said, not when everything is over.

She nodded, and he led her away, his touch at once gentle and unyielding. Lieutenant Irwin followed, and Sarah had the impression he would have gladly increased the pace if he had been allowed to set it. She

25

couldn't blame him for his eagerness to get away, not when she shared it.

Sarah glanced at Sergeant Tate, able to study him now in full daylight. He'd put his uniform hat back on, but she could still see his hair was the blue-black of an Indian brave and aggressively straight where it grew over his ears and down on his neck. He was tall, much taller than the Comanche men she had encountered, so perhaps he was of another tribe. His body was lean and straight and broad-shouldered, too, unlike the Comanche, who tended toward squatness.

His face did have the high cheekbones and heavy eyelids that bespoke his Indian blood, but his white blood showed, too, in the straightness of his nose and the curve of his mouth. His skin might just have been tanned more darkly than most, so if she'd met him under other circumstances, she might have thought him simply striking in appearance and missed the other hints of his lineage.

The residents of the village had begun to gather. They were always interested in whatever was going on around them, especially in novel events like watching one of their former slaves being escorted from camp by two of the blue-coated soldiers. They lined the way, their broad, bronzed faces set as they watched Sarah's progress through the village.

Sarah glared at them all, seeing here and there a face she particularly hated, a woman who had tormented her, a man who had abused her. Desire for vengeance roiled in her, the urge to grab the pistol out of Lieutenant Irwin's holster and begin firing to kill as many of these monsters as she could. The earth would be a much better place if each and every one of them was exterminated from its face, but Sarah knew how foolish she would be to try. Her feeble effort would only cause her own destruction and that of her child, as well as of the soldiers whose only crime was coming to claim her.

So she squashed her vindictive urges and walked on, content to simply hate them, each and every one. Finally she and her escorts reached the edge of the village where several enlisted men waited with the horses. How strange it looked to see horses weighed down with the heavy saddles the white man favored when for months she'd ridden practically bareback.

They'd brought a horse for her, a pretty little mare she supposed they'd chosen for its gentleness, never dreaming she'd ridden half-wild Indian ponies over half the country. One of the soldiers brought the mare forward for her.

"Here you are, ma'am," he said, not quite meeting her eye. She glanced around and saw the others had been staring at her, but they, too, looked away. For a moment she stood uncertainly, still holding the cradle board.

"I'll take that," Sergeant Tate said, removing the cradle board from her unresisting hands. "Do you need some help up?"

Sarah realized she would have to get used to normal life all over again. Not only would a Comanche man never dream of assisting a female into the saddle, he would consider her worthless if she even hinted she might need help. "No, I . . ." she started, then stopped, wondering if she should ask for help anyway, if the men expected her to, if they would think less of her if she didn't need it. Brushing the thought away, she stuck her moccasined foot into the stirrup and swung up into the saddle.

Below, she heard a slight gasp from the soldier holding her mare, and for a second she couldn't imagine what she'd done wrong. Then she knew. White women, *ladies*, didn't ride astride. Or perhaps he'd caught a glimpse of her naked leg beneath her doe-skin dress. Or perhaps he'd caught a glimpse of naked something else, since she wore nothing at all beneath it.

She felt her face burning and wondered that she could still blush after all she had endured at the hands of the Indians. True, they had humiliated her in every possible way, but she hadn't felt true shame until this minute, until she'd had to face her own people again.

For one insane second she wanted to jump down from the horse, grab her baby, and run back to Wita-woo ʔooki's lodge and hide herself away from their censorious eyes. But that truly *was* insane, and the urge vanished as quickly as it had come.

Sergeant Tate was tying the cradle board to her saddle horn so her daughter could ride safely, the way a real Indian baby would ride, the way her little one had ridden many times before in her short life. Then he and Lieutenant Irwin mounted their own horses and led them off.

Sarah didn't know quite where she would fit in this odd caravan, but when the enlisted men made no move to follow, she understood they expected her to go ahead of them. With newly learned skill, she guided her mare into line behind Sergeant Tate and rode out, holding her head up and her shoulders back, showing every last Comanche savage in the camp that they had not cowed her. Beside her, her daughter slept peacefully, totally unaware of how drastically her fortunes had changed in the past few minutes. When she woke up, she would be free, and she would never know how close she had come to being raised as a Comanche squaw.

After a few minutes, when they were well clear of the camp, Sarah began to notice her hands were shaking. Her heart seemed to be pounding ever more slowly in her chest, as if it were gradually slowing down and might eventually stop altogether. Her chest grew tight, until she had to struggle for every breath, and she felt the strength draining from her limbs.

"Mrs. Peters," someone said sharply.

Sarah jumped and looked up to see Sergeant Tate had dropped back to ride beside her. His dark face was set, his silver eyes full of concern.

"It's just reaction," he informed her. "Take a deep breath and let it out slowly."

She did as he commanded, forcing the air into her lungs and holding it there until she had to release it again. After a few deep breaths her heart no longer pounded laboriously and her hands weren't shaking quite so badly.

"We can stop, if you want," he said after a minute.

"No," she said, too quickly. "I mean, I want to get as far away as possible."

"They won't come after you, not with so many soldiers in the area. You're safe now."

Safe? Would she ever feel safe anywhere again? Once she'd thought herself secure in her own home, and how wrong she'd been.

"Where are you from?" Sergeant Tate asked.

"What?" Sarah asked stupidly, not really comprehending the mundane question.

"Where are you from?" he repeated patiently. "Originally, I mean. I know you were living in Texas when you were captured, but before that . . ."

"I . . . Tennessee," she said. How far away it all seemed now.

29

"Pretty state," he remarked. "I fought there, during the war."

Suddenly, Sarah realized what it was about Sergeant Tate that seemed odd: the contrast between his accent and his blue uniform. "You're from the South, aren't you?" she exclaimed.

"Yes, Texas, like you," he said with a small smile.

"Then how could you fight for the Yankees?" she demanded, outraged.

"I didn't. I was a Confederate for four long years."

"So you're a turncoat, then! A traitor!"

"There's nothing left to be a traitor to, Mrs. Peters," he said sadly. "The war is over. It's been over since April."

"April?" she echoed incredulously, and tried to do some figuring in her head. "What month is it now?"

"October," he replied.

She'd tried to keep track, but all she'd been able to do was count the full moons, and that wasn't exactly accurate. "The war is over," she murmured sadly, thinking of all the suffering the people in the South had endured. "I don't suppose the Confederacy won."

"No, we lost. General Lee surrendered at some little place in Virginia."

"And you turned right around and signed up with the Yankee army," she said contemptuously, unable to understand how anyone could do such a dastardly thing.

"Not exactly," he told her, a trace of irony in his deep voice. "I told you I fought in Tennessee. I was captured after we lost the battle of Nashville last December."

"The Yankees took Nashville?" she asked, outraged again.

"Nashville and Atlanta and practically everything

else," he told her. "After they captured us, they gave us a choice, either rot in a prison camp or sign up with the Army and go West to fight Indians. We'd never seen a Yankee prison camp, but we figured they didn't treat their prisoners any better than we treated ours, so we chose the Indians. If nothing else, we Texas boys figured we could escape and make it back home. Nobody told us how quickly the war would be over, though, or we might've chosen the prison camp instead. If we had, we'd have been home long since."

Sarah glanced around at the other soldiers. "Are . . . are all these men Confederates?"

"All the enlisted men, at least the ones in this outfit. We call ourselves 'Galvanized Yankees.' " He grinned at what was obviously a joke.

Sarah had never heard the word "galvanized" before and had no idea what it meant, but she didn't want Sergeant Tate to guess at her ignorance and have one more reason to look down on her. She returned his smile.

"Of course," he added, "the real Yankees aren't so kind. They call us 'Whitewashed Yankees,' and they make sure we never forget who won the war."

So the war was over. Sarah wondered what other momentous changes had taken place in the world while she'd been a captive, but she was afraid to ask. The ones she knew about, losing her family and now her country, were more than enough.

"Do you have any family left in Texas?" Sergeant Tate asked after a moment.

"No," Sarah said, feeling the familiar pang of loss. "My . . . they were all killed."

"I knew your husband and child were," he said, his voice gentle again, the way it had been when he had

31

spoken to her back in the lodge. "It was in the report. I thought maybe you had some other relatives, though, people you'd come with from Tennessee, perhaps."

"No, we . . . we came alone." How hopeful they'd been then, full of plans and dreams, contemptuous of the warnings of Indian attacks.

"Then I guess you'll go back to Tennessee now."

"What?" she asked in surprise.

"Now that you're free, I mean. You don't want to go back to Texas alone, do you?"

Alone? To rebuild the dugout the Indians had burned? To farm the land Pete had been working the day the savages attacked? The very idea made her blood run cold. "No," she murmured.

"I suppose you'll want to go to your family in Tennessee. You'll be able to forget it all back there."

Forget? She'd never forget, not if she lived to be a hundred years old. And go back to Tennessee? To what?

"I . . . I don't know . . ." Instinctively, she touched the cradle board where her child slept. What would her old friends back in Tennessee think of her bastard child? Could she possibly pass the baby off as Pete's?

"You *do* have family there, don't you?" he prodded.

Did she? Her parents were dead, along with her two brothers and three sisters, all victims of some mysterious fever only she had survived. Pete's mother was dead, and his father had been sickly when they'd left before the war. Surely, he, too, was gone by now. Pete's brothers and sisters were scattered, and she had no idea how to get in touch with them.

"No," she said at last. "I don't have family anywhere."

After that, Sergeant Tate seemed unable to think of anything to say, so they rode in silence. Sarah spent the time trying to envision her future, but what opportunities an ex-Comanche slave with a bastard half-breed child might have, she had no idea.

Sergeant Tate had been right when he'd said the main camp wasn't far from where they'd found her. After only about an hour of riding, she could see the orderly rows of tents that marked the encampment. Soon she could also make out the soldiers moving among the tents to their various duties. Wagons stood in row after row, wagons the likes of which Sarah had never seen before. Big and boxy, they were similar to peddlers' wagons but without the fancy paint.

In the middle of it all, someone had built a great brush arbor. Beneath it stood a row of tables and chairs, and Sarah could imagine the white men seated in them, conferring with the Indian leaders about the terms of the treaty. Which reminded Sarah of something.

"You said the Indians signed a treaty," she said to the Sergeant. "Does that mean the whites will be safe now? That they'll leave us alone?"

Sergeant Tate smiled again, but Sarah could see he wasn't amused. "That's what the treaty promises, but I don't think the Indians really understand that."

"What?"

"Well, the terms of the treaty are clear enough. The Indians have to give up their captives and stop making war and allow the white men to travel through their lands and build roads and railroads. In exchange, the Comanche get almost all of Western Texas and western Indian Territory, and the Arapahoes and Cheyenne get part of the Cherokee Outlet and Southwestern Kansas. The problem is, the federal government doesn't have the power to give away land in Texas because when

33

Texas became a state, she kept control of her own public lands. You can be sure no Texan will voluntarily give an Indian one square food of Texas land, and that's just the beginning of the problems with this treaty."

"They expect the Indians to let white men build *roads* through their hunting grounds?" Sarah asked incredulously.

"Somebody in Washington does," Tate told her grimly. "Trouble is, those same people don't have any idea how little control the Comanche chiefs have over their people. The chiefs will promise anything to get the trade goods the Army gives them for signing a treaty, but the young men don't feel the slightest obligation to keep the promises their leaders made."

"The Army gives them *presents* for signing a treaty they don't intend to keep?"

"I'm afraid so. You see those wagons?" he asked, pointing to the vehicles Sarah had noticed earlier. "A few days ago, they were full of blankets and pots and cloth and beads and all sorts of things the Indians like. Now they're empty, and all we've got to show for it is a worthless piece of paper and about a dozen captives."

"A dozen?" Sarah said in surprise. "You found others?" She hadn't seen another white during her entire captivity.

"Just those few. I hate to think how many more are out there that we don't even know about."

Sarah hated to think of them, too. How fortunate she'd been that her captors had chosen to attend the treaty negotiations. How much longer might she have languished in captivity, waiting for rescue that might not come?

The Army's camp was like the Indian village in that

everyone paused in their work to gawk at the new arrivals. Acutely aware of her Indian dress, her greasy hair, and the fact that she hadn't had a bath in months, Sarah felt the stares like barbs. What would they think of her? What were they saying about her?

She imagined she heard the word "baby" whispered among the ranks of blue-coated onlookers, or perhaps she hadn't imagined it at all. Suddenly, she began to realize the truth of the warning Lieutenant Irwin had given her. It was one thing for a female captive to return with everyone knowing she had been raped by the Indians. It was quite another to have her return with living proof of the violation.

Sarah wanted to cover her child from their prying eyes, to protect her from their judgments. Since she couldn't, she just stared blindly ahead, blocking out the sight of all those curious, contemptuous eyes.

She was so studiously ignoring her surroundings that at first she didn't realize the enlisted men had dropped out of their caravan and she was riding alone with the Sergeant and the Lieutenant. No sooner had she noticed this than she noticed they had taken her to the brush arbor and she saw who was waiting under it.

At first she thought they were Indians and knew a moment's panic at the prospect of being thrust back among them. But she soon saw they weren't Indians, only dressed as Indians. Two grown women and a bunch of children ranging in age from young childhood to early teens, all clothed in a combination of tattered calico and worn doeskin and staring at her from sunken eyes, their unsmiling mouths set between hollow cheeks. Their bony arms were covered with sores; their stringy, matted hair hung down to their bowed shoulders.

35

One woman sat off to the side, huddled on the ground, knees to her chest, her frail hands ceaselessly stroking her filthy arms as if she could wipe away some taint. Her eyes were blank, dull and unseeing as she continued her futile task.

The other woman had been moving among the children who sat or lay listlessly about, less like real children than statues of children, horrible wasted statues. The woman looked up at Sarah with eyes that seemed to burn with some inner flame, a fury being held in check only with great difficulty.

"You've found another one, I see," she said in a sharp voice.

"Mrs. McDonald, this is Mrs. Sarah Peters," the sergeant said. "We found her with the Comanches."

"Well, get yourself down from there," Mrs. McDonald told Sarah. "The soldiers'll get you something decent to eat. You got a baby in there?" She pointed to the cradle board.

"Uh, yes," Sarah replied uncertainly.

"Boy or girl?"

"Girl," Sarah said.

"You must've been with 'em a long time," Mrs. McDonald observed.

Sarah felt her face burning. "Over a year."

"At least you've still got your wits, not like Mrs. Sprague over there." Mrs. McDonald gestured toward to the woman stroking her arms. "Well, get down. Lieutenant, fetch her something to eat."

The lieutenant snapped an order, and a soldier went scurrying off as Sarah swung stiffly from her saddle. Now she could see the children more clearly. The older girls looked like frightened does, their eyes wide and wary, full of the terrors they had seen and experienced.

Sarah understood those terrors only too well and couldn't bear to look at them. One of the younger girls had her feet bandaged in clean white cloth that contrasted sharply with her other garments.

"Savages held her feet in the fire when she didn't understand what they was telling her to do," Mrs. McDonald explained when she saw the direction of Sarah's gaze. "Fair roasted 'em, they did."

Sarah fought off a wave of nausea and looked away. Busying herself with freeing her daughter's cradle board from her saddle, she took some extra time to compose herself. She should have been grateful to know she wasn't the only one who had suffered. Instead she found herself resenting these other victims because they mirrored her own misery and magnified it. They looked so awful, so pathetic.

Was that how she appeared to the soldiers? Was that why they had gawked at her? Heaven knew she was thin, like them. Who could eat the half-cooked swill the Comanches called food? And she was filthy. And wounded to the depths of her soul by all she'd endured. Did her eyes look that haunted? Or that blank? Would people know from simply looking at her what had happened to her?

When she took too long about her task, Sergeant Tate's capable hands took over for her, easily untangling the rawhide ties that bound the cradle board to the saddle and lifting it for her. He carried it to one of the tables under the arbor and laid it down there.

Having no other choice, Sarah followed him, trying not to stare at the other captives. A soldier appeared with a plate of beans and a tin cup of steaming coffee. Sarah's mouth instantly began to water. Awkwardly, anxious not to appear too eager, she pulled out a bench and sat down at a table for the first time since the day the Indians had dragged her, screaming, from her house on the Texas plains.

Sarah thought she'd never tasted anything so delicious as this plate of beans, and she didn't even care that everyone was watching her eat it. When she had finished, she wiped her mouth with the back of her hand and reached for the coffee that had now cooled enough to drink. It was strong and bitter, but Sarah didn't care. She gulped it down in one breath.

When she set the cup back on the table, she noticed that one of the little boys had come over and was staring at the cradle board. His brown eyes held a spark of interest, although his little body fairly quivered with trepidation.

"Baby?" he asked tentatively.

"He don't speak English so good anymore," Mrs. McDonald explained. "Yes, it's a baby, Jimmy," she said more gently to the boy. Then she turned to the lieutenant. "You'd best get this girl some more moss for her baby. She'll be needing it if we're going to spend another night in this godforsaken place. We would've gone on to the fort this morning, but they heard about you being out there, so we had to wait another day," she told Sarah.

Sarah felt an absurd desire to apologize to the woman, and she might have if the lieutenant hadn't snapped out another order to the soldier who had brought the food, sending him off to find Sarah some moss to replace what was packed into the cradle board. In the absence of diapers, the moss absorbed the baby's bodily waste inside the carrier and kept the baby surprisingly comfortable. Sarah couldn't say she'd missed washing diapers, either, although it would be a small price to pay for her freedom.

When the lieutenant turned back to her, Sarah saw his sunburned face had grown even redder than usual. The veins at his temples bulged and his eyes burned with fury. He held his lips together so tightly, they'd turned white, as if he were holding back something vile. Was he angry with her? Had she done something to offend him? Perhaps it was some civilized thing she'd forgotten about during her captivity.

"What is it?" she asked in alarm.

"That . . . that . . ." he sputtered, gesturing to the cradle board which still lay on the table and in which her child lay sleeping. At first she thought he meant the cradle board, that she shouldn't have put it on the table. Then he burst out, "That *whelp*, that spawn of Satan! *How could you?*"

"Lieutenant," Sergeant Tate growled in warning, but the lieutenant ignored him.

"How could a white woman ever let an Indian *touch* her?" he demanded, his face crimson with rage now. "Any *decent* woman would *kill* herself before she'd let some red vermin violate her!"

Sergeant Tate made a move as if to lunge at the lieutenant, but Sarah jumped to her feet, knocking the bench over and blocking his way.

"They don't *let* you die, Lieutenant," she screamed at him, the rage she'd suppressed for so long exploding like a tidal wave in her chest. "No matter how much you don't want to, they make you *live* instead. And they give you such pain, you'll do anything to make it stop. *Anything!* They slice off the bottoms of your feet and tie you to the back of a horse and make you run through cactus. They put red hot coals up your nose when

39

you're sound asleep. They cook parts of you over the fire until they sputter and pop, or they just cut off your male parts and stuff them down your throat and let you choke on them. How would you like that, Lieutenant? And when you're screaming in agony, you'll let them do anything they want if they'll only stop the pain."

Lieutenant Irwin's face wasn't red anymore. In fact, it looked decidedly green. He gaped at her for a long moment, then suddenly clapped both hands over his mouth and bolted, nearly tripping over his own boots in his haste to get away.

For a minute no one spoke, and Sarah realized she was trembling. Then strong hands gripped her shoulders. "There, now," Mrs. McDonald was saying. "Sit down, it's all over."

Sergeant Tate had righted her bench and was pushing it against the back of her knees, forcing her to collapse into it. Vaguely, she was aware of her daughter fussing. Indian babies were trained not to cry, but the sound of Sarah screaming had disturbed her.

"That bastard woke up the little one," Mrs. McDonald observed acerbically. "Sergeant, maybe you could arrange for that one's horse to step in a chuck hole so he'd fall and break his neck sometime soon."

"My baby," Sarah murmured, somehow too drained of strength to reach for her herself.

Mrs. McDonald freed the child from the cradle board for her and passed the dear little body into Sarah's eager hands.

"Better go in the tent if you're going to feed her," Mrs. McDonald advised. "No use showing these soldiers anything they don't deserve to see."

"Tent?" Sarah asked vaguely, feeling oddly detached

from everything, as if her outburst had robbed her of her will.

This time it was Sergeant Tate's hands that helped her. She knew his touch now, the gentle strength of his fingers, and she let him lead her to one of the Army tents nearby. It held two cots, and the Sergeant helped her lie down on one of them, her baby nestled beside her. Then he spread a blanket over them both, a scratchy woolen army blanket that felt better than satin against her skin because it didn't smell of Indian.

Beneath the cover, Sarah lifted her top and offered her breast to her baby's eager mouth. She closed her eyes and savored the many pleasant sensations of warmth and comfort and safety. As if from a great distance, she heard Sergeant Tate's deep voice.

"Everything will be all right now, Sarah. You can count on it."

Chapter Two

Hunter watched the woman named Sarah for a long time after she'd fallen asleep. She was, he supposed, the most pathetic creature he'd ever seen. Starved to gauntness and marked with the abuse she'd suffered, she reminded him of the countless corpses they'd buried on the battlefield during the war. She should have been dead, too, after all she'd been through, or at least worn down to the kind of mindless oblivion that woman Mrs. Sprague suffered.

But she wasn't, and Hunter didn't pity her, not a bit. Oh, her story was sad enough. Kidnapped when her homestead was attacked, husband killed with the usual savagery, young child destroyed before her eyes, raped and beaten and enslaved, then saddled with a bastard half-breed child that would forever remind her of her ordeal. None of that seemed to matter, though, because something inside of her remained unbroken, like a rod of steel running through her soul that enabled her to bear the kind of tragedy that would have crushed most people.

Hunter would never forget the first time he'd seen

her, fighting her way through the crowd at the village, desperate for them to find her. He'd noticed her eyes first, her wonderful blue eyes. They'd burned like the center of a flame as they sought him out, and then they'd softened with relief when she saw him. She'd known he'd come for her; somehow she'd known, and she'd trusted him.

That was how his mother must have been, he thought. He'd often wondered about it but had been unable to imagine his invincible mother as a Comanche slave, beaten and broken, nurturing her child until the day she could get him away to civilization again. This was the kind of strength she must have had, the strength of a Sarah Peters.

He couldn't help but admire Sarah, especially after the way she'd put Irwin in his place. The damned little fop was probably still retching his guts out. And Hunter admired more than her spirit, too. Oh, she wasn't much to look at right now, but he could see past the dirt and the skeletal thinness. Cleaned up and given a few weeks of good food, she'd be an attractive woman once again.

Imagining how her blond hair would look washed and shining in the sunlight and how her eyes might glow if they were lit with passion, Hunter smiled to himself. She was the kind of woman who should be dressed in silk and whose delicate hands should pour tea from a china pot. And whose lovely mouth should be kissed by someone who loved her very much.

Would that ever happen now?

"Better get that baby," Mrs. McDonald said behind him.

Automatically, he stepped out of the way and let her take the infant from beneath the blanket. Sarah stirred but didn't waken. He wondered if she were that exhausted or if she was suffering from some kind of shock.

"Can't be more'n a couple months old," Mrs. McDonald said, examining the child. "Didn't you tell her she didn't have to bring it?"

Hunter smiled again. "We couldn't stop her from bringing it." He glanced at the child and was surprised to notice how fat the baby was. The cubby arms waved excitedly at him and the round face broke into a cherubic grin. "She's a cute little thing, isn't she?"

Mrs. McDonald frowned. "Yeah, and she'll have a hell of a life, too."

Too shocked to answer, Hunter let her carry the baby from the tent. After a moment, he followed. "What do you mean?" he demanded, catching up with her.

"She's a breed," Mrs. McDonald reminded him. "You of all people oughta know what that means."

Hunter felt the old anger stirring in his chest. "It's not the worst thing that can happen," he informed her defensively.

"Maybe not to a man, although I expect that's bad enough, but for a girl . . . Well, you tell me, who's gonna marry that girl in there if they gotta take on an Indian bastard into the bargain? And when this'n grows up, who's gonna marry *her?*"

Her question stopped him in his tracks, and while she walked on, carrying the child back to the shelter of the arbor to return her to her carrier, Hunter relived the moment four long years ago when beautiful Eva had told him she was marrying a *white* man instead of him. Mrs. McDonald was right, as he knew only too well.

For four years Hunter had been running from his life, using the war as an excuse to delay facing the truths he had discovered that day under the willow trees. Since then, he'd seen enough death and suffering to put his own problems into perspective, but nothing would make them disappear completely. Someday soon he'd finally be going home, and he'd have to pick up the pieces of his life once more and try to make something out of them.

His family would expect him to settle down. In fact, lately their letters had spoken of little else beyond their desire to see him with a home and family of his own. Which meant a wife.

Which was what Hunter wanted, too, a woman to love him and help him forget the horrors of war. But who would that woman be?

"Sergeant!"

Hunter turned to see Kit Carson approaching.

"I hear you found the lady you were looking for," he called, loping over.

Carson looked exactly the way Hunter had expected the renowned plainsman to look, weathered and sinewy and sharp-eyed, but nothing at all like a commissioner for the United States government, which was what he'd been for the past several weeks during the treaty negotiations. Selected for his knowledge of the Indians, he'd helped notify the tribes of the meeting, then he'd helped work out the details of the treaty and ensured the Indians would sign it.

"Yes, sir, we found her," Hunter said.

"I'd like to meet her," he said, then lowered his voice discreetly. "How is she?"

"Oh, she's as fine as she could be under the circumstances. Nothing wrong a little soap and good food won't cure. She brought back a baby, though."

Carson swore. "That's a shame. Wouldn't leave it behind, I reckon. They hardly ever do, you know. It'd be sensible, but I guess there just ain't nothing stronger than mother love."

"No, sir," Hunter agreed, thinking of his own mother's refusal to leave him behind in a Comanche camp.

"Well, where is she?"

"In the tent, sleeping, I'm afraid. She was pretty worn out."

"Not too worn out to give young Irwin a tongue lashing, I hear," Carson said, grinning broadly.

Hunter grinned back. "Good news travels fast."

Carson's hawklike gaze drifted over to where the rest of the captives lounged beneath the arbor. "At least we accomplished something with this treaty."

"I'm sure those people and their families will think so," Hunter agreed.

"I only wish I thought some other good'll come of all this talk. There's just no way to make the Indians understand that we couldn't stop the whites from moving into their hunting grounds even if the government *wanted* to, which of course they don't."

"It would help if Leavenworth wasn't so set on being kind to everybody," Hunter said.

"Yeah, for an Indian agent, he don't know squat about Indians. Imagine, thinking they'll give up their whole way of life and live in peace, all for a few trinkets and the promise of a farm."

Hunter shook his head solemnly, thinking of the fight that was bound to come when neither side was able to keep the terms of the treaty they'd signed. "There's going to be a bloodbath," he predicted.

"If we could only convince these morons from Washington of that," Carson mused, referring to the other men who'd served as commissioners in the negotiations.

"Even if we could, they wouldn't care, not if the fighting happens far away from them. If they don't have to see it, they can pretend it's not happening."

"And you know who's going to win, don't you?"

Hunter nodded. "No matter how savagely the Indians fight, there just aren't enough of them, and the buffalo are already getting scarce. A few more years, they'll be starving."

Carson sighed. "Which is the only way we'll ever get them on the reservation."

"But it won't be for a few more years yet, and in the meantime . . ."

"And in the meantime, how do *you* feel about all this, Sergeant Tate?" Carson asked shrewdly.

"Me? I just told you—"

"No, I mean how do you feel about your people being slaughtered?"

Hunter studied Carson's leathery face, looking for some clue as to exactly what his question meant. "Are you talking about my mother's people or my father's people?"

"It'll be sorta like the late war for you, won't it, son? Brother against brother. Blood against blood.

47

I'm kinda surprised you signed up with the rest of these converted Rebels to fight your own kin."

Hunter felt the hot flame of anger burning in his chest again. "I don't feel any kinship to the Comanches."

"Don't you?" Carson asked slyly. "Or maybe you just don't *want* to. You've been pretty busy lately worrying about the Yanks and the Johnny Rebs and where you stood with them, but now that they've settled their fuss, you'll have a lot bigger problem to think about, especially when you get back to Texas.

"Soon's the winter's over, the young bucks'll be on the warpath again, looking for horses and scalps, and they'll be riding clear across Texas with nobody to stop 'em, what with all the old forts abandoned and only green, Eastern troops left to fight 'em. Be a lotta folks dead before too much longer, and their kinfolk'll just as likely blame you because of the Comanche blood you don't want to think about."

Hunter stared at Carson, speechless with rage, and before he could manage a coherent reply, Carson grinned and walked away.

"Oh, and tell Mrs. Peters I'll come by to pay my respects tomorrow, will you?" he called back over his shoulder.

When Sarah awoke the next morning, she at first didn't know where she was. Then the memories came flooding back, and she sat up quickly, startling her baby who started to fuss.

"I'm sorry, little one," she crooned softly, soothing the child.

Vaguely, Sarah recalled someone rousing her in the

night to feed the baby, and wondered who it might have been. Mrs. McDonald, she guessed, although when she glanced across the tent, she saw the pathetic Mrs. Sprague sleeping in the other cot.

During the night, someone had tied a rag around the baby for a crude diaper, but it was soaked now. "You're going to have a lot of new things to get used to," she told the baby as she peeled off the diaper and let it fall to the ground. "And so will I, I guess," she added as she offered the hungry child her breast, remembering the lieutenant's outburst yesterday. Had she really stood up and screamed in his face? What had come over her? Sarah Peters, who'd never spoken out of turn in her life.

And so long as she had her daughter, she would have to deal with a lot more of the same sort of questions, she knew. Like how could she have let the Indians rape her? A stupid question to anyone who understood them the way Sarah now did, although she might once have wondered how anyone could endure the abuses she herself had endured. And why hadn't she killed herself after she'd been violated? Surely, any decent woman would have. Or so she'd once thought. Now she knew the will to live was much stronger than any other force.

Soon she heard the sounds of others in the camp rising and beginning to prepare their breakfasts. The smell of cooking food made her mouth water, and she remembered she'd fallen asleep well before supper last night. How strange. She'd never slept so long in her life, what with farm chores to do and the like.

When her baby had finished nursing, Sarah rose and straightened her clothes as best she could and, being careful not to disturb Mrs. Sprague, slipped out of the tent.

Outside, the camp was alive with activity as soldiers cooked and packed and struck their tents. Apparently, the entire place had been simply waiting for her arrival before returning to the Fort.

Which fort? In which state? Sarah realized she had no idea where she was or even in which direction from her former home in Texas. Not that she planned to return there, or anyplace else in particular, but she found she did want to know where she was right now.

Nearby a soldier was serving the other captives their breakfasts under the arbor, so Sarah settled the baby in her arms and went over to join them.

" 'Morning," Mrs. McDonald called, motioning her to a seat next to her. Some of the children looked up shyly while others just continued to eat. The same little boy who had noticed Sarah's daughter yesterday pointed a grubby finger and said "baby" again.

"That's right, Jimmy," Mrs. McDonald praised him. "Now eat your breakfast."

A soldier set a plate down in front of Sarah, and when she looked up to thank him, she caught him leering at her, an insolent grin on his pockmarked face.

"Private O'Brien!" someone snapped, and the solder jumped back guiltily.

Sarah looked up to see that Sergeant Tate had once again arrived to rescue her. The soldier slunk away, but he was rude enough to cast one last smirk at her before he did so. Sarah shivered. Was this what she would have to endure from all men from now on?

"I must apologize for our enlisted men, Mrs. Peters," Sergeant Tate said, sketching her a small bow. "I'm afraid the Indian wars don't attract the highest caliber of soldier."

Sarah didn't think anyone had ever actually bowed to her before, and the act surprised her so much she almost forgot why he was apologizing to her.

"When're we leaving this hole?" Mrs. McDonald asked when Sarah didn't reply.

"As soon as we get everything loaded up," he told her. "We'll let the bulk of the men move on ahead, but a troop will travel with you and the children at a slower pace. Even still, we should reach Fort Larned by sunset tomorrow."

"Fort Larned?" Sarah asked. "Where is that?"

"About forty miles northeast of here," he said.

"No, I mean, what state?"

His fine eyebrows lifted in surprise, but he was much too polite to make fun of her ignorance. "Kansas," he said, as if the question were a perfectly natural one. "And about five hundred miles from Texas, or at least where I'm from in Texas."

His smile was warm, and it almost took away the chill his words brought. Would she ever get back to Texas? And if she didn't go there, where *would* she go?

"Don't let me keep you from your breakfast, ladies. I'll be back in a minute with Mr. Carson. He'd like to meet you, Mrs. Peters."

With military precision, he turned away. Absently, Sarah watched him go, feeling oddly bereft. That was silly, of course. Sergeant Tate was nothing to her, not even really her rescuer. He'd just been doing

51

his job, following orders the way any soldier would.

And she must be less than nothing to him. He was probably polite to everyone, not just her. And if he didn't leer at her like some of the other men, it was only because he wasn't rude.

A few minutes later, a group of men approached the arbor, led by Sergeant Tate. One of the men was a soldier, an officer of some sort but much higher up than Lieutenant Irwin, if Sarah could judge by the braid on his coat. The rest of them were civilians, several of them dressed in broadcloth suits and two of them in buckskins.

For a moment, Sarah couldn't imagine what they wanted, then she remembered Sergeant Tate telling her he was bring someone back to meet her. She'd thought he said only one man was coming, though, but she suddenly realized they were all approaching her.

Approaching *her*, in all her filth, in her horrible Indian dress that hung over her naked body, barely concealing her nudity but not her shame at what had been done to her. They would know. They would all know. Sarah felt a surge of panic.

Her baby lay on the table in her carrier, and Sarah instinctively rose from her seat and reached for it, ready to protect herself and her child as best she could, although how she might protect them she had no idea.

Sergeant Tate was smiling, as if to reassure her that everything was all right, although she knew perfectly well it wasn't. The men stopped before her, and the officer stepped forward and took off his hat. All the other men did the same.

"Mrs. Peters, this is General Sanborn," Sergeant Tate said.

A *general*. Sarah had never hoped to see a real general in her entire life, much less speak to one. Her tongue refused to move, but the general gave no sign that her silence was unusual.

"I'm pleased to meet you, Mrs. Peters, and on behalf of the United States Army, please allow me to apologize to you for all the hardship you have endured. I assure you, it is over now, and we will be returning you to your family as soon as it is humanly possible to do so."

Sarah's mouth felt as if it were stuffed with cotton, and although she knew she should speak, she couldn't seem to force any words through her constricted throat. The general's little speech had raised so many horrible memories and the prospect of such an uncertain future, Sarah could hardly even think. Then someone squeezed her arm, and she looked down to see Mrs. McDonald was trying to reassure her. Swallowing with difficulty, Sarah at last found her voice. "I . . . thank you," was all she could think to say.

Sergeant Tate was introducing the other men to her, now. He said something about how they were commissioners or something, and how they'd just negotiated the treaty that had resulted in her release. She felt she should thank them, too, but they were so finely dressed and so finely mannered, more mannered than any men she had ever met, that she couldn't seem to find any words to say.

Then Sergeant Tate introduced the two men in buckskins. One of them was a Mr. Carson, and Sarah remembered that was the name the Sergeant had said earlier. The other was a Mr. Bent. Sarah had heard of a fort in Texas by that name and wondered if there was any connection, but of course she didn't ask. She merely nodded, unable quite to meet their steady, penetrating gazes.

While the other men had intimidated her with their dress and manners, these men did so with their knowing looks. Sarah could tell from their weathered faces and their trail-worn clothes that they had lived on the plains. They knew the Indians, knew what they did to captives, knew what she had been through in gruesome detail. She saw pity in their eyes, and understanding. She didn't want pity, and she didn't want anyone to understand.

Sarah clasped her icy hands in front of her and willed herself not to run away.

The one called Carson was smiling at her now, a strangely gentle smile. "Do you have some family back in Texas, Mrs. Peters? Someone we can notify?"

Sarah thought of how alone she was, how very much alone, and for one horrible moment the loneliness loomed before her like a black pit, waiting to suck her in. But she fought off the darkness and forced herself to respond. "I . . . no, I don't."

"She's from Tennessee originally," Sergeant Tate offered.

"You'll be wanting to go back there, then, I expect," Mr. Carson said.

Sarah saw no reason to argue, so she simply nodded.

Mr. Carson's gaze drifted to the cradle board that still lay on the table. "Cute baby," he remarked. "Boy or girl?"

"Girl," Sarah said, truly frightened now. She didn't want them looking at her baby, thinking how she should have left it behind, maybe even telling her she should have. Maybe even taking it away.

Carson smiled and chucked the baby under her plump chin. "What's her name?"

Sarah almost uttered that horrible guttural noise that meant "Bluebird" in Comanche, but she caught herself just in time. She would never call her child by that word again, nor would she use the English translation, either. "I just call her Little One. She . . . she doesn't have an American name yet."

"Maybe you'll name her after one of us," Carson suggested, his dark eyes dancing. "I think 'Carson Sanborn' has a nice ring, although I'd stay away from something like 'Bent Steele,' if I was you," he added, combining Mr. Bent's name with that of another of the commissioners.

Sarah realized with a start that he was teasing her. She hadn't been teased in so long, she couldn't even remember how to react.

Before she could, she heard someone shouting and the sound of running. She turned to see a short, wiry man racing toward them, coattails flying, holding his hat on with one hand and a book or something in the other.

"Mr. Carson, is this the other captive?" he was shouting. "What's her name? Peterson, is it?" he demanded as he skidded to a halt in front of her. "How does it feel to be back, Mrs. Peterson? How many of your family members were killed in the raid in which you were captured? Is that your baby?"

He'd snatched a pencil from behind one of his ears

55

and started writing, as if he were taking down her answers although she hadn't said a word.

"Sergeant Tate, I thought we'd gotten rid of all these goddamned reporters!" Carson exclaimed, grabbing the little man by his lapels and lifting him to his toes. The little man gasped and dropped his pencil.

"Mr. Carson, don't you know we've got freedom of the press in this country?" the reporter piped, his voice shrill with fear in spite of his defiance.

"Sergeant, will you kindly escort this vermin to the river and drown him?" Carson asked.

"With pleasure, sir," the Sergeant said. He took the reporter by the arm and began to drag him away. The reporter's face was scarlet now as he poured invectives on Carson and the others for denying him his rights.

"I'm awful sorry, Miz Peters," Mr. Carson said. "I thought all them reporters had left yesterday. They've been about driving us crazy ever since we got here, asking us questions about everything that's been going on, then writing stories without a word of truth in them so the folks back East don't have the slightest idea of what's really going on here."

"It's all your fault, Kit," Mr. Bent said cheerfully. "They only came because you're so famous. They think he's a romantic figure," he confided to Sarah with a wink.

Sarah blinked in surprise. Kit Carson? The name did sound vaguely familiar, although she wasn't sure where she'd heard it before. Perhaps her husband had spoken of the man long ago, in her other life. At any rate, her mind was too muddled right now to sort it all out.

At the moment, she just wanted them all to stop staring at her and go away and leave her alone. Perhaps her feelings showed on her face because General Sanborn said, "We're very happy to have met you, Mrs. Peters, and we'll be seeing you again when we all reach the fort."

They took their leave and only when they were walking away did Sarah remember she hadn't actually thanked them for freeing her. Feeling unutterably weary, she sank back down onto the bench where she'd been sitting when they arrived.

"You did just fine," Mrs. McDonald assured her, patting her arm. "They just like to make sure we're still in our right minds. Makes 'em feel a little better about letting us get captured in the first place and all."

Sarah was barely listening. All she could think was that they'd come and gone and none of them had said a thing about taking her baby away. When she finally unclasped her hands, she found they were trembling.

On the trip back to the fort, they let Sarah and the other captives ride in the funny wagons she'd noticed before. The soldiers called them "ambulances." Sarah didn't care what they were called. She was too thankful for the concealment they provided her. Inside the sturdy wooden walls, no soldiers could see her, much less stare or leer at her and her child.

Sarah shared a wagon with Mrs. Sprague and several of the older children. No one spoke very much on the trip. Mrs. Sprague contented herself with rub-

57

bing her arms in that same futile motion, and the children either dozed or stared listlessly out the back of the wagon.

The caravan stopped at noon to eat, then continued until dark before stopping again. The children were fretting with hunger by then, all except Sarah's baby, who had already nursed herself to contentment.

The soldiers prepared a meal for them, and when Sarah looked around camp, she realized that the bulk of the men had indeed gone on ahead. Only about thirty remained to guard them, although that was probably more than enough to protect them under the circumstances, Sarah reasoned.

After they had eaten, Sergeant Tate came by to make sure they were being properly tended before going about his other duties.

"Did you get enough supper?" he asked Sarah, hunkering down beside where she sat on a blanket one of the men had spread for her and the baby.

"Oh, yes, everything was wonderful," Sarah assured him.

"You don't have to lie," he admonished her with a grin. "Army food is never *wonderful.*"

"It seemed like it to me, I'm afraid," she admitted, feeling a warm flush spreading all over her body. She couldn't imagine what was the matter with her. Maybe she was coming down with a fever or something, although she didn't feel a bit sick. "I was getting awful tired of half-cooked buffalo meat."

"I expect you were. And how about you, Little One?" he asked the baby who was lying naked on the blanket, enjoying her freedom from the cradle board. "Did you get enough to eat, too?"

"Oh, she doesn't eat real food yet," Sarah hastened to explain. "I still . . . I mean, she . . ." This time the warmth turned to fire as Sarah's face blazed with embarrassment. What on earth was she saying?

But Sergeant Tate was grinning, his gray eyes sparkling with silent laughter. "I know," he said, giving the baby one finger to grab. Delighted, the infant squealed and thrashed her arms and legs in excitement. "What I can't figure out is how she got so fat when you're so skinny."

Sarah hadn't been able to figure that out either, so she just had to sit there and blush in silent mortification while her daughter enjoyed his brief attention.

After a few minutes, he shook loose of the baby's grasp and rose to his feet. "Try to get some rest tonight. We should be at the fort by tomorrow afternoon unless something happens."

"What could happen?" Sarah asked in alarm, instantly forgetting her embarrassment.

"Oh, the usual things, a wagon losing a wheel, we get a late start or something." Then, seeing her fear, his silver eyes narrowed in the firelight. "You don't have to be afraid anymore, Mrs. Peters. You're safe now. I won't let anything happen to you."

Relieved, she laid a hand on her chest to still her clamoring heart. "Thank you," she whispered around the lump that had formed in her throat.

For a long moment he just stared down at her, his silver eyes unfathomable. "Get some rest now," he said at last and walked off to check on the other former captives.

When he left, Sarah released the breath she hadn't realized she'd been holding. Then she caught herself watching after him, admiring his tall, broad-shouldered figure, and jerked her gaze guiltily away. What had come over her? Just because a man said he'd take care of her . . .

Suddenly, she realized he'd said *he* would take care of her. Not the United States Army, not even this group of soldiers in particular, but he himself alone. The thought made a little flutter in her stomach, but she quickly squelched it. He hadn't really meant he was taking personal responsibility for her. That was probably just the way soldiers talked.

Although the promise did make her feel a whole lot safer.

Too bad he was part Indian, she told herself. Or perhaps it was good. At least she didn't have to worry about liking him. She could never really like an Indian, or trust one either. So she didn't have to worry about getting too used to his kindness or coming to rely on him too much. Or starting to think he was being anything more than kind. She knew he didn't care anything about her as a person, just as she didn't care anything about him. After they got to the fort, she'd probably never see him again.

As she prepared herself and her baby for bed, she tried not to wonder why that prospect made her feel sad.

As she lay in the darkness of the tent the soldiers had pitched for her and Mrs. Sprague to share, Sarah listened to the sounds outside, sounds totally unlike the sounds of a Comanche camp. Comforting sounds, like the rattle of harness and the thud of boots on the sun-dried earth.

Gradually, those sounds died, too, as the soldiers also settled in for the night, and Sarah savored the silence as well. Only after she'd lain there for a while did she realize why she hadn't fallen asleep yet. The coffee she'd drunk at supper—a beverage she was still getting used to drinking again—had finished its progress through her body and was now clamoring to be eliminated again.

With a sigh of exasperation, Sarah slipped out of her cot, being careful to tuck her baby in securely and being silent so as not to disturb Mrs. Sprague's slumber. Pulling back the tent flap, she looked to see if anyone was around to see her, but everything seemed perfectly quiet and peaceful.

Silent in her Indian moccasins, she stole out of the tent and hurried to the edge of the camp, skirting the other tents and the bedrolls of the sleeping soldiers. She knew where the latrines had been dug, but she didn't go there for fear of encountering a soldier in the dark. Instead she crept to the privacy of some sort of bush far beyond the outskirts of the camp.

Ducking behind it, she quickly hiked up her skirt and relieved herself. When she was finished, she shook her skirt back down and turned, in an equal hurry to return to the privacy of her tent. She cried out to see a dark figure looming up before her.

"Shhh," the man cautioned. "You don't want everybody in camp to know we're out here, do you?"

Sarah's heart was pounding in her chest. Had he followed her? Had he watched her? Humiliation warred with apprehension as she tried to decide whether or not she was in danger. "I . . . I have to get back to my baby," she said, stepping to the side to go around him.

"Not so fast," he said, reaching out an arm to block her way. "I been wanting to talk to you. You oughta be glad to talk to a white man for a change. You oughta be glad any white man *wants* to talk to you."

Sarah didn't think talking was what he wanted from her, and when he turned slightly, the light from the dying campfires illuminated his face and she recognized him as the soldier who had been leering at her this morning at breakfast. What had Sergeant Tate called him? O'Brien?

Fear coiled in her chest, but she forced it down. She was no longer alone and defenseless, as she had been with the Comanches. "Let me pass, please," she said as firmly as she could.

"You don't want to go anywhere, not until we've had a little fun." He threw out his other arm, in case she tried to dodge that way. "I always wondered what it'd be like to have me an Indian squaw, but I never could stomach those heathen bitches. You, now, you're a squaw but you're white, too."

Sarah wanted to scratch his eyes out, but she knew too well the futility of trying to fight for her honor. "If you don't let me alone, I'll scream," she told him. "Every soldier in this camp'll be here in a second."

He smiled, his teeth white in the fire light. "You'd like that, wouldn't you? Maybe you'd like to have every soldier in this camp. We could line up for it, take turns. What do you think? It's all right with me, so long as I get to be first."

She opened her mouth to scream, but he grabbed her and clamped a hand over her mouth, smothering the cry. "Don't make a sound," he hissed, his breath hot and stinking in her face. "If you do, I'll just say you told me to meet you out here but you got mad when I wouldn't pay you what you wanted. Then they'll *all* know you're a whore."

He held her tightly against his body, and she could feel the hard evidence of his lust. She squirmed frantically, trying to break free, but he was too strong and only seemed to enjoy her efforts.

"That's it," he said. "Them Injins taught you good."

She tried to kick his shins, but her moccasins had no effect against his boots. Struggling, she fought to free her mouth so she could scream. They wouldn't believe his story! They'd come to help her!

Or would they? Her fear turned icy as she clawed at his hands and felt her own helplessness against his strength.

"I'll give you a white baby to go with your red one," he snarled, forcing her backwards.

"Private O'Brien!"

His body stiffened, and he jerked around, still holding Sarah fast with one arm. "Wait your turn!" he snapped viciously.

Then they both saw Sergeant Tate step out of the shadows. "Take your hands off her," he said, his voice ringing with steel.

O'Brien released Sarah so quickly, she almost fell.

"This ain't what you think, Sergeant! She told me to meet her!"

"No!" Sarah cried in horror.

"You're wasting your time, O'Brien," Sergeant Tate said. "I heard every word you said to her, and I think the general might be interested in it, too."

O'Brien hastily stepped away from Sarah. "They won't believe you!" he insisted. "Not a Johnny Reb and a half-breed into the bargain. Everybody knows she's an Indian whore. She's got that baby, ain't she?"

Sarah cried out in anguish this time, but neither man seemed to notice her.

"You know I could shoot you where you stand, don't you, O'Brien? For trying to rape a civilian female under Army protection?" This time it was Sergeant Tate who smiled, and the sight chilled Sarah's blood.

"You'd never get away with it!" O'Brien tried, edging still farther away from her. "They'd hang you!"

"Maybe they would and maybe they wouldn't, but you'd still be just as dead."

"I didn't hurt her none," O'Brien said. He was whining now, and Sarah could smell the stink of his fear. "Hell, she's just a—"

"Don't say it," Tate warned. "In fact, if you're going to say anything at all, I think you'd better apologize to Mrs. Peters."

"What?"

"You heard me," Tate said. "Or maybe you'd like to be called up in front of the general to do it. Or maybe . . ." Very deliberately, he lifted the cover of his holster.

"I'm really sorry, ma'am," O'Brien blurted. "I didn't mean no harm."

Sarah gasped at the blatant lie and would have spit in his face if Tate hadn't distracted her.

"And I'd better not hear a word about this from anyone else, O'Brien," he warned, giving Sarah a whole new reason to be terrified of the soldier. "Because if I do . . . Well, just don't give me a reason to be sorry I didn't kill you right here. Now aren't you supposed to be on guard duty?"

O'Brien was gone in an instant, disappearing into the night shadows as swiftly as he had appeared. For a minute Sarah couldn't believe it was really over, that she was safe from that monster. Then reaction set in, and she began to tremble.

"Are you all right?" Sergeant Tate asked, hurrying to her.

She didn't want him to touch her. She didn't want any man to touch her ever again, but her knees wouldn't hold her up anymore, so when his arms caught her, she didn't resist his strength. Instead, she sank into it, gritting her teeth against the urge to weep out her terror and frustration.

"I thought it was over," she groaned against his chest. "I thought I didn't need to be afraid anymore."

He didn't say anything for a long time; he just held her and patted her shoulder. Then, finally, he said, "I didn't think so either."

Startled, she jerked away from him. She didn't know what she'd expected him to say, probably some drivel about how everything would be fine now, but she certainly hadn't expected him to confirm her fears. "What?" she demanded.

"You're going to have to be careful," he said, dropping his hands to his sides. "What on earth were you doing out here by yourself anyway?" Now he sounded angry. What did *he* have to be angry about, for God's sake?

"I was . . . I was . . ." she sputtered, gesturing helplessly and trying to think of a decent way to explain her purpose in coming out here.

65

Apparently, he got the point. "Then why didn't you go to the latrines?" he demanded.

"Because I didn't want to see any soldiers," she informed him. "Because I didn't want *this* to happen!"

"Well, you shouldn't have gone so far from camp," he countered.

"But I didn't want any soldiers to see me, either!" she cried in exasperation. "I didn't want anybody to think I was wandering around in the night looking for company! You act like this was *my* fault!"

"Of course it wasn't *your* fault! You should just be more careful!"

"I've been careful all my life, Sergeant, and it didn't stop the Comanches from killing my family and taking me away and it won't stop the Private O'Brien's of this world either!"

She was trembling again, this time with fury, but the weakness had vanished in the red haze of her outrage.

To her surprise, Sergeant Tate smiled again, a real smile this time. "I think it's my turn to apologize to you now, Mrs. Peters. You're absolutely right, I *was* trying to blame you for being a victim, probably because I'm angry at myself for not protecting you better and I didn't want to admit my own failing. I'm sorry, and I beg your forgiveness."

No one had ever apologized to Sarah quite so eloquently, and she didn't know exactly what he expected her to say, so she just stood there while the roiling of her own fury gradually boiled down to a bubble of resentment.

"Are you, uh, ready to go back now?" he asked after a moment.

"Yes," she said stiffly, then remembered she'd left her baby all alone. "Oh, I'd better hurry. The baby . . ."

He didn't need any more explanations. He took her arm just as he had in the Indian camp—had that only been yesterday? Sarah knew she should have resented his touch or at least objected to it, but her legs were still unsteady enough for her to appreciate the help. He guided her unerringly through the maze of tents and sleeping men to her own bed.

Listening at the flap of her tent, she heard only the soft sounds of sleep from within and sighed with relief. Then she turned back to where Sergeant Tate waited expectantly. The course of Sarah's life until this moment had never required her to exercise formal courtesies or even to learn what polite society might have called good manners. A poor farmer's wife seldom needed such skills.

Now she stood before a man who had rescued her, not once but twice. He'd saved whatever might have been left of her good name and certainly of her self-respect. Because of him, she needn't dread facing the morrow and Private O'Brien, and none of the other soldiers would hear stories about her, either. There were probably words to express the gratitude she owed him, but Sarah didn't know them. At the moment, she wasn't even sure she *felt* that gratitude.

She said the only thing she was certain was true. "I'm very glad you came along when you did tonight."

His smile brightened his face again. "I didn't just 'come along.' I was following you."

"*Following?*" she echoed in renewed alarm.

"Yes, it's my responsibility to keep you safe until

67

you're back home again, Mrs. Peters. I couldn't let you go sneaking around the camp all alone and unprotected, now could I?"

"I wasn't sneaking around the camp!" she informed him, outraged all over again.

His smile never wavered. "I thought you said you didn't want anyone to see you. Isn't that sneaking?"

She supposed it was, but still . . . "It's . . . it's late," she said at last, knowing she was taking the easy way out, but also knowing she'd never be able to best him in a battle of wits.

"You're right, and I'm keeping you from your rest. You aren't planning any more excursions tonight, are you?"

Sarah didn't know what an excursion was, so she certainly wasn't planning any. "No, I'm going right to sleep."

"Good, I'll see you in the morning then. Tomorrow you'll be sleeping in a real bed at the fort. You'll have some real clothes, too. The officers' wives will take good care of you and the other captives. You won't have a thing to worry about from now on, Mrs. Peters."

Sarah's heart turned to stone in her chest. *Officers' wives.* How would they look at her? And at her baby? What would they think? And more importantly, what would they say?

Nothing to worry about? Sarah didn't think she'd ever been so worried in her life.

Chapter Three

The next morning, Sarah didn't catch so much as a glimpse of Private O'Brien, much to her relief. Even still, she dreaded what else the day might bring. All the other captives seemed thrilled that they would finally be reaching the safety of the fort and that they would soon be returning to their homes and families. Perhaps if she'd had someone who would welcome her home, she'd feel the same way. Instead, she felt only apprehension when she considered the future.

As Sergeant Tate had promised, they reached their destination late in the afternoon. At first Sarah hadn't recognized the fort for what it was. She was used to stockades with high walls to protect the inhabitants, but Fort Larned had no such walls. It looked more like a regular town, a collection of buildings of various sizes built around a large empty square.

The children sharing her wagon began to chatter excitedly at the sight of it. Sarah wished she could share their enthusiasm, or at least express her apprehension to another adult, but Mrs. Sprague just stared vacantly off into space and continued to rub her arms, oblivious of the momentous change that was about to take place in her life.

All the occupants of the fort, including the soldiers who had been at the treaty negotiations and who had arrived much earlier, were gathering to watch the caravan as it wound its way onwards. The children hung out the rear of the wagon, waving at well-wishers along the way, but Sarah scrunched herself into the far corner, clinging to her baby's carrier, out of sight of curious eyes.

Acutely conscious of her tattered doeskin dress, her greasy hair, and her desperate need of a bath, Sarah cringed at the thought of being paraded past more soldiers and — even worse! — their wives. Sarah herself had felt pity when she had seen how bedraggled the other captives were and knew she must look just as bad as they. She didn't want anyone looking at her and her baby with pity.

Or the contempt she'd seen on Lieutenant Irwin's face.

For one crazy moment she wished for Sergeant Tate's strong arm to lean on, for his protection against whatever was to come. No sooner had she called herself a fool than the wagon stopped and the children bounded out, shrieking with joy.

A soldier Sarah had never seen before appeared at the back of the wagon and offered to help her down. On legs rubbery with trepidation, she accepted his help, clinging tightly to the cradle board and its precious burden, using it as a shield against prying eyes.

But she wasn't outside more than a second. The

70

soldier conducted her immediately into a large building, a hall of some kind, where the ladies Sarah had so feared were waiting.

They were everything she'd dreaded, neat and well-groomed and finely dressed, at least to Sarah's unschooled eye. She wanted to run, but before she could, two of them had descended on her, taking her by the arm and leading her away. At first she was too frightened to notice where they were taking her, and their soothing murmurs gave her no clue. Then they led her behind a blanket that had been hung from a rope strung across the room and she saw a bathtub.

"Oh!" she cried, suddenly realizing the room had been divided up into several such blanketed cubicles and all the captives were being escorted into them.

"Yes, I expected a bath is the first thing you'd be wanting," one of her escorts said matter-of-factly. "We'll have some hot water here in a minute. Is that a baby you've got there?"

Instinctively, Sarah hugged the cradle board more tightly, but the other lady was too strong for her and wrested it away from her before Sarah could even protest.

"I'll do that," Sarah tried when the woman began to unwrap the baby, but no one paid her any mind.

"We need some hot water here," the first lady called, then held back the blanket while a soldier carried in two steaming buckets. Sarah watched, mesmerized with longing, as he poured it into the tub.

"I expect it'll take more than one bath to get you really clean, but we'll make a start at least," the first lady said. "By the way, I'm Mrs. Wynkoop, Major

71

Wynkoop's wife. He was at the treaty negotiations. Perhaps you met him?"

"I . . . no, I don't think so," Sarah muttered absently, intent on watching the other woman unwrapping her baby.

"And this is Mrs. Sterling," Mrs. Wynkoop added, indicating the other woman.

Mrs. Sterling looked up and smiled briefly before going back to the task of freeing the child. "A little girl," she announced when she had finished and Sarah's daughter lay naked on a blanket Mrs. Sterling had spread on the floor. The child's raven hair shone in the afternoon sunlight and her coppery limbs flailed in a celebration of freedom, proclaiming her every inch a breed. "Isn't she . . . cute," Mrs. Sterling added. This time her smile seemed a little strained.

"You've been through a lot, haven't you?" Mrs. Wynkoop asked Sarah, her voice kind and her eyes soft with sympathy, and Sarah had to blink against the sting of tears. She wouldn't weep in front of these women. She wasn't ashamed of her baby or anything else, and she wouldn't let them think she was.

The soldier had finished pouring the water, and he slipped out between the hanging blankets.

"Now, let's get that filthy thing off you," Mrs. Wynkoop said, all business once more as she efficiently stripped off Sarah's dress, leaving her naked. Before Sarah could even think to be embarrassed, Mrs. Wynkoop was helping her into the tub. The delicious warmth enveloped her, and for one wonderful moment Sarah forgot everything else.

"This lye soap'll take care of just about anything," Mrs. Wynkoop said, startling Sarah rudely back to reality and reminding her of her shamefully filthy state.

"It was so hard to keep clean," she muttered, unable to meet the other women's eyes as she accepted the offered soap and rag.

"Of course it was. Why, even the soldiers get lice when they're in the field."

Sarah's face flamed, but she doggedly ignored her own humiliation and concentrated on scrubbing the lye soap over every inch of her body. The other lady slipped out and returned with another bucket of water, which she used to bathe the baby.

Sarah watched enviously from the corner of her eye as another woman gave her daughter her first real bath. The child thoroughly enjoyed the sensual experience and cooed through the whole thing.

"She's a good-natured little thing," Mrs. Sterling remarked.

"The Indians teach them not to cry," Sarah said without thinking, and when the other women looked up in surprise, she was forced to explain. "When a baby first tries to cry, they hold its nose so it can't get its breath and has to stop crying. After they do that a few times, the baby doesn't try to cry anymore."

"How cruel," Mrs. Sterling exclaimed in outrage.

"I don't know," Mrs. Wynkoop disagreed. "I think I'd like having a baby who didn't cry." She smiled at Sarah who tried to smile back, but she was too busy trying to see if their eyes held the pity or the contempt she so dreaded.

"I'll help you scrub your hair," Mrs. Wynkoop offered, taking the soap from Sarah when she'd finished lathering her face and body.

Sarah wanted to object. She didn't want a stranger touching her so intimately, but Mrs. Wynkoop was already scrubbing the soap over her head, building the strong lather that would cut through the bear grease and carry away the vermin. After a few seconds, Sarah's concerns evaporated under the blissful luxury of her ministrations, and Sarah gave herself up to the sensations.

Mrs. Wynkoop rinsed and lathered Sarah's hair twice more before she was satisfied, and by then Sarah saw that most of the ground-in dirt had soaked out of her hands and knees and elbows.

Mrs. Sterling had long since finished bathing the baby and wrapped her in a towel. Now she slipped out through the hanging blankets while Sarah got out of the tub and allowed Mrs. Wynkoop to help her dry off. Sarah had never realized how wonderful it could be simply to feel clean. Her hair actually squeaked as she rubbed it with the towel.

When she was dry and Mrs. Wynkoop had wrapped her in a clean blanket, Mrs. Sterling came back carrying some clothes draped over her arm.

"These aren't very nice, I'm afraid," she apologized as she separated the clothes into two groups. "It's only what the ladies at the fort could spare from their own wardrobes, but it will do until we can get you some new things made up."

With a smile, she offered Sarah the largest of the bundles. Almost afraid to accept it, Sarah took the

74

clothing. A quick glance told her it included a faded gingham dress, a threadbare petticoat and some stockings. She didn't think she'd ever seen anything so beautiful in her entire life.

"I've got a few diapers and a gown for the baby," Mrs. Sterling went on, oblivious to Sarah's reaction. "You can get some flannel sheeting from the sutler's store to make some more later."

Sarah's happiness evaporated. How on earth could she buy something from the store when she had no money and no way of getting any?

"I'm afraid we couldn't find any shoes, so you'll have to wear those until we can get you some," Mrs. Sterling added, indicating Sarah's discarded moccasins.

Sarah's heart sank completely, but she tried to match the enthusiasm of the other women as they helped her dress in her new finery. And the clothes did help, even if she still had to wear moccasins with them. The moccasins hardly showed under the too-long skirt, and from the ankles up, at least, she looked and felt like a white woman again.

Mrs. Sterling had a time of it putting the diaper and gown on a baby who had never worn clothes before and thought the whole process was some sort of new game. But at last the child, too, was clothed, and Mrs. Sterling placed her in Sarah's eager arms. Instinctively, the baby began to nuzzle her breast through the cloth of her dress, and the other women laughed knowingly.

"I reckon we'd better get you someplace where you can feed that child in private," Mrs. Wynkoop said. "What's her name, anyway?"

75

"I . . . I haven't given her a name yet," Sarah hedged, thinking she should do so and soon, although she couldn't seem to think about it right now. Maybe later when things had settled down a bit, and she wasn't so worried about everything else.

"If you don't mind, you can stay with my husband and me while you're here at the fort," Mrs. Wynkoop was saying.

"That's very nice of you," Sarah said, knowing her limited social skills had once again left her uncertain about how to properly express her gratitude to such a fine lady as Mrs. Wynkoop.

"Oh, don't worry," Mrs. Wynkoop said, misunderstanding her reticence. "You won't be here long. A local fellow, a Mr. Dunlap, has volunteered to carry you all back to Texas. As soon as everyone's had a chance to rest up, you'll be on the road back home again. Probably won't be more than a few days before you leave."

Sarah tried to return Mrs. Wynkoop's smile, but her heart felt like a stone in her chest.

Hunter had been right. Sarah Peters *was* an attractive woman when she was cleaned up. Her hair was even •blonder than he'd imagined and shined like a brand new gold piece in the sunlight. The dress wasn't too nice and it hung loose on her slender frame, but he could still see the potential.

He'd been waiting outside the dining hall for each of the captives to come out. One of his jobs was to make sure none of the soldiers loitering about made any rude remarks to them. Hunter couldn't blame the men for being curious, though. Sometimes the captives were interesting sights, with noses and ears burned off. Fortunately, there was nothing too horrible to see in this bunch. His other job was to make sure all the captives were being taken in by one or another of the officers' wives.

The children were the easiest to place. Everyone felt supremely sorry for them and wanted to mother them. The women were harder because, while everyone felt just as sorry for them, the fact that they'd been raped by the Indians made them less than respectable, at least in some folks' eyes.

So Major Wynkoop had asked Hunter to make sure the women weren't slighted. He wasn't too worried about Mrs. McDonald or Mrs. Sprague. No one would ever dare slight Mrs. McDonald, and Mrs. Sprague was in her own world where feelings no longer existed. But Sarah Peters was another matter. While he knew she could stand up for herself, as she'd done against Private O'Brien, damn him to hell, Hunter couldn't help seeing the pain and uncertainty in her lovely blue eyes whenever he mentioned the future.

Hunter felt a lot better when he saw Sarah being escorted by Mrs. Wynkoop herself, and before he could think about it, he stepped forward and greeted Sarah as she came out of the hall.

"Good afternoon, Mrs. Peters," he said, pulling off his hat.

She jumped a little in surprise at being addressed, but he was glad to see some of her wariness dissipate when she recognized him. "Hello, Sergeant," she said softly.

"You look very nice," he told her, ignoring Mrs. Wynkoop's disapproving frown. Probably she thought he was being forward or something. Maybe she even thought he might be disrespectful to a returned female captive. God knew, and Hunter did, too, that other soldiers would be.

At his compliment, Sarah hunched her shoulders self-consciously and shifted her baby uneasily. "Thank you," she murmured.

"Sergeant, I don't think Mrs. Peters wants to stand out here all afternoon letting people gawk at her," Mrs. Wynkoop informed him sharply.

He continued to ignore her. "Did you hear?" he asked Sarah. "A local man has offered to take all of you back to Texas in his wagon. They'll notify your family to meet you in Austin."

Once again he saw the flash of panic in her eyes. "I don't have any family left in Texas," she said.

"Oh, that's right, you're from Tennessee," he remembered, trying to reassure her. "Well, we'll be glad to make arrangements for you to get back there. If you'll just tell Major Wynkoop whom he should notify—"

"There's nobody," she blurted, the panic widening her eyes. "I mean, I don't have anyone—"

"Now don't you worry about a thing," Mrs. Wynkoop said, slipping an arm around Sarah's thin shoulders and giving Hunter one last glare. "We'll take care of you. Sergeant, I'll thank you not to upset our guests."

78

"Yes, ma'am," he said, giving her his most charming smile. It didn't seem to move her much, though. She just took a firmer hold on Sarah and led her away, toward the Wynkoop's house.

Glancing around, Hunter saw the men who were loitering in the area watching after her. He couldn't blame them, either. Fresh from her bath, she looked good enough to eat. Hunter pursed his lips as he thought about how sweet she'd taste, too.

Sweet and spirited. That's the way Hunter liked his women. For an instant he wondered what his mother would have thought of her and what she would have said to Sarah to dispel that haunted look in her eyes. "Now don't you worry about a thing," was what Mrs. Wynkoop had said, but that didn't seem like very practical advice for somebody with no place to go and no family to take her in.

Suddenly, Hunter felt an overwhelming urge to protect her somehow, to do something himself that would make Sarah Peters *really* stop worrying and maybe even smile. But that was silly. There was nothing he could do for her, and he had his own problems to worry about.

Like what he was going to do in a few weeks when his enlistment was up and he went back to Texas. The Tate family farm belonged to him now that his grandfather was dead, but he didn't want to be a farmer. He'd heard people were starting to run cattle, and the Tate holdings were certainly large enough for such a project, but having something to do with his life now that the war was over was only half of a solution. The other half was having somebody to do things *for*. That meant a family. That meant a wife. But he remembered dear sweet Eva's condemnation all too clearly. What decent woman would marry a breed?

Instinctively, his gaze darted to Sarah Peters who was now almost to the Wynkoop's house.

What woman indeed. Only a woman who was desperate. Only a woman who had no other options.

Only a woman like Sarah Peters.

The next afternoon, Hunter caught up with Major Wynkoop when he was walking across the parade ground.

"Afternoon, Sergeant," Wynkoop said, casually returning Hunter's brisk salute.

"Good afternoon, sir. I was wondering if I might talk to you a minute."

"Take as long as you like," Wynkoop said. "I'm heading for my office to do some paperwork, so I'm glad for any delay."

Hunter smiled. "Thank you, sir. It's about Mrs. Peters."

"Mrs. Peters?" he asked in surprise. "The lady who's staying at my house?"

"Yes, sir, we . . . we got acquainted on the trip back to the fort."

"I see," the Major said, although plainly he didn't see at all. "Maybe we'd better do this in my office," he suggested, pushing open the door to the crude building where he worked. Inside, a soldier rose as the major walked through the outer office into his private one and closed the door behind him and Hunter.

"Sit down, Sergeant. Would you like a drink?"

Hunter would have loved a drink, but he said, "If you agree to what I'm going to ask, I don't think I want to have whisky on my breath, but thanks just the same."

Now the major was thoroughly intrigued, but he waited until he'd sat down behind his desk, pulled a bottle and a glass from one of the bottom drawers and poured himself a drink. "Now what's this about Mrs. Peters?" he asked, taking a sip.

"I'd like to have your permission to call on her."

Major Wynkoop choked on his drink and had to cough for a few minutes before he could ask, "Call on her? By God, that sounds like you want to court her, Tate."

"I do, sir."

"But . . . but you've only known the woman a few days, and she . . . well, she's been with the Indians and . . ." He gestured vaguely, not wanting to be indiscreet.

"*I'm* an Indian, or at least I'm part Indian," he reminded the Major.

Major Wynkoop seemed nonplused for a moment, but he recovered quickly. "Yes, of course, but it's not the same thing. I mean, she's been through quite an ordeal and—"

"Do you think her mind has been affected?" Hunter inquired.

"Oh, no," Wynkoop hastily assured him. "She seemed perfectly normal when I spoke to her last

81

evening, but . . . well, there's the child, too. Have you thought of that?"

"A half-breed bastard? I've thought about that my entire life."

Wynkoop had the grace to flush, but he wasn't yet convinced. "Your intentions, Sergeant, are they completely honorable? I'm sorry to be so blunt, but the woman is under my protection, you see, and —"

"My intentions are completely honorable, Major. I have nothing but the utmost respect for Mrs. Peters."

"Well, then," Major Wynkoop said, seemingly at a loss for words. "Well, then, when did you . . . I mean, how soon were you planning to call on her? This evening might —"

"Right now, if I have your permission," Hunter said, straightening in his chair.

The Major looked at him in renewed surprise, then his eyes narrowed speculatively. "I thought there was something. . . . You've had a haircut, haven't you?"

"Yes, sir, and a bath and I got one of the laundresses to iron my uniform so I'd look respectable. So with your permission . . ."

"Oh, yes, of course, I . . . She seems like a nice girl, Tate," he added gruffly. "I wish you success."

"Thank you, sir." Hunter rose and saluted again.

Wynkoop returned it with a sly grin. "Oh, and be sure to tell my wife I sent you. She's very protective of her charge, you know."

Hunter did know.

* * *

82

Sarah carefully laid her sleeping daughter into the box that was serving as a makeshift cradle during their stay at the Wynkoop's house. The baby still fussed a little at being bound in clothes and laid in a bed instead of being carried all the time, but she was adapting. Soon, she'd behave just like a white baby. Except, of course, she'd never cry.

And she'd never *look* like a white baby, either, and no one would ever mistake her for one. What would happen to her now? Had Sarah been foolish to insist on keeping her child? Foolish and selfish when the girl might have grown up happy as an Indian? Whenever Sarah allowed herself to think about it, she wanted to cry, so she tried not to think about it. Besides, nothing could have compelled her to leave the baby behind in an Indian camp, so it was silly to even wonder about it. Just as silly as it was to wonder what would become of them now.

Sarah jumped at the sound of someone knocking on the Wynkoop's front door. Calling herself an idiot, she laid a calming hand over her clamoring heart and reminded herself she had nothing to be afraid of. Mrs. Wynkoop was doing an admirable job of keeping the curious away, even the other ladies of the fort who thought it their Christian duty to bring food or castoff clothing to Sarah and her child and who, by the way, wanted to see what the little bastard looked like and find out firsthand what it was like to be a Comanche captive.

So far, Sarah hadn't had to speak to or even see any of them. Now she sat quietly in the corner of the kitchen where Mrs. Wynkoop had fixed up a cot for her and the bed for the baby. The house was small, only three rooms, so Sarah could still hear everything very plainly while remaining completely out of sight.

The front door opened and Mrs. Wynkoop asked, "Yes?" in her haughtiest tones. If Sarah had been the visitor, she would have scurried away as quickly as her legs would carry her.

This visitor wasn't so easily intimidated, however. She heard a male voice say, "Good afternoon, Mrs. Wynkoop. I'd like to see Mrs. Peters, if you don't mind."

"About what?" she demanded imperiously.

"Well, it's a personal matter, ma'am," the voice said, and Sarah thought it sounded familiar, although she couldn't quite place it.

"I'm afraid Mrs. Peters isn't receiving visitors, Sergeant, and quite frankly, I'm shocked that you would be so forward as to—"

"Major Wynkoop gave me his permission to call on her," the voice said, and now Sarah's heart was hammering again as she recognized it as Sergeant Tate's. Why on earth was he here? What on earth could he want to talk to her about?

"Then Major Wynkoop will have to tell me so himself," Mrs. Wynkoop was saying. "When he has, you will certainly be welcome to do so, but until then—"

"Maybe you should ask Mrs. Peters if she'd *like* to see me," Sergeant Tate insisted.

Sarah hadn't even realized she'd risen, much less that she was walking into the front room until she heard herself say, "Mrs. Wynkoop?"

The other woman was as startled as she by the

84

sound of her voice. "Sarah, you don't have to do anything you don't want to do," Mrs. Wynkoop assured
her.

"I . . . I don't mind," she said, surprised to realize
it was true. In fact, not only didn't she mind seeing
Sergeant Tate, her stomach was fluttering with anticipation at the prospect. She clenched her hands over
it and tried to smile.

"Well, if you're sure," Mrs. Wynkoop said doubt-
fully, but Sergeant Tate didn't wait for a confirma-
tion. He very skillfully maneuvered around Mrs.
Wynkoop and stepped into the room.

Sarah blinked in surprise at the sight of his broad
smile. He looked different, much different, than the
dusty, saddle-weary soldier who had found her at the
Indian camp. Today his hair was neatly trimmed and
his uniform immaculate. In her faded gingham dress,
she felt suddenly as shabby as she had in her Indian
garb.

"Good afternoon, Mrs. Peters," he said.

"Good afternoon," she replied, much less confidently.

"I was wondering if I might speak to you." He
glanced at Mrs. Wynkoop. "Privately."

"I'm sure anything you have to say to Mrs. Peters
can be said in my presence, young man, and if it
can't, then you've got no business saying it in the first
place," Mrs. Wynkoop informed him.

"I appreciate your concern for Mrs. Peters," he replied, not the least disturbed, "and I assure you, I
have nothing to say that you or she would be embarrassed to hear. It's just that some things are best kept

85

between the two people involved." He grinned wickedly. "And if you're worried, I'm sure Mrs. Peters will call for help if I somehow manage to offend her. You're bound to hear her from the other room, aren't you?"

Mrs. Wynkoop's face was scarlet with indignation, but she couldn't seem to think of any arguments to the contrary. "Sarah, it's up to you," she managed finally. "I'll respect your wishes."

Sarah wasn't sure she had any wishes, but she was dying of curiosity to hear whatever it was Sergeant Tate had come to say. "It's all right," she said. "Really."

Obviously torn between what she perceived to be her duty to protect Sarah and Sarah's own expressed desires, Mrs. Wynkoop hesitated for a long minute before saying, "Won't you come in, Sergeant Tate? Would you like some coffee?"

"Thank you, ma'am. That would be very nice." He hung his hat on a peg by the door as Mrs. Wynkoop swept out of the small parlor to get the coffee.

"Won't you sit down?" Sarah said, unsure whether or not it was her place to issue the invitation but knowing she wanted to get on with it as quickly as possible.

"After you," he said, bowing slightly. This was the second time he'd done that, and Sarah found it every bit as disconcerting as the first time.

Awkwardly, she made her way over to the sofa and lowered herself onto one end of it. To her chagrin, Sergeant Tate chose to sit on the other end instead of in Major Wynkoop's wing-backed chair, which was far more comfortable. And much farther away. They sat in silence, listening to the clatter of dishes as Mrs. Wynkoop prepared refreshments. Sarah had ample time to notice everything about Sergeant Tate, how large and broad-shouldered he was, how neat and black his hair was, how straight he sat, and how brightly polished his boots were. His eyes were what she noticed most, though. In the afternoon sunlight, they shone like new silver dollars, and they seemed to be studying her the same way she was studying him.

After what seemed an eternity, Mrs. Wynkoop returned bearing an enameled tray holding two cups of coffee, a bowl of sugar, a pitcher of cream, and a plate of cookies. She set it down on the side table and motioned for Sarah to serve.

"If you need anything, Sarah, I'll be in the next room," she said, giving Sergeant Tate a warning glance. Most people, Sarah included, would have quailed under such a glance, but Sergeant Tate merely grinned.

"And if she screams, you'll be sure to hear her," he said, making Mrs. Wynkoop flush again.

For one terrible moment, Sarah thought she'd refuse to leave them alone after all, but then she drew herself up to her full height and strode into the bedroom, closing the door with a decisive click.

"She's just worried about me," Sarah felt compelled to explain.

"Of course she is, but she doesn't have to worry about *me,* too. I'd never do anything to harm you. You know that, don't you?"

Sarah wasn't sure she could possibly know such

a thing, so she chose to ignore the question. "Coffee?" she said instead, picking up one of the cups.

"Thank you," he said, but his eyes told her he knew she was avoiding the issue.

"Sugar or cream?" she asked.

"Just black, thank you." His eyes were dancing with amusement now, and Sarah's hands shook slightly as she handed him the cup.

She wanted to drink some, too, but didn't quite trust herself not to spill it in her lap, so she offered him the plate of cookies instead. He took one and wedged it onto his saucer.

When he'd taken a sip of his coffee, she said, "What did you . . . I mean, you said you wanted to talk to me about something."

"I do," he said, setting the cup carefully back into the center of the saucer again. "But first, I'd like to tell you a little about myself, if you don't think you'd be too bored."

"Oh, no," she said too quickly, then flushed in embarrassment. Truth to tell, she'd been dying of curiosity about him, too, ever since she'd realized he was a half-breed, but she hadn't dared ask and didn't know who else to consult on the matter. "I mean, I'd like to hear about you."

That, too, had been a blunder, but he was polite enough to pretend not to notice. "I told you my mother was a captive, too," he began, setting his cup aside. He laid his long-fingered hands on his thighs, and Sarah couldn't help noticing how tightly his uniform pants were stretched across them. She forced herself to look back at his face and nodded encouragingly.

"She was captured when she was fifteen years old. I was born less than a year later."

The words sounded so simple, but for Sarah they conjured a nightmare of horrors, horrors she herself had suffered. Humiliation and terror and pain beyond bearing. She'd hardly survived it herself. How had a mere slip of a girl borne it?

"She wasn't as lucky as you about being rescued," he was saying. His voice sounded as if it were coming from far away, and Sarah consciously pulled herself back from wherever her memories had taken her. "She was with the Comanche for seven years."

"Seven years!" Sarah exclaimed incredulously. "How could she . . . how did she stand it?"

Sergeant Tate's finely molded lips stretched into a small smile. "I never really asked her, but after four years of war, I've learned that a person can stand almost anything if he has to . . . if *she* has to."

That was true, as Sarah had learned. She nodded and dropped her gaze to her lap where her hands clutched each other. No one would ever know what she had endured. Certainly, it had been far more than she'd thought herself capable of enduring.

"But finally," Sergeant Tate continued his story, "a group of Comancheros came to the camp where she was living. One of them was a white man named Sean MacDougal. She asked him to rescue her, so he did."

"He ransomed her?" Sarah had heard of such

things and had fully expected that to be the way she was rescued when the time came.

"Not exactly." Tate's silver eyes crinkled at the corners with his reminiscent smile. "The way I heard the story, he tried to buy her freedom, but the man who owned her wouldn't sell me, too, and since she wouldn't go without me, MacDougal had to kidnap her."

"Kidnap?" Sarah echoed in surprise. How on earth could you kidnap somebody from a Comanche camp?

"Well, maybe I'm getting a little ahead of myself. He didn't actually kidnap her. Spirited her away would be a more accurate description. She pretended she was going swimming, left her clothes on the riverbank and waded down to where MacDougal was waiting to take her away. The Indians thought she drowned, so they didn't look for her."

Sarah returned his smile, sharing his amusement over the cleverness of the plan. But then she thought of something else. "And you went with her? They thought you both drowned?"

"No, I didn't go with her. She had to leave me behind."

"But . . ." Sarah was going to argue with him because obviously he *hadn't* been left behind, but he was one step ahead of her.

"I was the one who got kidnapped. Once MacDougal got my mother back to her family, he came to get me. He hired some Tonkawa braves—you know how much they hate the Comanche—to help him, and one day they just sneaked up and stole me right from the edge of the camp."

Sarah's jaw dropped in surprise. How could any-one even *dream* of sneaking up on a Comanche camp? And how could anyone actually get somebody away from there without being caught and slaughtered in the most hideous way imaginable?

"Pretty amazing, isn't it?" Sergeant Tate remarked. "Well, Sean MacDougal's a pretty amazing man."

"He's a real hero," Sarah agreed, awed by the thought of anyone taking such a risk for any reason.

"My mother thought so, too. She married him, and they lived happily ever after. Just like in the story books."

Sarah tried to smile at what he obviously meant as a joke, but she saw no humor in it.

"Don't you believe in fairy tales, Mrs. Peters?" he asked when she didn't respond.

"I don't have much reason to, do I?" she replied, thinking of her own uncertain future. Her wonder at the story faded into bleak despair.

"You know you can go back to Texas, don't you? Joe Dunlap's going to take all the returned captives to Austin. The state legislature will probably give you some money to get you started again, although God knows where they'll get it from since the state treasury is broke. You still have your land there—"

"I'll never go back there!" she cried, then covered her mouth in chagrin at her outburst. Swallowing down her sudden fury, she managed to say more calmly, "I can't go back, not after what happened there. And even if I could, I can't farm the land alone."

Sergeant Tate frowned thoughtfully. "And you said

91

you didn't have any family left back in Tennessee, either," he remembered.

"No . . . no one who could take me in," she murmured, dropping her gaze again.

"You could remarry," he suggested. "There's always a lot of men in Texas looking for a good wife."

Sarah smiled bitterly. "Men who'd take on a half-breed bastard?"

"Sean MacDougal did," he reminded her.

But Sarah shook her head. "I told you, Sergeant, I don't believe in fairy tales."

Sergeant Tate studied her for a long moment with those silver eyes that seemed to see everything while giving nothing of himself away. Then he said, "I'll be getting out of the Army in a few weeks. Did I tell you that I inherited the Tate family farm when my grandfather died? Actually, it's not just a farm. The holdings are quite extensive, thousands of acres, and since I'm not really interested in farming, I thought I might try my hand at raising cattle. Now that the war's over, there's talk of opening up some markets for Texas cattle in the North. It'll take some time to get established, and things will probably be hard the first few years, but I expect to prosper the way the Tates always have."

Sarah didn't know what she was supposed to say, anymore than she knew why he was telling her all this in the first place. "I'm sure you'll be very successful," she tried.

He smiled. "I just have one problem. You see, my family expects me to get married and start a family of my own."

Sarah stared at him blankly. Did he want some advice on the matter? From *her*, of all people?

"I can see you haven't figured this out yet," he said, shaking his head in dismay, "so I'm going to have to take the bull by the horns, as they say in Texas." He drew a deep breath and let it out in a long sigh, and Sarah saw his hands had curled into fists on his thighs. Suddenly, she realized he wasn't nearly as calm and confident as he had appeared, but before she could even begin to wonder why, he said, "Mrs. Peters . . . Sarah . . . I'd be honored if you would consent to become my wife."

The words were so unexpected, they didn't even make sense to her. "What?" she asked stupidly.

"I'm asking you to marry me, Sarah. I know this is sudden, and we haven't known each other very long, but under the circumstances—"

"Three days!" Sarah cried in amazement. "You've only known me three days!"

"Yes, but if I don't stop you now, you'll be gone in another few days, and we'll never see each other again," he reminded her.

"But . . . *why?*" It seemed the only possible question. "Why would you want to marry *me?*"

His smile vanished, and his eyes clouded. Plainly, this was the question he didn't want to answer. "I guess you wouldn't believe me if I claimed love at first sight or something romantic like that, so I won't bother. It's almost that simple though. I admire you, Sarah. Not many women could go through what you've been through and come out stronger."

"Mrs. McDonald did," she reminded him.

His smile returned. "Yes, but she's not young and pretty."

"I'm not pretty," she insisted. Of that much she was certain.

"I could argue with you there, but let's just say I'm satisfied with the way you look. If I wasn't, I never would have proposed to you in the first place. Now the real question is what you think of me. I've told you I can provide for you. You'll have everything you ever need, and I'll do my best to give you everything you'll ever want, too. I don't think I'm too hard to get along with, I don't have much of a temper, and I'm told I don't snore. Anything else you'd like to know?"

He smiled expectantly, but Sarah could see the tension radiating through him. For reasons she couldn't even guess, he was determined to marry her. She did have questions, at least a million things she wanted to know, but he'd already skirted the most important one. By his own admission he didn't love her, and admiration was hardly a reason to propose to a woman you hardly knew, but he wasn't going to tell her more than that.

And did he realize what he was offering her? A chance at a good life when mere moments ago she'd had no future whatever. Safety and security, a home for her and . . .

"What about my baby?" she blurted, remembering the most important thing in her life.

His smile didn't waver. "I've been thinking about that some, and I don't see any reason why we couldn't pass her off as my daughter. I've been away from home for over four years and in the U.S. Army here in Kansas for almost a whole year. We could have met here, gotten married and had the baby right away. She'll have my name, and . . ." He paused, then said the words that would change Sarah's life forever. ". . . and no one would ever have to know you were a captive."

Sarah felt as if a giant fist were squeezing the air from her lungs. She couldn't seem to get her breath, and her head was spinning. *No one would ever have to know she'd been a captive!* No shame to bear and none to pass along to an innocent child who couldn't help the circumstances of her birth. She'd be married to a half-breed, but this man was nothing like the savages who had captured her. If anything, he was more of a gentleman than any man she'd ever known. He was educated, too, if she could judge by his speech, and the future he offered was better than any she'd ever hoped to attain.

"I realize this is all very sudden, and you'll want some time to think it over," he was saying, and he started to rise.

Sarah stopped him with a cry. "No! I mean, don't go. I . . . I don't need to think. I just need . . ." She covered her burning cheeks with her hands and fought an absurd urge to weep. "You'd raise my baby as your own child?"

"A baby is easy to love, Sarah. Who could resist that chubby little sweetheart?"

Lots of people, thought Sarah, but she said, "Do you swear it?"

He smiled at that. "If it makes you happy, then

yes, I swear it." He even lifted a hand as if he were taking an oath.

Sarah knew she should ask more questions, exact more promises, but her mind was too full of them to be able to pick and choose which were most important. "I don't love you," she said instead.

"I don't expect you do, since you hardly know me," he said reasonably. "I don't love you, either, but I like you and respect you. Love has grown in rockier soil than that."

She considered his words, the beauty of them, and that more than anything won her. Then she remembered how he'd protected her the other night and thought about how it would feel not to be afraid anymore.

Quaking inwardly at the enormity of her decision, yet knowing she had no other choice, she somehow managed a tremulous smile. "All right, Sergeant Tate. I'll marry you."

They just stared at each other, the implications of her decision vibrating between them, and for an instant, Sarah thought he might take her in his arms.

It would have been the natural thing to do since she'd just told him she would be his wife for as long as they both should live, but since nothing about this union was natural, of course he didn't. Instead, he turned toward the closed bedroom door and called, "Mrs. Wynkoop, you can come out and congratulate Mrs. Peters now."

The door flew open and Mrs. Wynkoop rushed into the room, flushed with pleasure and not the least bit embarrassed at having been caught eavesdropping.

"Sarah, this is wonderful!" she declared. "I told you everything would work out. And for your information, one doesn't congratulate the bride, Sergeant Tate. One congratulates the groom on his good fortune at having won the lady of his choice, and one wishes the lady in question much happiness." She turned back to Sarah and took her hands. "You certainly deserve some happiness, too."

Sarah didn't expect to be *happy*. Happiness was a luxury in which she'd never been able to indulge. But she would be safe and secure, and her child would have a home and a name. That was more than she'd ever expected to achieve, and she would be more than satisfied with that.

Chapter Four

Since they had no reason to wait and every reason to proceed, Sarah and Sergeant Tate scheduled the wedding for the next afternoon. Hunter—at his insistence, Sarah started calling him Hunter the instant they were engaged—had a small, one room house where they could live until his enlistment was up. The army was letting him go a few weeks early so he could be home in time for Christmas. Home with his new bride and his new child.

As soon as he had left after settling the arrangements with Mrs. Wynkoop to be married in her parlor, Sarah discovered she was terrified.

"We'll have to get you a proper dress," Mrs. Wynkoop was saying. "One of the ladies is sure to have something you can borrow for the occasion. 'Something old, something new, something borrowed and something blue.' Isn't that what the saying is? Well, your dress will be borrowed and probably most of your other clothes since there simply isn't time to make you anything, but what on earth do you have that's old?"

Sarah thought *she* could fit the description. Suddenly, she felt ancient. But Mrs. Wynkoop hardly noticed Sarah's lack of enthusiasm and proceeded to make plans. Major Wynkoop would give her away, and Mrs. Wynkoop would stand up with her along with whomever Sergeant Tate chose as his best man.

All Sarah could think about was appearing before everyone and having them know Hunter Tate was marrying a virtual stranger who must be pathetically grateful for the opportunity. Would they laugh at his foolishness? Or feel sorry for him?

"Sergeant Tate is a fine man, even if he was a Johnny Reb during the late unpleasantness," Mrs. Wynkoop informed her. "A true gentleman. His mother was Rebekah Tate, but I guess he already told you all about her. She was famous, you know, even back East. One of the first white females taken by the Comanche. Everyone thought she must be dead, but her father never gave up hope of finding her. Imagine, her son is going to be married right here in my house!"

Famous? Hunter hadn't said anything about his mother being *famous*. Sarah had never heard of her, but that meant nothing. Not being able to read kept her ignorant of a lot of things, and the topic of discussion of an evening both in her family's home and later in her own had been primarily of crops and weather. Now she was marrying somebody who was famous, or at least the son of somebody famous. What on earth was she going to do?

But as it turned out, she hardly had time to do anything, certainly not to think much about the consequences of her decision. Mrs. Wynkoop came up

99

with a lovely dress of sapphire silk that had served one of the other officers' wives as a wedding gown a few years earlier. The hoops were a little large for current fashion, Mrs. Wynkoop explained, but Sarah would never have known the difference. The bodice of the dress was pleated with satin ribbon and fit snugly over her milk-laden breasts to emphasis her tiny waist. The log sleeves ended in lace cuffs that made Sarah terrified of catching them on something.

Because the Comanche had hacked Sarah's hair off the way Indian women wore it, it was too short to really pin up, but Mrs. Wynkoop fashioned a white lace veil that fell to Sarah's shoulders and disguised the shortness of her hair. When she was dressed to Mrs. Wynkoop and the other ladies' satisfaction, Sarah looked in the mirror and gasped, hardly recognizing the woman staring back at her. She was actually elegant, almost elegant enough to be worthy of a husband like Hunter Tate.

At least she wouldn't shame him, she thought with a sigh, and couldn't help remembering her other wedding, the one back in Tennessee in the little church where she and Pete had grown up. Her dress had been hers then, although it was only cheap calico and would serve her as a "best" dress for years to come. Pete had worn a borrowed suit that strained at the seams, and his face had been red from the moonshine he'd drunk the night before to celebrate, but his eyes had been shining with love, as she'd known hers were, too. They hadn't had much, hadn't expected much from life, but they'd had each other and they'd loved each other.

Hard work was the only way they'd known to get ahead, but when they'd reached out for something better, life had cut them down. Sarah still felt as if part of her had been sliced away when Pete and their son had died in the Indian raid, and although the wound was no longer raw, it still ached.

Now she was giving herself to another man, a total stranger and as different from Pete as a man could be. What on earth was she doing?

Mrs. Wynkoop informed her it was time for her to go out, and her stomach knotted in terror. She wasn't ready, might never be ready, but she could think of no excuse for delaying. She was dressed, the guests were assembled, and the groom was waiting. If she'd suddenly decided she might be making a terrible mistake, what did that matter? It wasn't as if she had any other choice, she told herself. This was her only chance, and she had to take it.

Someone was playing the wedding march on a squeaky violin, so they had to go. Taking a deep breath to still her hammering heart, Sarah saw her tiny daughter sleeping in a box in the corner of Mrs. Wynkoop's bedroom. She reached down and touched the baby's raven hair before accepting the bouquet of silk flowers Mrs. Wynkoop handed her.

"This is for you, little one," Sarah whispered to the sleeping child. Then the ladies were pushing her toward the bedroom door.

The parlor was full of soldiers and their wives, all decked out in their Sunday finery. The chaplain stood on the other side of the room at the end of an aisle left between the standing guests. Sarah didn't dare even glance at the faces on either side of her as she walked slowly past them toward where her groom stood waiting. Fixing her eyes resolutely on Mrs. Wynkoop's back, she made her way to the makeshift altar. Only when she had no place else to look did she risk a glance at Hunter Tate.

In his full dress uniform, he was even more formidable than she'd remembered from the day before. His jet black hair gleamed as brightly as his polished boots, and his silver eyes glowed with something that Sarah might have mistaken for love if she hadn't already experienced the real thing.

No, this wasn't love, but it was certainly something, something very fine. For sure, Hunter Tate liked what he saw and was thinking he'd made a pretty good bargain. Maybe it was just the dress, which made Sarah look as good as she ever had in her entire life. Then he took her hand in his, touching her naked flesh for the first time ever. Sarah felt a jolt of reaction from the warmth of his palm against hers and the possessive way his fingers closed around hers.

No, it wasn't love at all. It was lust, pure and simple, molten in those silver eyes and hot enough that she could feel it burning into her. Dear Lord, why hadn't she thought about *this* part of marriage when she'd been lying awake last night trying to imagine what her life would be like as Mrs. Hunter Tate?

Quickly, she looked away, her face flaming in response. Of course, she knew all about the marriage bed, and while she hadn't particularly enjoyed her husband's demands, she hadn't dreaded them either. Meeting his needs had been just one more chore on her list, a chore she'd willingly performed because she loved him.

But so much had happened in between. Pete's death. The Comanches and their violent assaults. The child she'd borne in shame and degradation. Could she ever lie with a man again and not remember?

But it was too late to question herself. The chaplain was asking her to promise to love, honor and obey Hunter Tate for as long as they both lived. Through lips stiff with apprehension, she made the promise, wondering how on earth she could ever keep it.

Then Hunter Tate was making promises of his own, vowing to cherish a woman he hardly knew and most certainly didn't love. Before Sarah knew it, the ceremony was over, and Hunter was lifting her veil. He was smiling, and his eyes were bright as he bent to touch his lips to hers for their first kiss. His mouth barely brushed hers, but she could see his desire for more shining on his face and felt the impact to her toes. This wasn't a man she could fob off with some excuse. He'd expect a real wedding night with all that meant. Sarah trembled at the thought.

In the next instant, they were surrounded by well-wishers, shaking their hands and kissing Sarah's cheek. Every once in a while, Hunter slipped his arm around her waist and gave her a possessive little squeeze that reminded her she now belonged to him body and soul. By the time Mrs. Wynkoop served the wedding supper, Sarah was too terrified to even consider swallowing any food.

Fortunately, everyone expected the bride to be nervous, and no one thought it odd that she didn't touch her supper. She couldn't avoid the wine, however, the first she'd ever tasted. It quenched her fear-parched throat but left her feeling dizzy and light-headed.

When her baby woke up a little later and demanded to be fed, Sarah gratefully escaped to the privacy of Mrs. Wynkoop's bedroom. At first she was too tense, and the baby cried when her milk didn't let down quickly enough, but after a few minutes of snuggling her precious child, Sarah felt herself relaxing again. Maybe it was the wine, she thought. Maybe she could get some to take with her tonight. She'd never been drunk before, but perhaps the time had come to try it.

She was smiling at the thought when the bedroom door opened and her new husband walked in. Chagrined, Sarah snatched up the baby's blanket to cover her exposed breast.

"No need to be so modest, Mrs. Tate," he scolded gently. "We're married now." The warmth of his smile made her blush and look away.

"I . . . I'm just not used to . . ."

"To me?" he guessed when she hesitated.

She nodded, unable to meet his knowing gaze.

"I suppose it'll take a little time, for both of us," he said, moving around behind her. "I've never been married before, so you'll have the advantage there."

Sarah jumped when he laid his hands on her shoulders.

"Now, now, nothing to be skittish about," he soothed, his voice as deep and soft as a feather bed while his fingers skillfully began to massage the tense muscles in her shoulders. "You've been wound as tight at an eight day clock all day. It's time to let it go and resign yourself to your fate."

His hands were magic, drawing the tension from her even while she resisted. "My . . . my fate?" she echoed uneasily.

"Yes, your fate to be married to me. It's too late now, even if you *want* to change your mind." He tried to make it sound like a joke, but Sarah heard the unspoken question.

"I don't want to change my mind," she said, uncertain whether it was a lie or not, but knowing she had no other choices.

"I hope not," he said. "Because I'm not going to change *my* mind."

"How . . . how can you be so sure?" she asked, fighting the lethargy his hands were creating.

"Oh," he said casually, reaching down to lift the blanket covering her naked breast for a quick peek, "it's easy."

Sarah gasped in surprise, and something between her legs clenched in response, but before she could even think to be embarrassed, he was rubbing her neck again, his fingers strong and impersonal and as disturbing as a thundercloud on the horizon.

"As soon as you're finished with the baby, we'll get out of here," he said. "You're probably as sick of all this as I am, aren't you?"

"Oh, yes," Sarah said in relief, although her relief

vanished in the next instant when she realized she would be going off alone with him to his house. Alone. With him. To his house.

"Could you . . ." She stopped and bit her lip in chagrin, her cheeks burning.

"Could I what?" he prompted and his hands stilled.

"Could you . . . bring some of that wine?"

"Oh, most definitely," he replied, a smile in his voice.

They left the Wynkoop's house with more ceremony than Sarah would have liked, with shouting and whooping and much throwing of rice. Since Sarah had to carry the baby, too, she had a time of it what with keeping her skirt from tangling around her feet and keeping rice from getting in the baby's face.

They ran down the packed earth street of the fort to Hunter's house, and when Sarah would have ducked inside, away from all the staring eyes, Hunter caught her arm and stopped her.

"You're forgetting an old tradition," he said, then scooped her up into his arms.

Still holding the baby, she couldn't even grab his neck, but he didn't seem to need any help as he maneuvered her through the narrow front door and kicked it shut behind him.

The silence of the room seemed deafening after their raucous departure from the Wynkoop's house, but it quickly grew into a roar as Hunter bent his head and pressed his mouth to Sarah's.

This was no quick brush but a full-fledged kiss that

claimed her mouth completely and stamped her as his as certainly as if he'd marked her with an iron. When he lifted his mouth, Sarah's lips tingled and burned and her whole body felt charged, as if she'd just sustained a fright. A pleasant fright, but a fright nevertheless.

Her breath coming in quick gasps, she stumbled slightly when Hunter finally set her on her feet.

"I hope my kisses always affect you that way, Mrs. Tate," he said, his eyes dancing with pleasure.

Sarah looked away and tried to regain her dignity, or what little of it she had left, and pretended to be brushing the rice out of the baby's hair.

"Well, I guess it's appropriate," Hunter said, watching her. "You got married today, too, didn't you, little one?"

His large, dark hand pushed Sarah's away, and he ever so gently took the baby from her arms. "There now, you weren't scared, were you?" he asked the child who had been fussing in protest from the jostling she'd received in their mad dash.

To Sarah's surprise, the baby quieted at once and stared in wide-eyed fascination at Hunter's face.

"Now that's more like it," he told the baby, holding her up at eye level. "You don't have anything to worry about. From now on I'll be your daddy, and I'll take care of both you and your mama. How do you like that?"

As if she understood, the baby suddenly grinned in delight and began flailing her chubby arms. Sarah felt tears starting in her eyes and quickly blinked them away. It wouldn't do to start blubbering, not here and not now. She had far more important things to worry about.

"We're . . . we're both very grateful to you," Sarah stammered, knowing she should have said this before and still sure she hadn't found the proper words.

Hunter lowered the baby and tucked her small body into the crook of one arm. "Grateful?" he asked as if he didn't understand the word.

She *had* said the wrong thing. She felt her face growing warm, but she forced herself not to drop her gaze. "Yes, for . . . for marrying me and . . . and everything."

He thought this over for a moment. "Maybe I'm grateful that you agreed. Did you ever think of that?"

Not for a second, she thought, but she said, "I'll try to be a good wife. I'm a hard worker and a good cook, too. You'll see. You won't be sorry you took us on."

"You make it sound like I hired you to keep house for me," he said with some amusement.

Now Sarah knew she really was blushing, but she couldn't do anything about it, so she covered by glancing around the room that was now her home. The place was small, but it didn't seem cramped because of the sparse furnishings. A fireplace covered one wall and obviously served for both heating and cooking. Several boxes had been nailed to the walls to serve as cabinets for dishes and cooking utensils, and a small table with two chairs stood nearby. A worn easy chair sat in the corner, a small chifforobe beside it. One of the soldiers had carried Sarah's meager belongings over earlier, and they sat in a heap in the middle of the floor. The only other furniture was a double bed that seemed to dominate the entire room. Sarah did her best not to stare at it.

"Everything's so neat," she remarked inanely.

"I'm not here much to mess it up," he said. "Would you like to sit down?"

Sarah could think of nothing else to do, so she pulled one of the straight-backed chairs from the table and sat down, carefully smoothing her beautiful dress around her. "I'll take the baby if you're tired of holding her."

"I'm not tired of her." He took the opposite chair and shifted the baby around so he could see her better. "Have you come up with a name for her yet?"

"Not yet," Sarah admitted guiltily.

"Well, there's no rush, I suppose," he allowed. "What did The People call her?"

Sarah almost asked, "What people?" until she remembered that was what he called the Comanche. "They called her . . ." She couldn't bring herself to say the Comanche word, so she said, "Bluebird."

He nodded. "Because of her eyes, I guess. They're just the color of a bluebird." His large hand gently stroked the baby's thick, dark hair which was so much like his own. "She's going to be a beauty, just like her mother."

Sarah was flushing again. She'd never received so many compliments in her whole life. The Bible said, "Favor is deceitful and beauty is vain, but a woman that feareth the Lord, she shall be praised." That was how Sarah had been raised, to fear the Lord and mistrust vanity, so she didn't even know what to say when someone hinted that she might be beautiful.

Of course she wasn't. Her own eyes had told her that much, but still, she found herself pleased to know someone else thought so. Or at least that he was willing to say so. Sarah felt the knot of tension in her stomach loosen ever so slightly.

"I was about six years old when Mac brought me back to my mother," he was saying. "I didn't have a white name, either, but they called me Hunter because that was part of my Indian name. The whole thing was Situ-htsi ʔ Tukeru, which means Little One Who Hunts Far From The Camp or something like that. Mac was too lazy to say the whole thing, so he shortened it to Hunter. I don't think that will work with *this* Little One, though. Can't go around calling her 'Blue' or 'Bird,' can we?"

Sarah's aunt, now long dead, had been called "Birdie," but it was only a nickname, so she didn't mention it. Besides, she didn't want to call her daughter by a heathen name, or even part of one.

"What was your name?" Hunter asked. "Your Comanche name, I mean."

Sarah shrugged, not wanting to think about that. "They never really called me anything in particular," she hedged.

Hunter looked like he didn't believe her, but he didn't press the issue. "What was the name of that old woman we saw outside your lodge?"

"Nūmū ruibetsū," Sarah said. "It means something about inviting your relatives. Her husband owned me," she added, trying not to think of the things he'd done to her.

"What was his name?"

"Witawoo ʔ ooki," she said bitterly. "I don't know what it means."

To her surprise, Hunter gave a whoop of laughter, making the baby jump.

"What's so funny?" Sarah demanded in dismay, thinking he was laughing at her.

"That name, what it means," Hunter said, still laughing.

Sarah still thought he must be making fun of her. "What *does* it mean?"

"It means . . ." He thought it over for a few seconds, plainly trying to get an accurate translation, or at least that's what Sarah had thought. Finally, he said, "As politely as possible, it means Barking Buttocks."

Sarah gaped at him for a second, and the next thing she knew, she was laughing, too. She hadn't laughed in so long, it felt strange in her chest, like a bubble breaking, and in spite of herself, she also felt some of her bitterness subsiding. That horrible man who'd mistreated her had been a joke.

When she'd stopped laughing, she glanced at Hunter, and she saw his eyes were shining with suppressed amusement. At least they could laugh together, she thought and some more of her tension eased.

Neither of them spoke again for a few minutes. Hunter concentrated on the baby, giving her his finger to play with and trying to make her grin. Sarah watched, fascinated to see such a large man so taken with such a small child. Pete had loved his children —

there'd been a little girl once, too, before she'd died of fever back in Tennessee—but he'd felt that caring for them was women's work, and he'd never been comfortable about holding them when they were this little.

In spite of his lack of experience, however, Hunter Tate didn't seem at all uncomfortable.

Perhaps it was watching someone else tend her baby that made her so uneasy. "I feel like I should be doing something," she said after a moment.

Hunter looked up. "Like what?" he asked, and the sparkle in his eyes made Sarah blush for what must have been the hundredth time today.

"Like fixing supper or cleaning your house or something," she said, pretending she didn't know he was teasing her.

"But we've already had supper and my house is clean," he pointed out, still grinning. "This is your honeymoon, Mrs. Tate. Try to relax and enjoy it."

That was precisely why she couldn't relax, and she didn't expect to enjoy it at all. "I guess I could unpack," she said doggedly.

"I guess you could," he replied, "since it's much too early for bed."

Not daring to meet his eye, Sarah jumped up and scooted over to where her belongings were stacked. One bundle held their clothes, hers and the baby's, the ones the good ladies at the fort had donated. The other bundle was extra diapers and some bedding for the box that served as the baby's bed.

"There's an empty drawer in the chifforobe," Hunter said.

12

Sarah nodded without looking at him and carried the bundle of clothes over. She pulled open the top drawer and found neat stacks of Hunter's underwear. She quickly closed it.

"It's the bottom drawer," Hunter explained, "but you can move things around any way you want, to suit yourself."

Sarah didn't feel she was ready to handle Hunter Tate's underwear just yet, so, cheeks burning, she opened the bottom drawer and laid her things in, then hung her two shabby dresses in the cabinet. The whole process took less than two minutes.

Feeling a little silly now, she hurried back over to where the box and the baby's bedding waited and began to make up the child's bed.

"Before you do that, maybe I ought to show you one of your wedding presents," Hunter said.

Sarah looked up in surprise. She couldn't have understood him right.

"It's on the other side of the bed," he told her smugly.

Almost afraid of what she might find, Sarah rose and crept reluctantly toward the bed she'd been avoiding up until now. She went only far enough to see what might be on the other side, and when she did, she cried out in delight.

"A cradle!" she exclaimed, hurrying to it.

"Just a minute, I'll get it out for you," Hunter was saying, but Sarah had already grabbed an end and was dragging it into the center of the room. The wood was dark and shiny and smelled of lemons. Clearly, other babies had slept in it before, but Sarah didn't care. Her baby had never slept in anything but a heathen carrier and a box, and now she would have her very own cradle.

"It's beautiful!" Sarah declared, running her hand over the smooth wood. Quickly, she laid the cast-off bedding into it.

"Somebody traded it at the store, and I thought, well, a baby needs a real bed," Hunter said, rising to carry the baby to it. With the same gentleness he'd used in playing with her, he laid the child in it.

Instantly, the baby began to squirm in protest at being abandoned, and just as instantly, her eyes widened in surprise at how her own movement caused the cradle to rock, soothing her again.

"Oh, Hunter, thank you," Sarah cried, perilously close to tears. She didn't think anyone had ever been so kind or thoughtful to her before.

"I wasn't trying to make you cry, Sarah," he teased, making her smile again. "In fact, I was sort of hoping I might get a kiss in appreciation."

Sarah's smile vanished. He had every right to expect a kiss, especially considering this was his wedding night. Considering this was his wedding night, he had a right to expect much more than a kiss. If only the prospect didn't terrify her so much, she thought wildly.

Taking a deep breath to still her quivering nerves and clenching her trembling hands in front of her so they wouldn't betray her apprehension, Sarah stepped around the cradle. Mercifully, her hoops kept her from getting too close to him, but when her skirts were brushing his legs, she stopped and closed her eyes and leaned her face up to his. Her heart hammered in her chest, and her breath burned like fire as she held it tight within her, and she waited. And waited. And nothing happened.

"I've seen soldiers face enemy fire with more enthusiasm than that, Mrs. Tate," Hunter observed, startling her eyes open again. He was walking away, and at first she was terrified that she'd offended him, but when he glanced back over his shoulder, she saw he was still smiling. "Maybe I should give you your other present first before demanding your appreciation."

She watched in confusion as he went down on one knee and retrieved something from under the bed. Something large and wrapped in a bundle and tied with string. He lifted it and set it up on the bed.

When she didn't move, he said, "Don't you want to open it?"

Sarah wasn't sure she did. If she'd almost cried over the cradle, how would she react to whatever this was? But he wasn't going to let her refuse, she could see that plain enough. Cautiously, she approached the bed, and he stood aside to give her room.

With hands that felt cold and fumbled with apprehension, Sarah clumsily untied the string and unwrapped the bundle. Instantly, she could see the present was many things, not just one. A stack of clothing. On top was a nightdress with a pink satin ribbon tied into a bow at the throat. Sarah couldn't help the strangled sound that escaped her.

"I don't know what's in there myself," Hunter was saying. "I asked Sergeant Emerson's wife to go to the

115

store and pick out everything you'd need in the way of clothes and personal items. She couldn't get you any ready-made dresses, of course, but she picked out some fabric. If you don't like what she picked, you can take it back and get something you do like. Anyway, at least you'll have the basic things you need."

Her head spinning, Sarah quickly shuffled through the stack. Petticoats, underdrawers, a corset, a comb, brush and mirror set, a packet of needles and spools of thread. On the bottom some lengths of calico, blue flowered and brown sprigged. And shoes, a pair of brand new shiny black shoes so she'd never have to wear the hated moccasins again. Replacements for all the belongings she'd lost in the Indian raid and more. More than she'd ever owned at one time in her entire life. Her mouth was dry, and her eyes stung.

"I . . . This must've cost a fortune!" was all she could think to say.

"I haven't had much to spend my money on lately," he said simply.

She couldn't seem to stop touching the beautiful things. They felt so soft and smelled so new, and she couldn't believe they belonged to her. Her stinging eyes began to burn, and she tried to blink it away, but blinking made it worse because the tears were welling now and she couldn't stop them, and they began to spill down her cheeks. He'd told her not to cry, but she couldn't help it, no matter how hard she tried. Her breath caught on a sob, and she clapped both hands over her mouth to catch it.

"Here now," Hunter said, and she tried to tell him

she was sorry, but she only sobbed again, and this time he put his arms around her and smothered her against his chest.

Men hated seeing women cry. She knew that, but she couldn't stop, and feeling his arms around her only made it worse. He was so strong, he made her feel even weaker, so she cried and cried, in great heaving gulps that tore at her chest and made her cry some more.

She wept out the pain and the sorrow and the agonies big and small. She wept out the humiliations and the grief and the loss she'd never let herself feel before. She wept for Pete and her lost babies and her family and her lost life and shattered hopes and the home she'd made and seen destroyed and for disappointments and things that couldn't be changed and things that could never be at all.

Hunter sat down on the bed and pulled her into his lap and rocked her like a baby while she sobbed and sobbed, until she was too exhausted to cry anymore and just lay limp in his arms.

She didn't know how long they'd sat like that, but when she opened her tear-swollen eyes, she saw the room was almost dark.

"Did that help?" Hunter asked when he felt her stirring.

Since nothing would ever help, Sarah didn't know how to answer, and she was too self-conscious at finding herself in Hunter Tate's lap on a bed to think of anything sensible to say. Although there was nothing sensual about the way he was holding her, he was still holding her, cradling her head against his broad shoulder and enfolding her in his strong arms as if he could protect her from all the evils of the world. Sarah found she wanted to let him. She wanted to snuggle into the warmth of his body and stay there forever. The desire frightened her, and she stiffened in his arms.

"I'm getting this dress all wrinkled," she said at last. "It doesn't belong to me, and I don't want to ruin it."

"Then take it off," Hunter suggested.

Suddenly, Sarah no longer wanted to be in Hunter Tate's lap. She scrambled to her feet. "No, I can't . . . I mean, the baby isn't asleep yet and—"

"I didn't mean *that*," Hunter said, his smile gleaming brightly in the dimly lit room. "I just meant you could take the dress off and put something else on until . . . Well, until later."

Sarah just stared at him, hardly daring to trust his assurance and not about to take her dress or anything else off while he was sitting there watching. Her heart was hammering again, and she laid a hand over it.

The gesture made Hunter frown. "Look, Sarah, I know this is awkward. It's awkward for me, too, and you don't have to worry about me making you do anything you don't want to do. There's no rush. If you like, we can take some time to get to know each other before we actually make love."

Sarah's face was burning again. "How . . . how much time?" she asked suspiciously.

He shrugged. "An hour?"

Sarah gasped and instinctively backed up a step.

118

"Hey, I'm only teasing," he assured her. "Trying to lighten things up a little."

"Maybe you should light the lamp then," Sarah said, misunderstanding.

"Yeah, maybe I should," he replied thoughtfully.

She watched as he rose from the bed and took the lamp down from the mantle, set it on the table and lit it. Then he used the same match to light the kindling beneath the fire that had been laid in the hearth. The warm glow from the flames reflected off the planes and hollows of his face, and Sarah tried not to think he looked sinister. It was just a trick of the light, she told herself, and turned quickly to tend to the baby who was still rocking herself peacefully in her new bed.

"Are you wet, little one?" she asked as she picked up the baby and checked her diaper. Finding she was, Sarah fetched a dry diaper and laid the baby on the table to change her. When she had finished, she looked up to find Hunter was watching her in turn, his silver eyes wary.

"I'll go outside for a smoke while you change your clothes," he said. "Then we'll talk for awhile."

Sarah had thought the prospect of going to bed with Hunter Tate was the scariest thing she would face tonight, but as he closed the door behind him, she realized she was equally frightened by the prospect of getting to know him better. Maybe because of what it would lead to, she guessed, glancing uneasily at the bed where she had sat with him just moments ago.

Now, *that* hadn't been too bad. He'd been gentle, at

119

least. She thought of Hunter's hands holding her so securely, so confidently, and remembered Pete's awkward fumblings on their wedding night. They'd both been virgins and totally ignorant, but somehow they'd figured out what to do and done it. The initial pain hadn't been too bad, and Sarah had taken pride in giving her husband so much pleasure. She tried to imagine feeling the same way about giving Hunter Tate pleasure and shivered instead.

Then she remembered why he'd left her alone and realized she'd better hurry if she hoped to be decent again by the time he came back. Laying the baby in the cradle, Sarah went to the chifforobe and opened the door, checking her meager wardrobe. For one brief moment she considered the lovely nightdress still lying on the bed but just as quickly decided against it. If he came back and saw her ready for bed, he'd get the wrong idea entirely. Instead she pulled out the least ugly of her two dresses, the faded blue gingham, and quickly stripped off the lovely wedding dress and hoop skirt.

The instant she'd buttoned the last button on the gingham, she released the breath she hadn't realized she'd been holding. How silly she was being. Hadn't he said he wouldn't force her to do anything she didn't want to do? And what if he *did* see her in her chemise? He was her husband, after all.

She only wished she felt like his wife.

When she'd hung her borrowed finery safely away and put her wedding gifts into the drawer, she busied herself by looking around the kitchen area of the room, checking the utensils and the food supplies.

Finding coffee and a pot, she poured water from the bucket by the fireplace and put it on to boil.

Hunter came in without knocking, making her jump, but she tried to smile to cover her nervousness. He smiled back and his silver eyes took her in from head to toe. Obviously, he liked what he saw, and for a heartbeat, Sarah thought he was going to come over and take her in his arms. Instead, he went to the table and sat down in one of the chairs. Fighting an irrational sense of disappointment, Sarah quickly set out the two tin cups she'd found.

"There's some sugar in that tin," he told her, pointing. Sarah fetched it and some spoons. Then, unable to think of anything else to do, she sat down in the chair opposite him at the table.

"Coffee smells good," he said.

"Yes, I . . . I missed it." She could have bitten her tongue. She hadn't wanted to remind him of her captivity.

"I guess you missed a lot of things," he said, studying her as if he were trying to see into her mind. "Tell me about yourself, Sarah."

"There's not much to tell," she hedged, wondering what he would want to know and how on earth she could make herself sound the least bit interesting to him. "I already told you I'm from Tennessee."

"How did you meet your husband? Your *other* husband," he clarified with a small smile.

Sarah bit her lip while she tried to think how to tell this without letting him know just how hideously poor she'd been, growing up barefoot in flour sack dresses and living on sorghum and corncakes. "I

121

never really met him," she began carefully. "I mean, I always knew him. He lived on the next farm."

"What was his name?"

"Pete."

"Pete Peters?"

"Well, his real name was Herman, but nobody ever called him that, at least not to his face," Sarah said, smiling slightly at the memory.

"Was he a big man?"

"Not big so much as tough. You could knock him down twelve times, and he'd get up twelve times. Wasn't no quit in him, not ever, not until . . ." Her throat closed, and she had to swallow down on the grief before she could speak again.

"Why did you go to Texas?" he prompted after a moment.

"Well, we wasn't doing too good and . . ." She cast about for a way to gloss over the grinding poverty of their farm but failed to find one. "And then our baby died."

Hunter frowned in confusion. "I thought your baby was killed in the raid."

Sarah's heart throbbed painfully. "That was our son was killed by the Indians. We had a little girl before that. She died of fever. Wasn't but three months old."

Hunter nodded solemnly. "So you decided to start over someplace else."

"They said things was good in Texas, that we could get free land there, so we went." She smiled bitterly. "But we found out nothing's free."

He nodded again. "How old are you, Sarah?"

Surprised by the question, Sarah had to stop and

think. "I'm about twenty, now, I guess." Then she had to wonder why he'd asked. "I'm still strong, though," she added, in case he thought she might be too old.

"I can see that," he said with some amusement, although Sarah didn't understand the joke. "I was just thinking that's awfully young to have buried a husband and two children."

Sarah felt the sting of tears again. "I didn't get to bury Pete and P.J. — that was my little boy. I don't even know where their graves are . . . or if they've got any."

"I'm sure your neighbors took care of them," he said, reaching out to lay his hand over hers where it rested on the table.

Sarah started at the unexpected gesture. Or maybe she was just skittish at being touched by him. Whatever, she felt compelled to jump up to pour the coffee. He watched her in silence, and when she was finished and had put the pot back on the fire to keep warm, he said, "You must have loved them very much."

She'd loved them all, all the ones who'd died. Her throat tightened again, and she could only nod.

They sipped on the steaming coffee for a few minutes in silence. Then Hunter said, "Tell me about your parents. What were they like?"

So Sarah told him, being careful not to admit that they'd never been to school or that they'd never even owned their own land. Instead, she remembered the good times and the love they'd shared as a family. While she talked about her childhood, the night outside grew darker and the hour grew later, and finally the baby began to fuss for her bedtime snack.

"She's hungry," Sarah explained at Hunter's puzzled look and felt herself flushing again. But there was no getting around it. She had to feed the child and would have to feed her every few hours from now on, so she'd have to get used to exposing herself in front of him.

Quickly, she picked the baby up, changed her diaper, and then looked around for the best place to tend to the baby's needs.

"Can you do it on the bed?" he asked, seeing her longing glance.

"Well, yes," but of course, she hadn't wanted to lie down on the bed she'd be sharing with Hunter Tate in just a short while. It might give him ideas she wasn't ready to deal with yet.

"Then go ahead."

Reluctantly, Sarah wrapped the baby tightly in her blanket, slipped off her borrowed shoes, then stretched out on the bed facing the wall, with her back to Hunter, and opened her dress. The baby suckled greedily, and after a few minutes Sarah was able to relax into the comfort of the straw mattress.

This wouldn't be so bad, she told herself. He'd already said he wasn't going to demand his rights tonight. He was a kind man, a gentle man. Hadn't the other ladies told her as much? He would take good care of them, and when she was ready, in a day or two or three, she would submit to him. It wouldn't be enjoyable, but when had she *ever* enjoyed sex? At least it wouldn't be as terrible as she knew it could be.

Then she jumped as the bed gave under his weight.

"What are you doing?" she cried over her shoulder, startling the baby and jerking her nipple out of the child's mouth.

The baby began to fuss, and Hunter laid his big, warm hand on Sarah's shoulder and said, "Relax. You looked so comfortable, I just thought I'd join you. We're a family now, aren't we?"

Not exactly, Sarah thought, but she wasn't going to argue, not with a man who now had the power of life and death over her. She gave the baby her nipple again and tried to settle herself once more but without much success. Hunter simply lay beside her, his body curved around her back without actually touching her, his heat radiating across the small space separating them.

Sarah might have felt safe and comfortable if she hadn't been so afraid of him. He seemed so huge, looming over her and taking up more than his fair share of space in the world and especially in this bed. Where were his hands? And what if he touched her? And what if he'd changed his mind and wanted her tonight after all? She couldn't have fought him even if she would have considered such a thing. But she wouldn't fight because he was her husband now, and he had a right to use her body. And because if she fought, he would only hurt her.

So she lay rigid, listening to the sound of his breathing and waiting for him to do something. Except he didn't do anything at all except lay beside her.

125

After a while, Sarah had to accept the fact that she'd have to turn over to give the baby her other breast, which meant she'd have to face Hunter on the bed. Gathering her bodice modestly over her breasts, she raised up and scooted the baby under her until the child lay like a barrier between them before turning toward him. Then carefully, so as not to expose herself too much, she offered the baby her other nipple.

Only when she had settled the baby did she dare to glance up at Hunter Tate. She found him watching in rapt fascination.

He lay on his side, head propped up on one hand, and he'd removed his shoes and his uniform jacket, so he wore only his pants and his underwear top. His face was in shadow, but Sarah could see his eyes shining in the dimness. She knew that look, knew what it meant, and her heart constricted in her chest. *Oh please, God, no,* she prayed as she watched the baby's eyes closing. Soon the child would be asleep, and there would be no more reason for him to restrain himself.

No reason except for his promise. But would that stop him? During the past year, Sarah had learned only too well what animals men could be. She'd never known a white man to behave like that, but then, Hunter Tate wasn't all white. *Please, at least don't let him hurt me!*

The baby suckled for a long time in her sleep, but finally her little mouth went slack and she relaxed away from her mother.

"At last," Hunter said with a smile, and gently

126

lifted the child from the bed. Before Sarah could protest, he added, "Stay right where you are," and carried the baby to her cradle and laid her in it.

"Put her on her stomach," Sarah instructed nervously, sitting up and hastily buttoning her bodice. Dear God, he didn't want her to leave the bed. What did that mean? And did she even want to know?

As if he'd been doing so all his life, Hunter laid the baby in the cradle and covered her with another of the hand-me-down blankets, tucking it in as carefully as a mother would have. Sarah might have been touched if she hadn't been so terrified.

"Don't look so scared," he told her as he came back to the bed. "I'm not going to jump on you."

Which was, of course, exactly what she was scared of. She tried to smile, but her face was too stiff with terror.

He lowered himself onto the bed again, stretching out beside where she still sat rigidly upright. "Here, lean back and make yourself comfortable," he suggested, fluffing her pillow and propping it against the iron headboard.

Sarah leaned back gingerly, although every muscle in her body remained taut, and braced herself for whatever was coming.

"You looked very beautiful today," he said, pushing up on one elbow and resting his head on his hand again. "I was very proud."

Proud? Of what? Sarah didn't think she wanted to ask. "You looked nice, too." She hazarded a glance at him. "You're getting your uniform all wrinkled," she

127

tried, thinking she could convince him to sit up in a chair instead.

"That's all right," he replied with a grin. "I've got a wife to iron it for me now."

Sarah had never ironed anything quite so fine as his uniform in all her life, but she didn't think she should say so. Instead, she folded her trembling hands in her lap and waited.

"Did you like the things Mrs. Emerson picked out for you?" he asked after a moment.

"Oh, yes," Sarah assured him, trying frantically to remember if she'd thanked him for them. Then she remembered he'd wanted a kiss. Maybe that's what he was hinting at now. Maybe he expected her to kiss him here on the bed. This time Sarah felt the flush spreading all over her body. "Everything was very . . . nice," she stammered.

"If she forgot anything, don't be too shy to tell me. I don't want you doing without something you need, either for yourself or the baby."

Sarah should have been grateful for his concern. Maybe tomorrow she would be. "All right." She drew in a deep breath and willed herself to relax, but her body simply wouldn't respond.

"Sarah," he said, gently prying one of her hands loose from where she was clutching them in her lap and taking it in his.

Sarah couldn't bring herself to wrap her fingers around his, so her hand just lay limp and cold in his palm, but he didn't let go.

"Sarah, look, I told you there's nothing to be frightened about," he said, his voice soft and soothing and terrifying. "Don't you think I'm nervous, too?"

"What do *you* have to be nervous about?" she blurted before she could stop herself, and quickly covered her mouth with her free hand.

Hunter smiled and squeezed the hand he held. "Lots of things. For instance, you were married to a man you loved very much and now you're married to a man you hardly know and for whom you probably don't have any feelings at all, one way or the other. So I'm worried that when we do make love—whenever that is—I won't be able to please you."

"Please me?" Sarah echoed uncertainly.

"Yes, you know, make you happy."

Sarah *didn't* know, but she nodded her head anyway. If he really wanted to please her and make her happy, he'd never lay a hand on her, but that was too much to hope for.

"And I've been a soldier for a long time," he continued. "I can't claim to have been celibate all those years, but I haven't been with a woman I cared about since I first joined up with Hood's Texas Brigade back at the beginning of the war."

Sarah had never heard the word "celibate" before, but she understood the gist of his remark. Amazingly, he was worried he might hurt her. At least they were concerned about the same thing. She felt a small part of the tension ease. Then she realized what he had really said.

"You . . . you've been with other women?" she asked uneasily.

"I'm afraid so. Are you jealous, Mrs. Tate?" he asked, and this time she knew he was teasing her.

"Should I be?" she countered.

"Not at all. In fact, I can quite honestly say I haven't even looked at another woman since the moment we met."

She couldn't help smiling at the outrageous claim. "That hasn't been very long," she reminded him.

"It seems like a lifetime to me, especially when you consider the changes you have wrought in my life. I surely never expected a week ago that I'd be married today."

"Why are you?" she asked without thinking, but when he didn't seem offended by the question, she continued. "I mean, you didn't have to marry me. You didn't have to marry anyone."

For a moment his silver eyes were troubled, but then he smiled until they crinkled at the corners and the trouble disappeared. "Let's just say that the time had come for me to settle down, and I knew as soon as I got back home my mother would be trying to fix me up with a wife. I prefer to make my own choices, so I chose you. I would have liked to court you a bit first, but since there wasn't time for it before, I'll do it now."

He lifted her hand to his lips and kissed the back of it. Sarah was so surprised, she almost didn't comprehend what he was saying.

"Have I told you how beautiful your hair is, Sarah Tate? It reminds me of gold coins, all shiny and bright. And your eyes are like the Texas sky after the rain has washed all the clouds out of it. Your smile— on the rare occasions when I have been privileged to see it—has brightened my life like the sunrise, and I intend to make you smile as much as possible in the years to come."

Sarah knew her mouth was hanging open, but she couldn't seem to do anything about it. If it bothered Hunter, he didn't let on. He just kept talking.

"And have I mentioned your figure? Now, if we weren't already married, I would never be so bold as to indicate I had even noticed you *had* a figure, but since we are, well, then, I can only say I have thought of nothing but your lovely form since the first time I saw it. At the moment, you're suffering from a lack of good, wholesome food, but I'm confident that within a few weeks, you will have filled out to the voluptuous fullness I'm sure you enjoyed in better times."

"I . . . I've always been thin," Sarah offered weakly, totally overwhelmed by this onslaught of flattery.

"But not too thin," he corrected, "at least in the important places." His appreciative gaze dropped to her bodice, and Sarah felt as if she'd been touched by a caressing hand. Her nipples tightened instinctively beneath the thin fabric of her dress, and she had an absurd urge to cover herself.

"And may I say how much I enjoyed watching you feed your daughter," he continued, "or *our* daughter, I should say, since she's also mine now, and how much I am looking forward to tasting your luscious sweetness myself."

Sarah gaped at him. He couldn't mean . . . no, a man wouldn't . . . "Tasting?" she echoed incredulously.

"Mmmmm," he said with an appreciative smile. "I

have visions of laying you down in this very bed and taking off every stitch of your clothes and proceeding to kiss you from the top of your golden head all the way down to your little pink toes."

Sarah couldn't seem to get her breath, and the blush that had been tormenting her all evening now burned like fire all over her body. He wanted to take off all her clothes! She didn't think anyone had seen her completely naked since she'd been grown, not even Pete, and although the very idea horrified her, she also felt strangely weak at the prospect of being kissed in places no one should ever even see.

Before she could get her breath, Hunter lifted her hand to his lips again and pressed a kiss to her palm. No one had ever kissed Sarah's palm before. She hadn't even suspected anyone *did* kiss anyone else's palm for any reason whatsoever, and then he touched the tip of his tongue to that extremely sensitive spot and Sarah gasped aloud as shivers of reaction raced up her arm.

"I was right, you *are* sweet," he murmured, his silver eyes glistening in the firelight as he looked up at her beneath his thick, dark brows.

Suddenly, the room seemed uncomfortably warm, and Sarah wondered vaguely if the baby would kick off her covers, but before she could decide if that was a problem, Hunter's lips touched the inside of her wrist, and she forgot everything else entirely.

"What are you doing?" she asked breathlessly in the second before his tongue traced a sensuous trail across her wrist and she lost the power of speech entirely.

"I'm getting a head start on kissing you," he explained languidly. "I figure if I kiss everything I can reach tonight, I'll get to the good parts that much sooner when I really do get started."

Sarah's heart was slamming against her ribs, and she wondered frantically if he could feel it thudding in her wrist. Probably not, she realized, because now he was kissing her fingers before taking the tip of each one into his mouth and sucking gently on it just the way he'd said he wanted to suck on her. . . .

Sarah's nipples puckered painfully at the thought, and she had to close her free hand into a fist to keep from reaching up to soothe them.

"I told you there's nothing to be afraid of," he chided her softly as he lifted her clenched hand from her lap and tenderly spread the fingers for a continuation of his sensual assault.

His head was almost in her lap now, and Sarah gritted her teeth to resist the urge to lift the hand he'd just finished kissing and touch the shining ebony of his hair. It looked so soft in the flickering firelight, soft and inviting, and Sarah found she couldn't resist the temptation to see if it was as soft as her baby's.

Slowly, barely breathing while Hunter continued to send shock waves up her arm by tasting each of her fingers, she lifted her other hand and lightly stroked the back of his head. She found it as soft as silk, or at least as soft as she imagined silk would be, and warm with life.

He froze at her touch, his lips enclosing her little finger in the heat of his mouth. His shining silver gaze lifted to meet hers.

Sarah's pounding heart lurched to a stop in her chest and her breath caught in her throat. She wanted to snatch her hand guiltily away, but she couldn't seem to move, caught as she was in the spell of Hunter's eyes.

Then he smiled around her finger and slid it slowly, sensuously out from between his lips. "It's all right, Sarah. You can touch me whenever you want and wherever you want."

Sarah should have said she really didn't want to touch him at all, except that she did, more than she'd thought possible. So instead of lifting her hand away, she slid it down the back of his head to where his silken hair met the warm flesh of his neck. He felt so vibrant under the hand he'd so recently caressed that Sarah couldn't stop touching him. Her hand moved on, slipping over the smooth flannel of his undershirt to explore the breadth of his shoulders and back where the steely muscles tensed beneath her fingers. Sensing his strength and power, she hesitated while her stomach made a small fearful flutter, but he didn't move, didn't even breathe. Emboldened by his acquiescence, she let her fingers play across his back, measuring him and knowing this was where her hands would rest when he lay on top of her and finally claimed her as his wife.

Once again she felt something clench between her legs and unconsciously pressed her thighs more tightly together. But the flush that was constant now seemed to have settled there and burned with disturbing warmth.

Hunter took the hand he held and laid it against

his cheek. She felt an answering heat smoldering there and gasped slightly at how smooth his jaw was beneath her palm. Vaguely, she wondered if he felt like that all over, and before she could be shocked by the thought, Hunter laid his hand over hers and turned his face, sliding his lips beneath her palm and planting a kiss there.

This time the reaction skittering up her arm jolted clear through her body, curling her toes and raising gooseflesh on her thighs. As if he felt it, too, he responded instantly, clasping her waist with both hands and pulling her down until she lay flat on the bed.

Just like he'd said he wanted to do, she thought wildly, except she still had her clothes on, although for some reason she no longer wanted them on. Probably because the room was so hot and her skin felt as if it were on fire.

She didn't have time to decide, though, because Hunter's face was over hers.

"If I remember correctly," he was saying, his breath warm and soft and delicious on her face, "you owe me a kiss."

Chapter Five

Sarah couldn't speak, probably because she couldn't breathe, even though her heart thundered in her chest until she thought it would burst. She trembled, but strangely, she wasn't afraid, or at least she didn't think she was.

Slowly, Hunter lowered his head until his lips touched hers ever so lightly, just the way he'd kissed her at the wedding, and when he pulled away, Sarah felt cheated and somehow empty.

Hunter smiled. "Oh, the look on your face," he marveled, then, mercifully, he kissed her again without being asked. Sarah had been terribly afraid she'd have to ask because she needed so very badly for him to kiss her some more.

Her hand still rested on his shoulder, so she slid it around his neck to hold him there so he wouldn't go away again, at least not until she was ready to let him go, which wasn't quite yet because his mouth felt so good against hers that she wanted to taste it for just a few more seconds.

"Mmmm, you're so sweet," Hunter murmured as he nibbled on her lower lip and sent chills racing over her. "Even sweeter than I thought you'd be."

Vaguely, she remembered something about him wanting to taste her, but she'd thought he'd meant something else, something terribly shocking that for some reason didn't seem quite so shocking now that her breasts were pressed against the solid wall of his chest and she could feel his heart pounding against hers.

Somehow, her other arm had gotten around his back, and she ran her palm down his spine until she touched the waistband of his pants, then she ran it back up again, savoring the hard masculine feel of him.

He made a noise in his throat in the second before he claimed her mouth again, and this time his kiss was far from gentle. Urgently, he parted her lips and thrust his tongue inside. Sarah had never seen the point of that kind of kissing, but this time was different. This time, her own tongue rose as of its own accord and met his like a lover, tangling with it in a moist embrace.

She couldn't believe how excited she was, how desperate for him to keep on kissing her, until his mouth finally slid from hers. She groaned in protest, but he ignored her, concentrating on kissing her face, her eyes, her ears, her neck. She thought she would choke when his teeth closed over her earlobe for a gentle nibble, and she thought her breath would stop altogether when his mouth trailed down her throat to find the pulse pounding just above the top button of her dress.

But he didn't stop there. Oh, no. His fingers found the button and worked it loose so his lips could move lower. Sarah wanted to help him with the second button because he was going much too slowly, but she was too busy kneading his back and burying her fingers in the rich thickness of his hair to assist.

Soon she felt his heated breath against the valley between her breasts, and when he jerked open the top of her chemise she felt not chagrin but relief at being able to offer herself to him at last.

His mouth was hot and wet against the fire of her skin, but instead of quenching that fire, he only stoked it, laving her breast with the rough softness of his tongue in ever narrowing circles until he reached the tender tip that had risen to meet his assault. Sarah cried out when he took her nipple in his mouth, and his hand cupped her other breast, as if to offer comfort, but his touch wasn't at all comforting. Sarah writhed beneath it in a confusion of fulfillment and need.

She'd never felt like this, never even known it was *possible* to feel like this. She wanted something, wanted *him,* wanted his kisses and his hands and his weight pressing her down, wanted to feed him inside of her filling the aching emptiness. When his lips found her other breast, she tore at his undershirt in the desperate need to feel his naked flesh against her own.

Hunter helped her, tearing at the buttons and stripping the shirt from his arms. For a single heartbeat, he hesitated, poised over her, and she saw his smooth chest gleaming coppery in the lamplight. Then he came to her, mouth to mouth and chest to breast in an orgy of lips and tongues and hands and arms that went on and on until Sarah thought she couldn't bear another moment.

Then Hunter lifted his mouth from hers, his breath rasping in his throat and said, "Sarah, I know I promised . . . to give you . . . some time but . . . unless

I stop now . . . I won't be able . . . to stop at all."

"Don't," she gasped, fingers clawing at his shoulders.

"Don't what?" he demanded.

"Don't . . . stop!"

He went perfectly still, as if he didn't trust his senses, but something in her eyes must have convinced him because he hesitated only an instant. The next moment, they were thrashing on the bed in a flurry of arms and legs and skirts and petticoats as they frantically stripped off the remainder of their clothes and each other's until, amazingly, Sarah found herself naked beneath a man she hardly knew and whom she was desperate to know completely.

She spread her legs, certain that was what he wanted and equally certain she wanted it, too, but he was kissing her again, exploring her mouth with his tongue while his hands explored the rest of her. His fingers were like flames as they stroked down her sides, grazing the breasts he had already so thoroughly adored and moving on to uncharted territory.

He lovingly traced the ridges where her ribs stood out too prominently, then the indentation of her waist and the small mound of her stomach. When he moved his mouth from hers, she tried to pull him back, but he broke her grasp and slid down her body, planting kisses as he went, until he reached the small cup of her navel where he made her gasp by laving it with his tongue.

Then she gasped again when she realized he was looking at her *down there*. It was shocking enough that she was naked, but for him to see *everything* up so close! Instinctively, she clamped her thighs together and reached down to cover herself, but Hunter brushed her hands away and traced the seam between her thighs from her knees up and up until he reached the mound of her womanhood, and he didn't stop. Oh, no, dear God, he didn't stop! His fingers grazed her, brushing lazily against the soft curls and sending shockwaves bolting through her.

"Wh . . . ?" she started to ask, but he touched her again, more firmly this time, and her question strangled in her throat as the burning sensation roared into an inferno.

Gently, he coaxed her legs apart, and Sarah might have been mortified if she'd been able to feel anything at all except the mind-numbing pleasure of his hands. What . . . ? How . . . ? But really, none of that mattered. Nothing mattered at all except that he'd found a way to give her pleasure so intense she wanted to weep and laugh and cry out and dance and lay perfectly still so he wouldn't stop, wouldn't *ever* stop touching her.

The heat he generated surged through her body, singeing her nerve endings until she tingled everywhere and thrashed restlessly in need of something she didn't understand.

"Please," she begged, not really knowing what she wanted, only knowing she wanted it so desperately she would die if she couldn't have it.

But Hunter seemed to know. He rose up until his face filled her vision and his body covered hers. "Tell me you want me, Sarah," he said, but it was a plea, not a command. A plea as desperate as her own.

"I want you," she gasped, praying those were the right words.

"Then touch me," he commanded this time. "Put me inside you."

She couldn't, she simply couldn't! But he didn't let

her refuse. He captured her hand and guided it downward until her fingers brushed the hot, silken shaft. Her heart thundered with passion and terror as her fingers closed around him, and she marveled at the wonder of him.

His breath caught at her touch, and for the first time in her life, Sarah felt her own feminine power. He was hers in that moment, hers completely, as weak and helpless as a babe. Wielding her power, she took him to herself, mating his hardness to her softness so he could fill the void she hadn't known existed until this moment.

"Yes," she sighed as he slid into her velvet depths, stirring the most delicious sensations she'd ever experienced. She'd never known it could be like this, never dreamed a man could give such pleasure.

When he had filled her completely, he went perfectly still except for the slight tremor of desire that rippled through him, and he rested his forehead against hers, gasping as if he'd run a mile.

"Sarah," he whispered, and she knew he shared her wonder. For a long moment, she simply held him, savoring their miraculous union, poised on the brink of a mystery and longing to jump but not wanting this moment to end.

Then he began to move inside of her in long, languorous strokes that sent her blood roaring through her veins and made her quake with wants and needs and a furious desire to cling to him and meet him thrust for thrust. So she wrapped him in her arms and legs and gave herself up in marvelous abandon, forgetting everything except for the overwhelming desire to be one with him.

But there was more, so much more that she hadn't known, passion so intense she felt as if her body were on fire with it. The flames filled her senses, swirling crimson and gold with the most exquisite heat that didn't burn but simply incited more heat and more until her very blood was molten in her veins and her nerve endings sizzled, and she wanted still more, so much more. She wanted everything he could give, and then it came like an explosion, all sparks and roar and mindless fury as her body shuddered with the quakes of ecstasy.

The aftershocks shook them for a long time, and they clung together, helpless against the echoes of their rapture and almost too spent to endure the stinging sweet pleasure of it.

When at last their exhausted bodies stilled, Hunter groaned, "Oh, God," and slid most of his weight off of her while still keeping her firmly in his embrace.

Her mind still swirling, Sarah held on to him, too, afraid of being cast adrift when she was still so weak and spent. They lay like that for a few minutes, clinging, side by side and sobbing for breath.

Then, when he could speak, Hunter asked, "Are you all right?"

Sarah didn't think she'd ever be "all right" again. "What . . . what happened?" she managed.

He made a sound that was meant to be a chuckle but which came out as a weak snort. "A good question. I thought we were just making love, but it's never been quite like that for me before. If this is what marriage is like, I'm starting to regret waiting so long to take the plunge."

"But it's not!" Sarah blurted without thinking.

142

"What's not?" Hunter asked, extremely interested.

Sarah could have bitten her tongue. "It's not . . . marriage isn't . . . I mean, I never . . ." She knew her face was scarlet, although how anything could embarrass her after the way she'd just behaved in this bed with this man, she had no idea.

He smiled that wonderful smile. "Are you saying it's never been quite like that for you, either?"

Which hardly covered it, but Sarah simply mumbled, "Yes," without meeting his eye.

Suddenly, she became acutely aware of the fact that she was completely naked and lying in the arms of a man who was also completely naked. What on earth had come over her to tear her clothes off like a wild woman? And to tear his clothes off, too, she remembered in chagrin. And now she was lying here and letting him look at her as if she had nothing at all to hide and . . .

"Are you cold?" he asked, sensing her discomfort.

"Yes," she lied, grateful for the excuse to seek refuge beneath the bedclothes. Within moments, they were under the blankets, but Hunter still felt compelled to hold her in his arms. The sensation of his long, hard body against hers only made Sarah feel more naked than ever.

"I . . . I need my nightdress," she said after a moment.

"All right," he said amiably, instantly loosening his hold on her. "You go get it, and I'll watch."

Sarah gasped in chagrin, making Hunter chuckle again.

"Still feeling a little modest, Mrs. Tate? I can't understand why after what just happened. You must

143

know you have no secrets from me now, or at least not very many, and—"

"I didn't have any secrets from the Indians, either, but that doesn't mean I want to parade around in front of them naked!" she snapped, then instantly clapped a hand over her mouth in dismay. Dear heaven, what had come over her? She couldn't seem to mind her tongue at all!

And now he was angry with her. She could see it on his face. He was frowning and his eyes were narrowed and she had no idea what he might do when he was angry. He might even hit her. A lot of men did. Instinctively, Sarah cringed away.

"I'm sorry!" she tried desperately. "I didn't mean—"

"What do you have to be sorry about?" he asked in surprise.

"I . . . I didn't mean to make you mad," she stammered, clutching the blanket to her chin. "I just—"

"No, my darling bride, I'm the one who made you mad, if I recall correctly, so I'm the one who should be apologizing. I was only teasing you, but I guess you aren't used to my sense of humor yet, and I'm truly sorry I offended you. Can you forgive me?"

Sarah hardly knew what to say, so she just nodded dumbly.

"Good," he said, his smile returning. "Now I'll get your nightdress for you. Where is it? In the bottom drawer?"

"Y . . . yes," she managed as Hunter threw back the blanket and rose from the bed, not exhibiting the least bit of modesty himself as he strode naked across the room to the chifforobe.

Sarah stared, open-mouthed, taking in the entire

length of his body which looked, in the firelight, as if it had been sculpted from fine oak. His broad shoulders and muscular back tapered down to a narrow waist and hips, firm buttocks, and strong, straight legs.

Just when Sarah thought she might never breathe again, he disappeared from view for a moment while he hunkered down to rummage in the drawer. When he rose, he was facing her, and Sarah's newly found breath lodged firmly in her throat at the sight of his manhood displayed so unselfconsciously. Of course, he wasn't aroused, but Sarah found the sight disturbing nonetheless and tried to pretend she was looking at his chest instead, an almost equally disturbing sight.

Like an Indian, he had no chest hair, and his smooth flesh looked as if it had been molded over the well-developed muscles beneath. His masculine nipples stood out darkly against his coppery flesh, almost as darkly as the raven hair crowning his manhood. Sarah had never seen a man stark naked before, and for a moment she thought she might faint.

"Here you are," he said, either oblivious to her reaction or choosing to ignore it. He handed her the nightdress, then crossed to blow out the lamp and bank the fire.

Quickly, clumsily, Sarah shrugged into the nightdress which was stiff with newness and resisted her efforts. She was trying to tie the ribbon at her throat when she noticed Hunter going over to the cradle to check on the baby. Tenderly, he adjusted her blankets, and Sarah's breath caught again, this time on a lump in her throat.

So far she'd misjudged him on every matter. Would she ever really know him? And how long would it take?

She'd known Pete nearly all her life, yet she'd still discovered new things about him after they married. She knew little to nothing about Hunter Tate, and what she'd thought she knew was apparently wrong. She always seemed to say the wrong thing to him, too. And to complicate matters even more, he also had some strange power over her body and the ability to make her feel things she'd never even dreamed about before. Already she felt helpless and weak with him. How on earth was she ever going to be a wife to him if she couldn't find some kind of common ground?

The bed sagged as Hunter climbed back in, and he immediately reached for her, as if it were his right, which she supposed it was. She went to him, determined if not eager to be the wife he expected, even though she would have given a lot to have him put on a nightshirt. At least *she* was now clothed, so when he pulled her against him, she could relax a little.

He settled her on his shoulder, his arm cradling her to him. "Comfortable?" he asked.

She nodded, not trusting her voice because the sensation of his naked flesh against her cheek and the musky scent of his body were so unnerving. Tentatively, she reached out and laid her arm across his chest. With a contented sigh, he laid his own arm on top of hers, and she felt the last bit of tension drain from him.

"Go to sleep now, Mrs. Tate. You've earned a good rest. Oh, and Sarah?"

"Yes?" she replied, unnerved all over again.

"I'm awfully glad you accepted my proposal."

Sarah had to bite her lip to keep from crying.

146

* * *

Hunter awoke first the next morning. Instantly, he remembered his wedding and, more importantly, his wedding night. He felt his renewed arousal and smiled into his new wife's hair. They were lying side by side, she with her back to him, and he was curled around the curve of her body. He reached over to pull her closer and snuggle her sweet little bottom against his desire when he encountered a foreign object in the bed.

Well, perhaps not so foreign, he realized, instantly recognizing Sarah's baby who was tucked in next to her mother's breast on her other side and sleeping soundly. Vaguely, Hunter remembered the child fussing in the night, and Sarah getting up to tend her. He'd been a little alarmed, but Sarah had assured him the baby was just hungry. Well, he supposed there were a lot of things he'd have to learn about being a father. And a husband, too, although he'd already learned what he considered the most important thing: Sarah Peters was a wildcat in bed.

At least she was a wildcat with him. If he remembered correctly, she'd been even more stunned than he over their lovemaking last night. They were certainly good together. No, more than good. Great. Terrific. Wonderful. And utterly amazing. He'd been as nervous as a harelipped schoolboy reciting poetry, but that hadn't seemed to matter. Nothing had seemed to matter once he started kissing her, not the fact that they were strangers, not her feelings for her first husband, not what had happened to her with the Indians. Nothing at all had been between them. And if that part of a marriage was sound, Hunter figured the rest would follow.

What had he ever done to deserve such good luck?

Burying his face in the back of Sarah's neck, he inhaled deeply of her sweet feminine scent and felt his arousal throb in response. He was nibbling on her ear in an attempt to waken her when he heard the first faint squawk. At first he thought it was Sarah, protesting being awakened, but then the squawk became a babble, and he realized it was the baby.

Sarah was already unbuttoning her bodice even though her eyes were still closed, and Hunter fell back onto his pillow, swearing silently in frustration. Yes, he certainly did have a lot to learn about being a father, and some of it wasn't going to be very much fun at all.

Sarah's first day as Mrs. Hunter Tate began as all her other days had begun for the past few months, with her baby's hungry cry. By the time Sarah was completely awake, Hunter was up and washed and dressed except for his uniform jacket. When she saw he was making coffee, she felt a small jolt of alarm.

"I can do that," she assured him, not wanting him to think her lazy.

But he smiled and said, "I'm sure you can, but you seemed a little busy at the moment. Besides, I'm used to making my own coffee."

Helpless to dispute his statement, Sarah lay in the bed, nursing the baby, while he went about not only preparing the coffee but breakfast as well.

"I was only able to get off duty today, so our honeymoon will be short, I'm afraid," he explained as he worked. "We won't be here much longer, though, only a few more weeks and then I'll be mustered out and we can go back home to Texas."

Sarah nodded, wishing they could leave today. She didn't relish the idea of being stuck here at the fort where everyone knew her story and surely must pity her at the very least. *Home* he'd said. What exactly would their home be like? And how would she fit in there?

When Sarah had finished nursing the baby, she got out of bed and changed the baby's diaper and put her back in her cradle, then washed her own face and hands. Briefly, she considered dressing, but the lack of privacy in the single room made her change her mind, so shivering a little from the morning chill in just her nightdress, she sat down to the breakfast Hunter had prepared.

"Looks like we forgot to get you a robe," Hunter observed. "Wait a minute." He went over to the chifforobe and pulled out his own robe, made of soft wool, then draped it over Sarah's shoulders.

The warmth was welcome, but his scent clung to the rich fabric and enveloped Sarah, conjuring visions of the night before and what had happened to her in Hunter's bed. Her body quickened in response, and she had to lower her eyes so he wouldn't see her reaction. Then Hunter's strong hands settled on her shoulders, and he leaned over to kiss her cheek.

"Good morning, Mrs. Tate. Did you sleep well?"

"I . . . yes," she stammered, wondering why it should matter to him if she had or not. "The baby woke me up, of course, but—"

"Does she do that every night?" he asked, taking his place across from her at the table.

"Yes, they—babies, that is—don't sleep through the night until they're a little older."

149

"Must be hard on you, getting up like that all the time," he observed. In the morning light, he looked even more handsome than she'd remembered, and his silver eyes glittered with contentment.

"It's not too bad. You . . . you get used to it," Sarah said, following his lead and picking up her fork to start in on the breakfast. Hunter was a good cook, and Sarah felt renewed alarm wondering if she could satisfy him with her limited culinary skills. She could make beans and fatback so delicious they could bring a grown man to tears, but what if he liked fancier dishes, the kind of food she'd never been able to afford to learn to cook? The worry spoiled her enjoyment of the meal.

When they'd finished eating, Sarah proceeded to clean up and wash the dishes in the pan she found hanging on the wall. Hunter brought her some water from the nearest pump outside, and while she worked, he went over and picked the cooing baby up out of her cradle.

"And how are you this morning, little Miss Bluebird?" he inquired, holding her up to eye level. Sarah started at the name and fought the urge to object to it and even to pluck her baby out of his hands. Don't cause any trouble, she told herself sternly. He didn't mean any harm, and she should be glad he was taking an interest in her child.

Indeed, as if the baby recognized him, she began to thrash and babble excitedly, making Hunter chuckle in delight. "I think she likes me," he told Sarah who watched in fascination as Hunter laid the baby on the unmade bed and stretched out beside her.

He gave her his finger to play with and gurgled nonsense to the baby's amusement. Sarah had never seen a man so taken with a child. She told herself she should be happy. Instead, she felt the unfamiliar prickle of jealousy, although she could not have said what she had to feel jealous about.

When she had finished her work and could delay no longer, Sarah went to the chifforobe and pulled out the clothes she would wear today. Using the door as a shield, she put on as much of her underwear as she could without removing her nightdress, then quickly pulled it off and put on the rest without looking to see if Hunter was watching.

From the fact that he'd stopped cooing to the baby, she figured he was, but she didn't let herself think about it, just as she didn't let herself think about the excited little shiver that raced up the back of her legs at the thought.

When she was decently clothed, she turned to find Hunter staring pensively at her. Was he remembering last night, too? At least he hadn't made any reference to her behavior. She thought she might die of embarrassment if he did.

"What would you like to do today, Mrs. Tate?" he asked after a moment. "It is your honeymoon, you know."

Sarah didn't want to do anything in particular, certainly nothing that required showing her face to the curious eyes outside Hunter's house.

"I need to do some sewing," she said, gesturing toward the faded dress she wore. "Maybe . . . maybe you could tell me about your home. Where we'll live, I mean. What it's like and all."

Pleased at the suggestion, Hunter plumped up the pillows, stacked them against the headboard and sat up so he could watch her as she worked at cutting out a new dress from one of the pieces of fabric he had given her last night. He raised his knees and propped the baby up in his lap so he could watch her as well.

Using one of her donated dresses as a pattern, Sarah began to cut while Hunter talked.

"Home . . . *our* home will be the Tate family farm. My grandfather, Zebulon Tate, settled it in '36, right after Texas won its independence from Mexico. The Tates were Hardshell Baptists—my grandfather was a preacher—and they were just waiting for the war to end to move in because they didn't want to live in a Catholic country. You remember how the Mexican government made all the settlers convert before they'd allow them in."

Sarah certainly didn't remember, but she nodded just the same.

"My grandfather laid claim to a huge piece of land, more acreage than he could ever hope to farm, but he felt the land would be valuable someday, so he held onto it. He gave a piece to Mac, my stepfather, to build a store on, and now a town's sprung up around it. They called it Tatesville, after my family."

Sarah's scissors faltered. Hunter Tate had a whole *town* named after him! Or at least after his family. She could hardly imagine such a thing. And now it was her name, too, hers and her baby's. What would that mean?

"My mother and stepfather lived in town, of course, because of his business, but I spent a lot of time out on the farm, too. I worked the fields right alongside my grandfather and his field hands, Dan and Enoch, which is why I know I never want to be a farmer."

Hunter smiled, and Sarah returned his smile, understanding perfectly how he could hate the backbreaking toil of farming.

"After Grandfather died," he continued, "Dan and Enoch kept working the land on shares, and I guess they still do if they're still alive, and Jewel will be keeping house for them. Jewel was my grandfather's housekeeper. That's where we'll live, I guess, out on the farm. The house isn't much, just a four-room log dogtrot, but as soon as we can, we'll build a proper house."

Sarah could easily picture the dogtrot, having seen many such structures in Texas. Two log cabins connected by a covered walkway which ran between them. Dogs liked to lay in the shade of the walkway, hence the name. How she'd longed for such luxury as wooden walls and a solid roof over her head and *windows* to let in the sunlight when she'd been living in that dark, filthy dugout on the Texas prairie.

"Does it have floors?" she asked.

"Floors?" he echoed in surprise. "The dog-trot, you mean? Of course it has floors."

"I mean *wooden* floors," she corrected, mentally crossing her fingers for luck.

"Sure," he said.

Sarah's heart leaped. She'd never lived in a house with proper wooden floors. "And glass windows?"

"Yes, and glass windows," he confirmed, smiling slightly in amusement. "I told you, my family's been in Texas for a long time. Wait until you see the house where I grew up. Sean MacDougal spared no expense in building it for my mother, and I intend to do the same for you some day."

Sarah had heard such promises before, and she knew

153

better than to trust them. The future—and life itself—was too uncertain. No, she would count herself lucky just to have a roof over her head and food to eat. She wouldn't know how to act in a fine house anyway.

Hunter entertained her all morning with tales of his childhood adventures, and after a while, Sarah felt confident enough to relate a few of her own, like how she and one of her brothers had once set the outhouse on fire when her father had been inside.

After they had eaten the noon meal that Sarah had prepared from the supplies on hand, she sent Hunter to the post's store for some things she needed. He didn't want to go without her, but Sarah couldn't bear the thought of showing herself out in the fort just yet where she would be a double curiosity for being both a returned captive and a new bride. So she begged off, saying she had to feed the baby and put her down for her nap.

"We're safe now, little one," she told the baby when they were alone. "*You're* safe, and nobody will ever know what happened to us or where you came from. You've got a fine father who'll look out for you. You'll just have to be nice to him so he won't be sorry he took us on."

The baby smiled around Sarah's nipple, as if she understood the warning, and Sarah smiled back tenderly at the only person in this world whom she dared to love.

A few minutes later, when the baby was asleep and nestled contentedly in her cradle, Sarah sat down in the one easy chair and for the first time since she could remember, enjoyed a single blissful moment of complete peace. She *was* safe now, safe and secure with a man to care for her and her child. He seemed nice and pleasant to be with, and although she might yet find out differently, he seemed to like her well enough. Pleasing him would not be difficult if her experience so far had been any indication. She had passed so quickly from abject despair over her future to this happy ending that she hadn't even had time to stop and catch her breath and savor the small miracle that had resurrected a new life from the ashes of the old.

Of course, she might come to care for Hunter Tate, but she'd certainly never love him. Loving was much too dangerous, as Sarah knew only too well, dangerous for the pain that losing cost her.

And dangerous to all those she loved who were now lost. Sometimes it seemed that . . . Well, that was silly. Her loving somebody didn't make them die. Her little one hadn't died.

Not yet. Sarah started at the thought and instinctively jumped up, rushing to the cradle where the baby lay. But the child was simply sleeping peacefully, her tiny back rising and falling with the regular rhythm of her breath.

Don't be a fool, Sarah scolded herself, moving purposefully back to her own chair. She didn't make people die. They just did. The fever that had taken her family hadn't been her fault, anymore than the Comanche raid that had taken Pete and P.J.

But she wasn't going to set herself up for any *more* pain by going out and *looking* for other people to care about. No, loving her little one was bad enough. If anything happened to *this* child . . . But she wouldn't think about that. Nothing was *going* to happen to this child. They had Hunter Tate to take care of them now,

155

and everything was going to be just fine. Sarah was overdue for some happiness, and she and her baby were going to have it now.

But she'd be real careful not to love Hunter Tate, too, so if life dealt her another terrible blow, she wouldn't have to feel Hunter's loss the way she'd felt Pete's. There was no use in asking for trouble when she'd already had more than her share.

The only problem was that Sarah had already begun to have feelings for Hunter. Not the kind she usually thought of as "love," but much different feelings, having to do with what had happened between them in bed last night. Dinner was hardly over and the sun was still directly overhead, but Sarah was already starting to think about climbing back into that bed with her new husband.

Her body tingled at the thought, and she wondered what on earth could be wrong with her. Although she'd prided herself on having kept her sanity while in captivity, perhaps she wasn't quite as sane as she'd thought. Women weren't supposed to enjoy sex. She'd always known that. Indeed, all her life she'd been hearing women complain about having to meet their husbands' needs. She'd complained herself. And since being with the Indians . . .

Which was why she couldn't understand the bolt of desire that shook her when the door opened and Hunter Tate came back into the room. He was carrying several bundles, so he had to close the door with his shoulder, but he took the time to find her and smile at her before he did.

Sarah's heart lurched in response and somehow she was on her feet and walking toward him without knowing exactly why or exactly what she planned to do when she got there. She only knew she had to get closer.

"I think I got everything you wanted," he was saying, still smiling at her as he set his packages on the table.

By then she was close enough to touch him, and she tried to pretend she was interested in what he'd brought, but she couldn't seem to tear her gaze away from his face, from his marvelous smile and the silver glitter in his eyes.

He must have seen something in her eyes, too, because he reached for her and pulled her into his arms and lowered his mouth to hers. His kiss was so warm, she felt as if she were actually melting into him, like soft butter, and she molded her body to his, instinctively clutching at his back so he wouldn't pull away.

This is crazy, she thought vaguely, but she didn't stop kissing him, didn't even think about it until he finally lifted his mouth from hers and stared down at her for a long moment.

He seemed surprised, or maybe he was just as shocked as she at her behavior. "Is the baby asleep?" he asked hoarsely.

Sarah nodded dumbly, not certain she could speak just yet because her heart was pounding in her throat.

"How . . . how long will she sleep?"

Sarah had never actually measured the length of her baby's nap in white man's hours. "I guess . . . most of the afternoon," she managed, sounding quite breathless.

Hunter's finely molded lips stretched into a wicked grin. "Then what are we waiting for?"

Taking her hands, he started walking, drawing her with him, toward the bed.

For a second Sarah couldn't imagine what he was doing and wanted to pull him back so he would kiss her again. Then the truth dawned on her, and she went rigid with shock.

"It's daytime!" she protested.

"So?" he countered, tugging her forward until she was forced to take another step.

"I . . . we can't . . ."

"Why not?"

When she refused to budge, he came back to her, slipping his arms around her and closing the distance between them until his body touched hers from chest to knees and her body trembled in response.

When he was this close, she couldn't think, but she knew it was wrong, so she managed to shake her head.

"Do you think there's some rule about not making love in the daytime?" he inquired. His silver eyes were dancing with amusement, but his expression was grave, as if he were really pondering the question.

Sarah was sure there must be some sort of rule, although she couldn't seem to remember it just then. "I . . . I never . . ."

"One of the Ten Commandments, maybe?" Hunter guessed. "Hmmm, let's see." He thought it over. "Nope, only thing about sex in that list is about adultery, and if you're married to each other, it's not adultery, is it?"

Sarah could only shake her head again. If he just wasn't so close that his musky scent was filling her senses and if his warm breath wasn't caressing her face while he talked, maybe she could think straight.

"Now I've listened to a lot of sermons in my time," Hunter reminded her. "My grandfather was a preacher, remember, so if there was anything at all in the Bible about this, I'd know, but truth to tell, about the only scripture verse that comes to mind just now is 'Husbands, love your wives.' I'm perfectly willing if my wife will just cooperate."

Then he kissed her again, and Sarah realized she was perfectly willing, too, even though she thought she might die of embarrassment when he started taking her dress off with the sunlight shining on them both like a torch.

But after a while, the sunlight didn't matter anymore, and Hunter didn't bother to take all her clothes off anyway, or his either. There simply wasn't time because when they finally got to the bed, neither of them could wait another second.

And when they were spent and Hunter was holding her to his pounding heart, gasping for his breath, he looked down and asked, "Do you still think it's a sin?"

"It must be," she replied, equally breathless, and before she knew it they were both laughing, clinging to each other and laughing until the bed shook almost as much as it had shaken just moments before.

When they were too weak to laugh anymore, Hunter settled Sarah onto his shoulder, and simply held her there. Sarah couldn't believe how wonderful she felt, so safe and secure and blissfully happy. So happy, in fact, that it wasn't long before she began to feel afraid again. Nothing this good ever lasted. Or at least it never had for Sarah.

And with the fear came guilt. "I've got so much to do," she said, knowing no respectable woman should be lying in bed in the middle of the day.

"You can do it all tomorrow when I'm on duty. This

is our honeymoon, don't forget, and I'm your husband. Your only job today is to please me."

Sarah didn't have to ask if she'd done that. His contented smile told her everything she needed to know. Funny, she couldn't remember marriage being like this at all.

"Ah, sweet, sweet Sarah," Hunter was murmuring, pressing a kiss to her forehead. "How did I ever get so lucky?"

Since Sarah considered herself the lucky one, she couldn't help wondering why he should be so happy with her, of all women. Surely, he could have chosen someone else, someone he really loved, someone he at least *knew*. And there *had* been others. He'd said so himself.

"Why . . . ?" she said before she could stop herself, then bit back the rest of the question she didn't dare ask.

"Why what?" he prompted, shifting slightly so he could look down at her face while her head still rested on his shoulder.

"Nothing," she insisted.

"You don't have to be afraid to ask me anything, Sarah. I'm your husband. We shouldn't have any secrets between us."

Sarah thought of all the secrets already between them, all the things that the Indians had done to her, things she'd never tell another living soul, not as long as she lived, and other things about her past, things she couldn't tell Hunter Tate lest he change his mind about how lucky he'd been to find her.

"It's not important," she lied.

"Then why can't you ask me?" he countered, his sil-

160

ver eyes telling her he wouldn't let it go until she did.

So she asked him something else, something she'd sworn she wouldn't ask at all. "You said you'd known other women. Who . . . who were they?"

To her surprise, her question delighted him. "I *knew* you were jealous," he said, smiling triumphantly. "But you don't have to worry. It was a long time ago, before the war turned my life upside down. And they weren't women, really, just girls. Silly girls."

Girls? she thought in dismay, wondering how many of them would be waiting when they got back to Texas. "How many?"

"Hundreds," he teased. "No, probably thousands. But they're all probably married by now, and besides, most of them were girls I met in Virginia, so they're too far away to even think about."

"In Virginia? During the war?"

"No, when I was there at school."

This was something new. "Why did you go to school all the way in Virginia?"

"Because Mac wanted me to have a good education, and he didn't think I'd get it in Texas. Mac is my step-father. Sean MacDougal, but we call him Mac. Remember, I told you?"

Sarah nodded, trying to imagine sending a child all the way to Virginia just to go to school. How old had he been? Old enough to like girls, at least. And she'd known he was educated from the way he talked, so different from the other men she'd known in her life. What kinds of things could a person learn at a school so far away that he couldn't learn just as well close to home? Sarah couldn't imagine, nor did she want to.

"And the girls in Virginia liked you?" she guessed.

161

To her surprise, Hunter frowned. "You could say that. On the other hand, you could say they just liked the idea of me."

"What do you mean?"

"I mean, they liked my being an Indian. They found it exciting."

Sarah had never found anything about Indians exciting. "Why?" she asked, genuinely confused.

His smile was bitter. "Because, my dear wife, they thought I was dangerous. Indians capture white women and use them for their pleasure. They wanted to be captured and used, except they knew I wasn't really dangerous, so they could enjoy the thrill of an Indian lover who was safe."

Sarah stared at him in horror. How could anyone imagine being captured by Indians was anything less than absolutely terrifying? And that being used by them was anything except total humiliation?

"I know," he said, stroking her cheek. "It doesn't make any sense if you know the truth, but I was a young man so I didn't mind taking advantage of such silly chits. I figured it served them right. So you see, you don't have to be jealous of them, not any of them."

Sarah considered his statement, then remembered he'd said "most" of the women he'd known had lived in Virginia. "Isn't there somebody . . . I mean, didn't you ever have a girl back home in Texas?"

He went perfectly still for several seconds, and just when Sarah began to be alarmed, he sighed. "Yes, I had a girl back home, but she's married now, too, long since. In fact, it's been so long, I can't even remember what she looked like."

"She was the only one?" Sarah prodded.

"The only one in Texas, yes."

"Did you . . . did you love her?" Sarah asked, hating herself for even wanting to know.

"I thought I did, but I was young, and when she married somebody else, I got over it. So if you're worried that I'm still carrying a torch for her, don't be. You're the only woman in my life now, Sarah. And," he added with another wicked grin, "you're about all the woman I can handle, so you needn't fear I'll have a wandering eye."

Sarah had feared so many other things, she hadn't even gotten around to that particular one yet, but she knew better than to believe him. Even men who married women they loved sometimes strayed. Sarah had no hope whatsoever of winning Hunter's heart, so she knew she would always have to be prepared to learn that some other woman had. Which was another good reason not to fall in love with Hunter Tate. Then, when he betrayed her, as he was bound to do, only her pride would be hurt.

"I should really get up and put those things away," she said to change the subject she never should have opened in the first place, glancing over to the packages that still lay on the table.

"In a minute," Hunter said, resettling her on his shoulder. "Just let me hold you for a little while longer."

And because Sarah feared this moment might never come again, she lay perfectly still and savored every second of its sweetness, storing it up so that in some distant, lonely time she could remember when Hunter Tate had wanted her above all others.

But if Sarah had feared Hunter would quickly tire of

163

her, he showed no signs of it during their remaining weeks at the fort. He absolutely doted on both her and the baby, paying them more attention than Sarah could ever remember receiving in her life. He made love to Sarah practically every night and sometimes in the afternoon, when he was home and they could steal an hour during the baby's nap. Sarah had expected he'd tire of her body after a while, but if anything he seemed even more eager for her each time, just as she was eager for him.

And as if that weren't enough, he spent every free moment of his time with them, coaxing her out whenever he could, to church or to visit with some of the other noncommissioned officers and their wives.

Although Mrs. Wynkoop was still friendly to them, Sarah quickly learned that a sergeant's wife didn't socialize with a major's wife. At least she felt more comfortable with the other sergeants' wives, whose backgrounds tended to be similar to her own, if not quite as poverty-stricken. They all supplemented their husbands' meager salaries by working as laundresses for the unmarried soldiers, too. Sarah would have gladly joined them, but Hunter insisted they didn't need the money for the short time they had left in the Army, and she should instead spend her time caring for her husband and child.

The weeks passed amazingly quickly, and no sooner was Sarah becoming accustomed to her new life than Hunter informed her they would be leaving for Texas even earlier than they'd planned. A wagon train of freighters was heading to Austin and would provide them protection if they traveled along, so the general was letting them go.

So Sarah had to bid good-bye to her new friends and pack her new possessions into a covered wagon and head out for Texas. She'd made this trip before, from a different starting point, with a different husband and child, and with far different hopes and dreams. Back then she'd believed her life would be better and happier. Now she hoped for nothing more than some measure of security.

The Indians wouldn't attack such a large company, or so everyone at the fort had assured her. Even still, she was mute with terror as the fort faded from sight and the long line of wagons lumbered over the winter-browned grasses.

The first night, Sarah woke up screaming from a nightmare of howling savages tearing her from her wagon and carrying her off again, and only Hunter's strong arms had kept her from snatching up her baby and running all the way back to the fort.

"You'll be all right now," he assured her, whispering into her hair as she sobbed on his shoulder.

"Promise me," she begged between sobs. "Promise me, if they come, if the Indians come—"

"They won't, I told you," he tried, but she couldn't trust him.

If they come, she insisted, "promise you'll kill me. Don't let them take me again! Swear it, Hunter! Swear it!"

She couldn't see his face in the dark, but she felt his horror. For a minute she was afraid he would refuse, but then his voice came to her, deep and strong in the darkness. "No one will ever hurt you again, Sarah. I swear it."

No, she promised herself, no one ever would because

she'd die before she'd let herself be taken by the Indians again. But they weren't the only ones she feared. Oh, no, If anything, she feared Hunter Tate even more. He'd promised to keep her safe and even made her want to believe he could, although she knew otherwise.

Because the Indians could only take her life. Hunter Tate could destroy her very soul if she let herself love him.

Chapter Six

The trip back to Texas was one long nightmare for Sarah, especially the time they spent traveling through Indian territory. Knowing she was surrounded by savages, even savages who had supposedly been civilized by living on the reservation, nearly drove her insane, and every time a group of them approached the freighters' wagon train to beg, Sarah hid in her own wagon, quaking with fear.

"They aren't going to hurt anyone," Hunter tried to tell her the first time it happened. He'd held her close and whispered soothingly, but no words could ease her irrational horror.

"Don't let them see me," she'd begged in return, and so no Indian had set eyes on Sarah Peters Tate since she'd left Fort Larned.

She'd been careful around the freighters, too, although her fears that they might scorn her as an Indian whore proved unfounded. Apparently, they had no idea of her past and knew her only as Sergeant Tate's wife. They treated her with exaggerated respect, probably to make up for the outlandish profanity they shrieked at their mules during the course of their driving. Sarah had been shocked until Hunter explained the mules had been trained to respond to those words, so the drivers couldn't moderate their language just because they happened to have a lady along on this trip. After a while, Sarah didn't even notice the profanity anymore, and she even felt a kind of affection for the rough drivers when the Indians came because she knew they were her protection.

So, although the trip seemed endless and the ever-present fear of Indian attack haunted Sarah, she grew accustomed to the routine of travel, the days riding on the wagon seat and the nights lying in Hunter's arms. She was so comfortable, in fact, that she almost forgot this was merely a passage into her new life. Then one night Hunter crawled into bed beside her in the wagon and whispered, "I just found out we'll probably reach Austin late tomorrow."

Sarah's heart constricted with brand new fears. Austin. The freighters' destination, which meant she and Hunter and the baby would be continuing on to his home alone. His home. His family. What would they think of her? And of her baby?

"How . . . how much farther is it to Tatesville?" she asked.

"A few days, but we'll stay in Austin a day or two to rest up first, get cleaned up and buy some new clothes. And gifts, too. Christmas is only a few weeks away."

Christmas. Memories of Christmases past bubbled up in her memory, times when they'd been so poor that their gifts had been only what they could make out of the meager scraps of their lives. But Hunter Tate didn't seem to have to worry about such things. So far, he'd bought her everything she'd asked for and a lot she hadn't. But surely, his Army pay wouldn't last forever.

"I thought your stepfather had a store. Won't he be mad if you buy things from somebody else?"

"Jealous, maybe, but not mad. From what my mother's been writing me, they had a hard time getting merchandise for the store during the war, and things haven't improved much since. They've got a bunch of Yankees running the state government, and things have been pretty unsettled."

"Yankees running Texas?" Sarah echoed in confusion. "How could that be?"

"After the war, the President appointed a new governor, A.J. Hamilton. He'd been a Texas congressman before the war, but he stood with the Union."

Sarah had never really understood government and wasn't following all this. "The President of what?"

"Of the United States," Hunter said, amused by her confusion. "Or rather, of what's left of the United States, since the Confederacy hasn't actually been re-admitted to the Union as yet. But that's enough of politics for one night," he added, slipping his arms around her and pulling her closer for his kiss. When his lips covered hers, Sarah had to agree she would much rather do this than talk about the government anytime.

Austin was the largest city Sarah had ever seen, and the streets were bustling with activity. Horses and wagons of every description jockeyed for position, and the sidewalks were crowded with people who all seemed in a hurry to get somewhere. Men in broadcloth suits jostled hunters in buckskins, and farmers in muddy boots made way for ladies in silk dresses and plumed hats.

So much was happening at once, Sarah couldn't seem to take it all in, even from the vantage point of the wagon seat.

"I'll put the wagon in a livery stable," Hunter was telling her as he drove carefully down the street, speaking loudly to be heard over the din, "but first I'll get us checked into the hotel."

"Hotel?" Sarah echoed in alarm. Sarah had never stayed in a hotel in her life. She'd refused Hunter's offer of one for the night they'd spent outside Dallas because she hadn't wanted to reveal her lack of experience, but now . . . "I don't mind staying in the wagon," she tried.

"Don't be a martyr," Hunter scolded cheerfully. "We're staying in a hotel, and we're getting ourselves a real bath and a real meal for once, so you might as well relax and enjoy it."

Sarah had no idea what a "martyr" was, but of course she didn't say so. Instead, she tried to match Hunter's smile in spite of the butterflies struggling in her stomach.

Fortunately, the hotel he selected didn't seem too fancy. They'd passed several much more elaborate buildings that had made Sarah hold her breath in apprehension, but this was simply a plain wooden box of a building with lots of windows and a sign over the door that Sarah imagined must be the name of the hotel. Men in suits were coming and going through the double front doors.

"Here we are," Hunter said when he'd managed to wedge the wagon into an open space in front of the hotel. He jumped down and waited until Sarah had picked up the baby from the cradle where she'd been sleeping in the back of the wagon. Then he helped Sarah down, too, right into the middle of that bubbling mass of humanity.

Instinctively, Sarah put her head down, shielding her

face with the brim of her bonnet, and hugged her baby closer to her breast. Hunter put his arm around her protectively and guided them safely across the busy sidewalk. A man just coming out of the hotel stopped and held the door open for her, but she didn't dare look up at him or at anyone else because the flutter of butterflies had become a storm of terror in her stomach, and it was all she could do to resist the urge to run right back to the wagon again and hide there the way she'd hidden from the Indians.

Once inside the hotel, she wanted to stop, but Hunter's arm was around her again, directing her to the other end of the room they'd entered. The room was large but crowded with men standing and sitting in groups of twos and threes. They all seemed to be talking at once, and they all seemed to be angry about something or another. Sarah couldn't make out what, though, because she was too busy trying not to panic.

At last they were at the other end of the room where a young man stood behind a tall counter. He was homely and pockmarked, but he wore a clean suit, in contrast to Hunter's dusty traveling clothes. He looked down at them with all the contempt people with something held for people with nothing. Sarah had learned to expect such contempt and would have fled from it if Hunter hadn't been holding her in place.

Oblivious to the man's opinion of them, Hunter said, "Good afternoon. I'm Hunter Tate, and I'd like a room for my wife and myself. We'll want a hot bath sent up, too, just as soon as you can manage it. What time will you be serving supper in the dining room?"

Hunter had dropped his arm from around Sarah and was reaching for the pen that stood in a little inkwell on the counter next to a huge book when the clerk

171

said coldly, "I'm sorry, we don't have any rooms available."

Good, Sarah thought in relief and was already turning to leave when Hunter said, "That's good news. I've never known this place to be full, but then, I've been away a long time and things seem to have changed a lot since before the war. Well, if you really are full, I guess you'll just have to throw somebody out. And if you're going to be clearing a room, make sure it's a big one. We'll be here a few days, and we want to be comfortable."

Sarah didn't know who was more shocked at his audacity, she or the clerk. Her cheeks were burning, but the clerk looked as if he might explode. His scarlet neck had actually swelled and was straining his collar button. "I'm afraid you don't understand," the young man said through gritted teeth. "We'll *never* have any rooms for a half-breed."

His muddy brown eyes narrowed as he glared first at Hunter and then turned to Sarah, looking her up and down as if judging her and finding her wanting. She was wearing one of the dresses she had made herself at the fort and knew she looked fairly presentable, but she couldn't help feeling ashamed, as if she stood before him in a ragged doeskin dress and moccasins and still carried her baby in a back pack. She wanted to run and hide, wanted to grab Hunter's arm and drag him away with her where no one would see their humiliation.

But Hunter didn't seem humiliated at all. Instead, he seemed furious, although Sarah wondered if anyone else could even guess since his expression had hardly changed at all. His face had only hardened, as if it had turned to stone, but the look in his eyes could have cut glass.

172

"You're new around here, aren't you, young fellow?" he asked with deceptive calm.

"I'm afraid I'll have to ask you to leave," the clerk said, trying to match Hunter's calm but obviously sensing his rage and desperate to avoid a scene.

"And I'm afraid I'll have to ask you if Mr. Stanton is still the manager here."

The young man stiffened defensively. "Yes, but—"

"Then be so good as to fetch him out here, will you?"

Sarah thought she might die of embarrassment. If the desk clerk wanted to throw them out, the manager might well have them arrested or something! The conversations around them had stopped and people were starting to stare, sensing the tension. Sarah wanted to sink through the floor.

"There's no need—" the clerk started to protest, but at that moment a wizened little man came out of a room behind the counter to see what was going on.

His bald head perched on a skinny neck that made Sarah think of a rooster's, and he peered at them over a pair of wire-rimmed glasses stuck on the end of his nose. He was frowning across the counter at Hunter, and Sarah knew an absurd urge to protect her husband from this man's critical gaze. Then, suddenly, Mr. Stanton's expression brightened.

"Mr. Tate, is that you?" he exclaimed in amazement, hurrying out from behind the counter to get a better look.

"It certainly is, Mr. Stanton. How are you?"

"I'm shocked out of ten year's growth is how I am! It's more'n a coon's age since I saw you last. Before the war, wasn't it? You was on your way to join up with Hood, if I recollect rightly."

173

"You recollect exactly right," Hunter assured him, shaking his outstretched hand.

Mr. Stanton was looking Hunter over from head to foot. "You don't seem none the worse for wear. Still got all your parts?"

"Never even got a scratch, unless you count the digestive disturbances common to all soldiers," Hunter replied with a grin.

"Amazing," Mr. Stanton marveled. "When you rode out of here that last time, I figured you was going off to get yourself killed for sure. And here you are, safe and sound and . . ." He had noticed Sarah, who was watching this exchange in wide-eyed astonishment. "Is this lovely lady with you, Mr. Tate?"

Hunter glanced over his shoulder at Sarah who still held the baby. He smiled with what Sarah could only call pride. "She certainly is. Sarah, may I present Mr. Ezra Stanton? Mr. Stanton, my wife."

"Your *wife!* Well, glory be! Who would've thought it? Pleased to meet you, Mrs. Tate, and welcome to our humble establishment. And what a cute young'un you've got there," he added.

"My daughter," Hunter said, and Sarah felt the words like an electrical charge.

"She'll be a beauty, just like her mother," Stanton predicted. "Lonny," he called, turning to the chagrined clerk, "what's the matter with you, keeping the Tates standing here like they was regular customers? Don't you know Mr. Tate owns this hotel?"

In a matter of moments, the clerk had gone from beet red to ghastly pale. "Uh, no, sir, I mean, yes, sir, I—" he stammered in an agony of embarrassment.

"Never mind," Stanton dismissed him. "I'll show

them up to one twenty. Then we'll see about their luggage. Right this way, Mrs. Tate."

Mr. Stanton bowed at his skinny waist and waved his arm with a flourish toward the carpeted stairway. Sarah blinked, uncertain about what he wanted her to do and still not quite able to believe what she had just seen and heard. Bare moments ago, the clerk had been about to throw them into the street because Hunter was a breed, and suddenly she had to deal with the fact that not only was the manager going to give them a room but that Hunter Tate *owned* this whole hotel. Sarah had never imagined it was possible for one person to own something so large. And he hadn't even *been* here for almost five years!

"Close your mouth, Sarah," Hunter whispered, slipping his arm around her shoulders again and directing her to the stairs.

Sarah closed her mouth with a snap and walked to the stairs. Somehow she managed to climb them without tripping, acutely aware that the entire lobby had now fallen silent and that everyone was watching their progress. When she reached the top, she encountered a long hallway running right and left and stopped dead, uncertain which way to go.

"To the right, please," Mr. Stanton directed, and Sarah turned to the right. "Room one twenty. It's our nicest one, so I don't rent it out often. Like to keep it for special guests, you know what I mean?"

Sarah would have walked right past it since she couldn't read the numbers, but Hunter stopped her. "Here it is," he said, pausing before one of the many doors lining the hallway. He threw open the door and stepped back for Sarah to enter first.

The room seemed enormous. Sarah judged it might

175

have been as big as the entire dugout where she'd lived on the Texas plains. It held a bed, a wardrobe and several chests, a washstand, a horsehair sofa and an overstuffed chair. A colorful quilt covered the bed, and the wooden furniture had been polished to a bright gleam. A red patterned carpet covered most of the floor, and although it was showing some wear, Sarah thought it the most elegant thing she had ever seen. Certainly, this was the most elegant room she'd ever been in.

"I hope everything is satisfactory, Mrs. Tate," Mr. Stanton said after a moment.

Sarah couldn't think of a thing to say. Fortunately, Hunter answered for her. "It's just fine, Mr. Stanton, thank you. I'll be down in a few minutes to see about getting my wagon unloaded. Would you have a bath sent up right away?"

"Certainly. Can I get you anything else?"

"No, that's fine . . . Oh, yes, there is something else," Hunter remembered. "Tell that boy Lonny that he's fired."

Sarah gasped, not because she was appalled—she agreed the boy should be fired—but because Hunter had the power to do it.

Mr. Stanton frowned. "I know you must be pretty mad at the boy, and he deserves it, sure enough, but jobs is pretty scarce now with so many men back from the war and all, and Lonny, he's got a mother and a sister to take care of. He's a good boy, Mr. Tate, and a good worker. I'd be hardpressed to find another half so good."

Sarah tried to guess what Hunter might do and realized she had no idea. She simply didn't know him well enough. She watched his face for some indication of what he was thinking and saw nothing.

176

After a moment Hunter said, "Then tell him if he wants to keep his job, he'd better get up here and apologize to me and my wife."

"Oh, yes, sir. Thank you, Mr. Tate. I know Lonny's mother'll be real grateful to you. Now you just come down whenever you're ready, and I'll get some boys to help you with your baggage. Good afternoon, Mrs. Tate. A real pleasure to meet you," he assured Sarah as he closed the door behind him.

Sarah turned to Hunter in astonishment. "You'd let him say he was sorry and then everything would be all right?"

"No, everything wouldn't be all right, but if I just fire him, he'll have a real reason to hate me, now won't he?"

"He'll hate you for humbling him, too," Sarah pointed out.

"But not as much, and he'll also be a little grateful when he doesn't have to go home and tell his mother he lost his job. And maybe he'll have a little of that overweening pride knocked out of him, so he'll be slower to judge other people next time."

Sarah might have argued with him, understanding as she did how difficult it was to respect people to whom you were beholden. Instead she said, "Do you really *own* this place?"

Hunter smiled at her amazement. "Not the whole thing, just a share, along with Mac and my cousin Andrew and some other investors." He glanced approvingly around the room. "I never thought it would amount to much, but business seems to be booming. I just hope they've been holding my share of the profits for me."

Since Sarah didn't understand business anymore than she understood government, she had no idea what he meant by "share" or "investment." She did understand profits, though. "I hope so, too."

Hunter chuckled and came over to where she stood in the middle of the room. "Planning on spending them all on shopping, Mrs. Tate?" he asked, slipping both arms around her and pulling her as close as he could with the baby in between them.

"No, I—" But he kissed her before she could finish. He couldn't seem to get enough of kissing her, and she didn't really mind because he did it so well.

A few moments later, he lifted his mouth from hers and grimaced. "Uh-oh, smells like somebody needs a new diaper, and they're all down in the wagon, I bet."

Sarah nodded regretfully.

"Well, I'll see about our things," he said, releasing her with obvious reluctance. "Meanwhile, you just have a seat and wait for your bath to arrive."

"They'll really bring a tub and hot water all the way up here?" Sarah asked. She hadn't actually registered before what Hunter had been asking for.

"Sure. Haven't you ever stayed in a really classy hotel? You can get your shoes shined and your clothes pressed, too. Even get your meals sent up, although I think we'll go down to the dining room tonight so I can show off my new family."

Sarah gaped at him. "How much does all that cost?"

Hunter smiled and kissed her nose. "Nothing if you own the hotel," he replied and then he was gone, leaving Sarah to marvel over the mysteries of her new life.

To Sarah's continued amazement, several young men carried up their trunk and the baby's cradle and the other things Hunter thought they would need for the next few days. Then they carried up a tub and some hot water. But before it arrived, the clerk Lonny knocked on the door.

Hunter let him into the chaos of their belongings which had just been dumped into the middle of the room until Sarah could sort them out. Lonny stood nervously before them, white as a sheet and sweating profusely.

"I'm real sorry for the way I treated you when you came in, Mr. Tate. I didn't have no idea who you was."

Hunter crossed his arms over his chest and glared at the boy, making him practically quake in his shoes. Even Sarah felt like quaking and vowed never to give Hunter reason to look at *her* that way. "Is that the only reason you're sorry, Lonny, because I have the power to get you fired?"

Plainly, it was, but Lonny knew better than to say so. He swallowed with a gulp that made his Adam's apple bob. "N-no, sir, I shouldn't've treated any customer like that."

"Not even a half-breed," Hunter added coldly, and Lonny could only nod his agreement. "I don't want to hear any more complaints about your work, because if anyone does complain about you, Mr. Stanton has instructions to let you go on the spot. Do you understand?"

"Y-yes, sir. Thank you, sir." He was backing toward the door before he'd even finished with the last "sir," and Hunter let him go without a word.

"You think that changed his mind about hating Indians?" Sarah inquired.

Hunter glanced at her in surprise. "I wasn't trying to change his mind, just his behavior." He grinned. "In this world, that's about all you can hope to accomplish."

Absently, Sarah bounced the baby on her knee and

considered. Maybe he was right, and in the future Sarah would remember to watch her behavior with Hunter Tate.

A few minutes later, the boys brought up Sarah's bath, and Hunter left to get his own at the barber shop down the street. When she was clean once again and dressed in fresh clothes and had bathed the baby and had dressed her again, too, Sarah put the baby in her cradle and sat down on the sofa to savor her good fortune.

Or at least that's what she started to do, but after considering what she'd just learned about her new husband, she began to wonder if her fortune had really been good. True, she'd discovered Hunter owned this hotel, or at least part of it, which meant he had some money, at least more than her father or her first husband had ever had. Maybe she wouldn't have to worry about how they were going to eat this winter or even whether or not she could afford a new dress. On the other hand, she had completely different things to worry about.

Like how she would fit into Hunter's life. What kind of woman would he have normally married? Someone who could at least read, she thought in dismay. Someone who understood what he was talking about more than half the time. Someone who knew how to act at a hotel. Sarah hadn't even known you were supposed to tip the boys who carried your things upstairs, so she'd challenged Hunter's claim about not having to pay for things in the hotel when she'd seen him giving the boys coins.

At least she could learn these things. Sarah wasn't stupid, just ignorant and inexperienced. Maybe she could even get interested in government or business, although the possibility seemed unlikely. In any event, those weren't her biggest problems. She thought her biggest problem might be the one they'd encountered downstairs in the lobby.

For all his money and education, Hunter Tate was still a half-breed bastard, and many people would hate him simply for that fact. They'd hate her, too, for marrying him.

No sooner had she reached that conclusion than somebody knocked on her door. Startled, Sarah jumped to her feet and was about to ask who it was when Hunter called, "It's me. Can I come in?"

She hurried to unlock the door which she'd bolted before taking her bath, and Hunter came in looking almost as handsome as he had on their wedding day. He wore a black broadcloth suit she'd never seen before with a shiny red ascot at this throat, and he carried a black bowler hat.

His hair had been trimmed and oiled and combed, and it shone as brightly as a raven's wing in the fading afternoon sunlight. When he walked past her into the room, she caught the faint aroma of bay rum, and he grinned at her reaction.

"Do I meet with your approval?" he inquired, turning completely around for her inspection.

"You look real nice," she said, at a loss to tell him her true feelings, which were much more shocking and impossible to explain. He was, without doubt, the finest-looking man she'd ever seen, but how could she say that? And how could she tell him she wanted him to kiss her and hold her and carry her over to the bed and . . .

But of course she didn't have to tell him to kiss her. He did it because he always kissed her when he came home. He kissed her and he held her but he didn't carry her over to the bed because just when she thought he might be considering it, her stomach growled and made him laugh.

"Maybe we ought to go downstairs and have some supper, Mrs. Tate. I don't want you to think I'd starve you."

"That's all right, if you want to . . . I mean," she stammered, catching herself just in time.

"If I want to what?" he prodded, pulling her close so she could feel his desire even through her petticoats.

"You know, if you can't wait," she tried, feeling her cheeks burning with embarrassment.

"I don't *want* to wait, but I will," he told her, setting her away from him. "Now get the baby, and let's go. You've given me a reason to want to hurry right through this meal."

Still blushing, Sarah went to get the baby, fetching her from the cradle and laying her on the bed to wrap her in a blanket. Then, seeing her daughter's black hair which shone just as brightly as her husband's, Sarah remembered what she'd been thinking about just before Hunter came in.

"Hunter?" she asked.

"Hmmm?" he replied, staring absently out the lace-curtained window at the busy street below.

"Don't you mind that . . . ? I mean, doesn't it hurt your feelings when . . . ?"

"When what?" he inquired, looking at her with those frightening silver eyes when she hesitated.

Sarah bit her lip, then decided she needed to know. "Doesn't it bother you when people call you a breed?"

Something flickered across his face, but it was gone before she could identify the emotion he'd felt. His face was stone again, she realized in dismay, but at least his eyes weren't angry. Instead they were as blank and hard as two silver dollars.

"My parents—Mac and my mother—taught me that it didn't matter what other people think about me. The important thing is what I think about myself, and I *know* that I'm as good as any other man, no matter who my father was. And if there was ever any doubt in my mind, I proved it in the war a thousand times. So no, I don't mind. I don't like it, but it doesn't hurt me."

Sarah studied his face, unable to believe his words because she'd seen how angry he'd been downstairs this afternoon and she'd seen his reaction just now, no matter how quickly he'd recovered. He minded, all right. He minded a lot, and Sarah, who'd suffered enough snubs and insults because of her poverty to know how it felt to be despised for something you couldn't help, knew it hurt him, too.

But she'd let him think she believed him. Better to keep the peace between them than to argue about something he would just deny and perhaps couldn't even admit to himself. So she finished wrapping the baby and picked her up, smiled and said, "I'm ready."

Hunter smiled back and offered her his arm, and she could almost have believed that he'd forgotten all about her question except that when she looked at his eyes, she saw they weren't smiling. No, they weren't happy at all.

The rest of their stay in Austin was like the honeymoon they hadn't had. They filled their days with shopping and spent far more money than Sarah had ever spent in her life. If people occasionally snubbed them because Hunter was a breed, he pretended not to notice and Sarah chose not to.

The nights were the best time, though, because they were alone together in that beautiful room with nothing to do after the baby fell asleep but love each other. Sometimes, in the light of day, when Sarah remembered the things they had done together in the dark, she actually blushed. Surely it was unnatural to feel the way she felt about Hunter's body, to want him all the time the way she did, but even if it was, she couldn't have done anything about it and didn't intend to try. After all, as Hunter often reminded her, they were married and could do whatever they wanted. It was nobody's business but their own.

Far sooner than Sarah wished, they'd finished shopping and had purchased Christmas gifts for everyone and two more new dresses for Sarah which she hadn't thought she needed but which she loved all the same. Unable to find any more excuses for delaying, Sarah had to agree with Hunter to leave for Tatesville the next morning.

That night, as they lay together in the tangle of covers, their bodies still damp from lovemaking, Sarah whispered to him, "Is it different for you? From the others, I mean?"

"What?" he murmured, half-asleep. "Is what different?"

"You know," she prodded. "What . . . what we just did," she clarified, glad for the darkness that hid her embarrassment.

His chest shook with a silent chuckle. *"Different?"* he mimicked. "Or *better?* That's what you really want to know, isn't it?"

Sarah knew her face was scarlet, but since he

couldn't see it, she didn't mind. "Yes," she confirmed as primly as she could.

"Well, now, that's an interesting question," he said, no longer drowsy at all. "I could ask you the same thing, if I wasn't afraid of the answer. You see, I'm competing with a loving husband, but your competition was just those silly girls I met when I was in college and—"

"*College?*" Sarah cried, certain she had heard him wrong. All her worries about those other women vanished from her mind in light of this horrifying new discovery.

"Yes, you remember I told you I went to school in Virginia," he said patiently. "I told you about the girls, too, and how they didn't mean anything to me and—"

"I didn't know you'd meant *college.*" Sarah couldn't believe it. She'd never even known anyone who'd been to college, or at least she'd thought she hadn't, and here she was lying in bed with Hunter, who . . .

"Well, I didn't graduate," he was saying. "I'd just finished my third year when the war started, and now of course, it's out of the question since I've got a family." He gave her shoulder an affectionate squeeze. "I don't suppose I would've gone back anyway, though. After the war, it just doesn't seem that important."

College. Sarah had always thought is sounded so mystical, so wonderful, like a dream that could never come true. What had Hunter learned there? He must be so smart, much smarter than she'd ever imagined. And so much smarter than Sarah who'd never even learned the alphabet, she realized with horror.

"I . . . I never went to school," she managed through her constricted throat.

"I never expected you had," Hunter assured her.

"Women don't usually go to college, anyway, so you don't have to be embarrassed about it."

She hadn't meant that, though. She'd meant she'd never been to school at all, not even for one day. But she couldn't explain that to Hunter. What would he think of her? Would he still look at her the same way? Or would he pity her? Maybe he'd even despise her. She couldn't let that happen.

"So, in answer to your question," he continued, "Yes, making love with you is different. It's wonderful, Sarah, and do I dare ask you the same question?"

Sarah was so upset, she almost didn't understand what he wanted to know. "I . . . yes, of course, silly," she managed, hoping her voice did not betray her. "I already told you, I never felt like this before."

It was true, too. Sarah had never been so terrified in all her life. She would have to make sure Hunter never learned the truth about her.

The trip to Tatesville was far different from the first portion of their journey. There was no cursing and swearing to get the mules started in the morning, no cloud of dust from the long wagon train to breathe everyday. There was just their wagon and them, alone beneath the broad Texas sky.

Sarah should have been frightened, far more frightened than she had been with all the freighters to protect her. Instead she wanted the trip to go on forever, because when it ended she would have to face Hunter's family. Then she would have a whole bunch of people to hide her secrets from, and she would find out for sure whether or not she could fit into Hunter's life.

The closer they got to their destination, the more excited Hunter became and the more subdued Sarah became. Hunter didn't seem to notice how quiet she was, though, because he talked all the time now, remembering his childhood, recalling all the wonderful things that had happened to him and some of the not-so-wonderful things, too. Sarah listened in silence, drinking it all in, memorizing his past in hopes of knowing how to conduct herself in his future.

But far sooner than she wanted, even though the trip had lasted several days, Hunter told her, "There it is!" He pointed to what looked like a shadow on the horizon. "That's Tatesville. We'll be there in time for supper."

"Stop the wagon!" Sarah cried, surprising Hunter who was already sawing on the reins before he could even think to question the command.

"What's the matter?"

"I have to change my dress!" she informed him, scrambling over the wagon seat the instant they'd stopped.

"Change your dress? For what?"

But Sarah didn't have time to explain. She was already digging in the trunk for the new garnet and green plaid wool she'd bought in Austin and which the clerk had assured her was the latest fashion. The hoops would be uncomfortable for travel, but since they were almost at the end of their journey, Sarah wouldn't mind.

"You don't have to get dressed up for my family, Sarah," Hunter was saying. "They'd love you if you came to them in rags."

But, of course, he had no way of knowing what his family would think of her, and Sarah's experience had been that no one paid her any mind at all when she was in rags. Ignoring his amusement and assurances and shivering in the wintery air, Sarah stripped off the gingham dress she'd been wearing and struggled into her hoops and then into the lovely gown.

"This is silly, Sarah," Hunter remarked, "although I can't complain about the show."

Sarah glared at him, which only made him chuckle, then she found her new black bonnet and gloves. Wrapping her heavy wool shawl around her shoulders again, she struggled back over the wagon seat while Hunter's chuckle disintegrated into genuine laughter over her fight with the unwieldy hoops.

It took some doing, but Hunter finally got her untangled and seated once again, just as the baby woke up and began to fuss to be fed. Hunter had to go back and get her, and by that time he was laughing so hard he almost couldn't pick her up.

"I don't see what's so funny," Sarah told him, thoroughly annoyed.

" 'Vanity of vanities, all is vanity,' " he quoted, a verse Sarah recognized from countless sermons.

"I'm not vain," she protested, taking the baby from him. "I just want to look nice. What's wrong with that?"

"I told you not to worry about impressing my family. They don't care about things like that."

But Sarah knew *everyone* cared about things like that, whether they admitted it or not. "Hush up and drive the wagon. I thought you were in a hurry to get there."

He grinned wickedly. "Not so much of a hurry that I can't take a minute to watch you feed the baby."

Sarah felt the heat of her anger slowly changing to another kind of heat entirely. "Is that all you ever think about?" she huffed in feigned indignation, unbuttoning her bodice.

188

"Lately, yes," he replied, watching appreciatively as she opened her dress and offered the baby her breast. Sarah knew she should have felt some embarrassment at the way he was staring at her and that she probably should have made at least an attempt at modesty, but for reasons she chose not to examine too closely, she did no such thing.

"You know," Hunter said after a few minutes, "I was right, you did fill out very nicely. A few more weeks of good food, and you'll be perfect."

"But you said," Sarah began, then caught herself, biting her lip as the flush of embarrassment spread down her throat and over her naked breasts.

"What did I say?" Hunter prodded, leaning down to nuzzle the breast closest to him while the baby suckled the other.

"You said . . . you said," she gasped as his teeth grazed her erect nipple. "You said I was *already* perfect."

"I was talking about something else," he murmured against her heated flesh.

"Hunter," she protested weakly. "You can't do this right out in broad daylight!"

"Why not?" he inquired.

"Because . . . because someone might see!"

But he'd already found where the edge of her hoop was wedged under the dashboard and had flipped it loose so her skirt flew straight up in front of her.

"Hunter!" she squealed in outrage.

"Just keep nursing the baby and mind your own business," he told her, taking her nearest leg and lifting it onto the seat while he dropped down onto the floor between her legs.

"Hunter, you can't!"

But of course he could and he did. With no trouble

at all, he pushed up her petticoats and found the opening in her pantelettes and the soft, secret place inside. She tried to protest again, but the words strangled on a gasp when his lips touched her most sensitive spot.

"Don't," she tried but so quietly, she didn't think he could hear. If he did, he paid no attention, and soon her breath came in ragged gasps as Hunter's lips and tongue played over her, working the magic that was as old as time, yet forever new.

Desire surged through her like liquid fire, curling her toes in her new shoes and raising gooseflesh everywhere else. This was wicked, she knew. It *must* be, what with the baby right here and all, but after a few more minutes, even that didn't matter anymore. Nothing mattered at all except the heat of Hunter's mouth and the answering heat in her own loins.

The fire roared, hotter and hotter, lifting her higher and higher while the flames licked her and Hunter licked her, until she couldn't stand it anymore, not another second, and her body convulsed in joyous release.

She cried out or thought she did, and then surrendered to the glorious aftershocks, one after another, each slightly less overwhelming than the last, until they faded completely and consciousness slowly returned. When it did, Sarah found herself sprawled on the wagon seat, her hoopskirt flung straight up in the air, completely exposing her bottom half, and the baby still nursing contentedly on her exposed top half, as if nothing at all had just happened.

"Hunter!" she wailed, knowing she should probably be furious at him and determined she would be just as soon as this blissful lethargy passed. Now he'd probably want to make love, right out here in front of God and everybody. . . .

Except he was very carefully putting her leg back down and gathering up her hoopskirt and tucking it back under the dashboard again. "Do you feel better now, Mrs. Tate?" he asked wickedly.

"I felt fine before!" she informed him, not trusting the satisfied gleam in his eyes. And when he made no move to embrace her, she was completely confused. "Don't you want . . . ? I mean . . . aren't you going to . . . ?"

"Take care of myself?" he supplied when she couldn't find the correct phrase. "I'm fine, at least for now. I can wait until tonight when we've got a nice big feather bed to enjoy ourselves in."

Sarah should have been angry that he'd taken advantage of her like that—because she was *sure* she'd been taken advantage of—but it was hard to get mad when your nerve endings were still singing with pleasure. Still, she managed a little outrage.

"How could you?" she demanded.

"Very easily. Want me to do it again?"

She did, of course, as her body told her by its thrill of reaction, but she certainly had no intention of telling him so. "That . . . you . . . What . . . what if somebody had come by?" she sputtered.

"Nobody did," he pointed out reasonably. "And I was paying attention to those things, even if you weren't . . . or couldn't," he added with a grin.

Sarah didn't know what to say or even what to think. He'd never pleasured her without pleasuring himself, too. In her experience, men never gave without wanting something in return.

Hunter's grin turned sly. "Isn't it time to change

191

sides?" he asked, indicating the baby in her arms.

Sarah glanced down to find the baby had stopped nursing and was watching them both in wide-eyed fascination. Quickly, she shifted the child over to her other breast and adjusted her shawl to cover herself, giving Hunter a glare when he sighed his disappointment.

"I'd think you'd be a little grateful and want to show your appreciation," he said.

"I don't have to show everything else along with it, though, do I?" she replied.

For a second, Hunter just gaped at her in surprise, and then he threw back his head and laughed in delight.

Sarah had no idea what she'd said to amuse him so much, and she didn't ask as he climbed into the back of the wagon to wash his face and hands before they continued on their way.

But however much she might protest, Sarah did feel much better, more relaxed and, amazingly enough, more self-confident as well. It was just having her new dress on, she told herself as the wagon jolted down the bumpy road again. She could face Hunter's family without having to feel ashamed of how she looked. And if she also felt warm and well-loved, well, what did that have to do with anything?

At long last the shadow on the horizon began to take shape and became a town.

"Everything looks just the same," Hunter remarked, slowing the wagon to take it all in when they were close enough to see. "It's all smaller than I remember, though. I wonder why that is?"

To Sarah's relief, Tatesville was indeed small, much smaller and quieter than Austin at least. It consisted of a single main street with a church at one end and what must be Hunter's stepfather's mercantile at the other with a row of businesses lining the street in between. Sarah recognized a blacksmith shop and a saloon among them. On the fringes of the town were scattered houses of various sizes where Sarah imagined the merchants and businessmen lived.

One in particular, the largest one, caught her eye and held it. She'd never seen such a magnificent house, three stories made of painted clapboard instead of rough logs, with an enormous wraparound porch. Wicker furniture sat on the porch along with several pots that held the remains of winter-shriveled flowers. Imagine having time to put flowers in pots just to set them on your front porch, Sarah marveled. The yard was fenced with wrought iron and neatly raked free of stones and debris. A huge live oak shaded the property, or would in the spring when its leaves blossomed again.

Sarah couldn't take her eyes off the house, and soon she realized they were heading right for it.

"Where are we going?" she asked in alarm.

"Well, Mac's probably still at the store, but my mother would kill me if I didn't come straight home first," Hunter said, his voice ringing with the happiness of finally being home.

Home? "Is that . . . ? Does your mother live in that gray house?" she asked with growing apprehension.

"She sure does," Hunter confirmed. "When they got married, Mac promised her he'd build her the most beautiful house in Texas. I always thought he succeeded."

Sarah had to agree, although her new self-confidence had suddenly evaporated. She'd hoped for a house with real floors and glass windows. She'd never even dreamed of a mansion. Before Sarah could begin to absorb it all, Hunter was stopping the wagon in front of the wrought iron gate and setting the brake and hopping down. The gate squeaked when he opened it, and just in case the occupants of the house hadn't noticed a fully loaded wagon lumbering up or the squealing gate, he shouted, "Hello, the house! Anybody home?"

He was only halfway up the walk when the front door opened and a woman stepped out. A beautiful young woman in a beautiful flowered dress, just the kind of woman who belonged in a house like this. She shaded her eyes with her hand, peering out to see who her visitor was. Sarah knew the instant she'd identified him. Her whole body went rigid with shock, and she clapped both hands over her mouth for an instant, then threw her arms wide and cried, "Hunter!"

Grabbing up her skirts, she ran down the porch steps and threw herself into his arms. He caught her up and swung her around with a whoop of exuberance, and Sarah felt the stabbing pain of loss. She had no idea who this young woman was, but she knew Hunter loved her, loved her the way every woman dreams of being loved.

Seeing the sun glinting off the woman's silvery blond hair as she pressed kiss after kiss on Hunter's laughing face, Sarah remembered in despair that Hunter had said he'd loved one woman in Texas. Surely, this was the one. Sarah laid a hand over the pain in her heart and wondered how she could suffer so much over losing Hunter's love, something she'd never had in the first place. Thank heaven she didn't love him herself. If it hurt this much to lose her pride, she might die if she lost her heart.

Hunter set the woman on her feet, and she was holding him at arm's length and gazing up at him adoringly, her pale eyes shining like stars. "Why didn't you tell me you were coming home?" she scolded, although plainly she wasn't mad. She wouldn't care about anything so long as she had Hunter.

And she did have him. Sarah could tell by the glow in *his* eyes as he looked down at her and by the way he held her firmly by her slender waist.

"Where's Mac?" he asked her.

"He's at the store," she said, gesturing toward the largest building in town. "Oh, wait, here he comes! He must have seen your wagon and decided to find out who our visitors are."

She started waving at the distant figure who broke into a lope the instant he'd recognized Hunter. At least Sarah didn't have to be jealous of him. He was only Hunter's stepfather.

Jealous? Where on earth had that come from? She certainly wasn't jealous of anyone or anything. She was just . . . what? Before she could decide, the tall red-haired man had reached his stepson, and the two threw their arms around each other. Sarah had never seen men hug, and the shock made her forget everything else for just a moment.

Now Mr. MacDougal was holding Hunter at arm's length and looking him over. "My God, I can't believe my eyes! How did you get out of the Army? We didn't expect you for at least two more months. And how did you get here?"

He turned and looked at the wagon while the woman pushed him away so she could hug and kiss Hunter again. Mr. MacDougal saw Sarah then and started.

Sarah went rigid on the wagon seat. She'd maintain

her dignity at all costs, even if she had to watch her husband kissing a woman more beautiful than Sarah could ever hope to be. She squared her shoulders and lifted her chin defiantly.

"And who's this?" Mr. MacDougal demanded, punching Hunter playfully on the arm.

Hunter looked up and smiled broadly, setting the woman aside. "This," he said, gesturing toward where Sarah sat on the wagon seat, "is my surprise, or at least one of my surprises. This is my wife."

"Wife!" they both cried in unison, but Hunter was already walking to the wagon. His eyes were still shining, and Sarah couldn't tell if it was just because he was so happy to be home and with them or because he was happy to be presenting her. He looked more than happy, though. He looked proud; although what he had to be proud about, Sarah couldn't imagine.

"Hunter, you have a wife, and you didn't tell us?" the woman exclaimed in outrage as she followed at Hunter's heels. "I'll never forgive you, not as long as I live!"

Sarah could easily believe it, she thought, slightly gratified that the woman finally understood her status.

Hunter had reached the wagon, and he smiled up at her just the way he'd smiled at the woman a few seconds ago. "Hand me down the baby first," he said, reaching up.

"Baby?" the woman echoed. Then fairly screeched: *"Baby!*

Yes, Sarah told herself as she reached back and scooped her child out of the cradle, a *baby,* my baby and Hunter's baby, and now you'll never have him, not ever.

Happy at the attention, Little One started to squeal

as Sarah passed her into Hunter's hands. He turned and placed the child in the woman's arms. "Merry Christmas," he said, laughing at her shock, then turning back for Sarah.

"Look, MacDougal!" the woman cried as Hunter lifted Sarah down from the seat. "It's our first grandbaby!"

"Is it a boy or a girl?" Mr. MacDougal asked, pushing the blanket back to better see the child.

"A girl," Hunter told them.

Grandbaby? Sarah must have heard wrong, but before she could decide, Hunter had thrust her in front of him, his hands planted firmly on her shoulders. "And this is my wife Sarah. Sarah, I want you to meet the two most important people in my life, my mother and father."

His *mother?* Sarah's mouth dropped open, but as she stared into the woman's blue eyes, now brimming with tears of joy, Sarah understood at last. She had finally come face to face with the legendary Rebekah Tate.

Chapter Seven

Sarah should have known. Now that she saw the woman up close, she could see the tiny lines around her eyes, and the silvery blond hair was really just blonde hair with some silver in it. But Rebekah Tate Mac-Dougal *was* beautiful and not at all like the elderly, white-haired lady Sarah had expected Hunter's mother to be.

And her smile was glorious, as Sarah knew because she was smiling at her now.

"Sarah?" Rebekah said, repeating her name questioningly. "You're really Hunter's wife?"

Sarah nodded and forced herself to meet the older woman's gaze. "Yes, ma'am."

"Then welcome home," Rebekah said, throwing one arm around Sarah's neck and pulling her in for a kiss. Since she still held the baby in her other arm, it was awkward, and Rebekah's kiss almost landed in Sarah's eye, so they both laughed, Sarah in embarrassment and Rebekah with pure joy. Tears were streaming down her cheeks now, but her smile still shone brightly.

Then Mr. MacDougal had his turn, taking Sarah by the shoulders and kissing her chastely on the cheek. "Welcome to our home, young lady," he said, smiling down at her. He was almost as tall as Hunter, and his light brown eyes were kind.

"Thank you," Sarah managed, although her throat felt tight.

"And isn't anybody going to introduce *this* young lady?" Rebekah demanded, holding up the baby. "And explain to me why I didn't know she existed until this minute?"

"Why don't you invite us inside where we can tell you everything you want to know, Mother?" Hunter inquired archly.

"Oh, dear, Sarah will think I don't have any manners," Rebekah lamented. "Please, won't you come in? You can see about your wagon in a few minutes, Hunter. First, you've got some questions to answer."

"Yes, ma'am," Hunter said, feigning meekness as he slipped his arm around Sarah's shoulders and they began to follow Rebekah into the house. Mr. MacDougal came along behind them.

"I'll carry the baby, ma'am," Sarah offered, feeling slightly bereft without her child.

"I won't hear of it," Rebekah told her over her shoulder. "I'm already several months behind on holding this baby, and why won't anyone at least tell me her name?"

Sarah and Hunter exchanged a glance. Good heavens, they still hadn't give Little One a real name yet! What had they been thinking? What had *Sarah* been thinking? And now the MacDougals would think she was a terrible mother and—

"Well, she doesn't really have a name yet," Hunter was saying. "I call her Bluebird, but—"

"Bluebird? What kind of a name is that?" his mother scolded. "And what do you mean, you haven't named her? How old is she, anyway?"

"About four months," Sarah supplied, her cheeks burning.

"Four months? What have you been thinking of to let a child go so long without a name?"

Sarah's flush deepened along with her humiliation, but she couldn't think of any way to explain.

"Can't you at least wait until we get inside, Mother?" Hunter asked as they climbed the porch steps.

"I told you, I've got a lot of catching up to do," she replied tartly, juggling the baby to push the front door open. She led them into the house.

If Hunter's arm hadn't been around Sarah, urging her on, she would have stopped dead in the entrance hall which seemed almost as big as the hotel room she'd thought so huge just a few days ago. The bottom half of the walls was paneled in dark wood and the top half was papered in a floral design. A massive set of stairs in the same dark wood started at the far end of the hall and wound up to the second floor. Sarah looked up and saw a shiny crystal chandelier hanging above her head, and just when she thought she couldn't take in any more, Rebekah pushed open one of the pocket doors that opened off the entrance hall.

"I'd take you into the parlor, Sarah, but the fire isn't lit in there, so we'll have to make do with the sitting room," Rebekah explained, leading them into the room.

"Rebekah is just showing off for you, Sarah," Mr. MacDougal said from behind her. "We never even go into the parlor from one year to the next."

"How can you say that, MacDougal," Rebekah chided him. "We use it every Christmas. We put the tree in there, as Sarah will see in a few weeks. Oh, I'm so glad you're here! Sit down and make yourselves at home."

Sarah knew she would never feel at home in such a

grand place, but she let Hunter direct her to a beautiful settee upholstered in red velvet and trimmed all around with elaborately carved wood. It must, she thought inanely, be difficult to dust.

Sitting down beside Hunter on the settee, she noticed Rebekah had taken her place in a large platform rocking chair made out of the same sort of wood as the settee and carved and upholstered just as elaborately. In fact, she realized, all the chairs in the room matched the settee, as did the carving on the side tables. Vases of dried flowers sat around on table tops, along with glass statues and assorted other bric-a-brac — some of which Sarah couldn't even identify — and pictures of landscapes too perfect to be real hung on the walls. Heavy red velvet drapes framed the windows, but lace liners allowed the winter sunlight to pass through.

A fire smoldered in the fireplace, and Mr. MacDougal went about stoking it into a roaring blaze to warm the travelers.

"Now let me get a good look at this baby with no name," Rebekah said, laying the baby in question on her lap and proceeding to unwrap her from her blankets. "Oh, Hunter, she looks just like you did when you were a baby! Look at her eyes, MacDougal! Have you ever seen eyes that color?"

As Mr. MacDougal obediently admired the infant, Sarah gave Hunter a desperate look. She couldn't lie to them, couldn't make them believe her child was Hunter's. It was just too cruel.

"How could you not tell us about her, Hunter?" Rebekah was asking, her pain obvious. "We've had letters from you, but you never even mentioned Sarah, much less —"

"Mother," Hunter said, stopping her. "The reason I

haven't told you about Sarah or the baby is because there hasn't been time. I've only known Sarah about two months."

Mr. MacDougal and Rebekah gaped at him, but he turned to Sarah. "We have to tell them the truth," he explained, as if he were trying to convince her. "But they won't tell anyone else, I promise you."

"The truth about what?" Rebekah demanded.

Sarah found she was frightened, almost as frightened of telling the truth and having this woman reject both her and her daughter as she was of lying and causing even more pain. But she nodded her permission to Hunter. He smiled slightly and patted her hand, then turned to his mother.

"I only met Sarah about two months ago. One of the ways I convinced her to marry me was by promising to raise her daughter as my own."

Mr. MacDougal abruptly sat down in the chair closest to Rebekah who was staring at Hunter as if she hadn't understood a word he said. Then she looked at the baby still lying in her lap. "But this baby looks just like . . ." Her voice trailed off as the truth dawned on her. "This baby has Indian blood," she said instead, raising her gaze accusingly to Hunter and Sarah.

Sarah dropped her head, too ashamed to meet her eye, but Hunter said, "Yes, Sarah was a captive of the Comanches for over a year. That's how we met. The Army got them to sign a treaty, and one of the provisions was release of all captives. My unit found Sarah and brought her back."

No one spoke, no one even breathed into the deadly silence that seemed to last forever. Sarah might have fled if she'd had possession of her child. Instead she sat frozen on the settee, her gaze locked on her folded hands, her face burning with humiliation.

Finally, Rebekah said, "Oh, my God," then muttered something that sounded like, "Hold the baby," before rising in a rustle of skirts.

Sarah looked up in surprise to find Rebekah descending on her. She swooped down onto the settee beside her, taking Sarah in her arms.

"You poor girl, you poor darling girl! I should have known! I should have *known!*"

Pressed against Rebekah's bosom, Sarah inhaled the faint scent of lavender and the motherly warmth she hadn't known in so many bitter years. Her eyes stung, but she blinked hard against the tears, not wanting to cry, only wanting to savor the indescribable bliss of comfort from one who truly did understand what she had been through.

The two women clung to each other for long moments, and as if from a distance, Sarah heard Mr. Mac-Dougal ask, "Where was she taken captive?"

"Someplace on the western frontier of Texas," Hunter explained. "She and her husband had settled there from Tennessee. They had a small child, but both her husband and the child were killed in the raid."

Rebekah's arms tightened around her, as if she could shield Sarah from this old loss or at least the pain of it. And surprisingly, Sarah found the pain bearable for the first time. Emboldened by having at last found someone with whom she could share her anguish, Sarah pushed away from Rebekah so she could see her face.

"They wanted me to leave my baby with the Indians," Sarah told her.

"Who did?" Rebekah demanded, outraged.

"The soldiers, the . . ." She glanced over her shoulder at Hunter, silently pleading for help.

"Some damn fool lieutenant we had with us," Hunter clarified.

"He said it would better," Sarah explained. "He said everyone who saw the baby would know I'd been a captive, but if I left her behind . . ."

Rebekah was nodding. She understood. "But you couldn't leave your child with them."

"Yes, I mean, no, I just couldn't."

Rebekah's gaze lifted to where Hunter sat beyond Sarah. "Of course you couldn't," she agreed, obviously remembering her own compulsion to have her son with her so many years ago. "I suppose when Hunter came along, it must have seemed like a miracle to you," she mused. "If you've only known each other for two months, it must have been a whirlwind courtship, too. How long have you actually been married?"

Instantly, Sarah dropped her gaze again. Their courtship had been even more whirlwind that Rebekah realized, and she didn't want to be the one to tell her.

"We've been married for two months," Hunter said, apparently not as loathe to admit it as Sarah was.

Sarah could feel the jolt of surprise go through Rebekah who was still holding her by the arms. "Then you . . . you didn't know each other very long before . . ."

"Only a few days," Hunter confirmed when his mother hesitated.

Plainly, Rebekah couldn't make sense of any of this. After a moment of silence, Mr. MacDougal said, "It must have been love at first sight then."

Love! Oh, dear, how could Sarah tell a lie like that?

But Hunter was saying, "The minute I saw Sarah, I

knew she was the woman for me. I'm afraid I took advantage of her unfortunate situation, but I don't think she's sorry she accepted my offer."

"Oh, I'm not!" Sarah hastily assured her mother-in-law. "I mean, Hunter's been very good to me, to *us*," she corrected. "And I'm very grateful and . . . and happy and . . ."

"And I'm sure you've been good to Hunter, too," Rebekah supplied when Sarah couldn't think of anything else to say.

"She certainly has," Hunter confirmed, making Sarah blush, although no one else could possibly know that he must mean the way she responded to him in bed, since she couldn't imagine how else she'd been good to him.

Rebekah studied Sarah for a long moment, as if she were searching her eyes for something she didn't see there. Sarah was beginning to feel very uncomfortable under the scrutiny when Mr. MacDougal said, "I really hate to mention it, but this baby seems a little damp . . ."

"Oh, my," Sarah exclaimed, jumping up to retrieve her daughter. She hadn't even noticed he was holding her, albeit a little uncomfortably. His wife must have passed the child to him when she went to Sarah, although Sarah knew she must be a terrible mother not to have even noticed. "I'm awful sorry. I don't know what I was thinking." She snatched the baby from him, looking around desperately for some way of escape.

But her hostess was already dealing with the situation. "I suppose the time has come for you to start carrying things in from your wagon, Hunter, and you'd best start with the dry diapers."

"Yes, ma'am," Hunter replied with the same feigned

meekness he'd shown her before. "Maybe you can give me a hand, Mac."

"Sure thing," Mr. MacDougal replied, following his stepson out.

"I'll show Sarah up to Hunter's bedroom," Rebekah called after them. "Just bring everything right on up." Then she turned back to Sarah. Her lips were smiling a welcome, but her eyes held a reserve, as if she hadn't quite made up her mind about Sarah yet. "Actually, we've got two other spare bedrooms if you'd like a separate room for the baby or—"

"Oh, no, ma'am, she still sleeps with us," Sarah assured her.

For some reason, this assurance seemed to mollify Rebekah somewhat. "Well, then, right this way," she said.

Sarah followed her out into the entrance hall and up the massive staircase. Sarah tried not to stare, but each new thing she saw was more beautiful or amazing than the last, so it was all she could do not to gasp aloud.

Upstairs, an oblong hallway opened into several rooms, and Sarah hoped she didn't get lost the next time she came up here and end up in the wrong place. Rebekah led her through one of the doors after indicating another which led to her and Mr. Mac-Dougal's room.

"This is Hunter's room," she said. "It's probably a little dusty, and we'll have to make up the bed, but I've left everything pretty much the way it was when he left."

The room was smaller than their hotel room in Austin, but it contained less furniture. A large four-poster bed covered with a colorful quilt sat against the far wall. The other furnishings were a wardrobe, a chest of drawers and a washstand. Built into one wall was a bookcase that held what Sarah imagined must be a hundred books. Could Hunter have read them all? Could *anyone* read so many? Even more amazing was the fireplace. A fireplace in a bedroom! What a luxury.

Lace curtains hung at the window, and the walls here were wallpapered, too, and more pictures hung on them. Framed photographs sat on the chest along with an assortment of junk a boy might have collected in his lifetime. The room looked as if it had been well loved by someone long ago, and Sarah might have felt at home there if she hadn't felt so intimidated by the richness of the furnishing.

Rebekah looked around and smiled sadly. "There were too many times when I was afraid he'd never live to sleep here again. And of course, I never dreamed that when he did come back he'd bring a family with him."

Sarah didn't know whether to smile or apologize, but fortunately, no response seemed to be expected.

"I've been meaning to tell you," Rebekah went on, visibly shrugging off her sad memories. "Your dress is beautiful."

"Oh, thank you," Sarah managed, not quite certain if that was the appropriate response. "Hunter got it for me in Austin."

"I thought it must have come from a big city. I haven't seen anything that nice in so long . . . Well, since before the war. Nothing's been very nice in the South since before the war."

"I still can't believe it's over," Sarah said, shifting the baby to a more comfortable position while trying to keep her wetness from soaking into her dress.

"Sometimes I wonder if it ever will be," Rebekah muttered, then consciously brightened. "Well, we'll have to get you a rocking chair up here, won't we? And a cradle."

"We've already got a cradle," Sarah offered.

207

"That's good," Rebekah said, moving to the fireplace. "I'll get this started to take the chill off. You're really lucky you didn't come in the summertime, you know," she added, taking a box of matches from the mantel and stooping down to light the fire someone had already laid in the hearth. "In the summer, it's just too hot to sleep up here at all. I tried to tell MacDougal that when he built the place, but he wouldn't listen. You know how men are. In the hot months we have to sleep downstairs on the porch."

Sarah remembered how cool the dugout had been in the heat of summer and almost said so before she caught herself. How could she tell a woman who lived in a mansion how comfortable she'd been living in a hole in the ground?

From downstairs, they could hear the men coming in the front door with their first load. Rebekah stood up and faced Sarah who still stood near the door, holding her baby like a shield.

"We'll talk about . . . about everything later," she said. "There's nothing you can't tell me, you know. I've been through it all, too, so you don't have to worry about shocking me. Oh, I know you don't want to; I can see from your face, and you probably won't believe me, but it helps if you do. If you can get it all out into the open, it won't seem nearly so bad, and after a while, you'll even stop having the nightmares. Believe me, Sarah, it's true."

But Sarah didn't want to believe her, because she knew she could never speak of those things, not even to Rebekah. Desperate to change the subject, she hurried out the door and over to the top of the stairs where she could see Hunter and Mr. MacDougal just starting up.

"I hope you brought me some diapers," she called

down to her husband.

"I brought *all* the baby stuff this trip," he called back.

And Sarah waited for him there so she wouldn't have to be alone with Rebekah again.

When the men had carried everything up and Hunter had gone to put the wagon away, Rebekah and her husband left their new daughter-in-law to unpack while Rebekah went to see about fixing supper.

"What do you think of her?" Rebekah asked her husband the moment they were alone in the kitchen.

"She's pretty enough, and she must be all right or Hunter never would have married her," Mac pointed out.

"But how would he have known?" she demanded. "He said they only knew each other a few *days* before they got married!"

"I only knew *you* a few days before I'd decided to marry you," Mac reminded her, taking her in his arms.

"But that was different," she protested, resisting the embrace.

"How was it different?" he insisted, holding her still in his arms.

"For one thing, we didn't get married right then. We didn't get married until we were both sure we were in love. Did you notice Hunter didn't say he loved her? Not even when you gave him a chance to. And she doesn't love him, I'm sure of it."

"Don't be a mother hen," Mac chided. "Hunter is a big boy now. He's been to college and fought a war, so he should be more than able to pick the woman he wants to marry."

"But why would he pick *her?* Why choose somebody

whose life is a shambles? Who's been married before and who has a child and who—"

"And who's been a captive of the Comanches, just like his mother?" Mac supplied. "Who even looks like his mother and who has a half-breed child like she did and—"

"MacDougal!" Rebekah cried in horror. "You don't think he married her because of that, do you? Oh, Lord, she doesn't really look like me, does she?"

"Well, no, except that she has blond hair and blue eyes, but you can't deny the similarities in her situation. Maybe he saw her and that baby and couldn't help thinking what a hard time they'd have and how he could make it easier for them, the way I did for you and him."

"I've never known Hunter to be quite so noble," Rebekah reminded him skeptically.

"Maybe the war changed him. Don't forget, we haven't seen him in five years."

"But how could he have changed so much he'd want to throw his life away on a woman he didn't even know just because he felt sorry for her?"

"I don't know, and who said he felt sorry for her? Maybe he just liked her looks. She is a fetching little thing. A tad skinny, maybe, but a few weeks of your cooking should fix her right up."

Rebekah frowned up at him. "Maybe I've been worried about the wrong thing. Maybe I should be worried because my husband thinks his daughter-in-law is a 'fetching little thing.' "

Mac grinned unrepentantly. "I thought it was my duty to notice so I could put your mind at ease about what might have attracted Hunter to her."

Rebekah playfully slapped him on the arm. "It's not

your duty to notice any woman but me, and don't you forget it."

"Yes, ma'am," he said, imitating Hunter's phony meekness.

"And that's something else!" Rebekah cried. "Hunter did every blessed thing I asked him to today without an argument. What's wrong with him?"

"Maybe he grew up . . . or maybe he's trying to impress his bride," he tried when Rebekah snorted at his first theory. "Whether he loves her or not, he certainly cares about her. Remember when you asked about the baby, he said they'd tell us about her past but that we wouldn't tell anyone one else? He reminded me of that while we were carrying their things in. It seems he promised her that no one would ever know she'd been a captive. They plan to tell people they've been married a little over a year and that the baby is his."

"Which certainly explains why *she* was so willing to marry *him*, but it still doesn't explain why *he* wanted *her* so badly."

"Maybe that's something only another man would understand, Rebekah Tate," he told her slyly.

"Do you think she's *that* fetching?" she asked skeptically.

"To a man who's been a soldier for as long as Hunter was? Without a doubt."

Rebekah considered the matter. "I suppose he must have been terribly lonely."

"More than lonely," he said, pulling her hips more snugly against his to illustrate his meaning.

"But would he *marry* her for that?" she asked, unconvinced.

"I don't know, but I get the impression he's pretty satisfied with his bargain."

211

"Did he *talk* to you about his relations with his wife?" Rebekah asked incredulously.

"Of course not, but didn't you notice how he let her boss him around, telling him what to get from the wagon and where to put it when he brought it in? And he smiled through it all. A man doesn't act that content unless he really is content . . . and there's only one thing I can think of that'll put a man in such a good mood."

"I hope you're right, for both their sakes. I just wish . . . Oh, Lord, you should have seen her face when I told her she could talk to me about what happened to her with the Indians. Her eyes were so haunted. . . . Was that how I looked when I came back from them?"

"I don't remember," her husband said tactfully. "Look, it's really none of our business *why* they got married. The fact is, they did, and we've got to accept it, and accept her and her baby."

Rebekah softened at once. "That baby! Isn't she adorable!"

"When she's dry," Mac agreed with a grin.

"I hadn't realized how much I missed babies until I had her in my arms. That's the only thing I really regret about our life together, MacDougal, not having any more children. I wanted to give you a houseful of little red-haired demons."

"I know, my darling, but you know I never minded. You gave me Hunter, and he's the finest son a man could want."

Rebekah reached up, pulled his face to hers, and kissed him soundly. "Now I remember why I love you so much, MacDougal."

"I can't imagine how I ever let you forget it," he replied, returning her kiss.

* * *

212

Just as Sarah had feared, Rebekah set supper in the formal dining room with real china plates and crystal glasses laid on a damask cloth and so much silverware, Sarah had no idea which utensil to use. Fortunately, the table was so huge, she could hardly see the other people seated at it, so she supposed they wouldn't see her, either.

From the corner of her eye, she watched her mother-in-law to see which fork she picked up while being extra careful with her coffee cup so she wouldn't lose her grip on the fragile handle and send it crashing to the floor or, even worse, spill it on the beautiful table cloth.

"Don't get the wrong idea, Sarah," Mr. MacDougal said when they'd been eating for a few minutes.

Sarah looked up in surprise. The men of her previous acquaintance wouldn't have considered interrupting the serious business of eating with conversation.

"The next time Rebekah Tate serves you a meal in this room will be Christmas day," he told her.

"That's right," Hunter agreed. "I can't remember the last time we used these dishes, either."

"Hush up, the both of you," Rebekah scolded good-naturedly. "Sarah will think we're white trash, eating in the kitchen all the time on chipped dishes."

"Well, we do," Mr. MacDougal confided with a grin. "She makes us wear our shoes, though."

Sarah smiled perfunctorily, aware she was expected to find this amusing. Instead, she felt her supper settling into a hard lump in her stomach at the realization that they would consider *her* white trash if they knew her background. Rebekah Tate MacDougal might serve meals in the kitchen of this mansion, but Sarah was sure those meals were nothing like the ones she'd served in her own kitchen which had also served as the parlor and the bedroom for her entire family.

When they'd finished sampling the two kinds of pie Rebekah produced for dessert, Sarah rose and began helping to clear the table.

"You don't have to do that, Sarah. You're company," Rebekah told her. "Go ahead and tend to the baby."

Sarah glanced at her daughter who lay quietly in the laundry basket Rebekah had filled with soft bedding for her.

"She's fine, and I'm not company," Sarah replied, carefully picking up several of the china plates and silently praying she wouldn't drop them on her way to the kitchen.

The kitchen was the biggest surprise of all in this house full of them. Sean MacDougal had spared no expense in equipping it, and Sarah saw every sort of modern convenience, including a cast-iron stove with a boiler over it so hot water would always be available and a pump right in the sink so no one would ever have to go outside and haul water on a wet or freezing morning.

Rebekah drew some water from the boiler and filled the sink, adding some soft soap and swishing it around to make suds. "Just put the plates right in here after you've scraped them," she instructed, returning to the kitchen for another load.

After a few trips, Sarah began to feel more comfortable performing this familiar task, and when the table was clear, she gladly began to dry the dishes Rebekah washed.

"Everything is so beautiful," Sarah remarked after a few minutes, admiring the rose patterned border of the plate she was drying.

"We've been collecting things for twenty years, don't forget, and when you're married to a storekeeper, you get first pick. Of course, what I usually get first pick of is the things that arrive damaged. Take this china, for instance. I only have five complete place settings because the rest arrived smashed, so I can only use it for family."

"Oh, dear, now I really am scared of dropping a piece!" Sarah said in dismay.

"Don't be," Rebekah assured her. "I've got some odd pieces to replace them with if you do."

Still, Sarah used extra care in setting the dried dishes on the table.

"Sarah, I don't mean to meddle," Rebekah began after a moment, carefully keeping her gaze on the dishpan, "but as soon as people hear that Hunter is home, they'll start coming by to see him and, well, they'll want to meet you, of course, and . . ."

Sarah froze in apprehension when Rebekah hesitated, obviously uncomfortable with what she had to say. Was she going to tell Sarah she wasn't good enough to meet Hunter's friends and family? Had she figured it out already that Sarah wasn't like them and might never be able to fit into Hunter's life?

". . . and they'll want to see the baby," Rebekah continued, "and, well, what are we supposed to say when they ask us what the baby's name is?"

She looked up at last, her lovely face simply concerned, not angry or judgmental at all. She just wanted Sarah to name the baby. Sarah felt almost giddy with relief.

"I . . . we just haven't . . . I mean, you're right, we should, but Hunter . . ."

"Hunter what?" Hunter asked from the kitchen doorway. He was carrying the baby, who had begun to fuss. "Looks like somebody's hungry," he added, holding the baby up.

"Your mother thinks, I mean, we should name the

215

baby," Sarah said, laying aside the dish towel and hurrying to take the child from him.

"What do you want to name her?" Hunter asked, handing the baby over.

Sarah hadn't allowed herself to even think about it. She'd had her own name for the child, Little One, and giving her a real name had seemed so . . . so final a step, a commitment of sorts that Sarah had been afraid to make because until now she'd never quite been sure she wouldn't somehow lose this child the way she'd lost the others. But now . . .

"I don't know," Sarah said, knowing her mother-in-law must think her simpleminded for not having at least considered the matter.

"Maybe you'd like to name her after your mother," Rebekah suggested.

Sarah didn't think she did, although it was probably a good idea.

"What was her name?" Hunter asked when Sarah didn't reply.

"Anne," Sarah admitted reluctantly. She'd always thought the name too plain.

"That's pretty," Rebekah said hopefully.

"I thought . . ." Sarah began, then stopped, wondering if her impulse was the right one or not. She didn't want to cause offense, but . . .

"What did you think?" Hunter prodded.

"Well, I know she's not really your grandchild, Mrs. MacDougal, but I thought, I mean, I'd like to call her after you. If you don't mind, that is."

For a moment Sarah thought she'd made a terrible mistake. Rebekah's eyes widened with shock, and then they filled with tears. And then she threw her arms around Sarah, wet hands and all.

MORE PASSION AND ADVENTURE AWAIT... YOUR TRIP TO A BIG ADVENTUROUS WORLD BEGINS WHEN YOU ACCEPT YOUR FIRST 4 NOVELS ABSOLUTELY *FREE*
(AN $18.00 VALUE)

Accept your Free gift and start to experience more of the passion and adventure you like in a historical romance novel. Each Zebra novel is filled with proud men, spirited women and tempestuous love that you'll remember long after you turn the last page.

Zebra Historical Romances are the finest novels of their kind. They are written by authors who really know how to weave tales of romance and adventure in the historical settings you love. You'll feel like you've actually gone back in time with the thrilling stories that each Zebra novel offers.

GET YOUR FREE GIFT WITH THE START OF YOUR HOME SUBSCRIPTION

Our readers tell us that these books sell out very fast in book stores and often they miss the newest titles. So Zebra has made arrangements for you to receive the four newest novels published each month.

You'll be guaranteed that you'll never miss a title, and home delivery is so convenient. And to show you just how easy it is to get Zebra Historical Romances, we'll send you your first 4 books absolutely FREE! Our gift to you just for trying our home subscription service.

BIG SAVINGS AND FREE HOME DELIVERY

Each month, you'll receive the four newest titles as soon as they are published. You'll probably receive them even before the bookstores do. What's more, you may preview these exciting novels free for 10 days. If you like them as much as we think you will, just pay the low preferred subscriber's price of just $3.75 each. *You'll save $3.00 each month off the publisher's price.* AND, your savings are even greater because there are never any shipping, handling or other hidden charges—FREE Home Delivery. Of course you can return any shipment within 10 days for full credit, no questions asked. There is no minimum number of books you must buy.

GET
FOUR
FREE
BOOKS
(AN $18.00 VALUE)

ZEBRA HOME SUBSCRIPTION
SERVICE, INC.
120 BRIGHTON ROAD
P.O. Box 5214
CLIFTON, NEW JERSEY 07015-5214

"Oh, Sarah, nothing would make me happier! I'm so *honored!*"

Sarah hugged her back, closing her eyes and breathing a silent prayer of thanks for having, for once, done the right thing.

"But maybe we should ask Hunter's opinion first," Rebekah added, releasing Sarah and turning to her son. "Maybe he had something else in mind."

Hunter grinned. "She'll always be little Bluebird to me, so I don't care what you decide her *real* name will be."

"Bluebird," Rebekah scoffed, dismissing his opinion with a wave of her soapy hand. "You should name her after *your* mother, too," she told Sarah. "It's only fair, and besides, Rebekah Anne Tate sounds lovely, don't you think?"

"We should probably call her 'Anne' to keep folks from confusing her with you, though," Hunter said.

But Sarah didn't want any references to her family who would be so unacceptable to the Tates if they ever found out about them. "No," Sarah insisted, surprising the others with her vehemence. "I mean, we can call her 'Becky.' Then no one'll get confused," she explained more reasonably when she saw their surprise.

"That would be fine," Rebekah agreed. "What do you think, Hunter?"

"I already told you I don't care, and a man's opinion doesn't usually count for much when women start putting their heads together anyway, so why are you even bothering to ask me?"

Both women gave him disgusted looks, then Rebekah turned back to Sarah. "Now I suppose you'd better go feed little Becky before she starves to death. I'll run and tell MacDougal the good news."

"The dishes," Sarah protested, knowing she shouldn't leave the kitchen before the work was finished.

"They'll be here when I get back. Go on, now." Rebekah started off, then abruptly turned back and kissed the silken top of the baby's head. "Enjoy your supper, Becky," she whispered to the child.

She left Sarah and Hunter in a swirl of skirts. For a moment they just stood staring at each other. Sarah knew she should have consulted Hunter about such a big decision and half-expected him to be annoyed with her. Instead, he seemed vastly pleased.

"That was a nice gesture, naming her after my mother," he said.

"She seemed to like it. I thought she might want to wait for a grandchild that was really hers, though."

Hunter's dark eyebrows shot up. "Is that a possibility?"

For a second Sarah didn't know what he was talking about, and when she did, she blushed. "Oh, no," she hastily assured him, "not while I'm still nursing. That is, until I get my health back and . . ." She trailed off in an agony of embarrassment.

"There's no hurry," he said, grinning wickedly. "I hope you don't mind if I keep practicing in the meantime, though. I want to be ready to do my part when the time comes."

Sarah didn't mind a bit, but no decent woman would dream of saying so right out like that. "I . . . I'd better feed the baby," she muttered, brushing past him through the door and heading for the stairs.

Later that evening, after Sarah had put her newly named child to bed, she came down to find Hunter and his parents in the sitting room.

". . . and business at the hotel was booming," Hunter

was saying. "I went over the books with Stanton, and we can expect a nice return this year."

"I was in Austin a few months ago," Mr. MacDougal said. "The place is crawling with Yankees, so I suppose it's their money we're taking. I figure they owe us."

"We'll get rid of them soon enough once we have an election and replace that scalawag governor the President saddled us with," Hunter said, but Mr. MacDougal was shaking his head.

"I wouldn't count on it. Didn't you hear? They refused to seat our duly elected congressmen and senators in Washington because they'd fought for the Confederacy. Seems the Congress has appointed a committee to decide the terms under which the South will be readmitted to the Union, and somehow I don't think those terms will be easy."

As if sensing Sarah's presence, Rebekah looked up from her knitting. "How's little Becky?" she asked when she saw her daughter-in-law hovering uncertainly in the doorway.

"Sleeping," Sarah said, moving into the room at last.

Hunter patted the cushion beside him on the settee and slipped his arm around her when she sat down there.

"I can't believe they refused to seat properly elected officials," Hunter said to his stepfather. "Don't they know we'll just elect more like them?"

"I have a feeling they're going to try to prevent us from electing anybody. So far it's just rumors, but they're talking about disenfranchising everybody who fought for the Confederacy."

"But that's almost every able-bodied man in the South!" Hunter protested in outrage. Sarah could feel his fury, and she looked up at him in alarm, wondering if she should do or say something. "They can't stop us *all* from voting! What about the Constitution?"

"The South isn't part of the United States anymore, remember?" Mr. MacDougal said. "So the Constitution doesn't apply to us."

Sarah had never seen Hunter so angry. "But—" he exploded, but his mother interrupted whatever he'd been about to say.

"That's enough politics for tonight," Rebekah said firmly. "I'm so sick of hearing about the Yankees, I could scream," she confided in Sarah who nodded her agreement. "If they'd just let women run the government, they wouldn't have these problems."

"I'm sure *you* could have the North and the South peacefully reunited in no time, my dear," Mr. Mac-Dougal said in amusement.

"I never would have let them split up in the first place," Rebekah informed him haughtily. "Men, they think the only way to settle something is to fight a war over it, and just look at what good it did. The South is in ruins and the North is in debt."

"The slaves are freed," Hunter pointed out.

"Freed to what? Thousands of them are wandering the roads, begging food and shelter, because they left their former masters and can't get anyone to pay them wages for their labor. And what are the Yankees doing about it? The Freedmen's Bureau just makes promises the government can't or won't keep, and meanwhile, people are starving."

"Maybe we *should* put her in charge," Mr. MacDougal told Hunter. "It would serve the Yankees right."

"Never mind about the Yankees," Rebekah snapped. "What I *am* in charge of is this house, and I think we need to plan a party here to welcome Hunter home and intro-

220

duce his new family to all our friends and relations."

Sarah went cold at the very thought of being held up for inspection by the other Tates and their friends, but her husband didn't seem to mind at all.

"That's a wonderful idea," Hunter exclaimed, hugging Sarah to his side. "I can't wait to see everybody and have them meet Sarah and the baby."

"Of course there are *some* people you'd better see right away or they'll never forgive you," Rebekah reminded her son.

"I know, Jewel will skin me if I let another day go by without paying my respects," he said. "I want to take Sarah out anyway so she can look the place over. We plan to live out there until I can get a proper house built."

"That's silly when we have plenty of room right here," Rebekah protested.

"But I'll need to be on the land while I get the ranching operation started," Hunter argued. "I want to go home to my wife at night, not have her stuck way out here in town."

He patted Sarah's shoulder, and she was able to smile up at him quite sincerely, grateful that she wouldn't be spending too much time in such a grand house under Rebekah's watchful eye.

"Who's Jewel?" she asked, figuring she should get to know Hunter's family members.

"She was my grandfather's housekeeper. Remember, I told you about her? She took care of me a lot when I was a kid."

"Oh, yeah," Sarah said, recalling some of the stories of how Hunter had bedeviled the woman in his youth.

"She kept house for my grandfather, and she keeps house for Dan and Enoch now. You know, the ones who work my grandfather's farm. Well, I guess it's really mine, now, isn't it? Jewel will be thrilled I've finally settled down, especially when she sees I've brought her a baby to take care of."

Suddenly, the true situation dawned on Sarah. The woman had been old Mr. Tate's *housekeeper,* which meant they had *servants.* Sarah had never even *known* a servant, much less dealt with one. And old Mr. Tate had worked his farm with hired hands, which meant he had more money than Sarah could imagine, perhaps even more money than the MacDougal's. Dear heaven, how was she ever going to fool them all? And then there were the friends and relatives who would be coming to meet her and look her over and judge her and . . .

"Anyway, about this party," Rebekah was saying, "I think we'll have it a week from Saturday. That's still a few days before Christmas, and people will love having another party to go to during the holidays. We can put the tree up early so everything looks festive. What do you think, Sarah?"

"That sounds fine," Sarah said, wishing her throat didn't feel so tight and hoping her apprehension didn't sound in her voice.

Apparently not, because Rebekah was just going on with her plans. "And there's no sense in you moving all the way out to the farm just yet. You won't be able to do anything until spring anyway, and why should you isolate poor Sarah all winter when she could be living in town?"

"You just don't want little Becky to be too far away," Mr. MacDougal accused, and Rebekah smiled unrepentantly.

"Of course I don't, and why should I when I can have her right here under my own roof? Tell Hunter you want to stay here with us, Sarah."

What Sarah really wanted to do was go someplace where she didn't have to be afraid of being found out for an impostor, but that wasn't an option. Helplessly, she looked to Hunter for guidance, but he only smiled down at her expectantly.

"It's real nice here, but I'm used to living on a farm, so . . . whatever Hunter thinks is best is fine with me," she hedged.

"Oh, ho!" Mr. MacDougal whooped. "Where on earth did you find this woman, Hunter? I don't suppose she actually *obeys* you, too, does she?"

"Not hardly," Hunter allowed, smiling his approval at Sarah. "But Mother is probably right about staying here until spring. Nobody's really lived in the house at the farm since Grandpa died, so it might need some work. We'll decide after Sarah's had a chance to look it over."

"One thing, at least," Rebekah added, "with Jewel there, it'll be clean enough, but Hunter's right, it may need some repairs. You don't want to take a baby to a house with a leaky roof."

Of course, Sarah had taken a baby to a house with a *dirt* roof, and dirt floors and walls, but she smiled weakly and didn't protest at all when Hunter suggested she might be tired and want to retire early.

She knew what he wanted—he'd already warned her this afternoon of how they'd spend their first night in his old feather bed—and she certainly didn't mind. She wasn't *that* tired. So she went with him up the broad staircase into the dark upstairs and for a short time, at least, she could forget that she didn't belong here and pretend Hunter Tate really loved her.

Later, when they snuggled together beneath the warm quilts in the blissful aftermath of passion, Sarah was already half-asleep when Hunter whispered, "First thing tomorrow I'll take you out to meet Jewel."

When the farm buildings finally came into view, Sarah could have clapped her hands with joy. After all that talk about servants, Sarah had almost expected one of those enormous plantation houses with white pillars in front. Instead she saw the simple dogtrot house that Hunter had described to her in one of their many conversations about his home.

"The old place looks exactly the same," he said with a nostalgic sigh, and Sarah could easily imagine him as a boy, running wild through the carefully plowed fields.

Those fields now lay fallow, and there was no sign of activity from the out buildings. Only the plume of smoke from the dogtrot's kitchen chimney gave evidence of life.

Soon, however, the noise of their approaching wagon drew a response from the house. A woman's figure, clad in a red calico dress and a white apron, appeared in the covered walkway, then two male figures emerged from the big barn, curious to see who the visitors might be.

At first Sarah thought the distance was playing tricks on her eyes, but when they were closer, Hunter stood up and shouted a greeting that caused the residents to come running out to meet them. As they drew nearer, Sarah stared at them in horror. Jewel and the two men were colored. Hunter Tate had been a *slave owner*.

Chapter Eight

The woman, Jewel, was waving furiously and crying Hunter's name while the men shouted greetings and all of them ran toward the wagon. Hunter pulled the horses to a halt and jumped down, scooping up the woman in the same exuberant embrace with which he'd greeted his mother.

Sarah had never known anyone who owned slaves, but she'd certainly never imagined the owners treated them with the same affection they did their own families. Startling her even more, Hunter hugged the two men just as enthusiastically, then laughed aloud when they all three started asking him questions at once.

"I'm just fine and out of the army and home for good and I've brought someone for you all to meet," he said when he was finally able to get them quieted down.

Three pairs of dark brown eyes turned instantly to the wagon seat where Hunter was pointing and where Sarah was sitting. She stiffened under the unexpected scrutiny and shifted uncomfortably on the seat. At least she was wearing her best dress, the same one she'd worn for the MacDougal's, so she didn't have to be self-conscious about her appearance.

The woman, Jewel, was the first to speak after the amazed silence that had followed Hunter's announcement. "I knew it," she said, coming closer to the wagon. "I dreamed something good happened to you, Mr. Hunter. I didn't know what, but I knew you was happy for the first time in a lot of years."

She was tall for a woman and slender, her skin the color of coffee with cream and her hair completely covered by a red bandana wrapped around her head. Her face was still beautiful, although age and hardship had lined it, and Sarah might have been warmed by her smile if it hadn't been set in a colored face. Because it was, she squirmed uneasily and tried not to follow her instincts to draw back from the woman's approach.

"Jewel, this is my wife, Sarah," Hunter was saying.

" 'Course it is," Jewel said. "Knowed that the minute I set eyes on her. Pretty little thing she is, too, all done up in that fancy new dress you prob'ly got her in Austin or someplace."

"And Sarah, this is Jewel Tate, and Dan and Enoch Tate."

Seeing Sarah's shock, he explained, "They took my grandfather's name when he gave them their freedom in his will. It was Grandpa's idea, and we always considered them members of the family anyway."

Sarah nodded as if she understood, although she knew she never would, and tried to smile. "Pleased to meet you," she said, although the words came out as little more than a whisper.

"Now you come right down and get inside out of this

226

wind," Jewel told her. "Ol' Jewel'll fix you some nice hot tea to take the chill off."

"Not so fast, Jewel," Hunter said. "I've brought you another surprise, too. Sarah, show her."

With greater reluctance than she knew she should feel, Sarah turned and reached down into the back of the wagon and lifted her sleeping baby from her box bed.

From below, she heard Jewel's gasp of surprise. "A baby! You got yourself a baby, Mr. Hunter? Oh, Lordy, this here's about the happiest day I've ever lived through. Just you hand that young'un down here, Miz Sarah. Whatever are you thinking of, Mr. Hunter, bringing a baby out on a freezing cold day like this?"

"She's been outside a lot," Hunter said. For one terrible moment Sarah thought he was going to tell them about her, about her captivity and how the baby had been *born* outside, but instead he said, "We carried her here all the way from Kansas in this wagon. She's used to it."

Jewel was reaching up for the baby, and Sarah saw how white the palms of her hands were, in contrast to the rest of her brown skin. She had to remind herself those hands had cared for Hunter and they certainly wouldn't hurt Hunter's child before she could relinquish her daughter.

"It's a girl, is it?" Jewel said, taking the child from Sarah's reluctant arms.

"That's right, and we named her Rebekah Anne Tate, after our mothers," Hunter said proudly.

"We call her Becky," Sarah added, knowing she should say something.

"That's a mighty fine name," Jewel declared. "Come

227

on in the house, now. Dan and Enoch'll take care of your horses."

A few minutes later, they were all seated around the kitchen table drinking the strong black tea Jewel had brewed. Hunter had given his former slaves a quick summary of the fictional story of how he and Sarah had met after her first husband, a farmer in Kansas, had died.

"Your mama must be ready to skin you alive for keeping this young'un a secret all this time," Jewel said.

"She forgave me the first time she held little Becky in her arms," Hunter replied. "Besides, I wanted to see your faces when you heard the news."

"Well, Miz Sarah, you being a farmer's wife already, maybe you can get this fiddle-footed drifter to settle down here where he belongs at last," Jewel said.

"The farm's doing real good," Dan offered. "We growed cotton last summer for a cash crop. First time since the war started we was able to sell it up North."

"Now that you's home, we can start work breaking more ground, too," Enoch added. "You'll be rich a' fore you die, Mr. Hunter, if'n you put all this land in cotton."

"Maybe I will die rich, Enoch, but it won't be from farming," Hunter said. "I'm not going to farm any more of the land. I'm going to fence off the fields from the rest of Grandpa Tate's holdings and run cattle on the grass."

"Cattle!" they all echoed in astonishment.

"That's right. Since the war took most of the men away, there's thousands of head of unbranded stock running loose all over Texas, just waiting for somebody to claim them. I've already got the grass to feed them.

All I need is some able-bodied men to help me gather them up."

"Ain't no money in cows, Mr. Hunter," Jewel warned him. "Everybody knows that. No place to ship the meat, and the skins is only worth a dollar or two."

"There wasn't anyplace to ship the meat before the war, but now the North is crying for beef, Jewel," he told her.

"How you gonna get it there?" she scoffed.

"Haven't figured that out yet, but if we have to, we'll *drive* it to the nearest railhead."

"And where's that?"

"Missouri, I think, but the tracks are moving farther West every day. It won't be long until they get to Texas itself."

The dark faces reflected the same doubt Sarah felt, although she didn't feel confident enough to argue the point, as Jewel obviously did. Every time the woman opened her mouth, Sarah wanted to gasp at her impertinence.

"Uppity nigger" is what Sarah's father would have called her. For a long time Sarah hadn't been able to imagine how a slave could be "uppity" or what a slave would have to be uppity about. But that was before she'd learned the way the slaves of the rich looked down on her and her kind. Poor white trash was what they'd called her people, and for all the freedom their white skin allowed them, Sarah and her family certainly had nothing else. Not like the slaves who had someone to feed and clothe and shelter them from the moment they were born until the day they died, even after they were too old to work anymore.

Now the slaves were free, too, and Sarah felt a per-

229

verse satisfaction in knowing how difficult they would find their new lives.

"Why don't you show Sarah around the house, Jewel? And Dan and Enoch can take me around the rest of the place. Sarah and I were thinking we'd live out here while I get the ranching operation started. Then I'll build Sarah a big house on the other side of the creek so I won't have to ride through all those cotton fields to get home at night."

Dan and Enoch rose immediately, and before Sarah could protest the men had left her alone with the intimidating Jewel.

But Jewel was smiling at her, and since she still held Sarah's baby, Sarah somehow managed to smile back.

"Well, this here's the kitchen," Jewel said, "but I reckon you already knew that."

Sarah nodded. "I'll take the baby if you're tired," she offered.

"Maybe you'd better carry her while we walk around. These old arms might get tired and drop her, and I wouldn't want nothing to happen to Mr. Hunter's baby girl."

Sarah felt her smile vanish at the reminder of her lie, but she took little Becky from Jewel, being careful not to touch the woman in the process, and rose to follow her hostess, trying not to feel like the servant.

This house belongs to your husband, she told herself sternly. If only she had the confidence that should go along with such knowledge.

Jewel showed her the small room off the kitchen where she had slept ever since old Mr. Tate had brought her here over twenty-five years ago. Then she took Sarah into the parlor which no one ever used anymore now that Mr. Tate was dead and Mr. Hunter had been gone so long.

Sarah lifted the sheets that covered the furniture and was relieved to find it worn and not at all luxurious. She could feel quite comfortable in this room.

"That's all on this side," Jewel said, leading Sarah out into the windy passageway that separated the two halves of the house. "Nobody's used the bedrooms since Mr. Hunter left for the war," she added. "A lot of folks come by, slaves on their way to the promised land or what they think is the promised land, meaning the big city and the Freedmen's Bureau to get their forty acres and a mule that they think the gov'ment's gonna give 'em, but I don't let 'em sleep in the house. Never know what kinda folks they are, so I make 'em stay in the barn."

"Forty acres and a mule!" Sarah exclaimed in outrage, quickly adjusting the baby's blanket to cover her against the wind whipping through the dogtrot. "Is that what they get from the Freedmen's Bureau?"

"Not a bit of it," Jewel replied in disgust, pushing open the door to one of the rooms on the other side of the house. "It's just a rumor got started somehow, and every slave in God's creation believed it, seems like. They all set out to get to a Freedmen's Bureau, and now they're all starving on the roads. Them that do find the Bureau finds out the truth and about gets their hearts broke. It's a mighty sad thing, Miz Sarah. All them colored folk what never been off the farm where they was borned and who been took care of all their lives, they all too innocent to know what the world's really like. They hates their masters for treatin' 'em like slaves and keepin' 'em from being free, but they don't

231

know things'll be a lot worse once they gets away from home."

Sarah thought about her own cruel lessons on the same subject and realized Jewel was right. She knew her father would consider her disloyal for feeling sorry for niggers, but she couldn't help it. Although she still wasn't quite comfortable being around Jewel, Sarah began to see her as a person for the first time, a person who'd known suffering just as Sarah had.

"This here's old Mr. Tate's room," Jewel explained, gesturing at their surroundings. "Next door is the room Mr. Tate built for his daughter, though Miz Rebekah didn't use it long. Mr. Hunter did, though, whenever he visited us." On this side of the house, the furniture was also covered with sheets and the bedding rolled up, but Sarah liked the rough log walls and the plank floors. This was the same kind of place she'd grown up in, although it was much more luxurious than her parents' home with its wooden floors and glass windows. This was the kind of home she'd dreamed of having one day.

"It's real nice," Sarah allowed.

"You got a lot of furniture to bring with you?"

"No, uh, we didn't carry anything with us from . . . from Kansas," Sarah said. "Hunter said we wouldn't need anything."

Jewel studied her a moment in the winter light filtering through the dusty window panes. "Did your folks own slaves, Miz Sarah?"

"No!" Sarah said. Too quickly, she decided, seeing Jewel's dark eyes grow wide. "I mean, they didn't hold with it."

Jewel considered this. "Where'd you say you was

from? Before you settled in Kansas, I mean."

"Tennessee," Sarah said, knowing she had no reason to feel defensive, yet feeling defensive all the same.

Jewel's dark eyes narrowed. "Your husband . . . your first husband, I mean, he didn't fight in the war?"

Sarah shook her head. "He said it was a rich man's war. That's why he . . . why we left Tennessee."

Jewel nodded slowly, as if she understood. "What'd he die of? Your first husband?" she asked suddenly.

Sarah opened her mouth to reply, then couldn't remember whether Hunter had said or not. Her stomach knotted in sudden panic. Had they decided not to tell people he'd been killed by Indians? There were Indians in Kansas who killed settlers all the time, just like in Texas. It could have happened there just as well as here. "I don't know . . ." Sarah hedged nervously, earning a frown from Jewel.

"You *must* know," Jewel insisted. "Did he get sick or was it an accident?"

"I . . . he was killed . . . by Indians," she said impulsively, knowing she had to say something.

"*Indians?*" Jewel echoed, clearly astonished. Hunter must not have said that before. "Comanches?"

"Uh, yes," Sarah agreed quickly, before she could lose her nerve. "They . . . they killed my baby, too, my son."

For a long moment, Jewel just stared at Sarah, her dark face unreadable, and Sarah was sure she'd said something terribly wrong, something that disagreed with Hunter's story.

"But they didn't kill you," Jewel said finally. "How'd you get away?"

How indeed? Sarah wasn't any good at this at all.

233

Her heart was thundering in her chest, and she was *sure* Jewel must know she was lying. "I . . . I wasn't home. I was visiting a friend," she improvised.

"You went visiting and left your baby at home?" Jewel asked, plainly disapproving.

"No, I mean, yes, I left him. I left them both and . . . and . . ."

"How long was this before you met Mr. Hunter?" Jewel asked suddenly.

The terror was screaming in her head, and Sarah couldn't think. She tried frantically to figure out what might be a reasonable length of time, but she couldn't, not with Jewel's accusing eyes staring at her, waiting, waiting.

"A few months . . . I mean, a year," she corrected, not wanting Jewel to think she'd remarried with unseemly haste.

"And where was you living all this time?"

"I . . . on my farm," Sarah guessed, desperate now and wanting to run.

"On your farm that the Indians burned, where they killed your husband and your baby, and you stayed there all by yourself?" Jewel asked skeptically.

"No!" Sarah denied, frantically trying to think of something less preposterous. "I mean, I lived with neighbors, on *their* farm."

"The same neighbors that you was visiting when the Indians come."

"Yes, yes," Sarah confirmed gratefully.

"And how'd you come to meet Mr. Hunter?"

Sarah wanted to cover her face from those searching eyes that seemed to see into her soul. Her throat felt as if it were clogged with cotton. "I . . . He came by one day, and we . . . we met."

"And he took to you right off, I reckon," Jewel said, nodding her approval.

"Yes! Yes, he did." Jewel seemed to be believing her, and Sarah was beginning to think she might pull this off, although she'd have to make sure Jewel didn't have a chance to question Hunter before Sarah could talk to him and tell him what he was supposed to say.

"And he took to your baby right off, too," Jewel guessed.

"Yes!" Sarah agreed, almost giddy with relief at how well she was fooling Jewel.

But then Jewel frowned. "Now wait a minute, I thought your baby was dead. Kilt by the Indians, you said."

Sarah felt as if someone had punched her in the stomach. Trembling in terror now, she could only gape at Jewel, too confused to even figure out what lie to tell to cover up the other lies or even if that were possible.

Clutching her baby, Sarah backed up a step, needing to flee and knowing she'd never escape from Jewel's all-seeing gaze. She quaked with fear and shame and the knowledge that she'd somehow betrayed Hunter.

But when Jewel spoke, her voice wasn't triumphant, the way it should have been for having caught Sarah in her web of lies. Instead she sounded kind, so kind that at first Sarah couldn't believe her ears.

"There's nothin' to worry about, Miz Sarah. Jewel won't tell nobody. I can't believe Mr. Hunter thought he could fool *me*, though. I seen right away something was troubling you. At first I figured it was because we was colored, and maybe some of that's true, but it's more'n that, ain't it?"

She waited, but Sarah couldn't answer because of the lump of unshed tears blocking her throat and burning her eyes.

"I know 'cause I know Mr. Hunter'd never get hisself married without telling his mama all about it," Jewel said when Sarah didn't reply, "and he for sure wouldn't never have a baby without his family hearin'. Now, that baby don't belong to Mr. Hunter atall, do it?"

Sarah wanted to tell her, wanted to confess everything, but when she tried to speak, the words came out on a wrenching sob that brought Jewel running to embrace her. Sarah should have resisted, should never have let a colored woman hold her, but she was crying far too hard to even think about protesting. Besides, Jewel's dark arms felt so good around her that Sarah didn't *want* to protest.

"There now, old Jewel didn't mean to make you cry," Jewel crooned, patting Sarah's shoulder. "Come on, let me take that baby, and we'll get you back into the kitchen where it's warm, and you can tell me all about it."

By the time Jewel had heated some more water and fixed them each another cup of tea, Sarah had sobbed out her entire story, or at least as much of it as she ever intended to tell anyone.

"I should've knowed just from looking at you," Jewel berated herself when Sarah was finished. "When I first set eyes on you, I thought how much you put me in mind of Miz Rebekah, though you don't favor each other atall. I figured it was your eyes being so blue, like hers, or something like that. Now I know, it *was* your eyes, but not them bein' blue. It's the look in 'em. Miz Rebekah had that look when she first come home,

236

kinda haunted like. From what she'd been through, I reckon. From what you both been through. I know enough about suffering I should've seen it right off."

Drained, Sarah could only nod and dab at her face with the towel Jewel had furnished her.

"And you was right to keep your baby," Jewel continued. "Ain't nothing worse than havin' a baby someplace and not knowing where or how it is or even if he's alive. That's how Miz Rebekah felt 'bout Mr. Hunter. She couldn't leave him out on the plains with the Comanche. She 'bout died from worrying over him 'til Mr. Mac went after him for her."

"I think I *would've* died if I'd had to leave my little girl behind," Sarah said.

"No, you would've lived, at least on the outside," Jewel assured her. "You just would've died inside, in your heart, like I did."

"You? Did you . . . ?" Sarah didn't even know what to ask.

But Jewel knew the answer. "I had me four babies, and they all was sold away soon's they could walk. That was my job, 'fore Old Mr. Tate bought me and I come here, makin' babies for the master to sell. An' I'll never see a one of 'em again, not in this world, at least."

Sarah felt fresh tears welling up, and instinctively, she reached across the table and took Jewel's dark hand in hers. The difference in the color of their skin didn't seem important, not anymore. They were sisters now. Suffering had bonded them.

Jewel squeezed Sarah's hand, then, as if embarrassed by her own show of emotion, she jumped up and fetched Sarah a cold, wet towel.

"Hold this on them eyes, now, to get the swelling

down. We don't want them men wondering what you been crying about, do we?" Jewel asked conspiratorially, and Sarah could only agree.

When she could speak again, Sarah said, "I . . . thank you. I never wanted anybody to know about . . . about what happened to me."

" 'Course you don't, honey," Jewel said. "Can't blame you a bit, neither, not after knowing what folks say about women who was with the Comanche. Miz Rebekah heard her share of it, even with Mr. MacDougal to protect her, but you and this little angel here won't never have to worry about that, not with Mr. Hunter to take care of you, no, sir. You know, I do believe this is about the best baby I ever saw," Jewel declared when Sarah had finally finished with the wet towel.

"They teach them not to cry," Sarah explained, clearing the last of the tears from her voice. "The Comanches, I mean."

Jewel nodded sagely. "I don't know much about that. Mr. Hunter was already six years old when he first come here, almost half-growed. More'n half wild, too. You should've seed him. Took three men to hold him down so's we could cut his hair, and him no bigger'n a jackrabbit."

Sarah found herself smiling right along with Jewel at her reminiscences, and suddenly she didn't mind that Jewel's skin was so much darker than her own. They were just two women whose worlds centered on one Hunter Tate.

"What was he like when you first saw him, Jewel?" Sarah asked.

Jewel didn't have to be asked twice. She was more than ready to regale Sarah with tales of Hunter's child-

238

hood, much different tales than Hunter had recalled, or at least different versions. By the time Hunter and the other men returned from touring the farm, Sarah and Jewel were laughing together like old friends in the cozy warmth of the kitchen, and Sarah had all but forgotten Jewel's skin was brown.

"You and Jewel seemed to be getting along well," Hunter observed as they drove back to town later.

Sarah wished she could tell him just how relieved she was that this was true. "She knows what really happened," she told him instead. "About me and the baby, I mean."

"She knows you were a captive?" he asked in surprise, and Sarah nodded. "You didn't have to tell her, Sarah. My parents would have kept the secret."

"You're right, I didn't *have* to tell her because she already *knew,* or leastways she knew that whole story you told her was a lie! Hunter, she said you never would've got married without telling your mother, or had a baby neither. She started asking me all kinds of questions about what happened to my first husband, how was he killed and all, and how we met and how long it was after Pete died, and where was I living, all sorts of things we never figured out!"

Hunter grinned at her outrage. "I guess it's a good thing she did, too, or we might've got caught by somebody else, somebody who'd thoroughly enjoy telling folks they caught us in a lie. Well, now, maybe we ought to add some details to our story, but you'll have to help me. I haven't got much of an imagination."

So on the trip back to the MacDougal's house, he and Sarah worked on their story.

"Just in time, too," Hunter pointed out when the town was in sight, "since everybody who comes to my mother's party next Saturday is going to want to know *everything*."

At the thought of the party, Sarah went cold to her bones.

When that dreaded Saturday night finally arrived, Sarah was feeling slightly more confident. She'd been in Rebekah Tate MacDougal's house for ten days and hadn't made any serious errors, or at least she hadn't once given her mother-in-law cause to raise her eyebrows in shocked surprise.

There had been an awkward moment when Rebekah had offered to write down the recipe for Hunter's favorite cake, but Sarah had asked to simply be shown how to make it instead, saying she would remember if she did it once. Rebekah had been impressed by Sarah's powers of recall and hadn't seemed to even suspect that Sarah had refused her original offer because she couldn't read.

Sarah's first Sunday in church had gone well, too. She'd been introduced to so many people, she couldn't be expected to remember all their names, and no one had more than a few seconds to talk to her, so she hadn't had to answer any questions. She'd known all the familiar hymns by heart, so no one noticed she couldn't read the hymnal, and when Hunter held up his Bible so she could follow along with the scripture reading, Sarah had simply stared intently at the indecipherable squiggles on the page.

Tonight would a little different, though, she realized as she dressed in her garnet and green plaid wool, the dress that she'd so far worn each time she'd needed confidence. Praying it would work again tonight, she gave herself one final check in the mirror.

"You look beautiful," Hunter assured her, coming up behind her and slipping his arms around her waist to give her a hug.

Instinctively, Sarah sank back against him, reveling in his warmth and his strength and wishing fervently that she could stay right there for the rest of the evening.

"Mmmm," he murmured, nuzzling the back of her neck. Sarah savored the familiar bliss of his lips pressing against her skin for a moment before common sense prevailed.

"Be careful of my hair!" she cried in dismay, leaning away to protect her carefully brushed coiffure. Her hair was only beginning to grow out from where the Comanches had chopped it off short, and Rebekah had suggested she tell anyone who asked that she'd burned her hair with a curling iron and had to cut it. Hopefully, no one would be rude enough to ask.

"I'm not going to mess up your hair," Hunter replied, swooping in to plant a kiss on the side of her neck. "At least not *before* the party. I won't make any promises about *afterward*, though."

"Afterward, I won't mind at all," Sarah assured him. She turned in his arms to face him, grabbing the labels of his suit anxiously. "Tell me again who I'm going to see tonight."

"There's nothing to be worried about," he assured her for at least the hundredth time. "Just some friends and family. Cousin Cecil and his wife Prudence, you saw them at church."

Sarah nodded, remembering the old couple. Prudence had frightened her with those gimlet eyes, but Rebekah had told her she had nothing to fear from Prudence.

"Cecil's son, Cousin Andrew, and his wife, Lilly, and their children. Cousin Andrew is Mac's business partner. Remember, I told you?"

"Yes, he has a store in another town," Sarah recalled, feeling slightly calmer because she hadn't forgotten anything so far.

"And the people here in town," he continued, naming the other merchants she had already met. "And a few other friends. I don't know who all Mother invited, probably everybody in the county."

"I'll never remember their names, and what if they ask me a question I can't answer?" Sarah moaned, leaning her forehead to Hunter's shoulder in despair.

"You don't have to remember their names, and if they ask you a question you can't answer, just say, 'I don't remember.'" Hunter wasn't sympathizing with her plight nearly enough.

"Promise you won't leave me alone for a minute! *Promise!*" Sarah pleaded desperately.

"I promise," he replied, kissing her soundly.

But of course he didn't keep his promise. He couldn't, because everyone wanted to talk to him and everyone else wanted to talk to her, so soon they'd been separated by the press of people crowded into the Mac-Dougal's house.

Sarah sat in Rebekah Tate MacDougal's formal parlor with its marble-topped tables and brocaded furniture and the Christmas tree, a large mesquite bush that had been decorated as if it had been a traditional pine.

242

The bush gave off a delicious fragrance, totally unlike the crisp scent of pine but wonderful, nonetheless.

After about an hour of meeting people, Sarah had begun to believe she might survive the evening when a woman she had never seen before approached her. With her was a tall, gaunt man with sunken eyes and cheeks whose thinning ash blond hair barely covered his scalp. He looked as if he might be consumptive, and his left arm ended abruptly just above the elbow. The empty sleeve of his coat had been pinned up.

The woman drew him along by his good arm, working her way through the crowd, her eyes set on Sarah as her goal. She was an attractive woman, about Sarah's age with the same blond hair and blue eyes, short and plump, her rounded figure draped in an expertly made forest-green bombazine gown. Or at least Sarah thought she was attractive until she got close enough for Sarah to see the expression in her eyes. It was pure evil, and Sarah instinctively drew back in her chair as the woman and her companion bore down on her.

"You're Hunter's wife," the woman said, although it sounded more like an accusation than a question.

"Yes, I'm Sarah Tate," Sarah said, trying to smile and offering her hand.

The woman ignored it. "I'm Eva," she said, straightening her shoulders proudly as if the name should mean something to Sarah.

"I'm pleased to meet you," Sarah said uncertainly, glancing hopefully at the man, willing him to say something to clear up the mystery of who they were.

He just stared back, his sunken eyes glowing with what looked to Sarah like anger. Or bitterness. Considering the loss of his arm, he probably had a lot to be bitter about.

"This is my husband, Owen Young," the woman named Eva said, seeing the direction of Sarah's gaze.

"Pleased to meet you," Sarah tried.

"An honor, Mrs. Tate," Mr. Young said, bowing slightly, although he didn't look as if he felt at all honored.

"Owen lost his arm at Gettysburg," Eva announced, as if this were some sort of accomplishment. "Not everybody got home from the war without a scratch."

Sarah thought she must be referring to Hunter, and she smiled apologetically. "Hunter was so lucky. He was in so many battles and never once—"

"I know," Eva assured her grimly. "I know *all* about Hunter."

Sarah felt her uncertain smile disappear completely. She was looking past the strange woman and her even stranger husband for someone to rescue her when Eva said, "Is that Hunter's baby?"

She gestured toward the cradle sitting beside Sarah's chair where Becky lay, contentedly watching the people milling around her.

"Yes," Sarah said, a little defensively.

"She looks like a little papoose, doesn't she, Owen?"

The comparison was not a compliment, and Sarah felt her hackles rising.

"She looks like her father, yes," Mr. Young agreed, although Sarah couldn't tell if he was approving or disapproving. "Eva, we need to pay our respects to our hostess."

"Yes, but . . . I'd like to speak to Mrs. Tate alone for

a few minutes," Eva said, wheedling. "That is, if you don't mind, Owen."

For a moment, Sarah thought he would refuse, but he glanced at Sarah suspiciously for a second, and then, as if he'd decided she was harmless, nodded his consent and turned to go find Rebekah.

Sarah felt an absurd urge to beg him not to leave, but of course she didn't. Instead she glanced frantically around again, looking for one of her in-laws or her husband for help. But none was forthcoming, and in the next moment, she was alone with Eva Young. Eva smiled slyly.

"He told you about me, didn't he?" she demanded in a fierce whisper.

"Who?" Sarah asked, totally confused.

"Hunter, of course. He told you about me, about *us*, about how he loved me first. He said he'd always love me, even after I married Owen. And now that I see the woman he finally married, I know he still does, because you look so much like me. Not as pretty, of course, and pathetically skinny, but probably as close as he could come." Her blue eyes glittered like broken glass. "How does it feel to know your husband only picked you because you reminded him of the woman he *really* loves?"

Sarah felt as if somebody had stabbed her in the heart, and she knew her agony must show on her face because Eva Young's evil smile grew triumphant just before she turned with a swish of her finely made skirts and waltzed away.

It was true, Sarah knew it was. Hadn't Hunter told her that he'd loved one woman in Texas and that she'd married someone else? He'd claimed not to love her anymore, but what else could she have expected him to say? And this explained everything, why he'd been willing to marry a woman he hardly knew, a woman who'd been a Comanche captive and who had a half-breed child. He'd wanted Sarah because she reminded him of the woman he loved, the woman he would always love. She'd been so easy to convince, too. What other choice had she had? And she'd been so grateful!

Well, she still was grateful, wasn't she? She had a home and a husband and a father for her child. That was all she'd needed, all she'd *wanted*. Why should she care *why* Hunter had chosen her? Why should she care *who* he loved since she didn't love him and never intended to? It was just her pride that was hurt. No woman wanted to know she'd been second choice. Sarah hadn't realized her pride was so sensitive, though. She'd never expected it to feel like a breaking heart.

Someone else was approaching her, Cousin Andrew's wife, Lilly, but Sarah couldn't talk to anyone just yet, not until she'd had a chance to collect her wits.

"I . . . I have to feed the baby," she muttered to Lilly, scooping up the baby and fleeing out into the crowded hallway and up the broad staircase to the refuge of her bedroom. The tears were leaking out of her eyes even before she got the door shut behind her.

Hunter was laughing when he saw her, laughing at a joke someone had just told, but at the sight of Eva's face, the laughter died in his throat.

She looked older, much older than she should have, he thought. Marriage to Owen Young must have been

246

harder even than he'd predicted. The gold of her hair had faded, as had the blue of her eyes, and her willowy body had thickened. When he compared her to Sarah, he thought Eva looked more as if *she'd* been the one who had endured a year with the Comanches.

Still he smiled a greeting when she insinuated herself into the group of men surrounding him.

"Hunter, don't you have a few minutes for an old friend?" she asked coyly. Apparently, she had no idea she'd lost her appeal.

"Certainly," he replied, curious to see what she would have to say to him after all these years. "It's good to see you, Eva," he said, offering her his arm as he led her to a less crowded area of the house.

"I knew it would be," she said, batting her eyes. "You're looking remarkably well, Hunter. Adversity seems to agree with some people."

Yes, Hunter thought, thinking of his lovely wife. "You're looking . . . well yourself, Eva," he manage in return, although he didn't think he sounded very sincere. "Have you met my wife?"

"Oh, yes," she said, dismissing Sarah with a wave of her hand. "Such a funny little creature. She hardly had a word to say for herself, but then, I suspect meeting me might have been somewhat of a shock."

"A shock?" Hunter echoed, puzzled.

Eva looked up at him out of the corner of her eye and smiled what he guessed she intended as a flirtatious smile. "She knows all about us, doesn't she, Hunter? I knew you'd tell her."

She turned, taking him by the arms, and leaned close, pressing her breasts to his chest. Mortified, Hunter glanced around and was surprised to see she'd led him into the library which was empty except for the two of them.

"*Eva,*" he protested, backing up a step, but she followed him, throwing her arms around his neck.

"You don't have to pretend with me, Hunter! I know you've never forgotten, and neither have I! I still dream about you, darling, about how it was with you! You were right, Owen wasn't half the man you are even *before* the war, and now he . . . he can't even do it at all!"

"Eva, don't do this!" Hunter begged, trying to pull her arms loose, but she was much stronger than she looked, and he couldn't budge her unless he wanted to hurt her, which he didn't, at least not yet. "I'm a married man," he tried.

Eva snorted in disgust and pressed herself more tightly against him. "I know why you married her, Hunter. It's because she reminds you of me, but you don't have to settle for a substitute! You don't have to lie in the dark and pretend you're with me, not anymore! I'm here now, Hunter, and I'm all yours!"

The only other time Hunter could remember being this angry was the day Eva had told him she was marrying a white man. He wanted to throttle her, but he settled for bruising her arms as he dragged them from around his neck and held her away from him. "Aren't you afraid of having a half-breed baby anymore, Eva? Or are you so desperate for sex that you just don't care?"

Her eyes widened for a fraction of a second, and Hunter braced himself for a flood of fury, but instead she smiled, a crooked, pathetic twist of her mouth. "I know how to keep from having a baby at all, so we don't have to worry about it!" she whispered fervently, reaching for him again. "No one will ever know! No one but us! It'll be just like before only better because now —"

Hunter shoved her away in disgust. The urge to strangle her was so strong, he had to close his hands into fists and thrust them into his coat pockets to resist it. Unable to think of anything hateful enough to say to her, he turned and strode toward the door and almost collided with Owen Young.

"Owen," he said in dismay, and behind him he heard Eva gasp.

"Good evening, Hunter," Owen said coldly, not offering his hand. "What's going on here?"

"Just saying hello to Eva," Hunter said, feeling absurdly guilty. Owen looked angry, probably at finding his wife alone with an old flame, but not as furious as he would have been if he'd overheard anything incriminating. Thank God for that, at least. "I heard about your arm," he added to change the subject. "Gettysburg, wasn't it?"

"Yes," Owen said, his haggard face tightening even more. God, he looked like he'd already been dead for three days. Was there something worse wrong with him that Hunter hadn't heard about? "I wouldn't mind, except it still hurts me sometimes, even though it's gone."

"That's tough luck. It hardly seems fair that some of us got off so easily, does it?" Hunter offered.

"No, it doesn't," Owen said, and Hunter heard the wealth of bitterness behind the words.

"Owen, dear, did you want me for something?" Eva asked with forced cheerfulness, hurrying over to them.

"Only to find you," he said icily, turning his cadaverous stare to her. "Someone said they saw you and Hunter come in here."

The accusation was plain. Thank heaven Hunter hadn't been tempted to take Eva up on her offer. If he had, Owen might have seen them doing exactly what he'd obviously expected to see.

"We were just talking about old times, weren't we, Hunter?" Eva was saying, clinging desperately to her cheerfulness.

"Yes," Hunter agreed, not helping her a bit.

"Are you feeling well, dear?" Owen asked his wife without the slightest bit of concern. "Your face is flushed."

She touched her cheek with fingers that were less than steady and then gave a forced laugh. "I'm feeling fine," she assured him. "It must be all the excitement of the party. I'm just not used to it, I guess. We hardly ever leave the farm anymore," she confided to Hunter who supposed Owen knew what he was doing by keeping Eva at home where he could keep an eye on her. "I . . . I was just telling Hunter that people were concerned about his Negroes," she added quickly.

Hunter glanced at her in surprise, but her husband seemed to know exactly what she was talking about. He stiffened slightly. "You should have left that to me, Eva, but since you've already mentioned it, I hope you also warned Hunter."

"No, I—" she began, but Hunter interrupted her.

"Warned me about what?" he demanded.

"Those niggers you've got living out on your farm," Owen said. "We were willing to overlook it during the war when all the white men were off fighting, but now

250

. . . Well, we can't allow coloreds to be doing business as if they were white, now can we?"

"Who is this 'we' you keep talking about?" Hunter asked, holding his temper with difficulty.

"Those of us who are concerned about the future of the South and the purity of the race."

"Purity of the race?" Hunter repeated incredulously.

Owen had the grace to flush himself, but he said, "Perhaps you won't be as concerned as some of us, considering your background, but now that the Negroes have been freed, they seem to think they are entitled to . . . to all the rights and privileges of a white man, including mating with white women. Every Southern white man is dedicated to ensuring they do not have the opportunity to defile our women."

"Are you crazy?" Hunter demanded, no longer bothering to hide his fury.

"Hardly," Owen replied. "You've been gone a long time, Hunter. Things have changed, and I'm here to warn you we have our eye on your people. They're more uppity than most because they were freed even before the war and because you've allowed them to use your name and continue to live and work on your property, doing business as if they had every right to."

"They do have every right to," Hunter reminded him. "They're as free as you are, Owen, and they're entitled to live their lives as they see fit."

"They may be free by law, but everyone knows the Negroes aren't capable of taking care of themselves. They're like children, and without white masters to manage them, they'll run wild, like animals."

"Nobody has managed 'my people' as you call them since I left for the war five years ago, and they're doing

251

just fine. Or maybe that's why you've got your eye on them, because they've already proven you wrong."

"Owen, Hunter," Eva protested gently, laying a hand on her husband's arm. "Old friends mustn't quarrel, especially at a party. You'll upset Mrs. MacDougal if she hears."

Owen shrugged off her hand as if he couldn't abide her touch. "Eva, join the ladies," he snapped. "This isn't for your ears."

For a second, fury flashed in Eva's eyes, a trace of her old spirit, but then her face went slack with resignation. She lowered her gaze demurely and left the two men alone.

"I'm giving you the courtesy of a warning, Hunter," Owen said when she was gone. His face was still expressionless, but his deep-set eyes smoldered in his face. "Either your Negroes leave the county, or we'll have to deal with them."

"What do you mean, 'deal with them'?" Hunter demanded.

"You know what I mean. Those of us who fought to protect the South from the Yankees will keep on fighting to protect it against corruption by the coloreds. And if anyone stands in our way, even a white man, we'll deal with him, too."

"What about half-breeds?" Hunter taunted him. "Where do we fall in all of this?"

Owen flushed again, but he wasn't deterred. *"Anyone,"* he repeated solemnly.

Hunter considered telling him he was already too late if he wanted to protect his own wife's purity, then decided it wasn't worth the small satisfaction. "Excuse me, Owen, I'd like to get some fresh air." Hunter pushed past him, wishing he didn't have qualms about punching a one-armed man. Dear Lord, was this what had been going on in Texas in the months since the war ended? If so, he was almost glad he'd been tricked into the Union Army.

"Yes, it's true," Mac confirmed a few minutes later when Hunter had tracked him down and taken him aside to tell him about his strange encounter with Owen Young. "There have been several incidents of former slaves being beaten up or whipped at night by hooded riders."

"Vigilantes?" Hunter asked, unable to believe it.

"Not exactly, since the victims really hadn't done anything worthy of punishment. The beatings are apparently just a warning for the Negroes not to get any ideas about equality. You say Owen threatened Dan and Enoch?"

"And Jewel, too, I suppose. He didn't specify. He just called them 'my people.' He said he'd have to deal with them."

"We should warn them, then, so they'll be ready just in case."

"Do they have guns out there?"

"Of course," Mac said. "I made sure of that during the war. They had to protect themselves and the crops. Anyone who attacks them will be in for an unpleasant surprise."

"Sarah and I should move out there right away. Surely, they won't attack the farm if we're living there."

"Don't be so sure, and if you're wrong, you'll be putting Sarah and the baby in danger, too. Maybe we ought to talk to some people first, see if we can't get cooler heads to prevail. Owen Young and his kind don't speak for all the men in the South."

Hunter thought perhaps Mac was right, and he certainly didn't want to put Sarah and the baby in danger. He couldn't stand the thought of Jewel being in danger, though, either. How could he protect them all?

The question was still bothering him when the party was over and everyone was leaving. As he and Sarah stood at the door wishing everyone a good night and a Merry Christmas, it was all he could do to smile at the guests. He kept scanning the crowd, looking for Eva and Owen, but he never saw them. Apparently, they had left earlier without saying good-bye, which was just fine with Hunter. If he never saw Eva Young again, it would be too soon. When he remembered her clutching hands and her desperate pleas, he felt sick to his stomach. And when he remembered her husband's threats, he felt ready to do murder.

So he wasn't feeling very sociable when the company was gone. He and Mac set to work straightening the furniture while Sarah and Rebekah cleaned up the food and the dishes. The women were still working when the men had finished, so Hunter went on upstairs and got ready for bed, glad for the solitude.

Little Becky was sleeping soundly in her cradle, which someone had carried up to the bedroom during the course of the evening. Not bothering with the lamp, Hunter stirred the coals of the fire and threw a few pieces of kindling on them to make a small flame to see by. Then he undressed quickly and slipped between the icy sheets, grateful for the shock of the cold which helped clear his mind.

The first thing he would have to do was find out who

supported Owen Young and his crazy ideas. It made sense that a man who was unable to make love to his own wife and who probably at least suspected she was looking for satisfaction elsewhere would be irrational on the subject of the purity of Southern women. But to take out those fears on poor defenseless Negroes was unconscionable, thought Hunter, and surely, there were many others who agreed with him.

As she helped her mother-in-law wash and dry the dishes from the party, Sarah kept watching the kitchen doorway for Hunter. He hadn't spoken a word to her since Eva Young had appeared, and he'd been grim and preoccupied, too. She didn't think anyone at the party would have noticed because he'd put on a good front, but Sarah knew him well by now and saw through his forced joviality.

Her heart ached, although she kept telling herself she wasn't really jealous. Hunter was her husband, and he would continue to take care of her and Becky, no matter what else happened and no matter how he might feel about another woman. That was all Sarah cared about.

Wasn't it?

At last the kitchen door opened, and Mr. Mac-Dougal came in. Alone, Sarah saw with a sinking heart.

"Where's Hunter?" Rebekah asked.

"Went on up to bed," Mr. MacDougal reported. "Guess all that company wore him out. He had a little run-in with Owen Young that upset him, too."

"A run-in?" Rebekah echoed in surprise. "What about?"

Sarah's poor heart stopped dead in her chest as she waited for the answer, but Mr. MacDougal glanced at her before replying.

"Uh . . . nothing important," he said after a moment's hesitation. "A little political disagreement."

Of course he wouldn't tell the truth in front of Hunter's wife, Sarah thought in despair.

"Owen Young hasn't been right since he came back from the war," Rebekah said. "Sarah, we're about finished here. Why don't you go see if you can't cheer Hunter up?"

Sarah knew she was the last person who could cheer Hunter up, but she murmured her good-nights, hung her apron up and hurried upstairs.

In their bedroom, she found Hunter had stirred the fire back to life. By its light, she saw that Becky slept soundly and Hunter lay still in the big bed. Now that she was here, she couldn't imagine why she'd hurried. Was she anxious to see her husband mooning over another woman? Or had she been hoping he would welcome her with open arms and dispel her fears?

Instead, he seemed to be asleep, and Sarah undressed and put on her nightdress as silently as she could so as not to disturb him. Then she banked the fire and checked to see that the baby was still covered before sliding into bed beside her sleeping husband.

But he wasn't asleep because the instant she lay down he reached for her, pulling her close.

"You're freezing," he said, running his hands over her back and warming her with his own body.

He still wanted her! Sarah bit back a cry of joy as she went to him, inhaling his wonderful scent and lifting her face eagerly for his kiss. But his lips only brushed

256

hers before he pulled her face to his shoulder, and as soon as she was warm, his hands stopped, too, and he lay perfectly still with her settled comfortably in his arms.

"Hunter?" she asked tentatively.

"Hmmm?"

"Don't you . . . don't you want to . . . ?" *Please!* she begged him silently. *Please make love to me!*

But he said, "It's late, and you're tired. Just go to sleep."

That was when Sarah knew the truth. He didn't love her and never would because he loved Eva Young. She didn't care, she was sure she didn't. She had so much else now that she shouldn't miss a love she hadn't sought in the first place.

So why was she crying here in the dark while her husband slept beside her?

Chapter Nine

Sarah had thought she could live without being loved. She'd thought it wasn't important or even necessary, not compared to being safe and sheltered. Perhaps it wasn't, so long as you didn't know your husband actually loved someone else. He didn't waste any time proving it, either.

The very next morning, first thing, he announced he was going out to the farm to visit Jewel and the boys.

"I'll go along," Sarah quickly offered, thinking of the hours alone with Hunter on the way there and back. The times she shared with him would be more precious to her now. She would enjoy another visit with Jewel, too. There were so many things she'd neglected to ask her about the farmhouse. She hadn't even seen the second bedroom, since Jewel had discovered her secret before they reached it, and after that, touring the house hadn't seemed very important.

"The weather looks bad, Sarah," Hunter said. "I don't think you should take the baby out. Anyway, I won't be gone long, and if I go alone, I can ride a horse and be there and back that much sooner."

She started to protest, but the words died on her lips

when she saw his impatient look and understood he simply didn't want her along. And not because he was in a hurry, either, she realized in despair. Because he probably wasn't going to the farm at all. He must have arranged to meet Eva someplace. Suddenly, Sarah couldn't bear to face the day, and she wanted to crawl back into her bed and pull the covers over her head so no one could see her shame.

But of course she didn't crawl back into bed. She had a baby to take care of, so she got herself and Becky dressed and went downstairs and spoke to her in-laws and pretended to eat breakfast so no one would ask her what was wrong, and stoically accepted Hunter's peck of a kiss before he left. For the farm. So he said.

How could she bear it? How could she hold her head up knowing her husband was seeing another woman? But how could she stop him? He'd never pretended he loved her, and Sarah had no right to expect him to. Love simply hadn't been part of their bargain. Oh, if only there were some way she could make herself more attractive to him so he'd want to be with *her* instead of Eva Young.

Hunter had called her pretty and even beautiful, but of course he thought she looked like Eva. Besides, those compliments had come in the heat of passion and probably didn't count for much. Still, they'd come, and so had the passion. He liked her body, liked making love to her whether he loved her or not. She had that much, and she would make the most of it. She would never be too tired to perform her marital duties. Oh, no, she would always be eager to comply with his wishes.

If he continued to have those wishes, she thought, despairing. Last night he certainly hadn't. And what if

259

he didn't want her at all anymore now that he had Eva again?

Haunted by these agonizing thoughts, Sarah wandered around the house in a daze, dusting and straightening up the rest of the party mess while her mother-in-law watched Becky in the warmth of the kitchen.

Finally, Sarah reached the library, the room that had surprised her most of all the rooms in this house. Imagine, having one whole room just for books! Well, Mr. MacDougal used it for his office, too, but mostly it was just books, shelf after shelf of them. Sarah hadn't known there were so many different books in the whole world, much less that one person would own them all. Or manage to read them all, either.

Sarah stared covetously at the neat rows of leather bound volumes. How much knowledge they must hold, knowledge that Sarah was too ignorant to begin to imagine. She couldn't even guess how much she didn't know.

But Hunter knew those things, all those things and more. He'd been to college, and Sarah couldn't even speak proper English. No wonder he couldn't love her. If he'd known she couldn't read, he probably never would have married her at all, no matter how much she looked liked Eva Young.

With trembling hands, she laid her dust cloth down on Mr. MacDougal's desk and reached for one of the books. Carefully, quietly, so no one would hear, she pulled it from the shelf. It was reddish-brown, the leather thick and soft to the touch, and golden letters had been pressed into the spine and the cover both. They glittered in the morning sunlight streaming through the windows, and Sarah stared at them hard, until her eyes watered, willing herself to understand them. But the harder she stared, the more incomprehensible they became, like so many squiggles, like insect tracks in the dirt.

In frustration, she opened the book, desperate to know what it contained, to learn its mysteries. To her surprise, the first page was blank, as was the second. Mystified, she turned another page until she found some printing. These letters meant no more to her than those on the cover, but she was surprised to see how few were on this page. Quickly she turned a few more pages until at last she found what she'd been expecting, a whole page filled top to bottom with line after line of printing.

Who could have so much to say that they'd need to fill up an entire page, much less a whole book? And how important it all must be for someone to print it and bind it in leather and for someone else to spend money to buy it. So much knowledge, and this was only one book among the hundreds here, perhaps the thousands in the world.

And Sarah couldn't read one word of any of them. The enormity of her ignorance brought tears to her eyes, blurring her vision so the squiggles on the page ran together like snakes racing back to their holes.

"Sarah?"

Sarah jumped and slammed the book shut guiltily. "I was just looking at it," she said defensively, clutching the book to her breast.

"That's all right," Rebekah assured her from the doorway. "I told you before, you're welcome to anything here. Just help yourself to whatever you want to read. I'm sure MacDougal would be glad to know the books are being used instead of just sitting here gathering dust. What is it that's caught your eye?" she asked, coming toward her.

"I just . . . I don't . . ." Sarah couldn't admit she had no idea what the name of the book was, so she simply thrust the book out for Rebekah to see.

Rebekah took the heavy book from her hands and held it up to read the letters on the front. Her pale eyebrows lifted in surprise, and Sarah wondered what was wrong.

"Are you interested in South American history?" Rebekah inquired.

Was that what the book was about? It must be, Sarah reasoned frantically. "Yeah, well, that's about all the history I know, being from the South and all."

She managed a smile, but Rebekah didn't smile back. Instead she looked puzzled as she handed the book back to Sarah. Quickly, Sarah returned the book to its slot on the shelf. When she turned back, Rebekah was still watching her, a quizzical expression on her face.

"Maybe you'd enjoy reading Dickens. We have just about all his novels. They're over there," Rebekah said, pointing.

Sarah glanced at the shelf where the well-worn volumes sat. "Yeah, well, I don't really have much time for reading books, what with the baby and all. I was just looking, you know, to see what was here."

Rebekah nodded slowly, although her expression reflected no understanding at all.

"Did you want me for something?" Sarah asked after a moment of awkward silence.

"Oh, yes," Rebekah said, shaking off her pensive mood. "I almost forgot. The baby was fussing. I don't know if she's hungry or if she's just teething but—"

Sarah didn't wait for further explanation. Grateful for the excuse to escape her mother-in-law's attention as well as all those books she couldn't read, she hurried off to the kitchen.

"I don't think Sarah knows how to read," Rebekah told her husband later when he came in for the noon meal.

"What makes you think so?" Mac asked as he washed his hands at the kitchen sink.

"I caught her in the library, looking at a book. At first I thought she was just trying to find something to read, but she acted so strangely, guilty almost."

"Maybe she was just afraid you didn't want her messing with the books."

"No, it was more than that," Rebekah argued. "It was the book. She'd picked up *The History of the Conquest of Peru*."

Mac lifted his coppery eyebrows in amazement. "That's pretty heavy reading for anybody, especially for Sarah."

"Yes, and when I asked her if she was interested in South American history, she thought I meant *Southern American* history. I don't think she even knows South America is a different place. Then I suggested she might enjoy Dickens, but she wasn't interested, so I don't think she was looking for a book to *read*. I think she was just looking, curious."

"Well, if you want to know whether she can read or not, why don't you just ask her?"

Rebekah frowned at him. "I can't *just ask her.*"

"Why not?"

"Because if she can't, she's bound to be embarrassed about it. I remember when I came back from the Comanches. I hadn't read anything in so long, I was afraid to even try, afraid I'd forgotten how. I was *ashamed,* MacDougal, and I already *knew* how to read. Imagine how difficult it would be to admit you didn't know how at all, especially to your husband's family."

"Then ask Hunter about it," he suggested.

"But what if he doesn't know? What if she doesn't *want* him to know? I can certainly understand that she wouldn't."

Mac glanced at her impatiently. "Then what are you going to do, Rebekah Tate?"

"I'm not going to do anything," Rebekah informed him. "But *you're* going to offer to teach her to read."

"I'm *what?"* Mac almost shouted.

But by the time Sarah came down for lunch, she'd convinced him.

"Hunter isn't back yet," Sarah observed with a sinking heart when she got to the kitchen where Rebekah had laid the noon meal.

"Jewel probably insisted he stay for dinner," Rebekah informed her cheerfully. Too cheerfully, Sarah thought in dismay. Does she know or at least suspect where Hunter really went? Oh, dear heaven, please no! Sarah couldn't stand the humiliation if she did.

Quickly, before she could see pity in Rebekah's eyes, Sarah laid the baby in the box they'd prepared for her in the corner and sat down at the table to eat.

During the meal, Mr. MacDougal entertained them with what news he'd heard at the store that morning, and Sarah listened with only half an ear. The rest of her was straining for sounds of Hunter's return. He didn't return, though, and still hadn't when they'd finished eating and Mr. MacDougal had returned to the store and Sarah had put the baby down for her afternoon nap.

When Sarah went back to the kitchen, she found Rebekah putting the bread dough she'd prepared earlier into pans to bake. "You know, Sarah, MacDougal was wondering if you might be able to go over to the store this afternoon for an hour or two while the baby's asleep and help him out."

"Help him do what?" Sarah asked in alarm, thinking of things like bookkeeping and making change for customers and other tasks she couldn't hope to perform.

"Oh, I think he just needed some tidying up. Just dusting and straightening, things like that. He'd be very grateful." Rebekah smiled hopefully, too hopefully. Sarah wondered why Mr. MacDougal hadn't asked her himself when he was here if this was his idea. And if it wasn't, why would his wife be so eager to get her over to the store?

"I suppose I could," she agreed tentatively, unable to come up with a reasonable excuse and thinking maybe she should try to keep busy. At least she wouldn't have time to be worrying about where Hunter might be.

"I know he'll appreciate it," Rebekah said, fetching Sarah's shawl herself and practically shoving her out the door.

The cold wind stung Sarah's cheeks, and she pulled the heavy shawl over her head, clutching it tightly at her throat. Hunter shouldn't be out in this wind, she thought angrily. Hunter shouldn't be out at all.

The bell over the door clanked when Sarah pushed it open and stepped into the relative warmth of the store. The delicious aromas of smoked meats and pickles and new clothes and cinnamon sticks assailed her, and she paused a minute to inhale it.

"Sarah," Mr. MacDougal called to her from behind the counter. "I'm glad you could come."

"I can't stay long," she said, slipping off her shawl. "Just until the baby wakes up from her nap."

"I know," he replied, smiling. His smile looked strange, a little strained somehow and oddly determined. "Why don't you come into my office where you can sit down, and we can talk."

The last thing Sarah wanted to do was talk to anyone just now, especially her father-in-law, when her husband was off God knew where. But she managed to smile back and follow him into the small room he used as an office.

He motioned to a chair that stood beside his desk, and Sarah sat down while he took the more comfortable chair at the desk.

"I hope you know how happy we are to have you with us, Sarah," he began, leaning back and making his chair squeak.

Sarah nodded uncertainly, wondering what this had to do with her helping him in the store.

"We consider you part of the family, and we want you to be happy with us."

Sarah nodded again, growing even more uneasy. Usually when somebody started out kind like this, they were building up to something bad, something you didn't want to hear. "I *am* happy, Mr. MacDougal."

"Please, call me 'Mac,' " he insisted. "Rebekah Tate said she saw you looking at a book in the library to-day —"

"I didn't hurt it, I swear!" Sarah blurted. "I just opened it for a minute, then put it right back where I got it!"

Mr. MacDougal seemed a bit disconcerted, but he recovered quickly and made himself smile again. "I'm not worried about the book, Sarah. I'm worried about you."

"But I'm fine!" she insisted, wishing she'd never come, knowing she should have refused Rebekah's request. What did he want? What did *they* want, since obviously they'd planned this together.

His smile was gone, and he didn't look as if he believed she was fine at all. "I have something I'd like to give you, Sarah." He picked up a small book that had been lying on the corner of his desk and offered it to her.

Sarah glanced at it but didn't take it. "What is it?" she asked instead, apprehension burning in her stomach.

He looked at the book, too, as if he wasn't sure himself. "It's a reader. It's a book that teaches people how to read."

Sarah felt the blood draining from her head, and fear was squeezing her chest so tightly she couldn't seem to get her breath. "Wh . . . why would you give me that?" she asked, her voice no more than a whisper.

He didn't really answer her question. Instead he said, "I'm not a teacher, but I can help you, Sarah. We can work together for a few hours every day while the

267

baby's asleep. Things are pretty slow in the store in the afternoon, so no one would bother us. No one else needs to know, either. It will be our little secret."

Sarah looked at his light brown eyes, so kind and gentle, then she looked down at the book that he still held out to her. She wanted it. She wanted the book and the knowledge it held so badly she could taste it, but no matter how badly she wanted it, she couldn't take it. She couldn't take it because then they'd know for sure. Because it couldn't just be "their little secret" because Mrs. MacDougal already knew. She'd certainly put him up to this in the first place, and if she knew and Mr. MacDougal knew, then Hunter was sure to find out. Sarah couldn't let him find out. She couldn't give him one more reason to despise her.

"I think . . . you've made a mistake, Mr. . . . I mean, Mac," she said slowly, carefully, fighting the sting of tears that threatened to humiliate her. "I don't need anybody to teach me to read."

For along moment he didn't move. He just stared at her, still holding the book, and waited, as if he were giving her a chance to change her mind. But Sarah didn't change her mind. She couldn't. So she just stared back and willed herself not cry.

Finally, after what seemed an eternity, he laid the book on the corner of his desk again. "I'll just leave this here in case . . . well, in case somebody wants to borrow it," he said.

Sarah couldn't speak for a few seconds because of the tightness in her throat. At last she was able to squeeze out the words. "What did . . . you want me . . . to do in the store?"

Mr. MacDougal's eyes were sad when he turned

back to her, but he said, "Things get so dusty just sitting around. I'll show you."

"Now you take care, Mr. Hunter, and don't you dare show your face around here again less'n you bring that baby with you, y'hear?" Jewel told him as he shrugged into his coat in preparation for the cold ride home.

"And you let me know if anything suspicious happens," he told her and the two men who were lingering over their coffee at the kitchen table.

"Don't you worry bout nothin', Mr. Hunter," Dan said. "Only folks them night-riders been bothering is the ones what's been wandering the roads. They ain't got no protection and nobody to care if they gets hurt or kilt. If'n they think they can run us off your place, they in for a nasty surprise."

"That's right," Enos agreed. "Mr. Mac, he give us good rifles and showed us how to use 'em. Them night-riders too yellow to tangle with somebody can shoot back."

"Mac and I are going to talk to some people, too," Hunter said. "I want to make sure everybody knows you're under my protection."

"But don't you even think 'bout moving out here 'til after Christmas," Jewel warned him. "Your mama'd never forgive me if I took that baby girl away from her 'fore Santy Claus comes."

"All right, you win," Hunter said, bending down to kiss her brown cheek. "But don't forget, I want to know if anybody gives you any trouble at all."

Hunter opened the front door and was halfway through it before he noticed the people huddled in the

269

shelter of the dogtrot. At the sight of them, he stopped dead. Dressed in rags, they were just waiting. Waiting to be noticed, Hunter supposed, looking at their dark faces. A man and woman and two small children.

"Looks like you've got more company, Jewel," he called over his shoulder.

Jewel came to the door and looked out. "Lord have mercy," she sighed wearily, but she said, "Don't you even have sense enough to knock on the door?"

"We was just wonderin' if'n you had some spare vittles. The young'uns ain't et in a couple days," the man said, pulling off his battered hat to show his respect.

" 'Course they ain't," Jewel said in disgust. "Now get 'em on in here outta the cold before they freeze to death on top of it."

Hunter stepped outside to allow them room to enter through the kitchen door, but instead of moving, they all four simply stared at him in mute terror.

"It's all right," he told them, but still they didn't move.

"You get along home now, Mr. Hunter," Jewel told him. "I reckon they too scared to come in with you here."

"Does this happen often?" he asked.

Jewel nodded. "Pretty regular. They's all looking for the Freedmen's Bureau or something."

"Here," he said, reaching into his pocket and pulling out some coins. He tried to press them into her hand. "Do what you can for them."

Jewel refused to take the money. "They's already eatin' your food," she scolded him. "Besides, word gets out you give me money, I'll get robbed. Now get along. Miz Sarah be mad if'n you late."

Hunter frowned, but he turned to go. "You'll send for me if anything happens," he reminded her over his shoulder as he headed for the barn. "Anything at all!"

"Anything at all!" she agreed.

By the time Hunter had saddled his horse and ridden out of the barn, the wandering family had disappeared into the warmth of the kitchen. So many lost souls, he thought, and remembered how Sarah had looked the first time he'd seen her.

Suddenly, he needed to be with her again. Kicking his horse into motion, he hunched his shoulders against the wind and headed toward town.

Eva Young sat in her parlor, listening to the relentless tick, tick, tick of the mantel clock, and thought she must be going crazy. It just wasn't natural for a woman to be without a man for so long. And it wasn't natural for a man not to bed his own wife. Eva could have understood it if Owen had a mistress, but her very proper husband wouldn't even have considered such a thing.

No, Owen Young wasn't doing it to *anybody,* especially not to his wife, and his wife was slowly losing her mind. Oh, she pleasured herself when the need got too bad, but that wasn't the same, not the same at all. Eva wanted a man's strength, a man's weight pressing her down and filling her. There was nothing else like it, nothing in the world, she thought with a sigh.

Eva needed a lover, that's what she needed. She'd managed it a few times when Owen had been off fighting the war, but since he'd been back, she hadn't dared even try. First of all, he watched her night and day, keeping her a virtual prisoner at their farm and never

271

leaving her alone when they were out anywhere. She'd been so lucky to catch a few minutes alone with Hunter the other night, and she'd been certain he'd still want her. He'd loved her so much when they were younger. How could he have forgotten?

He must be in love with his wife, Eva decided, although she could hardly credit it. How anyone could love such a drab, mousy, skinny little thing, she couldn't imagine. Oh, Sarah Tate was pretty enough, Eva supposed, but where was the fire that inspired a man's devotion? Eva just didn't see it.

Eva had fire, though. She had enough fire to scorch a man's soul if he'd just give her a chance. But where was she going to find a man to scorch? And even if she did manage a few minutes alone with one to suggest a rendezvous, how could she be sure he wouldn't run right back to Owen instead of taking her up on her offer? And if he did agree to meet her, how would she accomplish it? Even on days like today when Owen left her alone at the farm to meet with his "associates" as he called them, Eva couldn't go anyplace unless she wanted to ride horseback, and no decent woman went anyplace on horseback. If somebody were to see her and told Owen . . . Well, it didn't even bear thinking about.

Tick, tick, tick. Only the clock broke the oppressive stillness, and each tick was like a stinging blow to Eva's jangled nerves. All around her the walls rose up forbiddingly, holding her in, keeping her a prisoner in her finely furnished house. She was going to lose her mind if something didn't happen soon. She had to have a man. She simply had to.

The sound was faint, so Eva didn't recognize it at

first. A knocking, at the kitchen door, but so soft and tentative, she hardly heard it. Tap, tap, tap.

What on earth? Suddenly, she was alarmed. She hadn't heard anyone ride up, and she should have been completely alone. She *was* completely alone except for whoever was knocking on her kitchen door.

Heart pounding, Eva instinctively snatched up the poker that stood beside the parlor fireplace and started toward the kitchen. Through the dining room, slowly, slowly, clutching the poker in both hands and holding it in front of her, ready to strike.

The knocking was louder here. Tap, tap, tap, then silence. At least whoever was out there was knocking. Surely, they weren't a danger. A dangerous person would have just come in the unlocked door and attacked her. But who could be out there? And did she dare look to see, a woman alone and defenseless?

Tap, tap, tap. She had to go. She had to know. She would die of fright just standing here imagining. Slowly, slowly, she crept to the door between the dining room and kitchen and pushed it open a crack. From there she could see the back door, still shut tight. Soundlessly, she tiptoed across the kitchen floor to the window over the sink and looked out through the slit in the curtains.

She couldn't see who it was, but it was a man, that much she could tell from the shoulder that was visible from this angle. A big man. A strong man. And he was standing on her back porch, knocking for admittance, and Owen was gone and wouldn't be back before nightfall and she was here, all alone. What if he wanted to attack her? What if he wanted to *rape* her?

Except he wouldn't *have* to rape her because she was

willing. Oh, was she willing! Eva felt the familiar ache between her legs, and her nipples tightened beneath her bodice. Carefully, deliberately, she laid the poker down on the kitchen table. With hands that trembled slightly in anticipation, she reached up to pat her hair into place. Then she ran her fingers down her dress, smoothing it and stroking the nipples that tingled alertly. Yes, oh, yes. Her breath quickened.

Tap, tap, tap. He was calling to her, and every nerve in her body sang an answer. Smiling slightly, she strode to the door and threw it open.

The man jumped in surprise. Well, he was a boy, really, probably no more than twenty, if that, but fully matured to manhood already, the way the darker races tended to do. His smooth skin was the color of chocolate. His lips were full, and his dark eyes were frightened.

" 'Afternoon, ma'am," he said nervously. "I's wonderin' if you got any work I could do to earn a meal."

He was one of the wanderers, a former slave searching for freedom. From the looks of his clothes, which were no more than rags and hardly adequate for the cold, he'd been on the road a while, but his body was still strong and muscular. Eva's gaze dropped to his hands which hung at his sides, clenched into fists. Big hands, but her breasts would more than fill them. She shivered in anticipation.

He was perfect. She could have him, and no one would ever know. Certainly, *he'd* never tell, because if anyone found out he'd been with a white woman, he'd be castrated and hung.

She smiled. "You look cold," she said. "Why don't you come inside so I can warm you up?"

* * *

By the time Sarah had used the feather duster — a tool she'd never even seen before coming to Tatesville — on the shelves of bottles and jars and tins Mr. MacDougal had sitting behind the counter, she was in complete control of her emotions again. She wouldn't cry now, not even if Mac mentioned the reading book again. She was sure of it.

And when the bell over the door clanked and Sarah looked up to see Hunter entering, she actually felt joy at the sight of him. For just a split second, though, until she remembered where he'd probably been.

He seemed delighted to see her, though. "What's all this about you putting my wife to work, Mac?" he called to his stepfather, rubbing his gloved hands together to warm them. "I couldn't believe it when Mother told me. Come here and give me a kiss to warm me up, Sarah. I'm freezing!"

In spite of itself, Sarah's heart leaped as she hurried to do Hunter's bidding, and when he enclosed her in a bear hug and kissed her resoundingly, she felt the welcome surge of relief. He certainly didn't act like a man who'd spent half the day with another woman.

"Jewel said I wasn't to show my face at the farm again unless I brought you and the baby with me," Hunter informed her.

Yes, Sarah thought, that's exactly what Jewel would say. He *had* seen her today!

"And Mother said to tell you to get home because the baby's awake," he added.

"Oh, dear!" Sarah cried, not realizing how long she'd been at the store.

"You go along," Hunter told her. "I need to talk to Mac for a minute."

"All right," Sarah said, hurrying to fetch her shawl from Mac's office. As she reached for the shawl hanging just inside the door, she saw the reading book still lying on the corner of Mac's desk. He'd said he'd leave it there in case someone wanted to borrow it, meaning of course that she could borrow it. In fact, he wanted her to, or he wouldn't have left it out like that.

For one agonizing moment, Sarah hesitated, torn between her fears and the compelling desire for knowledge. Then, quickly, before she could change her mind, she snatched up the book and tucked it beneath her shawl.

"Thanks for the help, Sarah," Mac called as she ducked out the door. Sarah felt too guilty even to respond.

When the door clanged shut behind her, Hunter turned to his stepfather and sighed. "Dan and Enoch don't think there's anything to worry about, and Jewel agrees with them," he said.

"Why not?" Mac asked, coming around the counter toward him.

"They said so far none of the Negroes who live around here have been attacked, just the ones who are traveling through."

"That's true, but then, nobody's ever threatened any of the locals like Owen Young did the other night either."

"We need to talk to some people, find out who these night riders are, and stop them," Hunter said.

"That won't be easy. It's a secret society. Nobody will admit to belonging."

"Then we'll have to figure it out. Who are Owen Young's friends?"

The two men discussed the possibilities, then decided to meet with a few of them right after Christmas.

"But in the meantime, your mother's got enough work to keep us occupied getting ready for the holiday," Mac said.

"And with Christmas two days away, the night riders will be far too busy to even think about any mischief."

Christmas was just the kind of holiday Sarah had dreamed about when she was a child. Everyone got lots of presents, and the joy of giving wasn't tarnished by the strains of poverty. The Tate cousins came bearing more gifts, and the younger ones filled the house with shrieks of joy. Rebekah cooked a giant ham, and the table held so many dishes Sarah was afraid it might collapse.

After dinner, they drove out to the farm to exchange gifts with Jewel, Dan, and Enoch. Sarah was surprised to see they'd decorated a tree, too, and Jewel's kitchen was redolent of spices from the goodies she'd baked.

Jewel had made a doll for little Becky and a bonnet for Sarah. Once, in her old life, Sarah would have desperately needed a new bonnet. Now, of course, she had several, but none was as beautiful as the one Jewel had made for her.

"Jewel, you're so clever!" Sarah exclaimed as she tied the ribbon under her chin. "Can you teach me to sew as good as you do?"

"When you move out here, I'll teach you anything you like," Jewel responded, her dark eyes gleaming with pride over Sarah's pleasure.

"But that won't be until spring," Rebekah reminded them, bouncing Becky on her knee. "So don't you start thinking you're going to get your hands on my granddaughter before then!"

The two older women argued good-naturedly over who would be more important to the little girl while Sarah bit her lip and tried not to cry when she remembered how such a short time ago no one had wanted her *or* her child.

The next few weeks passed like a pleasant dream. The cold and bad weather kept Hunter close to home, and when he did go out, he took Mac with him, explaining that they had business to do. If he was thinking about Eva Young, Sarah saw no sign. He was just as loving and attentive as Sarah could have wished. She still had to be careful not to let her in-laws know how ignorant she was, though—and to keep the reading book hidden from Hunter so he wouldn't ask her about it.

Not that keeping it was doing her any good, of course. Somehow Sarah had hoped she could use the book in private and somehow learn to read all by herself, but the symbols on the pages meant nothing to her. She would need a teacher to guide her, and since she couldn't admit her need, she couldn't ask anyone to teach her. But she kept the book anyway, unwilling to give up the fragile hope that someday it might start to make sense to her.

And she had to be careful not to fall in love with Hunter, either, which was getting harder and harder every day because he was so nice to her. Oh, he had his faults. All men did, but he didn't drink or beat her, and he always spoke kindly to her and was gentle with the baby. Since this was far more than she'd ever expected, Sarah counted her blessings and tried to be the best wife she could be.

But she knew this was only a temporary situation. Nothing lasted forever, certainly nothing good, as Sarah had learned from experience. The first bad thing happened in January, when they found a young black man hanging from a tree, his body frozen stiff by the frigid north wind.

"Who was he?" Rebekah asked when Mac had told them the story as he'd heard it that day in the store.

"A stranger. Nobody seems to know," he said.

"A wanderer," Hunter said angrily. "I thought this would stop once we—" He caught himself before he could finish what he was going to say and wouldn't look Sarah or Rebekah in the eye.

Rebekah looked to her husband for an explanation, but he wouldn't meet her eye either. "Once you what?" she demanded of them both.

The two men exchanged a glance, then Hunter said, "Mac and I paid some visits to some of the men we thought might be involved in these incidents. They assured us there wouldn't be any more trouble."

"I guess we need to go see Owen Young after all," Mac said.

"Why would you need to see him?" Sarah asked in alarm, thinking of Young's wife and knowing she didn't want Hunter anywhere near the Young farm.

Once again the two men exchanged a glance, but Sarah was too upset to figure out the significance of it.

"Owen seems to be the ring leader," Hunter said after a moment.

"I can believe it," Rebekah declared in disgust. "He

just hasn't been right since he lost his arm. Mad at everybody and taking it out on people who can't fight back. Somebody ought to string *him* up if he's the one responsible for this. Now's when we really need the Texas Rangers."

"And since it doesn't seem like the Yankee government is going to let us call them up, we're going to have to take care of this ourselves," Mac said. Sarah knew Mac had been a Texas Ranger and had fought with them during the Mexican War, but the Yankees had disbanded the Rangers permanently, believing—and probably quite rightly—that they would be a threat to Yankee rule in Texas.

"What are you going to do?" she asked anxiously, not liking the idea of Hunter being involved.

"We're just going to talk to Owen," Hunter said, reaching across the table to pat her hand reassuringly. "I'm sure we can make him see reason."

But Sarah wasn't sure. She wasn't sure at all.

The north wind was still howling the next day when Mac and Hunter rode up to the Young's house. Hunter called out a greeting, but the wind seemed to snatch it away, and when no one came in response, they decided they hadn't been heard. Mac stayed with the horses while Hunter dismounted and started for the front door. He was on the porch when it opened. Eva Young's wary expression quickly brightened.

"Hunter," she breathed, instinctively reaching for him.

Just as instinctively, Hunter retreated a step, eluding her grasp. "Good morning, Eva. Is Owen home?"

"Yes," she whispered, "but he'll be gone all day tomorrow and—"

Hunter couldn't believe his ears. She actually thought he'd come to see *her!* "Could you tell him we'd like to talk to him?" he asked, interrupting whatever she'd been about to propose.

"Who is it?" Owen shouted from inside the house.

"We?" Eva echoed Hunter, ignoring her husband. Her anxious gaze darted past Hunter to find Mac still seated on his horse in the yard. Instantly, the hopeful glow in her eyes changed to fury, but before she could say anything, her husband appeared behind her.

"Tate, what do you want?" he demanded coldly. He looked much worse than Hunter remembered, as if the flame of bitterness Hunter saw in his eyes was consuming him from within. He was haggard, as if he hadn't slept much lately, and he hadn't shaved in several days. His hair was mussed, as if he hadn't combed it yet today. His collarless shirt hung open at the throat, and the empty sleeve dangled forlornly from his shoulder.

"Mac and I would like to talk to you for a few minutes, Owen," Hunter said. "About the man who was killed the other night." Hunter noticed Young's eyes were bloodshot, and he thought he detected the odor of whiskey.

"I hadn't heard about any man being killed," Young said.

Hunter glared at him, impatient with the pretense. "You know who I mean, that young black man somebody hanged from the big cottonwood by Sweet Springs."

Young smiled slyly in comprehension. "Oh, a nigger, why didn't you say so? I thought you meant a *man.*"

281

Hunter had already closed his hands into fists when Mac called, "Are you going to invite us in or not?"

Young let his gaze flick over Hunter contemptuously. "Not if you're just going to complain about some nigger getting hanged. Maybe you ought to be more careful about whose business you stick your nose into, Tate. There's lots of folks think the only good Indian is a dead Indian."

Hunter couldn't help himself. He didn't even know he'd raised his arm until the shock of his fist connecting with the solid point of Young's jaw jolted through his body. For an instant, Young seemed frozen in surprise, then his body collapsed, clattering down into the doorway in a heap. Hunter braced himself for a counterattack, but Young didn't move.

Eva had jumped out of the way, and when she looked back up at Hunter, she didn't seem the least bit disturbed. "He's drunk," she explained calmly. "He probably won't even remember you were here. I'll just tell him he hit his chin when he fell down."

"Was he involved in that hanging?" Hunter asked.

Eva shrugged. Plainly, the hanging was of no concern to her. "He was out night before last. I don't know where. He doesn't tell me what he's doing."

"Do you know who he was with?"

Eva shook her head. "He doesn't tell me that, either. Could you help me get him inside?"

Mac and Hunter carried Young into the house and laid him on his bed. By then he was snoring softly, and Hunter realized Young had had a lot more to drink than he'd realized. It was only ten o'clock in the morning, too. There really *was* something wrong with Owen Young.

Mac muttered his apologies to Eva as he left the room, but Eva caught Hunter's arm before he could go. "He leaves me alone a lot. I could send you word," she whispered. "We could meet like we did in the old days."

Hunter drew away in revulsion. "This isn't the old days, Eva," he told her as he followed Mac out.

He pretended not to hear her muttered curse.

People were restless. There were rumors and more rumors about the government. In February a bunch of men met in Austin and drew up a new Texas constitution. Carpetbaggers and scalawags, Mac called them, but Sarah didn't ask what that meant. She didn't want to appear ignorant. She didn't know what a constitution was, either, but she knew nobody liked the new one. Word was that anyone who had fought for the Confederacy wouldn't be allowed to vote in the June election, either, which meant virtually all the white males would be excluded from the process. Only the former slaves would be making the decisions.

So all over Texas the night riders took their revenge on innocent people. The local group burned out a poor black family who'd squatted in an abandoned shack where white people had lived before the war, and two black men were tied to trees and whipped into unconsciousness.

And one day, when her husband was away, Eva Young saddled a horse and rode out from her farm, taking the back roads and hiding whenever she heard someone coming so no one would see her, and she rode to the Tate farm to see Jewel Tate.

The two colored men who lived with Jewel were up on the barn roof when Eva rode up, but she ignored them. It was Jewel she needed to see. Eva called Jewel's name until the black woman came out of the house.

"What is it, Miz Young?" Jewel asked warily, not at all happy to see her visitor.

Eva jumped down from the horse and strode up to Jewel angrily. "I did what you told me," she whispered angrily, "but I still got a baby. Now you have to get rid of it for me!"

Jewel glanced anxiously around to see if anyone could have overheard. "Come in the house," she said, turning on her heel and walking off without waiting to see if Eva followed.

But of course she followed. She was desperate.

Jewel closed the door securely behind them. "You sure you got a baby?"

"It's been two months since I bled last," she hissed. "And I'm sick every morning."

"Did you wash yourself out right after, like I tol' you?" Jewel demanded.

Eva glared at Jewel for a second. "Well, not *right* after," she said defensively. "It was . . . I didn't get a chance until later."

Jewel shook her head in disgust. "I don't know why you so dead set against havin' a baby. Now your husband's home, you don't got to worry. He'll just think it's his."

"No, he won't!" Eva wailed. "He *can't* be the father! Don't you understand?"

"You mean he don't . . . ?" Jewel asked incredulously.

"I mean he *can't!* If he finds out, he'll kill me."

284

"You a knowing woman, Miz Young. If'n you try, you could prob'ly get him interested again. There still time for him to think it his baby."

Eva blanched. "No!" she cried. "He'll know it isn't even if . . . When he sees it, I mean. Then *everyone* will know!"

Jewel's eyes narrowed suspiciously. "What you mean, *everyone* will know? Who give you this baby anyway?"

"No one! I mean, no one you know! He . . . he was just passing through and . . ."

Jewel knew a moment of relief. For just a second there, she'd been afraid that Mr. Hunter . . . But no, she should have known he wouldn't be so foolish. Then she realized what Eva Young had really said.

"Passing through?" Jewel echoed in horror. There were, of course, lots of people passing through since the war, old settlers who were no longer safe from Indian depredations on the Western frontier, new settlers fleeing the ravages of the Old South, and former Confederate soldiers looking for work, but only one kind of wanderer could give Eva Young a baby that people would know wasn't her husband's just by looking at it. "Did you find yourself a colored man, Miz Young?"

"That's none of your damn business!" Eva shrieked, her face crimson. "Just give me something to get rid of it!"

And of course Jewel did, because if Eva Young gave birth to a black child, no Negro would be safe here ever again.

The herbal concoction Eva took home was the same one Jewel and the other women had used at the breeding farm where she had been years ago, consigned to the task of producing a baby every year that her master

285

could sell. When a woman could no longer face the thought of bringing another child into slavery, she would swallow the brew and murder the baby, sparing it the agonies of life on this earth. If a woman miscarried enough times, she would be sold down the river to almost certain death in the cotton fields of the Deep South, but many preferred that fate to the horror of bearing children that were snatched away.

As she watched Eva Young ride off, Jewel offered a silent prayer that Eva Young's foolishness wouldn't destroy them all.

Chapter Ten

In early March, the air turned warm and the first tender shoots of green began to appear across the prairie. The time had come for Hunter to start gathering cattle for his ranch.

"I've got several men lined up to help me," he told Sarah one morning as they were getting dressed. "We've just been waiting for the grass to get started."

"Hunter, are you sure you can do this?" Sarah asked. "I mean, just go out and *take* the cattle? Doesn't it belong to somebody?"

"Not exactly," he explained. "When the war started and all the men went off to fight, they left the cattle to fend for themselves, which they are perfectly able to do. In fact, that's how we got cattle in Texas in the first place. The Spaniards brought some when they first came exploring and left them behind when they moved on. They did what cows naturally do and made more cows and eventually somebody got the idea of rounding them up and claiming them."

"So somebody *does* own them," Sarah confirmed. "That means you'll be stealing!"

"No, not at all," Hunter assured her. "You see, during the war, with all the men gone, none of the calves that were born were branded, so nobody has any way of knowing *who* owns what. And since so many men didn't come back from the war, there's a good chance *nobody* owns a lot of the cattle anymore. The law says whoever brands a cow owns it, so I'm going out to brand some for myself."

Sarah still wasn't sure this was completely fair, especially to whoever really owned the cows, but obviously, her opinion didn't count for much. "When are you planning to leave?" she asked, already feeling depressed at the prospect.

"Tomorrow or the next day," he told her and seeing her dismay, he took her in his arms. "I'll only be gone a few weeks," he said, kissing her forehead. "I'll miss you."

Sarah would miss him, too, more than she wanted to admit, even to herself. "What should I do while you're gone?"

He smiled. "The same things you do when I'm here . . . or at least *most* of the same things," he added provocatively. "I don't think I want you making love with somebody else while I'm gone."

Sarah couldn't help smiling back, even though her cheeks were hot. "Why not?" she teased.

Instead of answering her, he gave her a playful swat on the bottom which she barely felt through the thickness of her petticoats. "I *was* going to ask you if you'd like to move out to the farm before I go, but now I don't think I trust you," he told her with mock austerity.

"Are you afraid I'll run off with somebody?" she taunted, sliding her arms around his neck.

"No, I'm afraid somebody will run off with you," he replied, pulling her close and lowering his mouth to hers.

His kiss was sweet but demanding, claiming her

mouth as his private domain, and Sarah eagerly surrendered to him. When he lifted his lips from hers, he moaned softly. "I can't ever seem to get enough of you, Sarah. You must be some kind of witch. Is that it? Are you a witch?"

Sarah shook her head, thinking *she* was the one under the spell because she couldn't get enough of him, either. "How long will you be gone again?" she asked sadly, clinging to him desperately.

"Too long," he replied as his lips closed over hers once more.

They didn't get around to deciding about Sarah moving out to the farm until much later that day, but when they did, Sarah decided to stay in town with her in-laws. As much as she was looking forward to escaping Mac and Rebekah's scrutiny—she knew she would feel much more comfortable around Jewel, from whom she didn't have to keep secrets—Sarah agreed she should let Rebekah enjoy the baby for as long as possible.

The days dragged during Hunter's absence, and by the time he returned, spring had fully arrived. The redbud trees were rosy with blossoms, and the prairies sported a purple carpet of bluebonnets. And they heard Hunter long before he really arrived.

"What's that noise?" Sarah asked her mother-in-law. Sarah had been sweeping the front porch and paused in her work to identify the sound. Rebekah had come from inside the house to hear it better.

"I don't know," Rebekah said. "I never heard anything like it."

The two women listened intently to the faint, bawling sound.

"Look there," Sarah said, pointing. "Is that smoke or a cloud?"

Rebekah strained to see. "Looks more like dust, but what could be churning up so much of . . ."

The two women looked at each other in the light of sudden understanding. "Hunter!" they both cried together.

"Oh, dear," Sarah said, looking down at her dingy house dress. Her hair was a mess, too.

"Here," Rebekah said, taking the broom from her, "you go get cleaned up. I'll—"

Then they heard his shout and looked up to see him riding hell-bent down the street. He was wearing a sombrero, and he pulled it off and began waving it over his head.

Sarah's breath caught at the sight of him. His coal black hair shone in the sunlight and blew in the wind, and his long, lean body moved with the horse as if they were one. Before she had time to think, Sarah was running, down the steps and across the yard to the gate which she threw open just as Hunter jerked his horse to a halt and vaulted from the saddle.

In the next second, she was in his arms, caught up off her feet while he swung her around and kissed her soundly right on the mouth. Then they were both laughing and talking at once.

"We heard you—"

"You're so pretty—"

"Are you all right?"

"Even prettier than I remembered—"

"You must have brought a thousand cows!"

"How's the baby?"

"She's sitting up all by herself!"

"All by herself!"

"Yes, but *are you all right?*"

"Don't I get a kiss, too?" Rebekah demanded happily, having caught up with Sarah.

Obligingly, Hunter released Sarah for a moment and gave his mother a kiss on the cheek.

"I'm fine," he told them both. "Just tired and dirty."

"You certainly are dirty," Rebekah agreed, wrinkling her nose. "I'll get you a bath ready right away."

"Not just yet," Hunter said. "We want to take the cattle on out to the farm. . . . I guess I should say 'the ranch,' which is what it will be now. I just stopped by to let you know I'm back."

"How many cows did you get?" Sarah asked. The din from the herd was growing louder by the minute.

"A few hundred, and that's just a start. We'll keep gathering them all summer, but we couldn't handle many more at one time." He grinned broadly. "But I'm officially a rancher now. No more grubbing in the dirt."

He kissed her again, and for a moment Sarah held his face between her two hands. His cheeks were downy with several days' growth of beard—like the Indians, he had little facial hair—and Sarah inhaled his delicious scent like one who'd been starved for a long time.

When he finally made it back to the house late that evening, he was more than ready for the bath Rebekah insisted he take before telling them about his travels. Sarah was only too happy to scrub his back, although Hunter was so delighted to be with her again that he got her almost as wet as he by the time he'd finished his bath.

"We weren't the only ones with this idea," Hunter told them when they had all finally settled in the family parlor to hear his story. "We saw another group doing a gather and heard about several others. I'm telling you, Mac, cattle is what's going to save Texas."

291

"I hope something will," Mac said gravely. "Have you heard about the Iron Clad Oath?"

"The Iron Clad what?"

"Oath. You've got to take it if you want to vote in the election in June. You have to swear you never took up arms against the United States of America."

"Nobody in Texas can swear to that!" Hunter said, outraged. Indeed, even Mac had fought in the local militia, as had all the older men who had stayed home.

"Very few white men, that's true," Mac agreed. "But the Freedmen's Bureau is seeing that every black man is registered to vote."

"And they'll vote the way they're told because they won't know any better," Hunter added sadly. "Damn. This isn't going to make people like Owen Young any happier about the slaves being free, is it?"

"No, in fact I'm afraid even more men have joined Young's nightriders, decent men whom you would never expect to get involved in something like this. They're angry and frustrated, and they don't see any other way to protect their families from what they imagine is coming."

"This is crazy," Rebekah said. "Killing innocent people and for what?"

"The war made a lot of people crazy, Mother," Hunter said. "Some of them just don't know when to stop killing. Has anyone bothered our people out at the farm?"

"No, why should they?" Sarah asked in alarm.

Hunter smiled and slipped his arm around her shoulders. "No reason," he said. "I was just wondering."

Sarah thought it was more than that, though. She'd never thought about Jewel and the others being in danger, but if they were . . ."Maybe we should move out to the farm now that the weather is nice," she suggested.

Surely, the nightriders wouldn't attack a place where whites lived, too.

"I'm still going to be gone from time to time looking for cattle," Hunter warned her.

Sarah thought about the loneliness and decided it didn't matter, not if she would be helping to keep Jewel safe. She smiled. "Still worried I'm going to run off with somebody else?"

Hunter studied her face for a long moment, and Sarah saw the subtle change come over him, the transformation from excitement to desire. She felt the answering frisson in her own body, the need for what she'd been without.

"Uh, Mother, Mac, if you'll excuse us, I'm pretty tired. I think we'll go up to bed now," he said, not taking his eyes from Sarah.

"I hope you're not too tired to let Sarah give you a proper welcome home," Mac said with a sly grin, but neither Sarah nor Hunter even noticed the grin. They were already up and heading for the door.

Just as they started to climb the stairs, Sarah heard Mac say, "Aren't you ready for bed yet, Rebekah Tate?" and Rebekah's answering laugh.

The potion hadn't worked. Eva should have known better than to trust a nigger. Jewel Tate probably thought it was funny that Eva was carrying a black baby. Eva had tried everything else she knew to get rid of it, too. Galloping on a horse. Throwing herself down the stairs. Hot baths. Cold baths. But nothing had worked. She was already more than three months gone, and soon she would start to show. She'd be able to hide it for a while under her full skirts, but sooner or later Owen would notice.

And then he would kill her.

There was just one last thing to try, the one thing she'd actually feared. It worked, though. She'd heard people say it was the only certain way. But when she actually picked up the knitting needle and held it in her hands, the horror of it overwhelmed her until she shook so badly she thought she might faint.

She'd have to do it, though, and soon, before Owen noticed something. He'd be going off to meet with his "associates" in a few days. That would be the perfect time.

If only she could bring herself to go through with it.

"You can still change your mind, you know," Hunter told Sarah a few days later as they drove the wagon up to the farm buildings. "Jewel will understand."

"I already told you a dozen times, I *want* to move out here," Sarah assured him. "Living with your parents is all right, but I want to have my own house. I'm ready for it."

"But it won't be all your own house, not with Jewel running it all these years," he reminded her.

"We'll work together," Sarah assured him. "Besides, it'll be nice to have some help for a change. Being a farm wife isn't easy."

"You're a *rancher's* wife now," he corrected her.

"Oh, I'm sorry," she said in mock repentance. "Just don't get so excited about finding cows that you forget your promise to build me my own house."

"Don't worry," he told her. "As soon as I get enough cattle gathered up, I'll start to work on it, probably in the fall. But you won't have any help when you move into the new house."

"I'll manage," she said quite confidently.

Dan and Enoch were working in the fields when they arrived, but they came running at Hunter's shout of greeting and were only too glad to help him unload their belongings from the wagon.

Jewel was just as excited as they, although she was too dignified to actually clap her hands or jump up and down.

"This boy's always been trouble, Miz Sarah," she said sternly. "He could've at least told me you all was coming. I got nothing fixed for dinner and the house is a mess and—"

"When have you ever had *nothing* fixed for dinner, Jewel?" Hunter challenged.

"Nothing special," she clarified, taking the baby from Sarah's arms. "Look how this young'un's growed. She'll be walking 'fore you know it."

"She's already trying to crawl," Sarah told her. "I have to watch her every minute."

"I'll bet Miz Rebekah is fit to be tied, you coming out here," Jewel guessed.

"She wasn't real happy," Sarah agreed. "I think she would've been fine if we'd left Becky with her, though, which shows who she thinks is most important in this family."

"Well, now, Li'l Becky *is* the most important one, ain't you, sweetheart?" The baby cooed her agreement, making everyone laugh. "You just come along with me while those mean ol' men get the wagon unloaded, and we'll see if'n we can't find something for your folks to eat."

By bedtime that night, Sarah and Jewel had made the main bedroom completely comfortable, so that when Hunter and Sarah snuggled down into the soft feather mattress, they felt as if they'd lived there forever.

295

"I have to leave again day after tomorrow," Hunter warned her in the dark. "There's a lot of men like me with the same idea. If I don't get the cattle now, someone else will."

"I know," Sarah said. "And you want to be rich, so you have to work hard."

He kissed her, long and lingeringly. "I already am rich," he murmured against her mouth. "I just need to make some money for us to live on."

The fading light told Eva it was close to suppertime. Owen would be home from his meeting soon. She should be getting up to fix him something to eat. She at least should be getting up to clean up the mess and hide it so Owen wouldn't see, wouldn't know what she had done.

Except she couldn't move. The pain was simply too bad. The only way she could bear it was to lie perfectly still and hardly breathe. She'd thought the agony of passing the baby was the worst she'd ever experienced, but she'd also thought the pain would end when it was out of her. Instead it had gotten worse. And the blood! She'd soaked the towels and the bedclothes and the mattress, but she couldn't get up to do anything about it. She couldn't do anything except lie here and pray to die.

She was cold, so cold. Odd how cold it was. Someone should light a fire. Owen would when he came home. She'd tell him to. She wanted to pull the covers over her, but she didn't dare move because that would start the bleeding again, and she didn't think she had enough blood left to lose any more.

After what seemed hours, she heard Owen clumping into the house. He was slamming doors and calling her name, and she tried to answer, but she didn't have the strength to call out. What would she tell him? Female trouble, that was it. She was bleeding more heavily than normal and would have to stay in bed a few days. That was all she needed, some rest and some time for the pain to stop.

"Eva!" Owen shouted impatiently from the hallway, then he burst into the bedroom. His face was flushed from whiskey and fury at not finding her waiting with a meal on the table. Instinctively, she cringed from his anger, but his wrath instantly changed to shock. "What the hell?" he gasped in horror.

Eva tried to answer him, tried to tell him the story she'd so carefully prepared, but the words just wouldn't come. It was too late, anyway. He could plainly see the crimson towels, and he'd found the bloody knitting needle. He held it up as if he'd never seen a knitting needle before.

"What have you done to yourself?" he cried, pale now, all traces of the whiskey flush gone. "Where are you bleeding?"

But of course Eva couldn't answer him, even though she tried. So he pulled up her nightdress and saw for himself. Cursing, he gingerly tossed away the soaked towels lying between her legs and reached for the only clean towel left. Or what he thought was the only clean one, lying in a bundle at the foot of the bed.

Eva tried to stop him, but he didn't hear her feeble protest, and when he picked up the bundle, he saw. He saw what was left of Eva's terrible mistake, of all the mistakes she'd made.

She knew real fear then, the terror of knowing she'd done something unspeakable. With a roar of outrage, Owen threw the bundle to the floor. *"You whore!"* he screamed, spittle flying. "You filthy whore!" Shrieking curses, he lunged for her, grabbing her by the throat to choke the life out of her. He shook her like a doll, each jolt causing shock waves of excruciating pain until she prayed he would kill her quickly. *Please, yes, just let it be over!*

But it didn't stop, it just kept on, the pain, the horrible, unbearable pain, and at last she realized he was asking her a question, shouting it in her face.

"Who was it? Who, Eva? Tell me or I'll kill you! I swear to God, I'll kill you!"

She wanted him to kill her, but she wanted him to stop hurting her, too. *Oh, please, make it stop!*

A name, he wanted a name. She thought of those who had brought her to this place. Hunter Tate who'd rejected her. Sarah Tate who'd replaced her. Jewel Tate who'd betrayed her.

Through the blood red haze of agony, she forced the word up and up, past Owen's clutching fingers, up and out on a whisper of sound.

"Tate."

Owen threw her down in disgust. "Hunter Tate never give you that piece of shit!" he screamed. "It's too black! It was a nigger! But which one, Eva! Which one!"

Eva heard the words only faintly and didn't understand a one of them. She said the only thing she could remember.

"Tate."

Owen roared again, an inarticulate primal howl, and then he was gone. Eva knew a vague sense of disappointment. He hadn't lit a fire or covered her up, and she was so cold, so cold. Except for the blood which was flowing again, warm and comforting. Eva closed her eyes and imagined herself drowning in it.

Sarah and Jewel were laughing so hard tears rolled down their faces. Sarah couldn't even sit up straight anymore, so she collapsed on the kitchen table, burying her face in her arms while Jewel doubled over in her chair.

"You made that up," Sarah accused weakly when she could speak again.

"I did not," Jewel insisted, wiping at the tears streaming down her face. "That's 'xactly what he said. 'Course he was only a youngun at the time and couldn't speak English too good yet."

"Hunter is going to be sorry he let me come out here when he finds out you've been telling me all his deep, dark secrets."

Hunter had left that morning, looking for more cattle, and after working all day together, the two women had spent the evening in the kitchen with Jewel telling Sarah all the funniest stories of Hunter's childhood.

"He won't know, less'n you tell him now, Miz Sarah," Jewel warned.

"I'm not sure if I'll tell him or not. He prob'ly wouldn't let us be alone ever again if he knew what you've been telling me." Sarah started to laugh again, but her sides ached so much, she moaned instead. "Oh, I reckon I'd better go to bed before I bust out my belly from laughing."

"It's late anyways," Jewel agreed. "That baby'll be up at sunup for sure."

Sarah nodded and leaned back in her chair, rubbing her aching ribs. "I can't remember when I laughed so much, Jewel," she said, thinking she'd been so right about coming out here to the farm. She'd never have to pretend with Jewel, never have to worry about impressing her or hiding her own ignorance as she had with the

MacDougal's. For the first time in months, she could relax and be herself.

"Me neither. Been a long time since there was anything to laugh about 'round here."

"Things'll be different now, though," Sarah predicted. "With the war over, people'll be happier."

Jewel's smile faded. "Maybe so," she agreed without much enthusiasm, and Sarah wondered what she'd said to spoil the mood.

"At least *we'll* be happy, won't we?" she tried, knowing it was true, willing it to be.

Jewel managed another smile. "For sure, Miz Sarah. Havin' a youngun around always makes for laughing."

Which reminded Sarah of something she'd been wondering about Jewel. "How come you never got married, Jewel? Since you been here, I mean. I reckon Dan or Enoch would've married you if you'd wanted, or some other man. Maybe you could've had more babies, ones you could keep."

Jewel's dark eyes grew somber as she considered Sarah's question. "I was too tired, I reckon. Too tired of loving and losing what I loved to take a chance. It's hard to go through life without lovin' *somebody*, and I couldn't help loving Mr. Hunter and Miz Rebekah and even Mr. Mac, but it wasn't the same kind of love as you got for your own. Know what I mean?"

Sarah nodded, knowing only too well.

"I couldn't do it no more. For one thing, I swore I wouldn't never let no other man have his way with me. After what I went through at that place where I was, them overseers always trying to get the women in a family way whether we was willing or not, I can't stand the thought of it anymore."

Sarah understood this, too, and she reached across

300

the table and took Jewel's dark hand in her light one. "I know. I thought I'd feel the same way after . . . well, after being with the Comanches, but with Hunter . . ."

"I know, Miz Rebekah says the same thing. She says if I was in love with some man, it'd be fine, but I ain't never met a man I could love. Never met a man I wanted to love, come to that. It's just too dangerous when you . . ."

Dangerous. Yes, Sarah knew about the danger, but . . . "When you what?" she prodded.

"When you're one o' them who's cursed or whatever it is. See, everybody I ever loved is dead or gone, my family, I mean. My folks, my brothers, my babies . . . It's me, Miz Sarah, something about me what makes it too dangerous for the folks I love. I just couldn't take a chance again. You know what I'm talking about?"

Oh, yes, Sarah knew exactly what she was talking about. *Cursed.* Was that what was wrong with Sarah? Was that why she'd left so many graves in her wake? And did that mean little Becky was in danger, too?

Her blood ran cold at the thought. No, not Becky! Nothing would happen to her now! They were safe, and Hunter would take care of them!

And nothing would happen to Hunter either. Oh, no, it couldn't, it just couldn't. They needed him too much.

But what if Jewel was right about there being some kind of curse? And what if Sarah really *was* cursed? What if her loving him could kill Hunter the way it had killed everyone else?

But of course she didn't love him. She'd already decided that, hadn't she?

Sarah didn't like sleeping in the big feather bed at the farm all alone. She tried to convince herself it wasn't any

301

different from being without Hunter at Rebekah's house in town, but she still couldn't seem to rest easy. She kept dreaming. Terrible dreams. Ugly dreams.

The Comanches were coming. She could hear their horses and their war cries. Terrified, she tried to run, to hide somewhere, but she had to find the baby first. She had to hide the baby, too, so they wouldn't kill him, but she couldn't find the baby anywhere. Where could he be? Where could he be? She was frantic, tearing the house apart, turning the cradle over and dumping the blankets, but the baby wasn't there. He wasn't anywhere, and the Indians were coming and they would kill them all! They were howling and screaming, and Sarah was screaming, too, screaming for the baby who wasn't anywhere, until her own cry jarred her awake.

For a long moment she lay there, gasping in the darkness, her body soaked with cold sweat, her limbs trembling with terror as she waited for the dream to end. But in the next instant she realized the dream wasn't ending, not all of it, because she could still hear them, the horses and the shouts and a woman screaming and . . .

Jewel! Sarah bolted from the bed, her bare feet slapping on the wooden floor as she raced to the door to the dog-trot and threw it open. Before her she saw a tableau of horror, fire blazed up from the outbuildings and from Dan and Enoch's cabin, painting the world orange and blood red, and three men in robes and hoods were dragging Jewel from the other side of the house.

The nightriders!

Jewel was kicking and screaming and fighting, but she was no match for them.

"Put her down here on the ground, boys, and hold her legs apart," one of the men was shouting. "Who wants to be first?"

"No!" Sarah shrieked, and instinctively, she grabbed the Henry rifle Hunter had left her for protection from the corner of the room. With a haste born of panic, she jerked down the lever and slammed it back up, injecting a live shell into the chamber, all this as she ran out the door into the dogtrot.

The roaring flames danced eerily, making everything look exactly like the nightmare from which she'd just awakened, but Jewel's screams were too real to be a dream. Sarah wanted to shoot the men carrying her, but Jewel was too close, so she aimed for the sky and pulled the trigger, blasting a hole in the bedlam.

The recoil almost knocked her off her feet, but Sarah instantly lowered the barrel of the gun, pointing it straight at the men again. In that instant, everyone had frozen in place and turned toward her, and the only sound was the roar and hiss of the fires and the frightened wail of little Becky in the house. But Sarah couldn't think of her baby now. She had to protect the rest of her family.

"*Let go of her!*" Sarah screamed at the men holding Jewel, hearing the note of hysteria in her voice and feeling her own fear for the first time.

The men holding Jewel dropped her as if she'd been a hot coal, and Jewel lurched to her feet, pulling her nightdress down as she went, shambling and stumbling to where Sarah stood.

"What's *she* doing here?" somebody demanded. "Nobody said anything about a white woman!"

Plainly, the men were disturbed by more than Sarah's rifle. They stood awkwardly in their white, homemade robes, about a dozen of them, with feed sacks covering their faces, holes cut out for eyes, nose and mouth. A few of the men had affixed cow horns to the sacks, probably

303

to make themselves look more like devils, to look more frightening.

It was working. Sarah was terrified and acutely aware of how vulnerable she was as the wind whipped her nightdress around her bare legs, but somehow she held the rifle steady, remembering all her father had ever taught her about hunting squirrels. *Aim for the head, girl, or the meat won't be no good.*

Then she saw them, Dan and Enoch, stripped naked with their hands tied and pulled up over their heads so they fairly dangled from the largest limb of the old live oak tree out in the yard. A robed man standing near them held a bull whip.

"Let them go, too!" Sarah screamed. "Cut them down, then get out of here! What do you think you're doing, bothering innocent people?"

"Innocent!" one of the men shouted, striding toward her from where he'd been overseeing what they were doing to Dan and Enoch and gesturing wildly with one hand. "Those men raped a white woman!"

The outrageous accusation hardly registered because Sarah had seen the empty sleeve of the man's robe lifting in the wind. It was Owen Young. Owen Young, a man she knew, a man who knew her. Did she know the others, too? Did they know her? How could they hurt her if they did? How could people she knew do such a horrible thing?

"You're wrong!" Sarah shouted, her voice quavering as she took aim at Owen Young's head. "Get out and leave us alone!"

"She didn't cock the rifle!" someone on a horse shouted, and Sarah realized her terrible mistake. Oh, no, oh, no, oh, no, her mind cried as her shaking hands fumbled with the lever, somehow pulling it down, but

304

just as it slammed back into place, something struck her, something huge, and sent her sprawling on the ground. The rifle flew from her hands as the horseman went galloping on.

Frantically, she scrambled for the rifle on hands and knees, but one of the robes swooped in and snatched it up, holding it high, just out of her reach, taunting her.

"You can rape her, too!" Owen Young shouted to the other men. "She's been with an Indian! She's no better than the other niggers!"

Sarah's heart lurched in terror, and she lunged to her feet, ready to run or fight, but no one moved toward her. No one moved at all except Owen Young who was still gesturing wildly with his one arm.

"What's the matter with you! Don't you remember what we came here for? These niggers raped my wife"!

Sarah gasped in horror, knowing it couldn't be true, knowing Dan and Enoch were far too gentle and timid to ever even contemplate such a thing. What could have made Mr. Young think it?

"That's a lie!" Jewel shouted, and Dan and Enoch's protests echoed hers over the roar of the flames, but no one paid them any mind.

"I don't like it," one of the robed men was saying. "You didn't say there'd be a white woman here." The man turned to Sarah, his eyes sparkling through the holes in his hood. "We didn't know you'd be here, Miz Tate. Where's your husband?"

"He . . . he'll be back any minute," Sarah tried, but she didn't fool them.

"Prob'ly off hunting more cattle," someone under another hood suggested.

"I expect him back directly though," Sarah insisted

frantically. She felt Jewel's hand on her shoulder, strengthening her. "You can't do this!" Sarah cried, desperate now. "My husband will hunt you down, every one of you!"

The men shifted uneasily, glancing at each other. Plainly, they believed her threat.

"Killing niggers is one thing, fellows, but she's right, if we hurt a white woman . . ." one of them said.

"But she's married to a breed!" Young insisted.

"He's twice the man you are, Owen Young!" Sarah shouted furiously. The men gasped, and she whirled on them. "I know who the rest of you are, too!" she lied. "Hunter told me! He knows all your names already! Hasn't he been to your houses, trying to talk sense to you? Anything happens to us, he'll kill every one of you!"

"Owen, cut those boys down, and let's get out of here!" the man holding Sarah's rifle cried.

"Cowards!" Young screamed. "Are you forgetting what they did to my wife? Are you going to let them get away with it?"

For a long moment, the question hung in the air, then one of the men finally said, "We only got your word for it, Owen."

"Yeah," somebody else added, "and that boy we hung last month, you said he was hanging out at your place, bothering your wife. We only had your word for that, too, and now I'm wondering if you just think *all* niggers is after your wife."

A murmur of agreement went through the crowd, then another man said, "These here boys have always minded their own business. Never knowed a bit of trouble from 'em. 'Less I hear Miz Young her own self accuse 'em, I say let 'em go."

"That's right, let 'em go," the man holding the rifle

said.

"You bastards!" Young shrieked. "All right, I'll cut them down, but you haven't heard the last of this!"

Whirling, his robe billowing out behind him in the wind, he strode furiously back across the yard toward where Dan and Enoch hung helpless.

Sarah could hardly believe it. It was over. They were leaving. Most of the farm buildings would be gone when the fires burned out, but at least everyone was still alive and unharmed. She couldn't believe it had been so easy.

Owen Young had reached the two black men, and he pulled an enormous Bowie knife out from under his robe. It flashed once in the firelight, and Sarah knew one blissful moment of relief before one of the black men screamed the most horrible scream Sarah had ever heard.

"No!" she cried, but the sound was drowned by the other black man's blood curdling howl of agony.

The other men were shouting now and racing to stop him, but even before Sarah's protest had died on her lips, the anguished screams abruptly ceased, one and then the other, replaced by a horrible gurgling. Then Owen Young turned, his one whole arm outstretched and dyed crimson, as if to embrace them all with his deed of horror, and holding up his bloody knife for all to see. The rest of his robe was streaked in scarlet, too, and everyone froze, knowing it was too late, too late to help.

Everyone, that is, except Jewel, who darted from behind Sarah and, before anyone could react, snatched Sarah's rifle from the robed man, lifted it to her shoulder and fired.

The robed man lunged for Jewel, but Sarah threw herself against him and they both plunged to the ground in a tangled heap. The instant they hit, another explosion shattered the night, and when Sarah looked up, Jewel was down, too.

"Jewel!" Sarah fought her way free of the robed man and scrambled frantically over to where Jewel lay sprawled like a discarded rag doll. A scarlet blossom had bloomed on the front of her nightdress, and Sarah gasped in horror as she dropped down beside her friend. "Jewel," she whispered brokenly, wanting desperately to help but knowing it was far too late.

"Did I get him?" Jewel asked weakly.

Sarah's head snapped up, and she saw that Owen Young also lay sprawled on the ground, a fresh stain spreading across the already stained white of his robe.

"Yes, yes, you did," Sarah assured her frantically. "He's dead, Jewel. He's dead."

"We all are, then," Jewel said.

"No!" Sarah cried, taking Jewel's dark hand and pressing it to her cheek. It already felt cold. "You can't die! Who'll help me take care of Becky? Listen, Jewel, she's calling for you!"

In the ominous stillness, they could hear the baby's wail of anguish.

"You'll do just fine, Miz Sarah," Jewel said, her voice hardly a whisper now.

Sarah could hardly see Jewel's face now because of the tears that were spilling out of her own eyes and down her cheeks. "Don't die, Jewel, please, don't leave me," she begged desperately.

"Don't be sad," Jewel whispered. "I'll see my babies now. I won't have to miss 'em no more." She smiled, the sweetest, saddest smile Sarah had ever seen, and then she was dead.

Sarah sobbed brokenly for a long time, still cradling Jewel's hand to her tear-streaked face, and then she no-

iced the silence, broken only by the baby's distant cry
and the crackle of the dying flames. When she looked
around, all the men in robes were gone, all except Owen
Young who lay just where he had fallen. Someone had
cut down Dan and Enoch's bodies and covered each of
them with one of the robes the men had been wearing.
But no one had covered Jewel, so Sarah staggered to her
feet and lurched blindly back into her bedroom.

The baby was still wailing in terror, so Sarah mechani-
cally picked her up, planting her on one hip, and used
her free arm to pull a blanket from her own bed and drag
it outside into the yard to drape over Jewel's poor, broken
body. She wanted to carry Jewel inside where she would
be safe, but she knew she wasn't strong enough. For
some reason, she barely felt able to hold her own baby,
and when Jewel had been decently covered from the
rude stares of the nighttime stars, Sarah staggered into
the kitchen and sank down into the old rocking chair that
sat by the fireplace.

The baby still wailed, so Sarah opened the bodice of
her nightdress and offered the comfort of her breast.
And waited numbly for the help that would come.

Because help always came, even if it was too late to do
any good.

Afterwards, no one ever questioned exactly how
quickly word of the tragedy had spread. Everyone knew,
however, that the very men who had caused it must have
been the ones to summon help. Someone who never took
credit for the deed rode down the main street of town
shouting, "Fire!" to waken and alert the residents, and
farmers who should have been sleeping soundly in their
own beds, blissfully unaware, arrived at the Tate farm

fully clothed within the hour to fight the dying blaze and wrap the mutilated bodies for burial before the ladies who came to help Mrs. Tate could see them.

When someone finally thought to ride over to the Young's house to tell Mrs. Young what had become of her husband, they found her cold and dead in her blood-soaked bed. Those who discovered her never spoke openly of what they'd seen, but rumors abounded, whispers of murder and worse.

And someone rode after Hunter and brought him back. By the time he got to his mother's house where they'd taken Sarah and the baby, he was frantic.

"How is she?" he asked the instant his mother released him from her welcoming hug.

"She's shattered," Rebekah told him. "She just sits and rocks, holding the baby. Sometimes she cries, but not out loud. The tears just roll down her face, and she doesn't even wipe them away, like she doesn't know they're there. She won't talk about what happened, either. Mac tried to get her to tell him who the other men were, but she just stared at him."

Without even bothering to greet his stepfather who stood beside his mother, Hunter bounded up the stairs, taking them two and three at a time, running until he reached the bedroom where Sarah was. He found her sitting in the rocking chair, cradling the baby in her arms. If Sarah heard him come in, she gave no indication. She just stared into the cold fireplace. His heart seemed to freeze with fear.

"Sarah?" he tried, and he thought her eyes flickered, but she gave no other response.

Slowly, almost reluctantly, he approached her. Glancing down, he saw that Becky was asleep, so he gently took the child and laid her in the cradle. Sarah didn't

310

eem to notice that either.

"Sarah?" he tried again, desperately wanting to hold her, to know she was safe. This time she looked up at him, her lovely blue eyes empty of every emotion except pain, and he cried out for her agony, reaching for her, grasping her arms, hauling her to her feet and into his arms.

She made a small, mewling sound, almost a whimper, and he hugged her more tightly, wanting to draw her into himself where nothing and no one could ever hurt her again.

Pressing a kiss to the top of her golden head, he scooped her up into his arms and carried her to the bed, where he lay down beside her and held her for long, silent minutes. Her breath was ragged against his shoulder and after a while it caught on a sob, and then she was crying, weeping as if her heart would break, and he just held her, crying, too, their tears mingling when he laid his face against her burning cheek.

She cried for a long time, until she was too exhausted to cry anymore, then she lay limp in his arms. Finally, she said in a small, weary voice, "They're dead, Hunter."

"I know," he told her. "When I first heard it, I couldn't believe it. I can't even remember my life before Jewel came into it. She's just always been there, like my mother and Mac. And Dan taught me how to plow a field, and Enoch showed me how to plant seeds, and how to tell a weed from a plant."

"He killed them," she told him dully. "He killed them with a knife."

"Tell me what happened, sweetheart. Tell me everything."

"I was asleep," she began, her tone flat, as if she were relating a very boring story by rote, but he listened intently, hearing all the horror she so carefully concealed. He stiffened when she told the part where Owen Young had urged the others to rape her, but he relaxed again when he learned they had refused.

"Nobody knew what he was going to do, Hunter," she told him earnestly when she got to the last, terrible part. "We all thought he was going to cut them down. We did, *they* did. I think the others would've stopped him if they'd thought . . . But before anybody knew what was happening, they were screaming, Dan and Enoch. He cut them with his knife."

"Yes, he cut their throats after he cut off their . . . Well, he had some crazy notion they'd raped his wife." Hunter's throat felt raw and sore.

"They were running to stop him, even though it was too late, and Jewel grabbed the rifle, the one I'd brought out, and she shot him. Then someone . . ." Sarah's voice broke on another sob, but she choked it back, forcing herself to go on. "Someone shot her."

"Who was it, Sarah?" Hunter demanded. "Who killed Jewel?"

Sarah stared up at him helplessly. "I don't know. I swear, I didn't see. Just someone. They all had guns, I guess. Maybe nobody knows except the man who did it."

"Who were they, Sarah? Tell me their names."

But Sarah was still back there at the farm, still remembering. "She said not to be sad, Hunter. She said she'd see her babies, and then she smiled." Tears filled her eyes and trickled out, one by one.

"Who were they, Sarah? Tell me their names," Hunter urged.

But Sarah only shook her head. "I don't know. Some of the voices sounded familiar, but they all had on hoods and . . . I don't want to know who they were, Hunter.

312

Can't you understand? *I don't want to remember!*"

"I know, I know," he soothed, pulling her close again. "Thank God, you're all right, at least. If anything had happened to you and the baby . . ." He shuddered, wondering how he would bear it. Losing his old friends was horrible enough, but how could he live without Sarah? And why would he want to?

The thought of her importance sobered him. When he'd taken her to wife, he'd never expected to feel this way about her. He'd wanted a partner, a bedmate, someone to be with, to keep loneliness at bay. But in a few short months, she'd become his whole world, more important to him than the people he'd loved his entire life.

"I'm here now, Sarah," he whispered into her hair. "I won't let anything bad happen to you ever again. Do you hear? I'll protect you, Sarah. I swear."

The next day, as she stood by the graves and watched them throw dirt on top of the boxes, Sarah remembered Hunter's promise.

Everyone, white and black, for miles around had turned out, which was unheard of for a Negro funeral. The white preacher even spoke over the graves along with the black man who served the same duty in the black community, although he was really a farmer by trade.

The whites came out of guilt, Sarah supposed, and to support the Tates and the MacDougals, whose loss this was. If she closed her eyes, Sarah could imagine she heard the same voices here that she heard at the farm that night, but she wasn't sure and never would be.

Already the men were planning a barn raising to replace the one that had burned..They were actually eager, much more eager than farmers should have been to leave their fields during the spring planting. Guilt was what drove them, Sarah knew. And she felt some of them watching her, waiting for her to point a finger and condemn them. But of course she didn't. She couldn't, even if she had known who to point out. But she didn't tell anyone that. She just let them worry.

And she remembered Hunter's promise to keep her safe and almost laughed aloud while the black preacher was praying. How could Hunter keep her safe? The way he had the other night when the nightriders came? The way Pete had when the Comanches swooped down and carried her off? No, she knew nobody in this world could protect her, not for one minute.

And no one could protect Hunter from her, either. Because Jewel had been right, Sarah was cursed. She'd let herself love Jewel, just a little, just a tiny bit, and look what had happened. Jewel was gone now, too, just like the rest.

Just like Hunter would be gone if Sarah let herself love him.

She would have to be careful now, very careful, so no one else would die. She felt as if her heart had been torn from her chest and nothing was left there but a hollow void. Which was just as well, she supposed, because she wouldn't be needing her heart anymore. She wouldn't be needing it at all.

Chapter Eleven

The Tate Ranch, August 1867

Even though a year had passed since he'd built the ranch house he'd promised Sarah — miles away from the site of the old Tate farm — Hunter still felt a flush of pride whenever he first saw it again after being away. A full complement of seasons had weathered the boards of the big barn and the bunkhouse and the other outbuildings, but the stone house still looked brand new and would for a long time to come.

Hunter had been gone several days, rounding up some of his cattle for his first real drive North to sell his stock in the new market that had just opened up in Abilene, Kansas. For the first time since he'd started ranching, he'd see some cash money for his efforts, and the prospect delighted him.

Or it would have if he hadn't felt so reluctant to leave Sarah for the month or more it would take to make the trip. Of course, the new baby would be here long before he had to leave — should have been here by now, in fact — so he wouldn't have to leave her behind still pregnant.

No, that wasn't what worried him. It was leaving her at all that bothered the hell out of him.

When he tried to figure out why, though, he couldn't actually say. Maybe it was just that he always felt so distant from her even when they were together. Even when they were making love and he was actually inside of her, she wasn't really there. It was as if she were holding him at arm's length, although her arms were wrapped around him.

And of course, they hadn't made love in months because of the baby she carried, so Hunter hadn't even had her physically close. Sometimes he felt like he was standing on the shore and Sarah was in a boat, drifting farther and farther away, slowly but perceptibly, and there was nothing he could do to stop her.

He'd tried to recall if she'd always been like that, and he thought he remembered her being different in the beginning, when they'd first married. Open and free and affectionate. Cautious, of course, because she didn't know him well, but still giving. Now she gave him nothing except her body.

He supposed most men would be thrilled to have a wife who never refused them. No matter how tired she might be, Sarah always responded when Hunter turned to her at night, and she was still as eager as she'd been in the early days of their marriage.

But that was all he ever got from her. If he tried to talk to her, to find out what she was thinking or feeling, she would just stare at him with those big blue eyes of hers. It was like she kept an invisible shell around herself that he could never break through. He could touch her body but never her heart.

When he let himself think back, when he was willing to remember the pain, he remembered when she'd left him, too. She'd left him the night Jewel and the others died. Since then, she'd never been the same. Who would have guessed that a woman who'd seen her own husband and child slaughtered and endured Comanche captivity would have been so affected by the deaths of three people she hardly knew? Certainly, Hunter wouldn't have, but he knew it was true, nevertheless. He'd lost Sarah that night. Even though he'd slept with her and made love with her and eaten his meals with her and worked with her each day for over a year, she wasn't really his anymore.

And the farther away she got from him, the more desperately he seemed to need her. Sometimes he asked her to make love even when he felt no desire, just so he could be close to her for a little while. Of course, she never refused him, but instead of feeling closer to her, he found her compliance more and more infuriating and felt more and more frustrated as month followed month.

Even the new baby hadn't brought her around. She'd seemed pleased by the pregnancy, but she hardly ever talked about it and resisted all his efforts to decide on a name for the coming child. Only Becky seemed able to break through her reserve and make her show a spark of her old spirit, so that sometimes Hunter found himself feeling jealous of the child he now considered his own daughter and of the tenderness her mother showed her.

Now, as Hunter and the men who worked for him rode toward the ranch, he felt the familiar longing for that old Sarah who would rush to him with joy shining in her eyes. Instead, as he reined up in the ranchyard and swung wearily down from his horse, he heard a childish voice piping, "Papa! Papa! Papa!"

Chubby legs pumping beneath her floursack dress, black hair flying in a tangle behind her, little Becky came charging down the porch steps and across the ranchyard, right into his waiting arms.

He scooped her up, unable to resist her naked adoration, and hugged her to his chest as she planted kiss after kiss wetly all over his dirty face. "How's my little Bluebird?" he asked. She smelled little girl sweet, and he buried his face in her soft neck, growling playfully, as if he would gobble her up while she squealed in delight.

"Kiss, kiss!" she cried, pulling away to grab the sides of his face with her tiny hands and squishing his cheeks until his lips puckered. Then she puckered her own and kissed him quickly on the mouth. They both laughed, Hunter feeling real joy for the first time in days at this shameless display of affection, and he gave her another big hug before swinging her up onto his shoulder so he could carry her back to the house.

"Where's your Mama?" he asked, hoping the concern he felt didn't show in his voice as he anxiously scanned the front of the house looking for some sign Sarah had noted his arrival and was coming to greet him. But the figure that appeared in the front doorway was his mother's. Rebekah had come to stay with Sarah so she'd be here when the baby finally came.

"Mama s'eep," Becky informed him, her two-year-old tongue tangling over the word.

"Mama is *sleeping?*" Hunter clarified in alarm, wondering what this could mean. Sarah would never be asleep in the middle of the day unless something was wrong. The baby . . .

"Papa! Papa!" Becky was announcing to her grandmother who nodded and smiled her acknowledgement.

"So I see," Rebekah called back. "Did everything go all right?" she asked Hunter.

"Yes," he replied absently. "What's the matter?

318

Where's Sarah?" he demanded as he climbed the porch steps, looking past her, hoping to see his wife coming down the hall to see what all the excitement was about.

"She's asleep," Rebekah informed him, accepting his kiss on the cheek and taking Becky from his shoulder.

"Asleep? In the middle of the day?" Then a new possibility occurred to him. "Did she have the baby?"

Rebekah glared at him and nodded meaningfully toward Becky who was listening in rapt fascination.

"Baby?" she asked curiously.

"Sweetheart, go tell Angelita to fix a bath for your Papa. He looks like he needs one," Rebekah said, setting the child down and pointing her in the direction of the kitchen where their Mexican maid worked.

"Bath! Bath!" Becky sang as she skipped off to do her grandmother's bidding.

"What's wrong with Sarah?" Hunter demanded the instant the child was out of earshot.

"Not a thing," Rebekah said, leading him inside and closing the front door behind him against the afternoon heat. The house was at least ten degrees cooler than outside, and Hunter instantly felt the relief. "It's just that that baby you gave her kept her up all night, kicking and carrying on, so I made her take a nap."

"I want to see her," Hunter said, heading toward the room they shared, but Rebekah grabbed his arm, stopping him in his tracks.

"Can't you at least wait until you get cleaned up? She's *sleeping*, for heaven's sake! Let the poor girl rest."

Grudgingly, Hunter allowed his mother to lead him through the house and out the back under the covered walkway that led to the separate kitchen area. Inside, Angelita, the plump Mexican woman who helped Sarah with the household chores was pouring hot water into a hip bath.

"Buenos dias, Señor Tate," Angelita said. "You and the men are back, yes?"

"Yes, and Pedro is as anxious to see you as you are to see him," Hunter told her. Angelita's husband worked as a cowboy for Hunter.

"You go ahead and say hello to your husband," Rebekah told her. "I'll take care of Mr. Hunter's bath and see that supper gets on the table."

"Gracias," the Mexican woman called as she hurried from the room.

With Becky and Hunter's help, Rebekah prepared Hunter's bath and drew the curtain around the corner where the tub sat. Behind the curtain, Hunter undressed and handed his dirty clothes out to his mother, then lowered himself into the blissful comfort of the tub and began to scrub away several day's worth of trail dirt.

"Is Sarah feeling all right?" Hunter asked after a moment, while Becky ducked under the curtain and announced, "I help."

Absently, he handed her an extra washcloth and let her splash around in the cooling water.

"Sarah is feeling about the way you'd expect a woman to feel when she's two weeks overdue and it's August in Texas," his mother told him while she bustled about the kitchen, continuing the preparation of supper. "It's hard to really tell, though. You know how Sarah keeps to herself. I don't think I've ever heard her complain about anything."

"How does she look?" Hunter asked.

"Mama fat," Becky informed him solemnly, and Hunter couldn't help smiling.

"I know, Little Bluebird. I'm the one who made your Mama fat."

"Hunter!" his mother scolded, outraged.

"She's too little to understand," he defended himself.

"I big!" Becky protested, as outraged as her grandmother. "I two!"

Not knowing exactly when Becky had been born, they had decided on August first as her birthday and had celebrated it last week. "I know, Bluebird. I just forgot," Hunter told her, chucking her wetly under her chubby chin.

She pouted for another second, then broke into a cherubic grin, and it was all Hunter could do not to grab her and kiss her sweet little face. But of course he'd get her all wet if he did, so he settled for patting her cheek.

She sure was a beauty. Not at all like her fair mother, but a darling just the same. Ironically, she looked like Hunter, or so people always said, probably because of her coloring. He didn't know how Sarah felt when people said so because she never discussed it with him, but it gave Hunter a sense of pride to be able to claim this part of Sarah. Now she'd have his baby, a child that was really his, and she'd belong to him that much more.

Or so he told himself.

"Here, Becky, give Papa these clean pants, then come out so he can get dressed," Rebekah called.

When Becky had vanished beneath the curtain again, Hunter got out of the tub, dried off and pulled on the pants. "Don't you have a clean shirt?" he asked.

"No, that's all I've got handy without going into your bedroom and disturbing Sarah. You can eat without a shirt. We don't mind, do we, Becky?"

Becky giggled and ran to Hunter when he emerged from behind the curtain, holding up her arms to him.

Rebekah had set out a sandwich and a cup of coffee for him. "This should hold you until supper," she told him.

Obediently, Hunter picked up his daughter and carried her to the table, then set her in his lap while he ate, allowing her to feed him the crumbs that fell from his sandwich.

He ate quickly, compelled to hurry because when he was finished, he could go to Sarah. But when he was finished, his mother said, "Becky, I think I hear your doll baby crying out on the porch. Why don't you go take care of her?"

For an instant, Becky looked at her father, considering her options, then decided it was safe to leave him and scrambled down from his lap. When she was outside, Rebekah turned to him, her expression somber. "Is Sarah all right? Is there something I don't know about? Some trouble between the two of you?"

Hunter thought about his vague dissatisfaction, his nameless longings, but of course, he didn't mention them. "No, nothing between us. Like you said, Sarah never complains, and she . . . she always seems satisfied with everything." It sounded lame to his ears, knowing what he did, but apparently, his mother believed him.

"When I first met her, I thought . . . Well, those months you lived with us before . . . before the tragedy, she seemed different somehow, happier. I thought you'd made a good choice, Hunter, that you'd found a woman who could make you happy, too."

"I *am* happy," he insisted, although he knew it wasn't exactly the truth. He wasn't unhappy, at least, which was all most people could really ask for in this life. If only it were enough.

"Sarah doesn't seem to be," Rebekah said sternly. "Has she said anything to you about not wanting this baby?"

Not wanting it? Hunter gaped at her. Where could she have gotten an idea like that? "No," he said carefully, betraying nothing. "Has she said something to you?"

"Oh, no," Rebekah assured him, patting his hand. "I didn't mean to upset you. It's just . . . I've been trying to figure out why she acts so strangely. She doesn't seem to want to make any plans for the baby at all. I had to force her to get the cradle out and fix it up, and she says you haven't even decided on names yet . . ."

"No, no, we haven't," Hunter confirmed reluctantly. Well, at least Sarah's moods weren't his imagination.

Rebekah considered for a moment. "Does she ever talk about Jewel and . . . and what happened that night?"

"Never," Hunter said. "I've asked her at least a dozen times who the other men were, but she claims she doesn't know. I think she just doesn't *want* to know. I can't blame her. I don't like to remember it myself, and I wasn't even there."

Rebekah sighed. "I just feel like she needs help of some kind, but if she won't even tell us what's wrong, how can we help her?"

Hunter knew exactly what she meant, but he didn't want to say so and worry her even more. "She'll be fine, Mother. You told me yourself women get moody when they're expecting. Once the baby comes, she'll be her old self."

Rebekah didn't look convinced, however. "You love her, don't you?" she asked suddenly.

"Of course," Hunter replied, surprised. "She's my wife."

Rebekah smiled wisely. "There's no 'of course' about it, you know. You didn't love her when you married her, did you?"

"How could I?" he asked her reasonably. "I hardly knew her."

"So it's reasonable to assume that when you did get to know her, you might not ever come to love her, but you did. Have you told her?"

He started to say that of course he had, but figured his mother might challenge him on that, too, particularly since it wasn't true. "Mother, I think you're meddling," he said instead, wanting to end this uncomfortable conversation.

"I know I am," she countered, unrepentant. "But that's my duty as your mother. You should tell her you love her, Hunter. It might make a difference."

What kind of a difference? Hunter wondered bitterly. Would it make Sarah love him in return? Because that was the real problem, he knew. She didn't love him, which was why she held herself back from him, why he could never get close enough to her. Probably even why she wasn't excited about his baby.

But he wasn't about to discuss all this with his mother. "I think I'll go see if Sarah is awake yet," he said, rising to his feet.

He half-expected his mother to stop him, but she let him go without a word, and he hurried back into the main house as if he were fleeing from something.

His bare feet made no sound on the wooden floors as he entered the center hall and crept to the door that led to the room he shared with Sarah. He hesitated a moment before opening it, listening for any sound from within. Hearing nothing, he turned the knob silently and pushed the door open.

The room was dark and cool, the windows shuttered against the summer sunlight and its heat. Hunter slipped in and closed the door quietly behind him, tak-

324

ng a moment to let his eyes adjust to the dimness.

When they had, he saw Sarah. She lay on the bed, motionless except for the faint rise and fall of her breath. Her golden hair, grown out now, was braided down her back, and tiny wisps clung damply to her forehead and cheeks. Her face was pale and puffy, a poor, blurred version of the loveliness he'd first seen in her, and her body swelled hugely beneath the sleeveless nightdress she wore. Even her once-slender ankles were swollen now.

Hunter had never seen her look worse, and he'd never wanted her more. Desire was like a burst of molten lava, hot and painful inside him, and before he could think better of the impulse, he was on the bed beside her.

"Sarah," he whispered, laying a hand on her bare arm just so he could feel her warmth and her softness. "Sarah."

He lay down beside her, stretching himself so his whole body was against hers, against the mound of his child and her yielding softness. When his face was beside hers, so close that he could taste the sweetness of her breath, he whispered her name again.

Her eyelids flickered, reluctant at first, then slowly opened. For a second, she couldn't focus on him, and when she did, he saw what he hadn't seen in so very many months. Sarah's beautiful blue eyes filled with joy, the kind of joy he'd seen on Becky's little face when she'd raced across the yard into his arms. Sarah wanted him, was happy to see him; maybe she even loved him, at least in that one instant.

Before he could see that spark die, he kissed her, closing his own eyes, knowing she would close hers, too, as if by doing so they could lock in the precious joy and keep it safe. Her mouth opened beneath his, and he devoured her sweetness while his hands explored the changes in her body.

He stroked her arms, her back, the curve of her bottom through the thin fabric of her nightdress. The baby kept him from pressing his desire against her, but his hands found the hem of her nightdress and lifted it, baring her secrets to him.

Starved for such sensual pleasures, he caressed every inch of her that he could reach, reveling in the contrast of his calloused palm against her smoothness. Her knees, her thighs, her taut belly, then down again to her center, the only place where he could really touch her now that she'd frozen her heart against him.

Gently but firmly, he cupped her mound and watched in delight as her eyes widened in surprise.

"We can't," she breathed, her thighs tightening instinctively against the invasion. But instead of blocking him, she only held his hand more tightly against her.

"I know," he told her, letting his fingers play over her, teasing and taunting.

"What are you . . . ?" she tried, but the question ended with a gasp when he found the sensitive nub and coaxed it lovingly erect.

"You know what I'm doing," he told her, his nose against hers so he could feel her breath quicken against his face. "Just relax and enjoy it."

"We shouldn't . . ." she tried but without much conviction. Indeed, she was opening to him now, her silky thighs spreading to grant him access, and he felt the dew of her awakening desire.

She was hot, so hot, and her hips moved restlessly against the pressure of his hand, seeking, wanting, lifting to him. Her breath came in labored pants, and she bit her lip and shook her head in silent protest, as if denying her own need.

But she couldn't resist it, couldn't resist him and his power over her, and when he knew she was as near to the edge as she could be without falling over, he said, "Look at me, Sarah. Look at me!"

Obediently, she opened the eyes she had shut against the pure pleasure of it just as her body shuddered in release, and he saw it again: her joy, her need, her longing just for him. He kept the spasms going for as long as he could, prodding and coaxing for just one more and then another, savoring each one that shook her and the way she gasped at his power over her and the way her face softened and her beautiful eyes glazed and the way her nipples hardened against his bare chest.

But at last, too soon, it was over, and she went limp, and the tension of release dissolved into the warm afterglow. He waited, still cupping her heat, watching as the dazed expression faded from her face and her eyes focused on him once more.

Her breath came slowly now, and her eyes were puzzled. "Hunter?" she asked.

"Who else were you expecting?" he teased, pressing a kiss to her love-softened mouth.

When he drew away, he saw the joy had died completely from her eyes. In its place was confusion and the wariness he'd come to hate. "Why did you . . . ? I mean, don't you want . . . ?"

Her hand found his hardness pressing against the front of his pants

"I could—" she tried, but he caught her hand and pulled it away.

"No," he said firmly, unwilling to let her see him as he had seen her just moments ago, completely vulnerable and exposed. "I should've let you sleep. Mother said you were up all night. Now pretend I'm not here and close your eyes again."

He pulled her close, settling her into the crook of his arm, and forced himself to relax and to forget the throbbing of his own unsatisfied desire. She resisted for a moment, holding herself rigid, as if she expected some other attempt to force her to feel pleasure. But after a few minutes, when he made no move to do anything except fall asleep beside her, she slowly surrendered to his cuddling and allowed herself to soften against him again.

Feeling her capitulation, he pressed a chaste kiss to her forehead and simply held her, vaguely aware of his child stirring within her even as she drifted back to sleep again. The moment was so sweet he could taste it, and in the seconds before he surrendered to sleep himself, he felt one instant of satisfaction, all hopeless longings gone.

"I love you, Sarah," he whispered into her hair just before sleep claimed him.

Sarah awoke with a start, not knowing where she was or even who she was for a moment. Disoriented, she looked blearily around, puzzled to find herself in bed when the setting sun was slanting through the shutters. Even more confusing was finding Hunter sleeping beside her. He'd been gone for days, and she hadn't even known he was back, much less . . .

Or wait, she *had* known he was back, she remembered in chagrin. The memories came flooding back, and Sarah's face burned in embarrassment at what he'd done to her, what she'd let him do to her. Guiltily, she slipped out of his arms, putting some distance between them so she could think.

What exactly had happened? Sarah couldn't remember anything very clearly except the way he'd made her body shudder with ecstasy again and again. Had she said anything? Had he? Surely not. What could she have said, after all? What could she have revealed? Certainly not her feelings. She didn't have any feelings, not anymore. Not since . . . Well, she didn't think about that. She didn't think about anything unpleasant in her past. She simply lived each day as it came, never looking back, never expecting anything of the future. Encased safely in the now of her life, she couldn't be hurt. And she couldn't hurt anyone else.

Suddenly, her stomach contracted, hurting her badly, and Sarah instantly knew what had awakened her. It was the baby. The baby was coming at last, but instead of relief, she felt stark terror. *The baby was coming.* Hunter's baby. Their baby. Another person she was going to lose. How on earth could she bear it?

For long minutes she lay perfectly still, not wanting to wake Hunter, not wanting anyone to know in case she was mistaken, in case she still had another hour or another day before she had to push this new life into the world and hold it in her arms. As long as it was inside her, it would be safe, but once it was born, the danger began. And the terror began. One more person to worry about. One more life to be in danger. How on God's earth could she bear it?

When the next pain took her, she knew it was too late. The baby was coming, and there was nothing she could do to stop it. Nothing at all. Nothing at all.

Despair gripped her heart like a vicious fist, and her eyes burned with tears she couldn't shed, but she reached over and shook Hunter awake.

"Huh? Wha . . . ?" He sat bolt upright, looking

around, disoriented as she had been. Then he saw her lying beside him, her knees drawn up, her face strained.

"Hunter, get your mother," she told him slowly, carefully, in case he wasn't quite awake and didn't understand.

"My mother?" he asked, plainly confused. "Why?"

Sarah closed her eyes and drew a breath. "Because, the baby's coming."

"The baby?" he repeated stupidly, then the truth dawned on him. *"The baby!"* He jumped out of bed and ran to the door, throwing it open before Sarah could tell him there wasn't *that* much of a hurry. *"Mother!"* he shouted, disappearing into the hall.

But Sarah no longer cared because she was having another contraction. It won't be long now, she thought. The pains were coming close together. This was her fourth time. She should really be an expert at judging by now, she thought bitterly. Four babies, two already dead. And Pete and her parents and Jewel and all the others. So many dead. So many reasons to be frightened for the life now struggling so hard to reach the light of day.

By the time Rebekah appeared in the doorway, Sarah's face was wet with tears.

"The pains just started?" Rebekah asked, moving to the bed.

"Yes, but they're close." She'd already told Rebekah that she'd only been in labor with Becky for most of the afternoon. Each baby had come more quickly than the last, so this one should be here before she knew it. Before she was ready. She gritted her teeth against the next contraction.

"Are they really bad?" Rebekah asked in alarm. "You're crying!"

330

But when the pain had passed, Sarah shook her head and brushed awkwardly at the tears.

"Mama! Mama!" they heard Becky shouting from the hallway, and the rumble of Hunter's voice as he tried to soothe her.

"You're going to Angelita's house to play," he was saying, his voice stiff with the false cheerfulness that never fools a child.

"Mama! Mama!" Becky insisted, crying now. "P'ease! Mama!"

How many times had Sarah told her that she could have what she wanted if she said please? But she couldn't have her Mama, not now. Sarah gritted her teeth again, this time against the urge to call back her only living child. *Please!* she prayed, hoping desperately that God played by the rules. *Please, don't let this one die, too!*

But no one answered, and Rebekah hadn't heard. She was too busy bustling around, pulling the blankets from the bed and preparing for the labor. She stuffed pillows behind Sarah's back.

"There, that should be more comfortable," she said, and Sarah laughed because she'd given birth on the ground in a buffalo hide lodge the last time. What did she care for comfort?

Hunter was back now, anxious and frightened, even more frightened than Sarah, and she noticed absently that he was only half-dressed.

"Put some clothes on," his mother told him, "and stop dancing around like a frog on a hot griddle."

Obediently, Hunter found a shirt and some shoes, but he forgot to button the shirt until his mother reminded him, and even then he didn't tuck it in.

"What's taking so long?" he demanded after a few minutes.

His mother shook her head in disgust. "Babies take hours to come. Now get out of here before you scare Sarah with all that pacing around. Did somebody send for MacDougal?"

"Oh, no, I'll send one of the boys," Hunter offered, hurrying out.

Rebekah slammed the door behind him, still shaking her head, and continued her preparations. She tied Sarah's hands to the headboard so she could bear down when the contractions came, and they were coming even faster now. Sarah hardly had time to catch her breath between them.

"Won't be long now," Rebekah told her, and Sarah knew it was true. She could feel the baby's head straining to emerge, and the urge to push was overwhelming.

Rebekah wiped Sarah's face with a cool cloth, and their eyes met. "Something's wrong," Sarah gasped, desperate now, knowing she had to warn Rebekah before it was too late.

"What?" Rebekah asked in alarm. "Does it hurt? Where? Tell me!"

"No," Sarah told her, shaking her head, then bracing against the onslaught of another pain. When at last it eased, she fell back panting while Rebekah wiped her face again.

"What is it? What's wrong?" Rebekah demanded, frantic now.

"The baby, something's wrong with the baby," Sarah said. "I've known for months. He . . . he doesn't move, not like the others." She gasped, trying to breathe before the next pain. "He's going to die!"

"No!" Rebekah shouted, as if the force of her will could stop the inevitable, but Sarah knew it was no use. She knew the only hope was to keep the baby inside her, but it was too late, too late.

Another pain sent her into delirium, and when she emerged, Rebekah's face was white, her lips set grimly, determined. Nothing would stop her from saving the child, and Sarah didn't have the strength to tell her it was useless, that Sarah's curse had already killed it.

They worked in silence except for Sarah's grunts of pain. Rebekah wiped her brow and spread the towels when Sarah's water broke and tended to her in every way through the long dark tunnel of her labor. Sarah welcomed each contraction she knew wasn't the last, knowing each second that passed was one second longer that her baby would live.

But finally the last one came.

"I can see the head," Rebekah said, her voice strained, infected with Sarah's fear. "Once more should do it."

No! Sarah's mind protested, but her body ignored the protest, laboring on, pushing and pushing to expel the child she didn't want to birth.

"I've got it!" Rebekah cried as Sarah felt the tiny body slide from hers. She lifted the baby, the cord dangling, still attached, and held it up for Sarah to see.

So pale and white and still, not like the others at all, not at all. Swiftly, Rebekah tied off the cord and cut it, then held the baby up by the heels and slapped it, once and twice and three times, but it didn't cry. Only Sarah was crying, sobbing softly, helplessly as she watched the futile effort.

But Rebekah wouldn't give up. She plunged the shriveled little body into the basin of cold water, then held it up again and gave it a resounding whack. The answering cry was so feeble, Sarah wasn't sure she even heard it, but slowly, ever so slowly, the tiny white body pinkened, and the wail, weak as it was, continued.

Crying herself now, Rebekah wrapped the baby in the blanket she'd had ready and cradled it to her bosom.

"He's crying," she told Sarah defensively. "He's alive!"

And Sarah didn't say what they both knew, that the cry was little more than a reedy squeak or that the baby who now lived was too frail, too thin, and too blue to survive.

Tenderly, Rebekah lay the child next to Sarah on the bed, then quickly untied her hands so Sarah could hold it while Rebekah cleaned up the afterbirth.

When Sarah was comfortable again and tucked up in the bed once more, Rebekah said, "Try to nurse him."

Slowly, almost reluctantly, Sarah opened her nightdress and offered the baby her breast, but the child was too weak to suckle and after a few minutes, she gave up.

"He's all worn out from being born," Rebekah said with forced cheerfulness. "Let him rest a little, then we'll try again."

And Sarah nodded, knowing it was no use, knowing Rebekah knew it too, although neither of them dared admit it to the other.

"I'll tell Hunter he can come in," Rebekah said at last, and Sarah nodded again, not trusting her voice.

But Sarah knew the instant she saw Hunter's face that Rebekah hadn't told him the truth. He glowed with pride and happiness.

"It's a boy," he told her, as if she hadn't already known. "We have to decide on a name now. We can't put it off any longer." He sat beside her on the bed and tenderly, reverently, pulled the blanket back so he could see his son.

Sarah wanted to weep at the sight of the pale little face with its blue lips, so wizened he looked like a tiny old man.

"He's not very pretty, is he?" Hunter asked, not understanding. "But he'll fill out, just like Becky did. Remember how fat she was?"

Sarah was crying, the tears running silently down her face, but Hunter still didn't understand. He took her in his arms and held her against his heart.

"You've given me a son, Sarah. You've made me the happiest man in the world. I . . . I love you," he added in a whisper.

The tender words were like a knife in her heart, and her breath caught on a sob at the stabbing pain. *He loved her.* What did that matter now? What did anything matter?

"Sarah, are you all right?" he asked, pulling away to look at her, his silver eyes full of confusion. "What's wrong, tell me?"

"I . . . I'm just tired," she managed, somehow holding back more sobs, somehow stopping the tears. "I'd like to rest now."

"Of course," he said, laying her gently back against the pillows, as if she were an egg that might break with harsh handling. "Do you want me to send my mother to you?"

Sarah shook her head, praying for him to leave before she lost control again. He didn't want to go, she could see that, but at last he did, after taking one final look at the baby who slept so soundly, too soundly, beside her.

What was she going to do? she asked into the dark when he was gone. What was she going to do?

Later Rebekah brought her some supper, but Sarah couldn't eat it. She tried to nurse the baby again, but without success. The child was so pale, so deathly pale, and his little breath was so labored and painfully slow.

Sarah cradled him in her arms, counting every breath and each beat of the fragile heart that she could almost

335

see through the translucent skin until she couldn't stay awake any longer. Then she lay beside him, her hand on his tiny body, willing her strength into him, willing him to survive.

Exhausted, she slept through until dawn. She awoke slowly, aware of the ache in her breasts from the milk no one had drunk. The front of her gown was wet from it, and when she touched herself, she found her breasts were hard and painful.

What was wrong? she wondered groggily through the haze of sleep, then she remembered. She remembered everything, and the truth overwhelmed her like a giant hand clamping over her face to stop her breath.

Dear God, no! her mind screamed, but she knew even as she denied it. Morning had come, and her child hadn't awakened to be fed. Hadn't cried at all, not once during the long night. Somehow she managed to turn her head to see him lying beside her, tiny in his blanket, and still, so still.

No, no!

Somehow she lifted a leaden hand. Somehow she moved it. Somehow she grasped the edge of the blanket and pulled it back. The little face was still there, wrinkled and old and white as death. Her fingers touched the waxen cheek and found it cold.

She heard a sound, a cry of anguish so pitiful she wanted to weep for whoever had uttered it, but she couldn't weep, couldn't move, couldn't tear her eyes from the face of her dead child to see who was crying, not even when the wail grew louder and louder still, filling the room, filling her head until she thought it would burst. The bedroom door flew open, and Hunter and Rebekah rushed in, still wearing their nightclothes. They'd heard it, too, and now they'd see the baby and they would know what she'd done.

Rebekah snatched up the baby, and Hunter took Sarah, gathering her into his arms.

"Don't cry, don't cry," he kept saying, over and over, like a litany, and Sarah wondered why he was saying it to her until at last she understood the wail of unbearable anguish was coming from her own throat.

Sarah hated them. She hated them all. She hated Rebekah for telling her she'd have other children. She hated Hunter for saying it wasn't her fault and they could try again. She hated Mac for patting her hand and telling her she was brave. And she hated all the people who came to bury her baby and who pretended they knew how she felt.

Hunter carried her to the little plot they'd carved out of the sun-baked ground so she could see them put her baby in the earth. As if she wanted to. As if she cared.

They expected her to cry. She could tell from the way they all watched her, but she wasn't going to cry. She'd already cried every tear she had, so she just stared dry-eyed at the hole in the ground and at the little box they put in it, and when they put dirt in her hand, she dropped that in on top, then watched them close up the hole again.

When it was over, Hunter carried her back and put her to bed, still handling her as if she were an egg that might break. But he didn't tell her he loved her again. Thank God, thank God, because she didn't think she could bear it.

And she didn't care if he loved her or not. She didn't need his love. She didn't need anything or anyone and never would again.

Sarah lay in her bed, in the darkness of her room, and

heard the murmur of voices as people discussed her, and didn't care. Sometimes Becky would creep in and crawl into bed beside her saying, "Mama, Mama," and Sarah would hold her small body tightly, as if she were drowning and only this little bit of humanity could save her.

But she didn't love Becky anymore, either. She couldn't because it hurt so much and the pain was too big. It filled her up and didn't leave room for anything else.

Days became nights and then became days again. Rebekah brought her food and took it away again. Finally, Rebekah made her get up and get dressed, but the sunlight hurt her eyes too much, so Sarah preferred to stay in her shuttered room, alone.

Alone because Hunter slept someplace else now. Sarah didn't even know where, nor did she care as long as he left her alone. So long as he didn't want to lie with her and make another baby she would be fine, because she didn't want another baby. It was much too dangerous, and Sarah felt much too fragile to go through it ever again. Sometimes she imagined she was only holding herself together by the strength of her own arms wrapped so tightly around her.

"Mama p'ay!" Becky demanded of Hunter and Rebekah after they'd finished dinner one day. "Mama p'ay!"

Hunter glanced at his mother who refused to meet his eye.

"I'll play with you, sweetheart," Rebekah offered. "Just as soon as I finish with the dishes.

"No, *Mama!*" Becky insisted, her brown face flushed with frustration.

"Mama's sick, Bluebird," Hunter said, picking her up and trying to set her in his lap.

But she stiffened and fought against him. *"Mama! Mama!"* she screamed, thrashing wildly.

Hunter struggled frantically to hold her, but it was a losing battle.

"Put her down," his mother shouted over the din of Becky's shrieks.

Obediently, Hunter laid the child on the floor, where she proceeded to kick and howl and beat her tiny fists on the floor.

"What's wrong with her?" Hunter demanded in horror.

"She's having a tantrum," his mother shouted back. "Two-year-olds do that. You'd better get used to it. Come on."

She motioned for him to follow her out of the kitchen.

"We can't just leave her like that!" Hunter protested.

"She'll keep it up as long as she has an audience." When he still didn't move, she grabbed his arm and hauled him out, shutting the kitchen door behind them.

The door muffled the sounds of Becky's howling outrage. Hunter ran a hand over his face. "What next?"

"I don't know, but one thing for certain, we've got to get Sarah out of her bedroom," Rebekah said, sounding as weary as Hunter felt.

Almost two weeks had passed since they'd lost the baby, but Sarah still just sat in her rocking chair or lay on her bed and stared. If she would cry, Hunter could understand it, but she just stared.

"I've tried to talk to her, but she doesn't even seem to hear me. I just don't know what to do anymore."

Rebekah nodded her understanding and patted him on the arm. Becky's screams were already fading. Apparently, his mother had been right about the audience.

"You've just got to love her," Rebekah said. "And be

patient. She's been through a lot in her life. She'll get through this, too."

Hunter looked at his mother, trying to judge whether she really believed that or whether she was just trying to make him feel better. "And what if she doesn't get through it?" he challenged.

But Rebekah had no answer. "I'll get Becky," she said instead. "She'll be ready for her nap now."

Hunter knew he should go back to work. He and his men would be leaving tomorrow, taking his cattle north to sell. But he was still sitting in the parlor when his mother returned from getting Becky settled down and to sleep.

"Are you worried about leaving her?" Rebekah asked him.

"Yes, but I don't have any choice," he replied.

"You know I'll stay here just as long as she needs me," his mother assured him.

Hunter nodded absently.

"Maybe we should take her into town, to our house," Rebekah suggested. "Maybe she needs a change of scenery."

"If you can get her to go," Hunter said without much enthusiasm.

Rebekah smiled sadly. "I'll get her to go. Maybe you leaving will be a good thing for her. She'll know she doesn't have you taking care of things while she hides in her room."

"I that case, maybe you should leave, too," he said, matching her sad smile.

"Does she know you're going?"

"She knew before, but I don't know if she remembers or if she realizes how much time has passed. I don't know anything that goes through her mind," he added in frustration.

"Then maybe you should go talk to her. Tell her so she'll be prepared. Tell her she can stay with us if she wants to. At least suggest it so she can be thinking about it."

Hunter nodded and reluctantly pushed himself out of his chair and left his mother, going down the hall to the bedroom where Sarah had been hiding herself.

He started to knock, then decided it was a waste of time since Sarah hardly ever answered anyway. He pushed the door open to find her sitting as she always was nowadays, in the rocker in the dark, staring at the wall. He went to her and knelt down in front of her. If she knew he was there, she gave no indication.

"Sarah," he said, taking her cold hand in his. She was so thin, just the way she'd been when he'd first found her. His mother said she didn't eat enough to keep a bird alive. Sarah's hand felt lifeless in his. "Sarah, I need to talk to you about something," he said.

For a moment, he thought she hadn't heard him, but finally her blank eyes moved until she was looking directly at him.

"Where's Becky?" she asked faintly. "She should have her breakfast."

A cold chill ran up his spine. Sarah didn't even know what time of day it was. "Becky's fine," he assured her. "My mother just put her down for a nap."

"Did she eat first?"

"Yes," Hunter said wearily. "She ate. She's fine. Sarah, there's something I have to tell you. I'm leaving tomorrow. I'm taking the cattle north to sell them. You remember, we talked about it before?"

Her lovely blue eyes registered nothing.

"You're leaving?" she echoed uncertainly.

"Yes, you remember. The cattle drive," he confirmed patiently.

"Tomorrow?" she asked, plainly disturbed. It was the first emotion he'd seen from her in weeks.

"Yes, but Mother will be here, or maybe you'd like to go into town and stay at her place while I'm gone. It would be more fun for you than being stuck way out here. You could see people and . . ." His voice trailed off when he realized she hadn't had the slightest interest in seeing anyone since the baby died.

"You're leaving tomorrow?" she asked again. She sounded like a lost child, like Becky when she didn't understand something and was afraid.

"That's right, and I'll be gone about a month. I'll come back as soon as I can, as soon as the cattle are sold, though, and then . . ." And then what? he asked himself bitterly. Was he going to promise her everything would be all right when nothing would ever be all right again?

How had Sarah kept her sanity after losing her first two children? Hunter could hardly stand to wake up each morning knowing his son was dead, knowing all the plans and dreams he'd had were useless and wasted. Sarah had carried that baby in her own body. No wonder she didn't want to come out of her room.

Hunter lifted her icy hand to his lips and kissed it, blinking back tears. "Sarah, when I get back, we'll start over. We'll . . . we'll be happy again, I promise you. And we've still got Becky. She's more than enough reason to keep going, isn't she? And we can have other children."

She made a small sound, a tiny cry, and Hunter's gaze flew to her face, but not in time to catch whatever emotion had passed over her. She was rigid but without expression.

342

"Sarah?" he asked, but she shook her head slightly, as if to deny her own feelings.

"You're leaving," she repeated quietly. "For a month."

"I'll miss you and Becky and . . . and everything," he tried. "I wouldn't go unless I had to, but you know how much we need to sell the cattle and—"

"Yes," she said calmly. "I'll be all right." For the first time she looked him directly in the eye. "Don't be afraid to leave me. I'll be all right."

And because he couldn't think of any way to reply, he left her.

When he was gone, Sarah sat in the dark, staring at the wall, and thinking she'd soon be truly alone, without Hunter, and she wouldn't have to worry about him wanting to make another baby, at least until he came back.

But when he did, she'd have to tell him. She'd have to tell him she'd never, ever go through this again.

Chapter Twelve

"Look, Mama, look!" Becky cried, and Sarah obediently looked up from her mending to see that her daughter had made a precarious tower out of her blocks.

"That's real good, sweetheart," she said. Then Becky kicked the tower with one bare foot and sent the blocks skittering across the porch where she and her mother had been sitting most of the afternoon.

Becky threw her head back and laughed, clapping her grubby hands in delight over her destruction, and Sarah smiled tolerantly.

"Now you'll have to build it all over again," Sarah pointed out, which was the whole idea, she knew.

Scrambling on hands and knees, Becky gathered the blocks and started her project over again. Sarah watched from her chair, admiring the way the afternoon sunlight made her child's dark hair shimmer with blue-black highlights. Her deep blue eyes sparkled with glee, and Sarah felt an almost overwhelming urge to scoop her up and hug her just so she could feel that precious body against her own and know Becky was really there, alive and well.

But of course she didn't. She didn't reach, didn't hug,

didn't move, even though her arms ached with emptiness. She couldn't, not if she hoped to keep her distance, not if she hoped to keep from loving this little person to death.

This was all part of her plan. She would seal herself off from them so they wouldn't die. They'd be safe then, Becky and Hunter, both of them, if only she could keep herself from loving them.

She was doing pretty well, too. She'd managed to shake off the lethargy she'd felt after the baby died so she could at least go through the motions of living her life. Finally, she'd done well enough that Rebekah had consented to go home to her husband, even though Sarah knew she hadn't wanted to, so Sarah and Becky were alone now. Well, not completely alone. Angelita and her husband were still here, helping to run the ranch while Hunter and the rest of the men were away. But at least no one was watching over Sarah anymore, playing nursemaid and trying to figure out what she was thinking or feeling.

Soon Hunter would be back, though, and her blissful solitude would be gone. When Sarah thought about it, she sometimes quaked in terror, but she would have to face him somehow, have to tell him the truth. He wouldn't like it, but there was nothing he could do. Well, nothing he *would* do anyway, she supposed, and once things were settled between them, Sarah could at last know some peace about the future.

"Supper is ready, Señora," Angelita told her from the front doorway.

"Thank you, Angelita," Sarah said, gathering her mending and rising from her chair. "You can go home to Pedro now. I'll see about cleaning up. Becky, pick up your blocks. It's time to eat."

Becky made the usual complaining noises, but she did as she was told and followed Sarah into the house. The contrast of the interior coolness wasn't as pronounced anymore now that the summer heat had finally broken, but Sarah savored the silence of her home, the comforting stillness of the solid stone structure that told her the turmoil of the outside world couldn't reach her here.

Or at least she'd thought it couldn't until she heard the shouting from outside. Shouting always brought back that terrible night when the nightriders had come, and for an awful instant Sarah caught a glimpse of the slaughtered bodies hanging from the tree. But then she recognized the voice, and a new terror gripped her.

"Papa!" Becky cried, recognizing it, too. She dropped her blocks and raced away, back outside, while Sarah laid a hand on her pounding heart and willed herself not panic. This is your *husband,* she told herself sternly. You don't have to be afraid of him!

But she was afraid, so very afraid that her feet dragged as she moved back to the front door that Becky had left hanging open. Outside she could hear the child's squeals of happiness and Hunter's deeper voice as he spoke to her. When she reached the door, she saw them standing out in the yard, the man holding the child in his arms while they laughed and talked and Becky kissed his face again and again.

Sarah's empty arms ached again, wanting to hold them both, wanting to feel the warmth of their joy and their love, wanting to fill the void in her soul. But then she remembered the danger and the terrible agony she almost hadn't survived. How would she bear it if she lost them, too? So she steeled herself against the longing. It was the only way to protect them.

"Where's your Mama?" she heard Hunter ask, and Becky pointed toward the house.

By then Sarah stood in the doorway, her arms and legs leaden with reluctance even while her nerves hummed at the sight of him. This was Hunter, the man who'd given her a life when she'd had none, the man who'd given her baby a father when she'd had none, the man who'd given her a home and who'd shown her passion she'd never dreamed existed. But the passion brought such pain. She couldn't let herself forget, she just couldn't.

"Sarah!" Hunter cried, bounding up the porch steps, then setting Becky down so he could take Sarah in his arms, which he did, those big, strong arms she'd dreamed about even though she'd fought against the memory every waking hour.

She had to close her hands into fists to keep from hugging him back, and when he kissed her, the wonderful taste of him brought tears to her eyes.

"There's no need to cry," he told her, not understanding. "I'm home now and everything will be fine."

Fine? What did that mean? Sarah didn't want to know, which was just as well because he didn't give her time to ask.

"I stopped in town first," he was saying. "I thought you might be there, but Mother said . . . she said you were all right." He cupped her face in his hands and looked into her eyes as if her could see into her soul. "Are you?" he asked softly.

"I'm fine," she assured him, giving him back the word she didn't understand. "We're both fine, aren't we, Becky."

"Fine, fine!" Becky cried, dancing around excitedly and reaching up for Hunter again.

At last Hunter released her, and she found she'd been

holding her breath while he looked at her. His silver eyes were still clouded, as if he didn't quite believe her, but he picked Becky up and let Sarah lead him into the house.

"You're just in time for supper," she told him dutifully, remembering how a wife should act. "Are you hungry?"

"Not really. Mother made me eat when I stopped there."

Of course she had, Sarah thought as they walked through the house and outside to the kitchen. Rebekah knew how to take care of Hunter, too. Feeling oddly detached, as if she were observing the whole scene from outside her own body, Sarah took her family into her kitchen and seated them at the table and served them their supper as if this had been a normal night, as if they were a normal family, as if she was a normal wife.

Becky was much too excited to eat, so Sarah had to keep reprimanding her, and Hunter wasn't hungry, and Sarah couldn't have swallowed a bite if her life had depended on it, so in the end, she put away almost as much food as she had set out in the first place. Hunter stayed in the kitchen with her while she cleaned up.

"I just want to look at you," he said, his silver eyes shining. And he talked, telling her about how much money the cattle had brought, enough to keep them for years, and about the hazards of the trail, stampedes and thunderstorms where lightning danced in huge balls across the backs of the cows and rain-swollen creeks and dried up creeks and cattle half-crazy with thirst.

Somehow Sarah managed to make the appropriate responses to each of his tales, and Becky sat in his lap, listening in rapt silence, her dark blue eyes wide with wonder. When Sarah was finished with the dishes, they moved to the parlor, Sarah's parlor, the one she'd furnished herself from the things they'd ordered new from back East. Nothing was too good for her then, Hunter had said then. How would he feel about her after to-night?

They sat in the parlor while Hunter continued to hold Becky on his lap and tell them what he'd seen as he passed through Indian Territory, the Reservation Indians who looked like ghosts of themselves, reduced to grubbing in the ground and living on inadequate government handouts, their pride gone.

"Nobody paid any attention to the treaty we made at the Little Arkansas," he told her.

"Nobody ever pays any attention to any treaties with the Indians, least of all the Indians," Sarah reminded him bitterly.

Hunter nodded grimly. "The raiding has definitely gotten worse. The Comanches have many more captives now than they did when you were taken, and hundreds of settlers have been killed on the frontier. They say the edge of civilization in Texas is being driven back a little bit everyday, and the Union army won't do a thing about it. They're too busy trying to keep the peace in the cities where they think us Confederates are going to start another rebellion to worry about what's going on with the Indians."

Sarah shuddered at the thought of other innocent people suffering at the hands of the Comanches. "What are they going to do? The Texans, I mean."

"Not much they can do," Hunter replied thoughtfully. "Only thing that would satisfy the Comanche is if every white settler left the state. The next best thing would be to stop settlers from moving any farther west and giving what's left of Texas to the Comanches with a promise no whites would enter it, which is what the Little Arkansas treaty provided, but—"

"—but no Texan is going to give a foot of Texas to a bunch of Indians," Sarah supplied. "And there's no reason they should! They ought to kill every last one of those stinking savages and be done with it!"

Hunter blinked in surprise at her vehemence, but he managed a strained smile. "Did you forget you're married to one of those stinking savages?"

"You're not one of them!" Sarah protested in chagrin. "You're . . ."

"I'm what? *Civilized?*" he demanded, even more bitter than she. "I'm a half-breed, Sarah, and just in case you've forgotten that, let me tell you that the broker who bought my cattle didn't want to believe I owned them. He couldn't believe a breed could be so prosperous. He even hinted I might have stolen them until he heard my name and realized who I was. I'm just lucky my mother was so famous, or I might've had some trouble up in Kansas. As it was, I slept out at the camp instead of trying to get a hotel room in town. I didn't want to take a chance of being kicked out."

Sarah gaped at him, remembering how the clerk was going to throw them out of the hotel in Austin until he found out who Hunter was. "That's awful," she whispered, glancing at her daughter's dark head resting on his shoulder. Would Becky suffer the same prejudice?

Seeing the direction of Sarah's gaze, Hunter looked down, too. "She's asleep," he said.

Sarah knew a moment of panic at the realization they were suddenly alone. "I'll put her to bed," she said in a strangled voice, jumping up to do so.

"I can carry her for you," Hunter said, rising from his chair and cradling the sleeping child in his arms. "I've missed doing this." He caught her eye and smiled provocatively. "I've missed a lot of things."

350

Sarah's heart stopped dead in her chest, but she forced herself to keep on breathing, keep on walking, keep on doing all the normal things she did every night to put her daughter to bed. When the sleepy child had been washed and dressed in her nightdress and tucked into her bed, Sarah knew the moment she had been dreading for over a month had finally come.

Hunter took her arm gently and led her from Becky's bedroom into the twilit hall. The instant the door closed behind them, he took her in his arms.

"I've been wanting to do this all evening," he whispered as his mouth closed over hers.

Her body responded instinctively, leaning into his kiss while her hands slid around his waist to hold him close and her lips opened to his. He felt so good, so strong and solid beneath her hands, and her blood rushed hotly through her veins. For one wonderful moment, she could almost believe he could protect her, that nothing bad would happen to them if she could only stay safe within his arms.

But then she remembered the curse, and she knew this was the most dangerous place she could be. Somehow she found the strength to tear her mouth from his. "I have to talk to you," she gasped, breathless from wanting what she didn't dare to take.

He smiled knowingly. "Fine, let's talk in the bedroom," he said, reaching down and lifting her high against his chest before she could even think to protest.

She wanted to weep, but she refused to succumb, refused to seek refuge in tears. Instead, she laid her head on his shoulder and let him carry her into the room they had shared.

Hunter kicked the door shut behind him, then carried her straight to the neatly made bed and laid her down

351

on it, following her as soon as he'd taken off his shoes.

Fighting the bulk of her skirts and petticoats, Sarah struggled up into a sitting position before Hunter could reach for her again. "We have to *talk!*" she insisted.

He smiled tolerantly even as his fingers worked the buttons of his shirt. "All right," he said affably.

"We can't do this," she told him baldly before she could lose her nerve, then swung her legs to the floor and pushed herself off the bed to create some distance between them.

"What do you mean?" he asked, his smile gone. Then his handsome face creased into a worried frown. "Is something wrong? Some complication from the baby? Mother said you were fine, so naturally, I thought—"

"No . . . yes . . . I mean . . ," Sarah stared at him in helpless confusion for a moment, willing herself to calmness. She wouldn't help anything by getting hysterical. "No, it's not some complication from . . ." She couldn't bring herself to speak of the baby, so she forced herself to go on. "I *am* fine, physically and . . . and mentally, too. I know your mother thought I was crazy but—"

"No one thought you were crazy," he protested, sitting up himself now. "You were just grieving for the baby. We knew that and—"

"I'm *not* crazy," she insisted, gritting her teeth against the agonizing memories. She wouldn't remember, she just wouldn't. "Which is why I know I can never have another child, not ever!"

She glared at him across the bed, daring him to argue, daring him to challenge her, but his expression was still puzzled. "You mean . . . ? Then there *was* some complication," he finally concluded. "Something that makes you think you can't have another baby, but that's all right, Sarah," he assured her, reaching out to her. "We'll

352

take you to a doctor, find out for sure. Maybe there's something that can be done to help you, and if not . . ." He shook his head sadly. "Then we've still got Becky, and if we never have any other children, I—"

"*No!*" she cried in frustration. "You don't understand! I *can* have other children, but *I'm not going to!* I'm never going to watch another baby die, not ever, not as long as I live! So that means I can't . . ." Her voice caught on a sob, but she swallowed it and went on. "I can't ever sleep with you again, Hunter. Do you understand?"

At first he didn't. She could plainly see his determined confusion. Surely, he'd misunderstood. She couldn't mean . . .

And then his silver eyes hardened, and his expression grew grim. "What you mean is that you'll never make love with me again, isn't that it, Sarah?" he demanded coldly.

She'd known he'd be angry, furious even. She'd been ready for screaming and shouting but not this frigid calm. Her mouth suddenly dry, she nodded, backing up a step. "I'm sorry," she tried, holding her hand up as if she would ward him off, although he'd made no move toward her.

"Let me get this straight, you're afraid of having another baby die, so you're not going to make love with me so you can't get pregnant again, and you're sorry."

"Yes!" she cried, terrified by the cold ring of steel in his voice. She could see he was holding his temper only with great difficulty.

"Sarah, this is crazy," he said at last.

"I'm not crazy!" she insisted wildly, backing away, out of his reach so he couldn't hurt her.

"I didn't say *you* were crazy, I said your idea was crazy," he went on doggedly, determined to convince her. He rose from the bed and was coming toward her, a looming shadow in the darkening room.

Frantically, Sarah backed away until she felt the rough stones of the wall behind her, and Hunter just kept coming, closer and closer. She threw her hands up in front of her. "No, don't touch me! Please, Hunter!"

His face was terrible, angry and hurt and baffled as he glared down at her. "What's wrong with you, Sarah?"

"I *told* you! I'm not going to have any more babies! You don't know! You *can't* know what it's like to watch them die time after time! I can't stand it! *I . . . just . . . can't . . . stand . . . it . . . any . . . more!*" she cried, her voice convulsing on sob after sob as the tears poured down her face. The pain was so fierce she doubled over with it, and she would have fallen if Hunter hadn't caught her.

Somehow he got her to the bed and laid her down on it, but she could give him no help. She could only cry now, cry and cry when she thought she was done with crying forever. Where the tears came from she had no idea, but she couldn't stop them, couldn't even slow them, and she certainly couldn't resist when Hunter cradled her in his arms, those strong arms, and absorbed her agonies with his broad chest.

Plainly, he didn't know what to do or say, but there was nothing he *could* do or say. Sarah could have told him that if she could have spoken, but she was crying too hard and when the tears finally stopped because she was simply too exhausted to weep anymore, she couldn't talk either.

Hunter brought a cool cloth and bathed her face, but when he tried to unbutton her dress, Sarah stiffened in alarm, so he settled for pulling off her shoes and dragging the bedclothes down and back up over her.

She lay limp and drained and unable to do anything

except close her eyes and surrender to oblivion. She didn't even hear the door shut when Hunter left.

The sun was high when Sarah woke up. Her eyes were sore and swollen, as if she'd been awake all night, and for a moment she couldn't figure out why. Then she remembered that Hunter was home and, dear God, she'd finally told him.

What had he said? What had he done? Sarah couldn't even remember his reaction, just her own terrible grief and the tears that wouldn't stop. Slowly, carefully, she rolled over but she found the other half of the bed hadn't been slept in all night.

Where was Hunter? Had he left her?

The thought paralyzed her. She'd never considered that possibility, never once. She'd only known she had to tell him, that he'd have to learn to live with her new rules because that was the only way to keep them all safe. But what if he chose not to? What if he simply couldn't? What was to keep him from leaving her? She had nothing to hold him now, not a child — Becky wasn't his and *his* baby was dead — and not her body which she couldn't give him anymore, and certainly not a love she refused to feel. What was left for them?

A brand new terror gripped her, and she bolted from the bed and raced out into the hallway. The house was deathly silent, but the quiet no longer felt comforting as it had yesterday. "Becky!" she called, her voice hoarse from sleep and weeping as she darted across the hall into Becky's room. The child's high-sided bed was rumpled but empty.

Dear heaven, where could she be?

"Becky!" Sarah called, panicked now and running

outside, heedless of her stocking feet, to the kitchen.

She threw open the door and found Hunter and Becky sitting calmly at the table eating breakfast.

"Mama!" Becky cried happily from her highchair.

Hunter stiffened defensively, but Sarah was too relieved to care just yet. Becky was safe; that was all she could think about for a moment. She sagged weakly against the doorframe, suddenly conscious of aches and pains she hadn't noticed before. She felt stiff and sore, as if someone had beaten her, yet she knew Hunter hadn't laid a hand on her except in kindness.

She forced herself to look at him, to try to judge his mood. The eyes that stared back at her were red-rimmed and bloodshot, as if he hadn't slept. She tried in vain to remember if he had looked this tired when he came home yesterday. Oh, please, she didn't want to have done this to him. She didn't want to have hurt him at all.

But she had, she saw at once from the coldness in those weary eyes. For a long moment they simply stared at each other across the kitchen table.

"Mama messy!" Becky crowed from her chair, breaking the spell.

Automatically, Sarah reached up to find her hair had sprung from its neat bun and hung half-up and half-down. Her dress was a mess, too, from having been slept in. Suddenly, she was ashamed, the way she'd felt when Hunter had first seen her in the Comanche camp in her filthy Indian dress.

"Do you want some breakfast?" he asked in a voice that sounded almost normal.

But Sarah couldn't face him another minute, not feeling the shame, the terrible shame. "I . . . I'll get dressed," she muttered and turned and ran back to the house.

A few minutes later, after she had washed and changed and combed her hair and pinned it back up, she made her way slowly, reluctantly back to the kitchen. Hunter still sat at the table, nursing a cup of coffee, but he had lifted Becky out of her chair and she sat on the floor, playing with her toys.

"Mama!" Becky announced just in case Hunter hadn't noticed.

Hunter had poured her a cup of coffee and it sat in front of her place. She edged her way into the chair and lifted the cup gratefully to her lips. The drink was lukewarm and bitter, but Sarah gulped it down, praying for it to restore her somehow.

"Are you hungry?" Hunter asked when she set the empty cup down.

The thought of food revolted Sarah, and she shook her head. She saw the empty plates from Hunter and Becky's breakfast still sitting on the table and thought she should get up and wash them. That was something she could do, something normal that would make it look like everything was all right. She would do that, in a minute, just as soon as she felt better.

"Sarah," Hunter said softly. She heard pain in the sound and other things she didn't want to identify. Longing and lust and maybe even love.

Somehow, she made herself look at him. He was dressed, his hair neatly combed. Anyone would think he was fine unless they looked in his eyes. Sarah thought she might not be able to breathe anymore if she looked at them too long.

"Sarah," he said again when she met his eye. "We can work this out. I understand how you feel. I feel the same way, but we can't . . ."

His voice trailed off as Sarah rose from her chair,

swelling with rage. *"You don't know how I feel!"* she informed him. *"Nobody* knows how I feel!"

She saw Hunter glance at Becky to see if she was paying attention to them, but Sarah no longer cared. Satisfied, he looked back at Sarah. "What I meant was, I lost the baby, too. He was my son, too, Sarah. I can understand—"

"No, you *can't* understand," she insisted slapping the table in frustration. "Nobody can understand. Nobody!"

Hunter was going to argue with her, but something distracted him, some noise from outside. Sarah didn't notice it at first, and when she did, she just wanted to put her head on her arms and weep.

"Sounds like we've got company," Hunter said, rising with noticeable reluctance from the table.

"Company!" Becky echoed, scrambling up and running toward the door.

Just what Sarah needed.

By the time they reached the front porch, they could see who was in the buggy which was pulling up into the ranchyard. It was Rebekah and Mac, and with them, on horseback, rode a soldier in a dusty blue uniform.

Hunter and Becky went to meet them while Sarah remained on the porch and tried to put her ragged emotions into some kind of order so she could face her in-laws.

"We're so sorry to bother you on your first day back," Rebekah was saying as Hunter helped her down from the buggy, "but the sergeant here arrived yesterday just after you left, and his business is urgent. We made him wait until this morning so at least you'd have a quiet evening at home your first night."

She looked up and frowned to see Sarah still on the porch. Of course Rebekah would know something was wrong. She'd know just by seeing Hunter's eyes. Sarah made herself smile, but it felt stiff on her face, and she knew she wasn't going to fool her mother-in-law.

"This is Sergeant Vincent," Mac was saying, introducing him to Hunter. "My son, Hunter Tate, and his wife."

"Pleased to meet you, Sergeant Tate," the soldier was saying as he shook Hunter's hand.

"I'm not a sergeant anymore," Hunter assured him. "Haven't been for at least a year and a half."

The sergeant, a stocky, weathered man in his late thirties, smiled his acknowledgement. "The Army sent me to find you, Mr. Tate. We need your help."

Whatever he needed Hunter's help for, Mac and Rebekah weren't at all pleased, as Sarah could easily see from their grim expressions.

"Won't you come in?" Sarah asked perfunctorily, remembering her duties. "I'll get some coffee for everyone."

A few minutes later, they were all sitting in Sarah's parlor, drinking the remains of the big pot of coffee Hunter had made for breakfast and staring at each other awkwardly.

Rebekah held Becky in her lap and had given her a handkerchief to keep her occupied while the grownups talked. Rebekah didn't look any happier than she had when she first arrived and neither did Mac.

The sergeant hemmed and hawed a bit, but finally he got down to business. "We're going to make another treaty with the Indians," he said, as if this news should please them.

Instead they all groaned.

Doggedly, he hastened on. "This will be the most important treaty ever," he insisted. "Washington is sending the Commissioner of Indian Affairs and Senator Henderson, who is the chairman of the Senate Committee on Indian Affairs. This treaty is supposed to put the Indians on the reservation permanently and stop all the raiding that's been going on since the war." When no one responded, he added, "It's the only way Washington can think of to make peace with them."

"And what does the Army want me to do?" Hunter asked without much enthusiasm.

"Just what you did before, at the Little Arkansas treaty," Sergeant Vincent said. "Interpret, serve as a liaison . . ." He gestured vaguely.

"Show my half-breed face and give the proceedings my blessing?" Hunter suggested contemptuously.

Sergeant Vincent flushed, but to his credit, he didn't back down. "I think that's what they had in mind, yes, but Mr. Tate, that's not why I took this assignment. When I heard what they're planning to do, I figured you might be the only one who could stop them. They're going to give the Comanches a reservation in Indian Territory and tell them they can't hunt below the Red River or above the Washita."

"What?" both Hunter and Mac demanded in unison.

"And they'll get houses and schools and doctors and teachers who'll teach them how to be farmers—"

"The Comanches will never be farmers!" Mac cried.

"And they'll never give up hunting!" Hunter added. "This treaty would cut them off from the best buffalo ranges, the ones in Texas! They won't agree to that!"

"They won't have any choice, not unless somebody explains to these politicians how Indians think and why all this won't work," Sergeant Vincent said. "A treaty like this'll never stick. You know it and I know it and every man who's ever fought Comanches knows it. The government's got some fool idea that if we're nice to the Indians, they'll be nice to us, and we can all live in peace."

Everyone stared at him in open-mouthed amazement.

"Now you see why we need you, Mr. Tate," he said after a moment.

"Who's in charge of all this? Who in the army, I mean?" Hunter asked.

"General Sherman," Sergeant Vincent said.

"William Tecumseh?" Hunter asked in distaste. The Union general who had burned Georgia had no admirers in the South.

"The very same," Sergeant Vincent confirmed. "The President put him in charge of this whole region. He's the one who sent me to find you."

"Sherman? He doesn't even know me," Hunter scoffed.

"He knows about you, though. He didn't like the idea you was a Johnny Reb, but he heard you was at the Little Arkansas and how you tried to convince the army they was making a mistake. He don't like this anymore than I do. He needs some help persuading the politicians, though."

"Sergeant, my son just got back home," Rebekah pointed out. "He was away from his family for over a month. You can't expect him to turn around and head right back to Kansas, can you?"

"No, ma'am, I can't expect him to do anything. All I can do is ask." Sergeant Vincent grinned at Hunter. "I've done that, so now it's up to him."

Sergeant Vincent tactfully returned to town alone so the family could discuss the matter in private. Rebekah didn't think Hunter should go.

"You don't owe the United States government anything!" she pointed out. "They won't even let you vote because you fought for the Confederacy."

Mac disagreed. "We're talking about people's lives here, Rebekah. What about all the settlers who are being slaughtered and taken captive? Don't we owe them a chance to live in peace?"

"But no treaty will let them live in peace," Hunter insisted. "The only thing that can protect them is the Army standing guard, keeping the Comanche on one side of the line and them on the other."

"But the Army *won't* stand guard," Rebekah reminded them. "That's why we've got this trouble in the first place."

"And then there's the problem of the Comanche," Mac said solemnly, looking straight at Hunter. "If they don't get a treaty settlement they can live with, they'll fight, and if they fight, the Army will have to destroy them."

Hunter just stared blankly back at him, but for the first time Sarah felt compelled to speak. "So what?" she demanded. "This country won't be fit to live in until they're all dead! You know that as well as I do! The Army should have killed them off years ago!"

Mac's light brown eyes were kind when he looked at her. "We know how you feel, Sarah, and you have every right to, but —"

"She's right," Rebekah said. "You're foolish if you think you can make deals with Indians. They only know how to raid and kill. No piece of paper will ever change that."

"But they are my people," Hunter reminded them all grimly.

"No!" Rebekah and Sarah cried in unison.

"How can you say that!" Rebekah demanded furiously. "You're a white man! You've lived like a white man your whole life!"

"Not my whole life," he reminded her. "And the whites don't consider me white. I'm a half-breed and I always will be to them. The Comanche have never done me any harm."

"No harm!" Rebekah cried. "Are you forgetting they killed your grandmother and my baby brother and took me captive? And they killed Sarah's family and took her captive, too! Don't you consider that harm?"

"They were only doing what they've done for thousands of years, attacking the people who dared to invade their land," Hunter pointed out reasonably. "Civilized people do exactly the same thing and no one considers them savages for protecting what is rightfully theirs."

"This land was *never* theirs!" Sarah argued. "They don't own anything!"

"Not by the white man's laws, but by their own laws, they own the whole state of Texas and a lot more. Who are we to tell them they can't hunt the buffalo here the way they have for centuries?"

They argued all morning and all through the noon meal which Angelita served them, but they still didn't reach any conclusions. When they'd finished eating, Mac insisted that he and Rebekah should leave so Hunter and Sarah could discuss this between themselves. It was, as he pointed out, Hunter's decision, after all.

Rebekah didn't want to leave, and Sarah supposed it was because she didn't trust Sarah to convince Hunter not to go. Sarah didn't know how she could, either. All she had was her hatred for the Comanches and the hope that her husband would respect her wishes. Considering what she'd told Hunter the night before, she had no hope he would pay any attention to her wishes at all.

When Mac and Rebekah were gone, Sarah put Becky down for her nap and returned to the parlor to find Hunter sitting in his big, overstuffed chair. He glanced at Sarah when she came in, but she couldn't meet his eye. Hastily, she took a seat on the sofa opposite him.

"You don't have to go," she reminded him tentatively. "And . . . we need you here."

He raised his dark eyebrows at this. "To do what?"

Sarah's mouth went dry as she considered the possible answers to that question. Not very long ago, she could have gone over and kissed him, then lured him off to bed. Then he would have known exactly what she wanted him here for. But of course she didn't want him for that anymore, or at least she wasn't going to do that anymore. "Well, there's things to do at the ranch," she tried.

"Not this time of year. Pedro and the other men could handle it all for me just fine for a few more weeks."

Sarah twisted her fingers together nervously, wracking her brain for some other reason why he shouldn't go. She jumped when he rose from his chair and crossed the room to sit beside her. His body so close to hers was like a magnet, drawing her to him, and she almost had to lean away to keep from flinging herself into his arms. Instead, she sat rigidly erect, trembling inside because she knew if he reached for her, she would be helpless to resist.

"Sarah," he said gently, more gently than she deserved and far more gently than she had any right to expect, "we've had some hard times lately. I knew you were upset about losing the baby, but I didn't know how bad it was until last night." Sarah stiffened defensively, but he didn't seem to notice. "I can understand how you feel—I know you don't think I can, but I do just the same. I can understand why you wouldn't want to take another chance. I don't want to go through that again myself, but what you're asking . . . it just isn't possible. How can we live together for the rest of our lives and never . . ."

His voice trailed off, and Sarah knew he must have seen how she was trembling. She'd clamped her hands between her knees to hold herself still, but it wasn't helping. Why couldn't he understand? Didn't he know it was the only way she could protect them? But of course he didn't and he never would. Unable to look at him, she stared doggedly at the far wall, willing him to stop talking about this.

"Sarah," he tried, slipping his arm around her, but she cried out in alarm at his touch, and he drew back instantly. "Sarah, let me help you," he pleaded, but she could only shake her head frantically, praying he wouldn't touch her again.

He sat there for a few moments, helpless and baffled and frustrated. Then finally, he said, "Sarah, I have to go."

She started at that, certain she'd misunderstood, but when she looked at him, she saw the steely determination she knew too well.

"Two years ago, at the Little Arkansas, Kit Carson told me I'd someday have to decide how I felt about my Indian blood, and now I have. Whether I like it or not, the Comanche are my people, and I can't just sit back and let the government do something crazy that will mean death to hundreds of people, Indian and white alike, without at least trying to stop them."

"There's nothing you can do! You know how they are! They won't pay any attention, the government or the Indians either!" Sarah protested.

"I have to try. I won't be able to live with myself if I don't."

Don't leave me! she wanted to cry, but what right did she have to ask when she'd already told him she didn't even want to be a wife to him anymore? "You just got home," she said instead, remembering Rebekah's argument.

"I know, and I don't want to leave you when . . . when there's so much unsettled between us." His gray eyes shone like the sun on still water as he stared at her for a long moment. Then he said, "I want you to go with me, Sarah."

Sheer terror froze the protest in her throat, and she could only stare at him in mute horror as he went on, persuading her.

"It's just what we need," he was saying. "Some time away, alone together, and a change of scenery for you. Mother will keep Becky for us. It could be just like when we were first married, remember?"

Sarah remembered perfectly, except then they'd been going *away* from the Comanches, not toward them. "You want me to go to a *Comanche camp?*" she asked incredulously.

"It won't be a *Comanche* camp. There will be other tribes, too, and the army with hundreds of soldiers. You'll be safer there than you are at home."

Safe? Sarah almost laughed out loud. When had she ever been safe anywhere? "Don't you remember what they did to me?" she demanded. "How can you even *think* I'd ever want to go back to them again?"

"You won't be going *back* to them; you won't be a captive," he argued, so reasonable Sarah wanted to smack him. "You'll be there as my wife, as an honored guest."

Sarah stared at him, her eyes wide with amazement. She still dreamed sometimes she was back with the Indi-

366

ns, a prisoner again, a helpless slave, and sometimes
when she caught a whiff of something spoiled or the
scent of woodsmoke on the night air or the warm smell of
leather, she *was* back there again in that filthy place with
those filthy savages for a heartbeat of terror.

"I won't go!" she told him, shaking her head frantically. "I can't!"

"Sarah, listen," he insisted, taking her hand. His palm
felt hot, which meant her hand must be icy. "I told you, I
have to go, but I don't think I can face it without you. I
need you with me, Sarah. I need my wife beside me.
You're the only one who really understands what I'll be
going through, and I can't do it without you. Don't you
understand? You *have* to go with me."

Sarah felt as if someone were smothering her, as if
something were pressing against her face so she couldn't
get her breath. And then he said the thing she feared
most in all the world.

"Sarah, I love you."

"No!" she cried, jumping up and wrenching her hand
from his. "You don't love me! If you did, you wouldn't
ask me to do this!"

"There's nothing to be afraid of!" he insisted. "I'll be
with you, the army will protect us, and I need you,
Sarah. Surely, you understand. I can't do this alone! If
you care about me at all, you'll—"

"No! No!" Sarah put her hands over her ears, as if she
could shut out the sound of his voice, but he was on his
feet now, facing her, taking her by the shoulders so he
could hold her still.

"You're my *wife*, damnit, and I need you! Can't you
understand that? Don't you love me at all?"

Sarah stared into the face she'd seen above her when
she cried out in passion, the face she'd seen beside her in

367

sleep, the face she'd seen express joy and grief and tenderness and anger, and every emotion in between. But this time she didn't see the face of her husband. This time she saw the high cheek bones, the dusky skin, the raven hair, everything that said he was an Indian. He was her enemy, everything she had feared most in her entire life.

"No! I don't love you!" she screamed in terror. *"I hate you! You're nothing but a dirty, stinking savage!"*

For a heartbeat, he simply stared at her, his eyes terrible, full of pain and fury, then he thrust her away and was gone.

Alone in the room, Sarah covered her face with her hands and slumped to the floor, weary beyond words. Only when she tasted the salt tears did she realize she was crying, but she was too tired to brush them away. All she had strength enough to do was wonder what on earth she had done.

Sarah didn't know how long she had been sitting on the parlor floor when she heard the front door slam shut. Not long, she judged, although she couldn't be perfectly certain. Becky wasn't up from her nap yet, at least, so it couldn't have been long.

Who had slammed the door, though? There was only one other person in the house, and Hunter shouldn't be going anyplace. Feeling detached again, as if she weren't quite in her body, she forced herself to her feet and staggered to the parlor door.

The hall was empty, and their bedroom door hung open. Sarah listened and heard no sound, nothing but the silence of an empty house, a house without Hunter. Then, faintly, through the thick stone walls, she heard the sound of a horse galloping away. Her chest burned as if she'd swallowed lye, and her legs seemed hardly able to bear her weight, but somehow she made it to the front door and threw it open.

She saw the horse and rider growing small in the distance and the plume of dust rising behind them. Hunter had left her.

How long had it been since Sarah had first thought Hunter might leave? Just this morning, although it seemed more like years. She'd wondered then what she would do, and now she knew: she would sit and rock and somehow try to live from one minute to the next and pretend she didn't feel as if she were being ripped in half.

It was all Hunter's fault, she tried to convince herself. He'd forced her to say the words. If he hadn't insisted on loving her and making her love him in return, it never would have happened. They could have gone on like before, pretending everything was fine, living their lives, and Hunter would have grown old before he died. Not like the others.

Life just was too dangerous to take chances like loving. Didn't Hunter know that? Well, she supposed he did now. She'd shown him. She'd made him feel her pain, so now she could never accuse him of not understanding again. He understood, and he'd left her.

Of course, he hadn't left her for good. This was his house, his ranch. He'd be back. He'd just gone off for a while to cool down. People did that when they were angry. Hunter never had, but then she'd never made him quite that angry before either. When he was calm again, he'd come home. That was when she'd have to be afraid, because he might tell her *she* had to leave. Or he might tell her she could stay. Whatever he decided, nothing would ever be the same, and they would never live as husband and wife again. Sarah had settled that when she told him she'd never sleep with him, but she'd sealed it when she told him she didn't love him either. The pain of it was almost unbearable, but Sarah would bear it because the pain of watching Hunter die would be so much worse.

Hours passed, hours during which Becky woke up and wanted to know where her Papa was and Angelita came to prepare supper and asked if Señor Tate would be back to eat and they sat down to the table without him and then sat on the porch and watched the sun set, and for all that time, Sarah told herself she was glad it was settled. If she would never love Hunter, wasn't it better for him to know?

But she didn't feel glad, not a bit, and nothing was better, nothing at all. Hunter didn't come home, not even when it was dark, and Sarah put Becky to bed, ignoring her questions about her father. Then Sarah sat in her bedroom and rocked some more, trying to make sense of it through all the pain.

She didn't love Hunter. She knew she didn't. Hadn't she spent every day of her life since she'd met him trying not to? Especially this last year, since Jewel had warned her about what could happen if she did? Yet she felt as if her heart had been torn from her chest and carried away with him, just as she'd felt when she found her new baby cold and dead beside her the morning after his birth. Just the way she'd felt when Jewel died in her arms. And just the way she'd felt when Pete and P.J. were slaughtered and when her first little girl had taken her last, feverish breath, and . . .

Sarah had been so sure that if she just stopped loving

people, the pain would stop, too, but it hadn't. Oh, God, it had even gotten worse because Hunter wasn't dead, just gone, and she could hardly breathe for the agony of it. Why? Why?

Long hours passed before she could finally accept the truth. Realization came slowly because she resisted it, fighting every traitorous thought until she was too emotionally exhausted to deny it anymore. *She loved Hunter Tate.* The truth was as simple and as terrible as that. She'd tried to prevent it, tried to deny it, tried to convince herself it was possible to share herself with a man as good and kind as he and not love him.

But she'd failed. She'd wanted to keep her heart from him so he wouldn't be cursed like the others and so she wouldn't lose him, too, but by denying him her heart, she'd lost him anyway. And of course the reason she didn't want to lose him was because she really did love him and would always love him, danger or no danger. The irony of it was bitter in her throat.

Perhaps Sarah had been wrong to insist she wasn't crazy. When she thought it through, completely through, she realized she hadn't been behaving rationally at all, not since Jewel died and maybe not even before that. How could she not have known she loved Hunter? How could she not have recognized that her desperate desire to protect him had been born of that love?

And of course, if she'd loved him all this time, he'd somehow managed to survive in spite of it, at least so far. So why was she trying to keep him at arm's length, making them both miserable, when that wasn't helping anything at all, only hurting? None of it made any sense to Sarah, but at least she understood it now. Now, before it was too late.

371

No, she told herself, it wasn't too late, not yet. Hunter wasn't really gone. He'd be back, if not tonight, then tomorrow. She could explain, make him understand about the curse and everything. She could beg him to forgive her. He was good. He'd loved her, and he must love her still, just the way she loved him, and he would take her back, give her another chance. He had to, he simply *had* to.

Sarah was pacing the floor now, planning what she would say, how she would tell him. He wouldn't believe her at first. He might even hate her because of what she'd called him, a dirty, stinking savage, the one thing she'd known would destroy him. But she would convince him somehow. He would have to believe her, if only because it was true. And she would even make love with him. Yes, she would, because she loved him so much she was willing to risk anything. She was willing to risk *everything* if only she could have Hunter back for one more chance.

What time was it? Late, she knew, too late for him to return tonight. She should try to rest, get some sleep so she'd be able to face him in the morning. But as she paced down the length of the room she saw something she'd been too upset to notice before. Or rather she didn't see something—she didn't see Hunter's saddlebags, the ones he'd carried with him on the cattle drive, the ones that he hadn't even had time to unpack when he'd gotten home yesterday. They were gone.

And so was Hunter. And then Sarah knew: he'd gone to Kansas without her.

Chapter Thirteen

Sarah never closed her eyes all night, and by dawn she'd decided what she must do. She couldn't do it alone, and she had no idea who might help her, but she was going to do it nevertheless.

Becky protested when Sarah woke her up and dressed her and packed her clothes before the sun was even over the horizon. By the time Angelita arrived to prepare their breakfast, they had already finished eating, and Sarah was ready to leave.

"Would you ask Pedro to hitch up the wagon, Angelita? Becky and I are going to town."

"So early?" Angelita marveled, but something in Sarah's expression kept her from protesting the odd request. She hurried out to find her husband, and before too long, Sarah and Becky were seated in the wagon, their baggage stowed in the rear.

"I don't know when we'll be back," Sarah told her housekeeper. "I'll send you word when I know."

"But where are you going, Señora?" Angelita asked anxiously, obviously disturbed by Sarah's unusual behavior. "You can leave Becky with me, if you want. You know I will take care of her."

"She'll be staying with her grandparents," Sarah explained. So far, that was the only detail of her plan of which she was certain.

Angelita didn't like even that detail, but before she could question Sarah any further, Sarah slapped the team of horses into motion and started on her journey.

Maybe she was wrong. Maybe Hunter had changed his mind and she'd meet him on the road as he was returning home. The hope kept Sarah going even as she tried to figure out what she would say to Rebekah and Mac. How could she explain without telling them what a fool she'd been? Well, maybe she couldn't. Maybe that was her punishment. Somehow, she didn't care so long as she could get Hunter back.

The long ride into town seemed longer even than usual, especially with Becky whining and asking her questions she couldn't answer the whole ride, but at last the buildings of Main Street came into view. Sarah should have taken her horses and wagon to the livery stable first, but she went straight to Rebekah's house just in case she'd been wrong and Hunter hadn't left yet.

The sound of the wagon pulling up at her gate brought Rebekah out onto the porch. "Sarah!" she called in surprise. "What are you doing here?"

Sarah was already climbing down from the high seat, and by the time she had lifted Becky down, Rebekah had reached them.

"How's my girl this morning?" Rebekah asked her namesake, reaching for the child who went to her eagerly.

"Fine," Becky answered by rote, although her pout contradicted her words.

Rebekah gave Sarah a quizzical look, and Sarah said, "Can we go inside? I . . . Hunter's not still here, is he?"

"Why no, he and Sergeant Vincent left this morning

at first light. He didn't say anything about you coming here to stay, though, but of course, it's perfectly all right," she assured Sarah hastily.

"No, that's not . . . I mean, can't we talk about this inside?" Sarah asked, feeling the urgency now that Rebekah had confirmed her fears.

"Oh, I'm sorry, yes, come in." Still puzzled, Rebekah carried Becky and led Sarah into the house. "Can I get you something? Some coffee? It's cool this morning and—"

"No, nothing, I just . . . I have to go after Hunter," she announced baldly the instant the front door slammed shut behind them.

"Go after Hunter?" Rebekah echoed incredulously. "What on earth do you mean?"

"Just that. He asked me to go with him to the meeting, but I wouldn't do it. We had a terrible fight and I . . . Oh, Mother MacDougal, I just have to go!" The tears she'd been fighting ever since she'd realized Hunter had really left her started now, and Rebekah slipped her free arm around her.

"Come into the parlor and sit down and tell me everything," Rebekah said, "and then we'll decide what to do."

Becky was still pouting and wanted to cling to Rebekah, but eventually she got the child settled with some toys to keep her occupied. By then Sarah had regained her composure and began her tale. The first part of the story, about how she and Hunter had gotten married and Sarah had known she shouldn't ever love him, was fairly easy to tell. When she got to the part where Jewel died and Sarah had decided it was too dangerous for her to love Hunter, the telling got harder. By the time she got to the part where her baby died, both women were openly weeping.

"I tried not to love that baby!" Sarah insisted between sobs. "I wouldn't let myself because I knew what would happen! I couldn't help it, though, and when he died, it hurt so much that I thought I'd lose my mind!"

"I thought you had," Rebekah told her, dabbing at her eyes.

"So I couldn't go through that again, could I?" Sarah argued. "I couldn't stand it anymore, so when Hunter got home the other night, I had to tell him before . . . I had to tell him I couldn't have anymore babies!"

Rebekah gaped at her. "You told him that? But how did you propose to . . . Oh, no!" she cried when she realized the truth. "You didn't tell him you wouldn't sleep with him anymore, did you?"

Sarah wanted to cover her face in shame, but she nodded, forcing herself to face her mother-in-law's scorn. But Rebekah didn't scorn her. Instead she shook her head in despair. "No wonder, no wonder," she murmured. "What did he say? What did he *do?*"

"Nothing," Sarah said, forcing the shameful words past her constricted throat. "At least, I don't remember him doing anything. I was pretty upset and he . . . he just left me alone for the rest of the night. I didn't see him until the next morning and then . . . then you came with that soldier and . . ."

Sarah would rather have died than tell Rebekah the rest of it, but Rebekah was waiting, her cheeks wet with tears, her eyes full of Hunter's pain, and Sarah couldn't hope to make any of it right until she'd told it all.

"He wanted to go with that soldier, you know he did," Sarah reminded her defensively. "I couldn't've stopped him, no matter what, but he . . . he asked me to go with him."

"What?"

376

"He said he needed me," Sarah explained anxiously. "He said he had to go, but he couldn't do it without me. He said he loved me, and . . . and that if I loved him, I'd go with him."

Rebekah's face was stony. "And of course you don't love him, do you?"

"I *said* I didn't! I told him I didn't, but it isn't true, Mother MacDougal! I tried and tried not to love him, but I couldn't help it, I couldn't stop it! But I *told* him I didn't and then I . . . I called him . . . I called him a terrible, terrible thing and—"

"*What did you call him?*" Rebekah snapped, furious now.

Now Sarah really did want to die, and tears of shame coursed down her face. "I called him a . . . a dirty, stinking savage."

"My God!"

"I *know!*" Sarah wailed in anguish. "I know that's the one thing that could hurt him! I didn't *want* to hurt him, but I couldn't help it! He wanted me to go to *them,* to the Comanches! And I was so scared and I couldn't think about anything but that and I couldn't stand the thought of it and—"

"So you called him a dirty, stinking savage and sent him on his way alone," Rebekah said coldly. "So why are you here? You should be happy."

How could she explain? And why should Rebekah even want to understand how Sarah felt? Hunter was her son, after all, and she'd only see his part.

Sarah took a deep breath and tried to clear the tears out of her throat. "I told you, I tried not to love Hunter, but it didn't work. I . . . I love him anyway, and I can't . . . I can't let him go away thinking that I . . . after what I said . . . He's just too hurt. How could he ever forgive me after that? I have to go after him. I have to tell him the truth!"

Rebekah didn't answer for a long time, so long that Sarah became afraid. Finally, she said, "And what happens then? You tell him you love him and you expect everything to be all right? Sarah, you told him you'd never sleep with him again!"

Sarah felt the hot rush of tears again, but she choked them back. "I know, but I . . . I realize now I was wrong. I thought if I didn't have anymore babies, I would be safe, but I'll never be safe, not ever, because even when you don't want to love somebody, you can't always stop yourself. I tried not to love the baby that died and I tried not to love Hunter, but it happened anyway. I was so afraid before, and now . . ."

"And do you really believe that if you love Hunter he'll be cursed or whatever it is you said? That your love will kill him?"

"I don't know! I don't know anything anymore, but I can't stop loving him, no matter what, so the least I can do is make him happy or try to. And I will, Mother Mac-Dougal, I swear it! If I can get him back, I . . . I don't think I'll ever be scared of anything else again."

At first Sarah was afraid she hadn't convinced her mother-in-law, but then Rebekah smiled. Ever so slowly, her lips curved up and her eyes brightened. She dabbed away the last of her own tears. "Well, then, I suppose we ought to figure out a way for you to go after Hunter. Do you have any ideas?"

Sarah shook her head miserably. "But I'll walk if I have to! I just have to go after him!"

"I don't think you'll have to walk," Rebekah said, rising from her chair. "Let me go to the store and talk to Mac. You wait here. We'll figure something out."

Sarah couldn't imagine what they'd figure out, and every second that passed took Hunter farther and farther away from her. The waiting was agony, but finally she heard the front door open and Rebekah and Mac came in.

Squealing with delight, Becky ran to her grandfather, who scooped her up and greeted her with a big hug.

"Have you come for a visit?" he asked.

She nodded happily. "Visit you!"

"Well, maybe not me," he replied, lifting his gaze to where Sarah stood, waiting anxiously. "You'll stay with your grandmother. I think your mama and I are going on a trip."

"It's the only sensible thing to do," Mac argued a few minutes later when they were all seated in the parlor, Becky firmly ensconced in his lap. "I used to be quite a traveler, you know. Made my living as a freighter in the old days and then as a Comanchero, so I guess I can get one woman from here to Kansas without too much difficulty."

Sarah hadn't know what to expect, but this certainly wasn't it. "I can't ask you to—"

"You *didn't* ask me," Mac reminded her. "I'm offering, and only someone very rude and ungrateful would turn me down. I'm soon going to be an old man, Sarah, and this might be my last chance for an adventure like this. You wouldn't cheat me out of it, would you?"

Sarah didn't feel the least bit ungrateful, but she thought she might cry again if she wasn't careful, so she just shook her head.

"Cousin Andrew's boys can mind the store," Rebekah was saying. "They're always looking for an excuse to take over anyway. And Becky and I will have a wonderful time together, won't we, sweetheart?"

Becky nodded uncertainly, sensing their tension but not yet able to decide how it affected her.

"We'll leave first thing tomorrow morning," Mac said. "We can stop at the ranch and pick up your things, Sarah, and then—"

"I've already got my things with me," Sarah told him. "But can't we leave right away? If we wait until tomorrow, they'll already have a full day's head start on us. We'll never catch up with them."

"We'll never catch them up anyway," Mac pointed out. "They're on horseback, and we'll be in a wagon. Even if we'd left at the same time, they'd beat us by several days, and before we can leave, we've got to pack the wagon with some supplies and put a canvas cover on it. But don't worry. They were going to Fort Larned first, then riding out to the council grounds. We'll go directly to the council grounds and meet them there."

The thought of riding right up to thousands of Indians made Sarah tremble in terror. And she didn't want her first meeting with Hunter to be in the middle of a Comanche encampment, but then she realized how silly she was being. Her first meeting with Hunter *had* been in a Comanche encampment. Although the prospect of being surrounded by Indians again turned her blood cold, her fear of losing her husband was much greater. If she could survive them both, perhaps there was a chance the rest of her life might be worth living.

The first night, after Sarah and Mac had made camp and eaten their supper, they sat by the dying fire for a few minutes, waiting until it was time to go to bed.

Sarah looked at her father-in-law across the flickering flames and tried to picture him as he must have looked twenty years ago, his hair flame red instead of faded orange and streaked with gray, his face unlined, his body young and vigorous. He'd been brave then, too. He'd stolen Rebekah Tate right out of a Comanche camp. No wonder she'd fallen in love with him. Sarah'd had a man like that, and she'd driven him away.

"Mac?"

Mac looked up and smiled. "Yes?"

"I . . . I don't know how to thank you for doing this," Sarah tried, wishing she were eloquent enough to say what was really in her heart.

"I should be thanking you," he said. "I was getting a little set in my ways, keeping the store and all. I'd almost forgotten what it's like to ride all day and sleep under the open sky." He took a deep breath of the crisp night air. "Makes me feel young again."

Sarah wasn't fooled. She'd seen how stiff his bad leg had been when they'd finally stopped for the night, the leg some Mexican soldier had filled with lead years ago, during the Mexican war. This wasn't the first time he'd done something nice for her, either. "I . . . I never thanked you for . . . for what you offered to do for me before."

"What was that?" He really didn't know.

"For offering to teach me to . . . the book, remember?"

He nodded solemnly. "I remember."

"I took it off your desk," she admitted.

"I know. I said you could."

Sarah twisted her hands in her lap, embarrassed but knowing she shouldn't be. Sean MacDougal knew almost everything else about her. Why shouldn't he know this, too? "I lied to you when I said I could read," she said, not quite able to look him in the face.

"I know you did," he replied gently.

Sarah looked up in surprise. "You did?" She'd thought she'd fooled him.

He nodded again, waiting.

"I thought you wouldn't like me if you knew," she explained.

"Why would you think that?"

How could she explain that people had always despised her because she was poor and ignorant? "I don't know," she lied.

"Sarah, you were the woman Hunter chose as his wife. That was all we needed to know about you."

Sarah bit her lip, working up her courage. "I'd really like to learn how to read," she said finally.

"My offer still holds," he said.

Sarah had to blink at the sting of tears. Why did everything make her want to cry lately?

Mac smiled. "Too bad you didn't bring the reader with you. We'll have lots of time on this trip to—"

"I did bring it," Sarah told him eagerly. "I don't know why, but when I was packing, I saw it and—"

"Well, why don't you get it out," Mac suggested. "We can start tonight, if you're not too tired."

Sarah wasn't tired at all anymore.

In spite of her reading lessons to help pass the time, the journey seemed endless. Sarah missed Becky dreadfully, and she missed Hunter, too, although she couldn't figure out why, since he'd just been gone for over a month and she hadn't missed him at all then.

In Austin, Mac found some freighters traveling

through Indian territory to accompany them for security, since lone travelers were no safer now than they'd been when Hunter and Sarah had made the trip to Texas two years earlier. Hearing them shouting to their mules each morning reminded Sarah painfully of traveling with Hunter during what had been their honeymoon and made her ache not only for him but for that brief time when they'd been happy together. Would they ever know such a time again?

The first Indians Sarah saw approached the freighter's camp one evening after the train had entered Indian Territory. Her first reaction was terror to see the blanketed figures riding up to the circle of wagons, and she would have run to her wagon to hide had Mac not held her where she was.

"You don't have to be afraid," he whispered to her as his fingers clasped her shoulders firmly to keep her from fleeing.

Indeed, when the Indians rode into the light from the freighter's fires, Sarah saw that what Hunter had observed was true. These weren't the arrogant masters of the plains who had slaughtered Sarah's family and taken her captive. These were ragged scarecrow Indians, dressed in mismatched government issue calico and wrapped in moth-eaten government issue blankets so thin a white man wouldn't have used them for saddle blankets.

Mac and the freighters communicated with them in sign language and broken Comanche. Sarah remembered enough of the language to know they were begging for food. Their children were crying with hunger, they said, and the first snows hadn't even fallen yet. The beef the agents issued was never enough to feed their families and was usually rotten and infested with maggots. Their starved faces offered silent proof of their claims, and in spite of herself, Sarah felt pity for them.

The freighters offered them a bag of flour and sent them away. Then they rounded up their horses and mules and penned them within the circle of the wagons for the night.

"They'll come back and steal the animals if we don't," one of the freighters explained. Starving or not, Comanches were still expert horse thieves.

Sarah slept little that night, disturbed by dreams of Indians attacking and carrying her away while Hunter tried to get to her and failed. In the days that followed, she saw more Indians coming to beg, and her wagon train passed their reservation homes, squalid cabins around which ragged children with bloated bellies played.

"How can the government expect the wild tribes to come in when they see how the reservation Indians live?" Mac remarked as they passed yet another Indian "town."

"Hunter was right, they'll never give up without a fight, not while there's still buffalo on the plains, free for the taking," Sarah said.

"That's one thing the Indians are going to be mad about when they come to this meeting; the white hunters who are killing off the buffalo. They'll never agree to limit their own hunting to above the Red River, and they'll want the whites to stop hunting in Texas. They don't know that's the whole plan, to let the white hunters kill off the buffalo and starve the Indians into submission."

"They'll never be able to kill off the buffalo," Sarah scoffed. "It's impossible! Everybody knows that."

Mac's face was solemn. "The northern herds are practically gone already. It's just a matter of time now, Sarah, before the southern herds meet the same fate."

Sarah couldn't even imagine such a thing. The buffalo had always been a part of life in the West. Millions of them roamed the plains, providing food and clothing and shelter to generations of Indians. If all those years of hunting hadn't harmed the herds, how had the whites been able to in the short time they'd been here? But if Mac's prediction were true, then it really would be a mercy to persuade the Indians to come into the reservation now instead of waiting until they were starved out and hundreds of white settlers had been killed by their raiding.

Yes, she concluded, Hunter was right to go to the negotiations, to make his voice heard and perhaps convince those in power that they were about to make a terrible mistake. If it wasn't already too late.

They smelled and heard the treaty encampment long before they reached it. Their escorting freighters had turned off a few days earlier, but they were no longer necessary. It seemed every Indian alive — at least all those who had successfully avoided the reservation thus far — was moving toward Medicine Lodge Creek, where Indian councils had been held forever. None of these Indians were interested in attacking a lone wagon of whites when the government was going to be doling out gifts to those who hadn't caused any them any trouble lately.

And these Indians were different than the ones Sarah had seen on the reservation. These were the wild, bold savages feared by every white settler, and they'd come prepared to impress the white negotiators with their power and might.

Smoke from their camps rose like fog in the clear, blue

sky, and the odors of cooking and animals and massed humanity wafted across the prairie along with the rumble and clank of the heavy military wagons carrying the trade goods and the huge guns the army had brought to do their own impressing.

When at last Sarah and Mac's wagon topped a rise and the entire scene came into view, they were both completely awed. They were also terrified, because they saw that the Indian warriors, thousands of them, were massing for battle at one end of the huge open field.

The spectacle took Sarah's breath. Warriors of every tribe present had painted their faces and their bodies and their horses in bold hues of white and black and blue and vermilion. On their heads were warbonnets, some made of feathers, others from buffalo horns. Multicolored streamers trailed from their long black hair and decorated the manes and tails of the fierce war ponies. Shields and lances hung with trailing scalps and other relics of battles fought and won glinted in the brilliant sunlight.

At the other end of the field, the soldiers stood in ranks, backing the civilians — the government officials and their minions — who were lined up in front as if they didn't know they were about to be devoured by the most fearsome killing machine in the world. Hunter was down there, she knew he was. He was one of them who was waiting to die.

With a scream that froze Sarah's blood in her veins, the Indians attacked, charging forward at breakneck speed, a wedge that would cut through the army's lines like a scythe.

"*No!*" she shrieked, jumping to her feet, but the roar of the attack swallowed her protest, and Mac held her fast so she could only watch.

But just when she thought it was too late, the huge wedge miraculously reformed itself, somehow becoming a giant wheel made of five concentric circles of savage riders who raced each other round and round yet somehow managed to move forward, too, because the wheel was rolling across the prairie, straight toward the white enemy who still stood fast, unmoved by the spectacle.

The noise filled Sarah's head, pounding and pounding, and the dust cloud seemed to envelop her, snuffing out the air and filling her lungs so that she couldn't get her breath. They were going to be killed. They would all be killed, butchered and slaughtered, their hair ripped from their scalps to hang in some Indian's lodge, their fly-blown, mutilated bodies left to rot in the blazing sunlight.

The curse had struck with a vengeance, and Sarah would have to watch Hunter being killed, right before her very eyes!

Terror clogged her throat, and she couldn't breathe, couldn't breathe, and then it happened. The giant wheel stopped before the row of commissioners, a monster that had finally reached its prey, and the circle opened, like huge jaws spreading wide, closer and closer until they closed on the commissioners and their companions and swallowed them up.

"Hunter!" Sarah screamed as the beast devoured him. Then it swallowed her, too, and she fell into the blackness of its maw.

Sarah came slowly up out of the blackness, vaguely aware of the urgent voices around her but not caring much. Everyone seemed upset about something, but she couldn't imagine what, and she felt mildly annoyed that they were disturbing her with their ruckus.

"Who is she?"

"What happened?"

"Where's Mr. Tate?"

"Here he comes!"

The voices were muffled, as if she were insulated from them somehow, and she felt insulated, as if she were in some kind of cocoon, a dark safe place where nothing bad could reach her.

"Mac, what's going on? What are you doing here?" she heard someone shout, someone familiar, someone dear.

More voices, more talking, and Sarah just wanted to sleep, but then the familiar voice demanded, "Where is she?" and suddenly sunlight flooded her cocoon and stabbed her still-closed eyes.

"Sarah!" the dear voice called to her, pulling her completely out of the darkness.

Struggling, she lifted her weighted eyelids and saw that she was in the wagon, lying on the bed Mac had made for her there beneath the canvass wagon cover. Sunlight poured through the opening in the back through which someone had just stepped, and that someone stood over her.

At first he was just a dark shape silhouetted against the canvass, but then she blinked and his face came clear.

"Hunter?" she asked, not really believing her eyes.

"Sarah," he breathed, dropping to his knees on the pallet beside her. "My God, what on earth are you doing here?"

Was he angry? She couldn't tell, and his silver eyes revealed nothing. And she still couldn't believe he was here. Then she remembered why.

"The Indians!" she cried in renewed alarm. "They had you! I saw it!"

But Hunter didn't seem alarmed at all. "They were pretty frightening, weren't they?" he said grimly. "Mac said that's why you fainted. Even the commissioners were scared, I can tell you that, and some of those reporters probably wet their pants, but that was the whole idea. The army brought their guns and their troops to let the Indians know they meant business, and the Indians wanted to make the point that they're a force to be reckoned with, too, not some poor helpless creatures who need the government to take care of them."

"Didn't they kill anybody?" Sarah asked in amazement, remembering the war paint and the insane yells.

"No," Hunter assured her bitterly. "It was all for show. I'm afraid this whole thing is all for show, too. I've been trying to talk some sense into the commissioners, but most of them aren't the least bit interested in sense. General Sherman and the other army men agree with me, but there's nothing they can do. The only hope now is to get the Indians to listen to reason. But none of that matters right now, Sarah. Right now, I just want to know what the hell you're doing here."

This wasn't the way it was supposed to happen. Sarah wasn't supposed to be lying on her back after suffering a case of the vapors with her brains still scrambled. She'd made up a speech on the long trip and practiced it time and again so she was sure the words were right and Hunter would understand why she'd done what she'd done and know she was sorry and forgive her. But at the moment she couldn't remember one word of it, not one single word, except for the very last part.

She started crying because she was so stupid and Hunter would never understand now and so he'd never forgive her, but she had to say something, so she said the only thing she remembered.

"I love you!"

Hunter blinked in surprise, as if he hadn't understood her. "What?"

Maybe he hadn't heard her, so she said it louder. "I love you, Hunter! I didn't mean it, those things I said! I was just so scared and afraid you'd die and it hurt so much and I just wanted it to stop, but I didn't know it would hurt even more if I lost you and I never thought you'd leave and I couldn't wait until you came back and—"

"Whoa!" he said, stopping her by laying his fingers gently over her lips. "Slow down so I can make some sense of this."

Sarah didn't think she could make sense, so she grabbed his hand and kissed it the way he'd kissed hers so long ago. "I love you, Hunter, I really do!" she insisted, desperate to make him believe her.

He didn't look as if he believed her, but before Sarah could say anything else, he said, "I can see we've got a lot of talking to do, but we can't do it now. Everyone is waiting to find out if my wife is all right, and if you are, they'll be wanting to meet you."

"Everyone?" she echoed in alarm.

"The commissioners, the generals, the reporters—"

"Oh, no!" she cried in dismay.

"Oh, yes. You caused quite a stir when you fainted, especially when Mac told somebody you were my wife and to send for me. The opening ceremonies should be just about over, and the chiefs will be lining up for the gifts, so if you're feeling up to it, I should present you to the commissioners."

Sarah couldn't tell if he was pleased by the prospect or annoyed. The last thing she wanted to do was meet a bunch of strangers, especially with nothing settled be-

390

tween her and Hunter, but she certainly didn't want to annoy Hunter by refusing, either.

"I . . . could I get cleaned up first?" she asked.

"I'll get you some water," Hunter replied, rising to his feet. She still held his hand, and when he withdrew it, Sarah felt a sense of loss. "Take all the time you need," he added before he ducked out through the flap in the canvass and jumped down from the wagon. His voice held not a trace of warmth, and Sarah began to wonder if there was any hope at all for them.

But the least she could do was not embarrass him in front of the commissioners, so she quickly made use of the bucket of water Mac handed in to her. When she felt more presentable, she let Hunter lift her out of the wagon. His touch was impersonal, his expression guarded as he took her in his arms, and Sarah realized he hadn't even kissed her yet.

Mac was standing nearby. "How do you feel?" he asked, taking her arm solicitously.

"Fine," she lied. Her stomach felt as if it were full of angry butterflies and every nerve in her body tingled with apprehension.

"You look a little pale," Mac said. "If you'd rather wait until later—"

"No, I . . . . I want to get it over with," Sarah insisted. So Hunter and I can go someplace alone and talk, she might have added if they'd been alone right now. Instead she offered Hunter a tentative smile which he didn't return, and let him take her other arm and lead her toward a brush-covered arbor, just like the one she remembered from two years earlier, where about a dozen middle-aged men in suits waited.

Now that she noticed, Hunter wore his suit, too, and seeing men dressed so formally for a meeting out in the middle of nowhere was slightly disconcerting. Putting on a show was what Hunter had called it, and she supposed he was right.

"Gentlemen," Hunter said as they approached, using a formal tone of voice she's seldom heard. "Allow me to present my wife and my stepfather, Sean MacDougal."

The men instantly came to attention, and one of them, obviously the leader, stepped forward to greet them.

"Mrs. Tate, Mr. MacDougal, it's truly an honor to meet you," he said, bowing slightly to Sarah and shaking Mac's hand.

"This is Mr. Taylor, Sarah," Hunter said. "He's the Commissioner of Indian Affairs."

Sarah had no idea what a Commission of Indian Affairs did, but she guessed it must be very important.

"Pleased to met you," she murmured.

"We're so happy to see you've recovered from your . . . uh, little indisposition. The redmen can indeed be a formidable sight in all their splendor, particularly when they are on horseback. I don't believe I've ever seen quite such a spectacular display as the one to which we were treated this afternoon. I can't say I blame you for being frightened. Only your husband's and the other scouts' assurances prevented us from running for our very lives, I assure you. We were convinced our red brothers had determined to use this opportunity to ensure no one from the United States government ever had the temerity to meet with them again."

He chuckled at his own foolishness, and Sarah blinked, trying to determine how she should reply to this amazing speech. Fortunately, no reply was expected, because another of the gentlemen was presenting himself for introduction.

"This is Mr. Tappan," Hunter told them.

"So pleased to meet you, Mrs. Tate," Tappan assured her, bowing also. "As Mr. Taylor said, we are all relieved to see you are over your fright, although I daresay I may never be."

Indeed, he still looked as if he might faint himself. Sarah managed a smile and a murmur of acknowledgement and when he turned to Mac, Sarah turned to the next gentleman.

"Mr. Sanborn," Hunter said.

Stocky and somewhat owlish, Mr. Sanborn welcomed her profusely. "I'm sure I speak for everyone when I say how pleased we are to have a representative of the fairer sex among us," he concluded after going on at length. "Perhaps yours will be a calming influence in this time of . . . uh, disagreement." He gave Hunter a meaningful glance, and Sarah wondered if he expected her to straighten Hunter out.

A fourth man came forward. He'd been hanging back, waiting for Mr. Sanborn to finish his lengthy greeting, and now Hunter gestured to him. "Senator Henderson," he said.

If Sarah didn't know what a Commission of Indian Affairs was, she did know what a senator was and felt the color coming to her cheeks as he sketched her a bow. "Very pleased to meet you, Mrs. Tate," he said simply.

"The Senator is the Chairman of the Senate Committee on Indian Affairs," Hunter explained.

"We're very glad to have your husband advising us, ma'am," the senator said, and Sarah believed he meant it. Of all these government appointees, he was the only one who seemed capable of really considering the problems involved.

The other men in suits were secretaries and assistants and a few reporters who wanted to ask Sarah why she'd come.

"To be with my husband," Sarah replied, not knowing what else to say.

Hunter's fingers tightened on her arm, but before she could even look at him to judge his reaction, another reporter was asking her another question. "Aren't you afraid to be around so many savages, Mrs. Tate?"

Afraid? Sarah marveled that the word hardly covered her terror, but she said, "Everybody who's lived on the frontier is afraid of Indians. It's only natural when you know what they can do. But I'm not worried, if that's what you're asking."

The reporters scribbled down her words as if they were profound pronouncements, and before someone could ask her another question, Hunter drew her away.

"Just a few more introductions," he whispered to her as they turned to see several soldiers approaching. No, not soldiers, Sarah mentally corrected. Officers, and high ranking officers, too. Her brief experience as a sergeant's wife had educated her in such things, so she wasn't at all surprised when Hunter presented her and Mac to Generals Harney, Terry and Augur and to the infamous General Sherman.

Perfect gentlemen, they greeted her properly and didn't bother with the kind of flowery speeches the bureaucrats had felt compelled to make.

Finally, when Sarah had met them all, Hunter said, "If you will excuse us, gentlemen, I'd like to get my wife settled in my tent. She's very tired."

"Of course, of course," they all murmured and one of them told her to be sure and join them for supper that evening.

Mac was deep in conversation with Senator Henderson, so Hunter hustled Sarah away, leading her toward the small tent city the soldiers had erected.

Hunter didn't say a word to her until they had reached one of the tents that looked just like all the others and just like the tent Sarah had used when she'd been ransomed two years ago. Hunter pulled up the flap and gestured for her to go inside.

Ducking beneath the flap, Sarah entered the tent. Immediately, she knew it was Hunter's from the sight of his clothes hanging from the center pole and his belongings neatly stacked in the corner. She turned to face him as he entered behind her, dropping the flap into place to close out the rest of the world.

Suddenly, Sarah was afraid again, almost as afraid as she had been when she'd thought the Indians were attacking. Her heart lodged somewhere in her throat, and she couldn't seem to get her breath.

"Now, Sarah, tell me again why you came here," Hunter said, crossing his arms over his chest in silent challenge.

Sarah stared at him for a long moment, studying his face for some clue as to what he was feeling, but he offered none. His silver eyes were like two mirrors reflecting back only her own image, and his firm lips were straight and expressionless.

"I . . . I lied to you before, when you left," Sarah began, forcing the words past the tightness in her throat. This was part of the speech she'd memorized, although it wasn't the beginning. It would have to do, though, since it was all she remembered. "I said that I didn't love you, and that was a mean thing to say, I know, but I was so afraid."

She gestured helplessly, her eyes already filling with

395

tears, but Hunter seemed unmoved.

"What were you afraid of, Sarah?"

So many things, she didn't know where to start to tell him, but she said, "Of losing you." Seeing he didn't understand, she hastened to explain. "It started right off, when we first got married. I'd lost everything I ever had, everyone I'd ever loved — my parents and my family and my husband and my babies and my home, everything. I started to wonder if it was me, if I was going to lose everyone I ever loved, and then Jewel said —"

"*Jewel?*" he echoed incredulously.

"Yes, she told me that everyone she'd ever loved had died or been lost, that it was a curse some people had, and then she died, and I thought I must be cursed, too, because I'd only just started to love *her* and —"

"Sarah, that's crazy!"

"I *know* it's crazy, but that's what I thought, so I decided I wouldn't love you, *couldn't* love you because I might kill you, too!"

His face seemed to harden, as if he were steeling himself for something terrible. "I see," he said, but Sarah knew he didn't see at all.

Sarah swallowed down hard and continued. "It was hard not to love you, Hunter, because you were so good to me and Becky. I was starting to think maybe it would be all right, though, especially when we moved out to the farm. I didn't have to worry about your mother finding out about me or —"

"Wait a minute," he interrupted. "What could my mother find out about you?"

"That I'm not a fit wife for you," she told him impatiently.

"What on earth are you talking about?" he demanded.

"Because I'm poor and ignorant!" she exclaimed. "Be-

396

cause I never lived in a house with a wooden floor before I married you. Because I couldn't even read!"

He seemed surprised at this. "What does that have to do with anything?" he asked as if he really didn't know.

But Sarah didn't want to go into all that. "I couldn't let your mother find out, but I didn't have to pretend with Jewel. She didn't care whether I could read or not or anything else. And then when Jewel . . ."

She didn't have to explain. She could see her own pain reflected in Hunter's eyes.

"So then I decided it was too dangerous to love *anyone,* and when I found out about the new baby, I knew I couldn't love him either. I tried not to. I wouldn't even think about a name for him because I knew there was something wrong, even before he was born, and then when he died . . ." Her voice broke on a sob, and only then did she realize tears were streaming down her face.

At last, Hunter took her in his arms and held her to him, smothering her sobs against his chest as they both relived the grief of losing their child. After a while, Hunter drew her to the cot and sat down beside her, his arms still around her while she wept out the last of her pain.

"That's why . . . that's why I couldn't stand the thought of . . . of having another baby," she managed when she could speak again. "But now I . . . I know that's crazy." She looked up at him, praying he could see the love in her eyes. "It's all so crazy! Hunter, I didn't mean it when I said I'd never make love with you again. I was still grieving for the baby, but now I . . . now I know we can't live like that. I don't want to lose you, too, Hunter. I want to be a wife to you again!"

He looked so sad, Sarah wanted to cry all over again because she knew he didn't believe her. "All right," he said quietly, and reached up to brush a stray lock of hair from her damp forehead.

"Hunter, don't you understand?" she asked desperately. "I love you!"

"Yes, I understand," he said, but she knew he didn't, not if he was still so sad.

How could she convince him? What could she do? And then she knew. Tentatively, she reached up and put her arms around his neck. He stiffened slightly in surprise — she'd never been the aggressor before — but she didn't hesitate. Instead, she pressed her lips to his. He didn't respond, so she pulled him closer, pressing her breasts provocatively against him and opening her mouth beneath his.

She knew the moment he surrendered. He groaned, deep in his throat, and his arms came around her, crushing her to him. His tongue swept her mouth, as if he'd been starving for her and couldn't get enough.

Sarah felt her own blood leap, and almost forgotten responses began to spark along her nerve endings. Yes, yes, she thought as his hand found her breast through the thick layers of her clothing. Her nipple hardened instantly, and her body dewed in anticipation.

In the next few minutes, they tore off their clothes in a frenzy of wanting until they lay naked on the narrow cot. There was no time for touching or tasting or teasing. Old hungers, too long denied, roared to life, and they devoured each other with kisses, legs and arms tangling in a desperate dance only they knew.

Gasping with need, Sarah found the strong shaft of his manhood and guided him to her, moaning as she filled herself with him. Hunter moaned, too, with pleasure and desire, as he stroked her and stroked her, plunging in and withdrawing so he could plunge again.

Sarah had forgotten how it could be, how wonderful love could be, and the blissful abandon of possession and possessing. While passion raged, she clung to him with hands and legs, holding him to her as if she would take all of him into herself so they could never be parted again.

But before she was ready, long before she was ready for it to be over, her body betrayed her, convulsing in the ecstasy of release that pushed Hunter over the edge so that they rode out the last fiery cataclysm together.

When it was over, long after the last aftershocks had faded and nothing was left except the golden glow of fulfillment, they lay together, basking in that glow. Or at least Sarah was basking. She wasn't sure what Hunter was feeling. He moved slightly, easing most of his weight from her but unable to move far because the cot was too narrow.

So they were close, as close as two people could be unless they were one, and Sarah could feel his every breath, every heartbeat.

Then why did he seem so very far away?

Before she could figure it out, Hunter was levering himself off the cot.

"Hunter?" she asked in alarm.

"I've got some things to do this afternoon," he said, already sorting through the pile of castoff clothing to find his own. "You should rest. Nobody will bother you here, so just sleep for awhile. I'll come back and wake you in time for you to get ready for supper."

Sarah watched as he dressed, covering the body she'd so thoroughly loved just moments ago without even glancing at her, the woman he'd once adored so much he'd been content sometimes just to gaze at her naked body.

399

"There now," he said, pulling the edge of the blanket over her. "Go to sleep." Perfunctorily, he kissed her forehead, then he was gone, leaving her there in the half-light filtering through the canvas tent, her body sated but her mind in turmoil.

She'd explained everything, and she'd told Hunter she loved him. She'd even made love with him. Surely, he knew how she felt about him now.

But it wasn't enough. It wasn't nearly enough.

Chapter Fourteen

At supper, Sarah sat with her husband and Mac and listened while the men held forth, offering their opinions on the best way to settle the Indian problem. The generals, naturally, felt the only way to deal with them was to fight, but the politicians would not support an Indian war. The American people, it seemed, were heartily sick of war, and Congress would approve no more funds for fighting.

Sarah herself was heartily sick of talking about the Indians, particularly when they were so close at hand and particularly when she had much more important issues on her mind, such as how to win back her husband.

She didn't have much opportunity to do anything in that direction, however, because when the hour grew late, Hunter asked Mac to escort Sarah back to their tent while he continued his discussion with the commissioners.

Someone had brought a second cot to the tent, so Sarah prepared for bed alone and lay down on it, waiting for Hunter. The next thing she knew, it was morning, and Hunter was up and dressed and ready for the first round of meetings with the Indian chiefs.

"You don't have to get up yet," Hunter told her when he saw she was awake. "You can sleep for awhile longer. There's a soldier outside. Just tell him when you're ready, and he'll bring your breakfast to you."

"But . . ." she tried, but Hunter kissed her on the forehead and left the tent before she could say more.

Well, what had she expected? He had a job to do; that's why he'd come here in the first place. And she'd already told him she loved him and that she'd make love with him. She'd even proved it. What else could she do?

Knowing she couldn't stay alone in the tent any longer than she must, Sarah got up and washed in the water Hunter had thoughtfully left for her. Then she dressed herself, choosing a dress from the small trunk she'd carried with her from Texas and which some unseen hand had placed in the tent.

When she was decently clothed and had pinned up her hair, she stuck her head out of the tent flap and discovered that, indeed, a soldier waited outside to do her bidding. He was a young man, his face still pimply, his body still lanky and awkward with immaturity. He brought her a breakfast which she forced herself to eat, then asked him to escort her to where the meetings were being held.

He didn't want to. She could see he felt it would be improper for her to go there, but she had to be with Hunter. When she threatened to go without him, he relented and accompanied her through the long, confusing rows of tents back to the brush arbor underneath which the Commissioners sat behind their tables, listening to the Indians complain about the ill treatment they had received.

And the Indians. Sarah's breath caught at the sight of them, hundreds of them seated on the ground listening to their leaders. For a moment, everything went dark, and

402

she thought she might faint again, but she willed herself to remain conscious, and after a few seconds she knew she would be all right.

Sarah saw Mac first, sitting on a bench at the edge of the crowd of civilians composed of the secretaries, reporters, scouts and other hangers-on that had assembled to watch the proceedings.

"I see my father-in-law," Sarah told the soldier. "I'll go sit with him."

The soldier waited until Sarah had approached Mac. Her father-in-law looked up and, seeing her, moved over to make room for her on the bench.

"Are you sure you want to be here?" Mac whispered to her.

Sarah nodded, searching the crowd of men in suits standing and sitting around the commissioners' table for Hunter's familiar figure. She found him at last, sitting behind Senator Henderson. As she watched, she saw the senator taking notes on what the Indian speaker was saying. Occasionally, he would consult with Hunter about something, then go back to his note taking.

The other commissioners weren't taking notes. They were only listening and asking questions that were sometimes longer and always more eloquent than the answers they got. At first Sarah couldn't figure out why the commissioners were asking questions as if they were really giving speeches, but then she saw that the reporters were writing down everything everybody said. No doubt someone would read the commissioners' words someplace and be impressed. Sarah was simply bored until she really began to listen to what the Indians were saying.

The Indian speaking was a member of the Kiowa, the tribe that had volunteered to be first. He was insisting, as the interpreter explained, that he was a man of peace, but he wanted it understood that all the country south of the Arkansas River belonged to the Kiowas and their allies. This included all of Southern Kansas, Indian Territory, and Texas, and he and his people did not want this land disfigured by soldiers' camps and "medicine homes."

"This building of homes for us is all nonsense," he continued. "We don't want you to build any for us. We would all die. Look at the Pena tuhka," he told the commissioners, naming the southernmost tribe of the Comanches, who had been on the reservation for years. "Formerly they were powerful, but now they are weak and poor. I want all my land even from the Arkansas south to the Red river. My country is small enough already. If you build us houses, the land will be smaller. Why do you insist on this? What good can come of it? I don't understand your reason. Time enough to build us houses when the buffalo are all gone; but do you tell the Great Father that there is plenty of buffalo yet, and when the buffalo are all gone I will tell him. This trusting to the agents for my food I do not believe in."

Sarah frowned at his words, glancing at Mac to see his opinion. "I guess he doesn't know about the plans to wipe out the buffalo," she whispered.

"I guess not," Mac agreed.

Much later, when the commissioners had finished questioning the Kiowa and hearing their complaints about the white settlers taking their land, the negotiations broke for the noon meal. Sarah found Hunter in the crowd, but he didn't seem pleased to see her.

"What are you doing here? You didn't have to come," he said. "You could have stayed in the tent."

"I know, I . . . I just wanted to see what was happening," Sarah said anxiously.

Just then, a group of Indian braves walked past, close

enough to touch, and Sarah shrank back instinctively from them, gasping in terror.

"It's all right," Hunter said, catching her arm and leading her away. The braves didn't even seem to notice her, but Sarah's heart was pounding all the same. Just the smell of them had been enough to trigger the terrible memories she'd sworn never to recall again. "They won't hurt you, Sarah," Hunter was saying. "Are you all right? You're white as a sheet. Come on, I'll take you back to the tent so you can—"

"No!" she protested, forcing the fear from her voice. "I want to be here, with you. Please!"

He frowned as he looked down into her face, his silver eyes reflecting his confusion. "But you're scared to death!" he protested. "You're shaking like a leaf!"

"I want to be with you," she told him desperately. "Please, let me stay!"

"I'll take care of her," Mac told him. "Besides, she'd probably be more frightened alone in the tent."

Hunter didn't reply for a long moment, so long that Sarah thought he'd refuse Mac's offer. Then finally, he said, "Why did you come here at all if you're so afraid of them?"

"Because I wanted to be with you!" she told him, certain she'd already explained this, certain he should have known.

He still didn't look as if he understood, or perhaps he didn't believe her. Sarah couldn't read his expression. At last he said, "We'd better go get something to eat."

Again the men monopolized the conversation over their dinner with talk of what they had heard that morning from the Kiowas. Most of the commissioners, all except Senator Henderson, seemed to think the Indians had been mistreated and would respond to fairness and

405

kindness from the government. The generals disagreed, as usual, insisting the only way to keep the Indians in line was with force.

With everyone still convinced he was right, they returned to the afternoon session of negotiations.

The Comanches spoke next, and they had chosen a civil chief named Ten Bears as their representative. The instant he began to speak, the assembly fell silent, mesmerized by his eloquence, although at least half of them couldn't understand a single word he said until the interpreter translated. Even Sarah, who hated the man on sight because he was a Comanche, found herself leaning forward on her seat to catch every word.

"My heart is filled with joy when I see you here," he began, "as the brooks fill with water when the snows melt in the spring; and I feel glad as the ponies do when the fresh grass starts in the beginning of the year. I heard of your coming when I was many sleeps away, and I made but few camps before I met you. I knew that you had come to do good to me and to my people. I looked for benefits which would last forever, and so my face shines with joy as I look upon you.

"My people have never first drawn a bow or fired a gun against the whites. There has been trouble on the line between us, and my young men have danced the war dance. But it was not begun by us. It was you who sent out the first soldier and we who sent out the second.

"Two years ago, I came up upon this road, following the buffalo, that my wives and children might have their cheeks plump and their bodies warm. But the soldiers fired on us, and since that time there has been a noise like that of a thunderstorm, and we have not known which way to go.

"So it was upon the Canadian. Nor have we been made

406

o cry once alone. The blue-dressed soldiers and the Utes came from out of the night when it was dark and still, and for campfires they lit our lodges. Instead of hunting game, they killed my braves, and the warriors of the tribe cut short their hair for the dead.

"So it was in Texas. They made sorrow come in our camps, and we went out like the buffalo bulls when the cows are attacked. When we found them, we killed them, and their scalps hang in our lodges. The Comanches are not weak and blind, like the pups of a dog when seven sleeps old. They are strong and farsighted, like grown horses. We took their road, and we went on it. The white women cried and our women laughed.

"But there are things which you have said to me which I did not like. They were not sweet like sugar, but bitter like gourds. You said that you wanted to put us upon a reservation, to build us houses and make us medicine lodges. I do not want them. I was born upon the prairie, where the wind blew free and there was nothing to break the light of the sun. I was born where there were no enclosures and where everything drew a free breath. I want to die there and not within walls. I know every stream and every wood between the Rio Grande and the Arkansas. I have hunted and lived over that country. I lived like my fathers before me and like them I lived happily.

"When I was at Washington, the Great Father told me that all the Comanche land was ours, and that no one should hinder us in living upon it. So, why do you ask us to leave the rivers, and the sun, and the wind, and live in houses? Do not ask us to give up the buffalo for the sheep. The young men have heard talk of this, and it has made them sad and angry. Do not speak of it more. I love to carry out the talk I get from the Great Father. When I get goods and presents, I and my people feel glad, since it shows that he holds us in his eye.

"If the Texans had kept out of my country, there might have been peace. But that which you now say we must live on is too small. The Texans have taken away the places where the grass grew the thickest and the timber was the best. Had we kept that, we might have done the things you ask. But it is too late. The white man has the country which we loved, and we only wish to wander on the prairie until we die. Any good thing you say to me shall not be forgotten. I shall carry it as near to my heart as my children, and it shall be as often on my tongue as the name of the Great Father. I want no blood upon my land to stain the grass. I want it all clear and pure, and I wish it so that all who go through among my people may find peace when they come in and leave it when they go out."

When Ten Bears had finished his speech, he sat down again, and for a long moment no one broke the hushed silence. This untutored savage had put to shame the eloquence of the white politicians, and from the way the reporters were scribbling in their notebooks, they planned to report it, too. Even Sarah, hating him as she did, was awed, and once again a small part of her actually felt sorry for this mighty race of people who were being driven from the land of their forefathers. It simply wasn't fair, but then, neither was what the Indians had done to her family. Life was never fair to anyone, and the Comanche were just another faction being crushed under the wheels of progress.

The rest of the day, the commissioners listened to the Comanches make virtually the same complaints against the whites as the Kiowas had made that morning. Inspired by Ten Bears's eloquence, the politicians waxed profound with their speeches of assurance to the Comanches, promising that the Great Father would take care of them for all eternity if only they would come to the reservation and stop their raiding.

Might as well ask a rattler to quit striking, Sarah thought sadly. As the negotiations went on, even Sarah, as ignorant of such things as she was, began to realize there was no possibility of compromise between what the Indians wanted and what the whites wanted.

That evening, after supper, Mac once again escorted her to her tent while Hunter consulted with the commissioners. After a few minutes, Sarah noticed her father-in-law was uncharacteristically silent.

"It's not going too well, is it?" she remarked, thinking he must be as discouraged as Hunter.

"No, it's not. The government has its own agenda, and they're going to force their will on the Indians no matter whether it means war or not." He sighed. "I just keep wondering if there isn't something I could do."

"Like what?" Sarah asked.

"Like . . . well, I saw a familiar face today. Among the Comanches," he clarified.

Sarah winced. She'd been trying *not* to see familiar faces among the Comanches, uncertain how she might react if she recognized one of her former captors. "Who did you see?"

"Hunter's father."

Sarah gaped at him stupidly, stopping dead in her tracks. What on earth did that mean? *"Hunter's father?"* she echoed.

"Yes," Mac confirmed grimly, stopping beside her. "Well, not his natural father. Rebekah Tate never knew who . . . Well, you know how captive women are treated," he added apologetically.

Sarah shuddered, knowing only too well. She had no idea who her daughter's natural father was, either.

409

"But this is the man who took Rebekah Tate to wife after she was with child. He wanted a son, and his previous wives were barren. You know the Comanche aren't as particular as the whites about who actually sires a child. The man who rears that child is considered his father, and the man who reared Hunter, Isatekwa, is here at this meeting."

Sarah felt her revulsion as a cold, empty spot in her stomach. "Does Hunter know?"

"No, and I doubt Isatekwa would recognize him after all these years, especially since he probably thinks Hunter is dead. I don't think he even recognized me."

Sarah cringed at the thought of how pleased Hunter would probably be to find his Indian father, a man he must remember kindly. He'd probably want her to meet him, to show off his blond bride. "Are you going to tell Hunter?" Sarah asked in dismay, figuring she already knew the answer and wondering why he was bothering to discuss this with her at all.

Mac smiled slyly. "Are you serious? Rebekah Tate would probably murder me if I did. You know she didn't want him to come here in the first place, and she hates for Hunter to feel any kinship with the Comanches. If I introduced him to Isatekwa, a man she despises, I'd never be able to go home again. Besides, what good would it do?"

Since she shared Rebekah's feelings, Sarah felt relief, but she also felt confusion. He'd asked her what good it would do, but something in his tone belied the question, as if he were sending her some kind of message, as if he wanted *her* to do something. Unfortunately, she didn't understand what it was.

Seeing her bewilderment, he smiled and took her arm. "Come on, it's late and you're tired."

He led her back to her tent and saw her safely inside. Then he disappeared into the twilight, probably heading back to the wagon where he'd been sleeping. Certainly not heading to the Comanche camp for a chat with the Indian Isatekwa. Sarah smiled grimly when she realized the name meant "Liar." A good name for a Comanche. Perhaps they should have chosen *him* to deal with the commissioners.

But why had Mac told her about him? Surely, he didn't expect *her* to tell Hunter; she hated the Comanches as much as Rebekah did and had just as much reason to want to prevent Hunter from feeling his kinship to them. Still troubled, Sarah prepared for bed and lay down on her narrow cot in the darkness, wishing Hunter would come in before she fell asleep so they could talk or at least so she could kiss him.

She didn't know how long she'd been lying there in the dark when she heard them coming. The sound was faint at first, but still unmistakable. The whooping and screaming of a Comanche raid. Sarah wanted to run, but fear paralyzed her, holding her in a web of terror so she couldn't move, couldn't run, couldn't hide.

Maybe they wouldn't find her, she thought wildly. Maybe they didn't even know she was here. Or maybe Hunter would protect her. She had to call him, had to warn him. But when she opened her mouth, her scream strangled in her throat and came out as a faint croak.

And then they were there, throwing open the tent flap. She could see them clearly, even in the darkness, their painted faces red as blood, their eyes gleaming like flames, their teeth bared in a hideous snarl.

Sarah tried to scream again, desperate now. *Hunter, Hunter!* But her throat wouldn't work and no sound came out, and they were on her now, grabbing her arms, dragging her from the cot.

No! No! She fought them, flailing her arms, struggling mightily against them, but they were too strong, too strong. . . .

"Sarah, wake up! Sarah!"

The Indians shook her hard, until her head snapped, and her eyes flew open and the Indians were gone and only Hunter was there, sitting on her cot, holding her arms and shaking her and calling her name.

"Wake up, Sarah! It's only a dream!"

She was sobbing, gasping for breath, and she grabbed the front of Hunter's nightshirt with both hands and leaned her head against his chest.

"It's all right," Hunter assured her, patting her back. "It was only a dream."

Only a dream. Only a *nightmare,* one from which Sarah wondered if she'd ever really awaken. Hunter held her while she caught her breath and stopped her tears and calmed herself again.

When she had settled down, he gently laid her back on the cot. "What were you dreaming, anyway?" he asked, brushing a stray hair from her damp cheek.

"The Indians," she said faintly, drained from the terror. "They were coming to get me again, to take me away."

Hunter sighed wearily. "Sarah, why did you come here if you're still so frightened of them?"

"I *told* you," she exclaimed in frustration. "I wanted to be with *you.* I love you!"

"Shhh," he soothed her. "Go back to sleep now."

Sarah stared up at him, trying to make out his expression in the darkness and failing. He didn't believe her, she knew he didn't, but how could she convince him? What could she do to prove she hadn't meant the hateful things

412

she'd said? She thought of seducing him again, but she'd already tried that. What else . . . ?

Then suddenly she knew. She knew exactly how to prove to him how much she loved him, and the knowledge was bitter as gall. She'd rather cut her own throat than to speak the words, yet she understood it was the only way. The *only* way to prove she truly loved him.

He was getting up now, going back to his own bed, but Sarah grabbed his arm. "Hunter, wait!" she cried.

She felt more than saw him turn back to her. "Yes?"

"I . . . there's something I have to tell you, something I found out today."

"Can't it wait until morning?" he asked, sounding tired.

"No, I mean, you might leave before I wake up or something. I have to tell you now. Your . . . your father is here," she said, the words almost sticking in her throat.

"My father? You mean Mac?" he asked, as confused as she had been earlier.

"No, your . . . your Comanche father. The man who . . . Do you remember? His name was Isatekwa." Sarah waited, holding her breath.

"My father is *here?*" Hunter asked incredulously. "How do you know?"

"Mac told me," she said. "He saw him, but you can't tell your mother. Mac's afraid she'll kill him if she finds out."

"She probably would, too. My father," he repeated, and for the first time since she'd found him again, she heard excitement in his voice. "I thought . . . But I guess I didn't think, not about seeing him again. He taught me to ride a pony before I could even walk. I can hardly remember him, except for a few little things. I was only about six years old the last time I saw him."

But Sarah was thinking, imagining what their reunion

413

would be like and how they'd talk about Mac stealing him away and stealing Rebekah, too, right from under their noses, and the old Indian would be impressed with his son and with his son's stepfather. He'd be proud, too, so proud that he'd listen to his son, to what he had to say, and he'd believe him the way he couldn't believe the other white men, and maybe, just maybe . . .

"Hunter, you have to talk to him!" Sarah said, grabbing his arm.

"I will," he assured her. "I'll find him tomorrow and—"

"No, don't you see? This is your chance! You can tell him everything, about how the government is going to put the Indians on reservations whether they want to go or not and how they're going to let the white hunters kill off the buffalo and how they're not going to stop the settlers from taking the land and how they have to lose in the end no matter how hard they fight. You can tell him everything, and he'll believe you! He won't believe the others, but he'll believe you because you're his son! And he'll convince the other chiefs and—"

"You're right," Hunter said, taking her in his arms. "Sarah, you're absolutely right! I've been so angry and frustrated because I could see nothing was going to be settled here, but now . . . Now there's a chance! Now I can do something!"

He hugged her to his heart, and Sarah clung to him fiercely, tears stinging her eyes. But she could feel he wasn't thinking of her. He was thinking of tomorrow, when he'd see his Indian father, and planning what he would say and hoping, hoping . . .

"Will you stay with me until I fall asleep?" she whispered, desperate to keep him close to her. Without a word, he lay down beside her, cradling her in his arms. But he was still far away, thinking about making a lasting peace between both his peoples.

The next morning, Hunter found Mac eating breakfast in one of the mess tents. Joining him with his plate
and cup, Hunter said, "As soon as you're finished eating,
you can take me to my father."

The look Mac gave him wasn't surprised. Instead, it
was long and considering. "I didn't expect to feel jealous,"
he said after a moment. "But I did always consider *myself*
your father."

"You are," Hunter assured him, laying a hand on his
arm. "I'm sorry, Mac. I didn't mean—"

"I know," Mac said, lifting his coffee cup to take a sip. "It
was just a shock, I guess, hearing you say it like that."

"If you don't want to take me, I'll understand. I can ask
one of the scouts—"

"Oh, no," Mac said, grinning. "I'll take you all right. I
can't wait to see that old bastard's face when he finds out
how I stole his wife and son." His grin disappeared. "What
are you going to tell him?"

Hunter frowned. "You mean about the treaty?" Mac
nodded. "The truth, I guess. And try to make him see
reason, try to get him to convince the others they have to
come in now, before it's too late."

"Fine. Eat your breakfast, and then we'll go."

Hunter was too nervous to eat much, so within minutes, the two men were striding through the army's camp
toward where the Comanches had erected their lodges.

"I didn't think I remembered much," Hunter remarked
as they passed the first tent. "But this brings it all back.
The lodges seemed so much bigger back then, though,
like mountains."

"You were a lot smaller back then," Mac reminded
him.

"And the cooking smells. I remember a little old woman leaning over the fire, yelling at me about something. And somebody lifting me onto the back of a horse and seeing a dead buffalo up close and watching while the women skinned it." Hunter shook his head, marveling at all the memories he hadn't even known he had.

They stopped once to ask directions and were directed to a lodge that looked like every other lodge in the camp. In front of it, a thickset woman used a stick to stir a pot of cornmeal hanging over a fire. She looked up in alarm at the white men approaching her and ducked back inside the lodge, chattering a warning.

By the time they'd reached the lodge, a man had come out. He was probably only middle-aged, but his face was as wrinkled as a dried-up potato, and his body thickened and stooped with the years. Hunter tried to recognize him, but he had changed too much.

Mac lifted a hand in greeting and said in Spanish, "My name is MacDougal. Do you remember me? I used to come to your camp to trade."

As Mac had suspected, the old Indian understood the universal trade language. "I remember a trader with hair the color of fire," he said. "The flames are frosted now."

Mac smiled. "I am growing old."

The Indian returned his smile and glanced at Hunter, his gimlet gaze instantly registering Hunter's mixed heritage. Hunter sensed his curiosity, but the Indian was too well-mannered to inquire outright as to the purpose of their visit or the identity of his other guest. Instead he said, "Come inside. We will talk about old times."

They followed him into the lodge. He barked an order at the young woman who was probably his wife, and she left the lodge, scurrying past the visitors.

When they were seated in a circle on the buffalo-skin

416

floor, the old Indian filled and lighted a pipe and took a puff, passing it politely to Mac who sat beside him. Each of the men in turn took a puff and passed the pipe on until all of them had smoked.

"I remember you, MacDougal," Isatekwa said. "You tried to buy my wife, Huuwuhtukwaʔ, the one with the yellow hair."

"And you wouldn't sell her," Mac confirmed.

Holding back a smile, Hunter waited for Mac to tell him the rest of the story.

"She was unhappy with the People," Isatekwa said. "She killed herself, in the water."

Mac didn't bother to hide his own smile. "No, I stole her from you," he said.

He had the old Indian's attention now. "You are making a joke."

But Mac shook his head. "No, we planned it. She left her clothes on the bank and went into the water. Then she walked upstream, in the water so you couldn't track her. I was waiting with clothes and a horse for her, and I took her back to her people."

Isatekwa shook his head in wonder. "This is true?"

"This is true. She is my wife now. She has been with me all these years."

Grudgingly, Isatekwa smiled, showing his few remaining teeth. "You are a mighty warrior, MacDougal, to steal one from out of a Comanche camp. We never even looked for her. How could a white woman escape from us? Such a thing could never happen, so we never tried to find her. We thought she was dead."

"But you did look for her son, didn't you?" MacDougal guessed. "You sent a party of men after him, but you never found him or the Indians who stole him."

Isatekwa's smile vanished. "How do you know about my son?"

"Because I stole him, too."

Plainly, this was more than the old Indian could believe. "He was stolen by our enemies."

"He was stolen by men I hired. Tonkawa braves. They brought him to me, and I took him back to his mother. He has been my son ever since, and he has grown into a fine man, don't you think?"

Mac gestured to Hunter, who felt his breath catch when the old Indian turned his dark gaze toward him. He searched Hunter's face for a trace of recognition, and Hunter felt himself drawn to the longing in the dark eyes.

"It is true," Hunter said, speaking in Spanish. "I was playing with some other boys on the edge of camp one day." He named a few of those boys, as many as he could remember. "We heard a turkey gobbling, so we decided to shoot it with our arrows. We followed it into the tall grass, but it wasn't a turkey. The Tonkawas had tricked us, and they captured us. They carried us off to a white man with red hair. We rode until nightfall, then they left all the other boys behind so they would be found. I was the only one they kept. The Tonkawas rode away, and MacDougal took me to my mother."

"This is just how it happened," Isatekwa said in amazement. "Only my son could know these things." He stared at Hunter, his black eyes moist with emotion. "Yes, I can see it. Your eyes are the color of smoke, just like his. What is your name?"

"The whites call me Hunter Tate, but the name you called me was Situ-htsi ɔ Tukeru."

With a cry, Isatekwa embraced him, and Hunter felt the sting of his own tears as the older man wept openly with his joy.

418

"My son who was dead is now alive!" Isatekwa cried. Then he was jabbering in Comanche, calling his wife who hurried into the lodge leading a boy whom Hunter guessed to be about fifteen.

The boy was wary, obviously uneasy about entering a lodge filled with white men, but Isatekwa introduced him. "This is my son Ketse nab ? bo, Painted Feather. He is your brother."

The boy was as skittish as a deer, but he sat down beside his father and stared across at his "brother," a man everyone there knew shared no drop of blood kinship with him, yet who by right of adoption was his closest relative.

Hunter stared back, thinking of what his life would have been like if Sean MacDougal hadn't stolen him away one sunny afternoon. He would have grown up like this boy, wild and free, riding the plains in search of buffalo like generations of Comanche before him. Yet he would also face the same, uncertain future all the Comanches now faced. If Hunter didn't do something, this boy who was his brother would die either from fighting the white soldiers or from starvation on the very plains that had nurtured his kind for thousands of years.

Resolutely, Hunter turned back to Isatekwa. "Father, I must talk to you about this treaty. There are things you must understand, things you must tell your people before it is too late."

And Hunter told him. He told him the buffalo would soon be gone, perhaps before Painted Feather even reached manhood. He told him the soldiers were just looking for an excuse to make war on them. And he told him about the politicians who were only pretending to be their friends and who really just wanted to get this over with so they could go back to Washington and tell the

419

Great Father they had done everything possible to make peace.

Hunter explained it all as clearly as he could, and when he was finished, Isatekwa summoned some of the other Comanche chiefs to hear him. They listened stoically, revealing no reaction, and when they had heard Hunter's warnings, Isatekwa said, "We will think on these things, my son."

After the demands of etiquette had been met and Hunter and Mac had been fed and entertained, they were dismissed.

As they strode back to the army's camp where the commissioners were still hearing testimony from some of the other chiefs in attendance, Hunter asked Mac, "Do you think he understood?"

"I'm sure he did. They all did. The question is, what will they do about it?"

The rest of that day and the next, the Indians made speeches and told the commissioners over and over again how unfairly they had been treated and how they wanted things to be like they were before the white settlers had come and stolen their land. Then the commissioners made their flowery speeches, explaining they could do nothing to stop the white settlers and the railroads from taking the land, and the Indians' only choice was to accept the reservation the government was offering them.

General Sherman, speaking for the army, was more straightforward and painfully blunt. He told the chiefs that no matter what they wanted, they really had no choice except to give up the old ways and follow the ways of the white man. They could not stop the roads and rails coming into their hunting grounds. They would have to learn to live like white settlers, farming and ranching.

"The former agreements you made with the Great Father had not made allowances for the rapid growth of the white race," Sherman told them. "You can no more stop this than you can stop the sun or moon; you must submit and do the best you can."

He did not have to say that the alternative was a war that would destroy the tribes. Everyone understood why the five hundred soldiers and their howitzers were present at the council.

That evening Hunter and Mac returned to Isatekwa's lodge. When the formalities were over, Hunter finally asked him point blank what the Comanches planned to do.

The old man looked at his lost son with eyes full of sadness. "We believe you when you tell us what will happen if we do not come to the reservation the whites have made for us, but why should we come? We can see what has happened to our brothers who have followed this road, and we do not want this to happen to us and our children. As long as there are buffalo on the prairies, we will hunt them. We will roam free as our fathers did, and if the whites make war on us, we will fight. But until the people on the reservations are better off than we are, we will not come in.

Hunter and Mac exchanged an alarmed glance. "Then you aren't going to sign the treaty?" Hunter asked, wondering what the Army would do in such an event.

"We will sign," Isatekwa told him solemnly. "We will get our presents and go in peace so we do not have to fight the soldiers in this place. But we will never come in to the reservation."

Sarah was waiting in their tent when Hunter came

421

back from meeting with his Comanche father. She knew the instant he ducked into the tent that things had not gone well.

"What happened?" she asked.

He hardly glanced at her. "Get packed. We're leaving."

"Now? Tonight? It's almost nightfall," Sarah protested, wondering what could have frightened him into wanting to escape the camp so hastily. Were the Indians going to attack the whites? Were the soldiers going to attack the Indians? "What's wrong?" she demanded in alarm.

At last, he looked at her and saw her fear. "Nothing," he assured her. "I just want to get out of here. I've had enough of this farce, and I won't stand by tomorrow while they go through the motions of signing a treaty that isn't worth the paper it's written on."

"Couldn't you convince the Indians—?"

"I convinced them all right," Hunter snapped impatiently. "It just didn't make any difference. They'd rather die than live on a reservation, and it looks like the army will give them that opportunity."

"But . . ." Sarah tried helplessly while Hunter started throwing things into his duffel bag. Then she remembered the one single event she'd been anticipating of this whole council. "What about when they release the captives? Shouldn't we be here for that? I could help, we both could, and . . ."

Something in Hunter's expression stopped her, and she knew an eerie sense of foreboding.

"Sarah," he said, and Sarah didn't like the tone of his voice, not one bit. "There won't be any release of captives."

"*What?*" Sarah was sure she'd misunderstood him.

"The treaty doesn't make any provision for them. I know because I saw it even before we came out to the council grounds. I tried to tell them. I argued and fought, but it was no use. They just don't think it's important."

"Not important!" Sarah cried. "What about all those women and children? What about their families? How can the government just leave them with the Indians?"

Sarah wanted to scream. She wanted to run outside and find the commissioners and tell them what a terrible thing they were doing.

Hunter reached up and touched her face. "They don't care, Sarah. They just want to get the treaty signed and go home. They don't care about anything or anyone else."

Sarah remembered what it was like to be a Comanche slave, not knowing if anyone even knew she was still alive but hoping, praying that someone, somewhere was trying to find her. No one was trying to find the ones who were still lost. The horror of it — along with her own helplessness — overwhelmed her.

Moving as if in a fog, she helped Hunter pack their things, then helped carry them to the wagon where Mac waited to take them away. No one spoke as they loaded their baggage, then climbed up onto the seat.

Sitting between the two men, Sarah felt insulated but not quite safe from all the horror. The council grounds looked so peaceful in the twilight. Smoke drifted up from hundreds of campfires among the Indian lodges and the soldiers' tents, and the smell of hundreds of meals being cooked filled the evening air.

Seeing the two forces side by side like this, few would have guessed that soon, in another place, they would be killing each other. Sarah closed her eyes so she wouldn't have to see it anymore.

They traveled as far as they could before darkness forced them to stop. They could still see the glow from the huge encampment on the horizon, but the camp itself was no longer visible. In silence, they made camp and cooked their supper.

By the time they'd finished eating, the stars were out. Mac made himself a pallet beside the dying fire and told Hunter and Sarah to sleep in the wagon. Sarah retired first so she could enlarge the bed inside to accommodate two people. Then she quickly stripped off her clothes and slipped into her nightdress and crawled into her pallet.

Hunter joined her a few minutes later. The light from the dying fire outside hardly penetrated the canvas cover of the wagon, but Hunter still had enough illumination to see to undress. Stripping down to his drawers, he didn't bother to find his nightshirt in the dark but just crawled into bed beside Sarah.

His flesh was chilled from the night air, and instinctively, Sarah drew close to warm him. At first she wasn't sure how he might react. After all, they hadn't shared a bed for months. But to her relief, he took her in his arms and pulled her close.

"I'm sorry you couldn't help them," she told him.

"A lot of people will be sorry," he said with a sigh. "At least we tried, though. I won't ever have to wonder what might have happened if I hadn't."

Sarah wanted to weep at the sorrow in his voice, but she held back her tears. No use forcing him to comfort her when he was the one who needed comforting, so she simply held him there in the dark.

"Sarah?" he whispered after a long moment.

"Yes?" she replied, a little apprehensive over the tentative tone of his voice.

"Will you tell me again why you followed me here?"

Sarah wanted to weep again, this time in frustration. "Why?" she asked, determined to find out once and for all how he truly felt about her.

"Because when you told me before, I had a lot of other things on my mind, and I don't think I really understood what you were trying to say."

"What did you think I was trying to say?"

Hunter sighed again. "Well, you claimed that you followed me because you were sorry for . . . for the things you'd said—"

"I *am* sorry, Hunter!" she assured him. "I never meant it when I called you . . . what I called you. I was just so scared and—"

"What were you scared of?"

"I told you, I was scared of the Indians, and you were going to make me go with you, and I just couldn't stand it and—"

"But you came just the same," he reminded her. "Why?"

Sarah strained to make out his expression in the dark, but she couldn't quite see his face. "Because I was more afraid of something else than I was of the Indians."

"What?"

How could she explain? "Of losing you, I guess. When I realized you'd gone to Kansas without me, I . . . I was afraid you wouldn't come back, to me anyway. That you'd never want to see me again after the things I'd said."

"So you followed me, even though you were afraid of the Indians," he mused. "I don't think I realized just how afraid you were, either, until I saw you there at the camp with them. You haven't had a nightmare like that for a long time, either, not since we first got married."

She'd had other dreams, of course, but Hunter was right, not such bad ones.

"But," he continued, still trying to understand, "are you really more afraid of being a deserted wife than you are of being recaptured by the Comanches?"

425

"No! Not of being *deserted!* Of *losing* you, of not having you anymore, of not having you to *love*," she finally admitted.

"But what was all that about you being afraid I'd die if you loved me, something about a curse — ?"

"I don't know if it's true or not, Hunter, but if you think about it, it *seems* true. I mean, everybody else I ever loved has died, my family and Pete and my babies and —"

"Not Becky," he reminded her. "Don't you love her?"

"Of course I do! I tried to stop after Jewel died, tried to pretend I didn't, just like I tried to pretend I didn't love you, but I still did. I don't know, maybe it's true about the curse, but I do know I can't stop loving either one of you, so if you're in danger, there's nothing I can do about it. The only thing I'm sure of is I don't want to live without you. I didn't mean to hurt you, and I'm sorry, and I want you, Hunter, more than you'll ever know, but if you're afraid of me now, I'll understand and —"

"Afraid of you?" he echoed.

"Yes, afraid of the curse," she explained, trembling now because she was giving him every reason in the world to leave her.

"I'm afraid, Sarah, but not of some silly curse or whatever you think it is."

"Then what are you afraid of?"

She waited, holding her breath for fear of what he might say, but he didn't answer. Instead he said, "Why did you tell me about my Comanche father?"

"So you could talk to him. So you could do something to help them," she explained impatiently.

"Why? You hate the Comanche. You'd like to see them all dead."

"But *you* don't! You wanted to save them, so I told you, so you could at least try. It was the only thing I could do!"

"Not the only thing. You didn't have to tell me. I never even would have known you'd kept the secret."

"But *I* would've known! You were so discouraged, I had to do something to help you."

"Even if it meant helping the *dirty, stinking savages?*"

Sarah cringed and tried to pull away from him, but he held her fast. "I told you I was sorry for that!" she cried. "What else can I do?"

"Nothing," he said, "except you can tell me again why you followed me to Kansas."

Sarah felt the frustrating sting of tears and blinked them back furiously. "Because I wanted to be with you!"

"And why did you want to be with me?" he insisted.

What did he want from her? she thought wildly. What could she say that he would believe? All she had was the truth, so she said it again.

"Because I love you!"

For several heartbeats he didn't speak, didn't even breathe, and Sarah knew she had failed. She'd been a stupid fool, and she'd lost the most important person in the world to her.

And then he said, "I love you, too, Sarah."

For an instant, she couldn't move, afraid to believe he'd actually said the words. Then, with a cry, she threw her arms around him. "Oh, Hunter, Hunter, Hunter," she whispered over and over as she rained kisses on his face.

Then his mouth captured hers and held it for a long, deep kiss that took Sarah's breath and stopped her heart and made her urgently aware of the length of his strong, hard body pressed against hers. Her blood quickened, racing through her veins and roaring in her ears.

Then he lifted his mouth from hers and said, "Tell me again, Sarah. Say it again."

"I love you, Hunter. I love you! I love you!"

She would have gladly said it a hundred times, but he kissed her again so she had to stop, and when that kiss ended, he told her, over and over until she stopped him in turn.

His hands were everywhere, caressing her back, her shoulders, her breasts, her hips, through the fragile barrier of her nightdress until she wanted to rip it from her body and offer herself to him completely.

Then he went still and pulled his lips from hers. "Sarah?" he asked breathlessly.

"Yes," she said, trying to find his mouth again, but he eluded her.

"Did you mean what you said before?"

"About loving you? Yes, of course—"

"No, about having another baby, because if you're still not ready . . ."

Now Sarah went still, remembering the pain and the heartache and wondering how she could ever bear it again. And then she knew. She wouldn't have to, at least she would never have to bear it alone, because now she had Hunter. His love would give her whatever strength she needed for whatever she had to face.

"I'm ready to make love with you, if that's what you're asking," she told him.

His lips smiled against hers. "That's exactly what I'm asking."

His mouth covered hers and his body covered hers, and Sarah took his weight gladly, holding him to her as she thought of all the years ahead that they would share.

There would be pain and loss and suffering. Hunter's two peoples would fight each other and both would lose. Forging a life in the new world would be the most difficult thing they had ever done, but they would do it together.

And Sarah wasn't afraid anymore.

Author's Note

Many of the events in Sarah and Hunter's lives actually occurred. There were treaties signed in 1865 at the Little Arkansas River (actually Bluff Creek, Kansas) and in 1867 at Medicine Lodge Creek, also in Kansas.

The terms of both treaties were pretty much as I described them, and the attitudes of the signing parties were also as I described them. There really were eleven captives exchanged at the Little Arkansas (Sarah, whom I created, made twelve), and the names I used were the real names of those captives. I invented personalities for them based on what I knew happened to returned captives. Far too many of them came home like Mrs. Sprague.

No one except perhaps some officials in Washington actually believed the Medicine Lodge Treaty would succeed in bringing a lasting peace to the plains. Indeed, in the next few years, Indian depredations increased dramatically, and the Texas frontier was driven back a hundred miles. The army fought valiantly to protect the settlers, but only the destruction of the buffalo by white hunters — who killed them for their hides and brought the Indians to the verge of starvation — finally drove the Indians to surrender.

The activities of the night riders in this book are based on real events in Texas and other Southern states during the Reconstruction period. I did not call them the Ku Klux Klan because the Klan did not yet exist. There were, however, many groups of hooded riders terrorizing the newly freed slaves long before they called themselves by any formal name.

This is the second book in the Tates of Texas Series. The first, *Wild Texas Wind*, tells how Sean MacDougal rescued Rebekah Tate. If you missed it, you can ask your bookseller to order it for you or you can order it directly from Zebra Books. And watch for the third book of the series, *Winds of Destiny*, which will tell Becky's story.

Please let me know how you liked this book. For a newsletter announcing the publication of the next installment of the Tates of Texas series, send a long SASE to:

Victoria Thompson
c/o Zebra Books
475 Park Avenue South
New York, NY 10016

DISCOVER DEANA JAMES!

CAPTIVE ANGEL (2524, $4.50/$5.50)

Abandoned, penniless, and suddenly responsible for the biggest tobacco plantation in Colleton County, distraught Caroline Gillard had no time to dissolve into tears. By day the willowy redhead labored to exhaustion beside her slaves . . . but each night left her restless with longing for her wayward husband. She'd make the sea captain regret his betrayal until he begged her to take him back!

MASQUE OF SAPPHIRE (2885, $4.50/$5.50)

Judith Talbot-Harrow left England with a heavy heart. She was going to America to join a father she despised and a sister she distrusted. She was certainly in no mood to put up with the insulting actions of the arrogant Yankee privateer who boarded her ship, ransacked her things, then "apologized" with an indecent, brazen kiss! She vowed that someday he'd pay dearly for the liberties he had taken and the desires he had awakened.

SPEAK ONLY LOVE (3439, $4.95/$5.95)

Long ago, the shock of her mother's death had robbed Vivian Marleigh of the power of speech. Now she was being forced to marry a bitter man with brandy on his breath. But she could not say what was in her heart. It was up to the viscount to spark the fires that would melt her icy reserve.

WILD TEXAS HEART (3205, $4.95/$5.95)

Fan Breckenridge was terrified when the stranger found her near-naked and shivering beneath the Texas stars. Unable to remember who she was or what had happened, all she had in the world was the deed to a patch of land that might yield oil . . . and the fierce loving of this wildcatter who called himself Irons.

Available wherever paperbacks are sold, or order direct from the Publisher. Send cover price plus 50¢ per copy for mailing and handling to Zebra Books, Dept. 4184, 475 Park Avenue South, New York, N.Y. 10016. Residents of New York and Tennessee must include sales tax. DO NOT SEND CASH. For a free Zebra/Pinnacle catalog please write to the above address.